THE MENDICANT PRINCE

Aruna Chakravarti has been Principal of a prestigious women's college of Delhi University for ten years. She is also a well-known academic, creative writer and translator with fifteen published books to her name. Her novels, *The Inheritors*, *Jorasanko*, *Daughters of Jorasanko* and *Suralakshmi Villa*, have sold widely and received rave reviews. She is the recipient of the Vaitalik Award, the Sahitya Akademi Award and the Sarat Puraskar.

THE MENDICANT PRINCE

A NOVEL

Aruna Chakravarti

PICADOR INDIA

First published in India in 2022 by Picador India
an imprint of Pan Macmillan Publishing India Private Limited
707 Kailash Building
26 K. G. Marg, New Delhi 110001
www.panmacmillan.co.in

Pan Macmillan, The Smithson, 6 Briset St, Farringdon, London EC1M 5NR
Associated companies throughout the world
www.panmacmillan.com

ISBN 978-93-90742-38-7

3 5 7 9 8 6 4 2

Typeset in Fournier MT Std by R. Ajith Kumar, New Delhi
Printed and bound in India by Replika Press Pvt. Ltd.

Praise for *The Mendicant Prince*

'Aruna Chakravarti's *The Mendicant Prince* is a lively retelling of the Bhawal sannyasi case … a real-life mystery which continues to intrigue to this day'

Amitav Ghosh

'In her reconstruction of the Bhawal case, Aruna Chakravarti intersperses authentic records and legal data with fictional interludes. The case was fought at the Calcutta High Court: AIR 1942 Cal 418 and Privy Council (1946) AC 508. Descriptions of events, locales and interpersonal relationships, combined with self-revelations of the women characters, imbue the facts of this famous legal trial with dynamic life'

Justice Ruma Pal (retd)

'In her well-researched novel, Aruna Chakravarti presents the facts of the Bhawal case, familiar to many of us, in a new form. Seen through the light of her imagination, the characters and events become real and living in a memorable way. I enjoyed reading the book very much and am sure that all her other readers will do so'

Bangabir Kader Siddique

'A riveting story of royal intrigue and a long legal battle. The author enthrals us with her lyrical language and exquisite descriptions. Each image is like a piece of impressionistic art'

Sanjay Bhattacharyya

'With her forte for historical fiction, Aruna Chakravarti retells the story of the sannyasi who claimed to be the dead kumar of Bhawal. Melding the factual with the fictional, the novel brilliantly captures the ambience of the early decades of the twentieth century'

Professor Niaz Zaman

'*The Mendicant Prince* spans multiple genres: historical fiction, real-life mystery and a legal drama that inspired a long-drawn-out pamphlet war in pre-Partition Bengal. Aruna Chakravarti breathes life into the Bhawal sannyasi case that has fascinated generations in Bengal and Dhaka, in yet another novel that demonstrates her mastery over the genre of fiction about colonial Bengal' ***Book Review***

'The queen of historical fiction … evokes the past of a united Bengal – long before the Partition along religious lines in 1947 – repeatedly giving us a glimpse of an age where culture superseded beliefs' ***Borderless Journal***

'Indian writer Aruna Chakravarti has carved a special place in Bangladesh through her notable historical fiction about Bengal of different eras … We know how [this] story ends. And yet I could not put the book down till the last resonant page, where an inevitable end is made poignant yet jubilant. Such is the promise of Chakravarti's fictionalized version of our Bhawal story' ***Daily Star***

'This is the ultimate familiar "whodunnit" crime thriller in all of Bengal's history … A historical hysteria devoured by generations. Only Agatha Christie could have concocted an equally brilliant fictional account of a masterful mystery … Aruna Chakravarti provides a fresh eye in decoding the immersive saga of an extended family's agony and sadness, conflicting takes on the veracity of a mendicant's sudden appearance following a decade-plus absence, the slow recollection of his ancestry, his past life … [as the prince] of Bhawal … Aruna Chakravarti has admirably recounted the not-so-hidden history, while simultaneously engaging in the endurance of a tale' ***Dhaka Courier***

'A meticulously constructed work of historical fiction that reimagines the several intriguing characters embroiled in this age-old mystery and court battle' ***Firstpost***

'Aruna Chakravarti's deftly crafted historical novel marries the factual details of the Bhawal case with a fictional dramatization of the characters – their thoughts, motivations and interactions with each other. The result is a treat, as the dramatis personae of the mysterious affair take on a life beyond the pages of history and transport us right into the heart of one of the most gripping legal cases of all time … Meticulously researched and vividly rendered, *The Mendicant Prince* manages to capture the irresistible draw of the Bhawal sannyasi case, and will doubtless charm a new generation of readers, as well as those who have known about the story that has now passed into lore' ***Hindu***

'A classic retelling of legendary Bhawal sannyasi case … [Aruna Chakravarti] has perfectly blended history with fiction. This novel is unputdownable' ***India Today***

'After meticulous research, [Aruna Chakravarti] has dramatically brought alive this intriguing tale of dual identity and the inexplicable quirks of fate' ***Morung Express***

'Aruna Chakravarti displays a masterful restraint as she delves into the minds of the key players of the legal battle … What emerges is a fascinating, absorbing story. There's mystery here, and the suspense of a court case where the opposing parties had two radically different stances (and often, it appeared, equally iron-clad evidence in support of their stance). By imagining the intricacies of the relationships and the emotions involved, Chakravarti also works into it heartbreak, betrayal, familial loyalty and more … [The] novel examines, with feeling and compassion, what that period might have been like for those involved' ***Scroll.in***

'An addictive vintage of a racy old wine has popped up with *The Mendicant Prince*, a teasing, fictionalized and compelling retelling of the Bhawal sannyasi case' ***Telegraph***

For my lawyer grandson, Nirbhay

Contents

PART TWO

Author's Note

A HUNDRED AND FIFTY YEARS AGO, BHAWAL WAS A PROSPEROUS zamindari in the eastern part of undivided Bengal, its size and income next only to that owned by the Khwajas, the nawab family of Dhaka. Spread over five hundred and seventy-nine square miles, it covered 2,274 villages and boasted a population of 500,000 people, many of whom were tenant farmers. Pristine forests, dense with sal and piyal trees and the habitat of the beautiful blue-skinned deer called neelgai, bordered the estate. Nestling deep within was an ancient fort known as Bhawalgarh and a baganbari or pleasure villa where the Bhawal zamindars relaxed, far into the night, with their wine and women.

The earliest known ancestor of the family was a brahmin named Balaram Roy. He hailed from the village of Bajrayogini in Munshiganj district and served as dewan to Daulat Ghazi, zamindar of a large part of the Bhawal pargana. The Ghazis were slothful and pleasure-loving and left the administration of the estate almost entirely in the hands of their able dewan. But ability and ambition tend to go together and, soon the inevitable happened. Balaram Roy's equally competent son Srikrishna Roy managed to wrest the zamindari from his master and set up his own rule. This he was able to do with the active assistance of Murshid Quli Khan, founder of the nawabi regime in Bengal. Murshid Quli Khan had come to Bengal as Naib Nazim or Governor, with a charter from His Imperial Majesty of Delhi, in the first decade of the eighteenth century. But, within a few years, he became the virtual ruler. He started minting coins in his own name and shifted the capital from Dhaka to Muksudabad, renaming it Murshidabad. But despite the fact that the Mughal empire was crumbling, nearly teetering on the verge of extinction, he was loyal to his imperial masters and sent the revenues owed to them regularly and faithfully.

The Ghazi estate was one of the many Muslim zamindaris that lost their rights as a result of the administrative policies of Murshid Quli Khan. It may seem strange that a Muslim would connive at robbing other Muslims of their legitimate inheritance. But Murshid Quli Khan was a Hindu by birth, a brahmin who had gone by the name of Suryanarayan Mishra, until his conversion to Islam. Unlike most other fledglings in the new faith, he did not follow it with fanatical zeal. Never losing sight of his Hindu origins, he used Islam only to further his own ends. A man of ambition, exceptional financial acumen and administrative ability, he had caught the eye of Emperor Aurangzeb who appointed him Governor of Bengal, Bihar and Orissa with expectations of enhanced revenue coming into the imperial treasury.

Murshid Quli Khan proved equal to the task assigned to him. He formulated a policy of ousting those Muslim zamindars who were habitual tax defaulters, having lost control over their estates from years of indolence and dissolute living, and replacing them with hard-working Hindus who were more grounded and would serve his purpose better. The estate of the Ghazis was one of those that came under the governor's scrutiny. Shortly afterwards, Daulat Ghazi was booted out and Srikrishna Roy installed as the zamindar. Srikrishna Roy fulfilled Murshid Quli Khan's expectations to a degree that surprised even the wily and ambitious Naib Nazim. Within a few years, rental collection from the estate doubled, even tripled. Over the next century, Srikrishna Roy's successors were able to expand the holding by acquiring several estates adjoining their own, the most notable of them being an indigo plantation known as the Wise estate. This was in 1851. Through this purchase, the family became the owner of the entire Bhawal pargana. By judicious management and keen supervision, Srikrishna Roy's successors held uninterrupted sway over the pargana for the better part of the next century.

At some point of time the family earned recognition as the legendary Roys of Bhawal. In 1878, the British conferred the title of Raja on Kalinarayan Roy and his successors. Unlike many others of their ilk, the Bhawals were not absentee landlords who abandoned rural living in favour of the bright lights of the city of Kolkata. They preferred to live in their grand mansion situated at the heart of their estate in Jaidevpur.

The Bhawals were unique in another way. Unlike most zamindars who depended solely on dewans and stewards to manage their properties, the rajas of Bhawal travelled extensively, kept an eye on every inch of their estate and regularly attended meetings with official representatives of various moffusils at the cutcherry in Jaidevpur. In consequence, the fortunes of the Bhawals swelled with every passing year. Their wealth and power rose to phenomenal heights and they came to be universally acknowledged as one of the premier zamindar families of Bengal. Kalinarayan Roy had married three women but only his second wife Satyabhama was capable of giving birth. She bore him two children, a son, Rajendranarayan, and a daughter, Kripamayi.

However, every rise has a decline, and it wasn't long before the Roys' glory began to fade. With Rajendranarayan's death, the Bhawal sun started sinking, slowly but surely, and the shadows of twilight began to gather. Rajendranarayan Roy died the last great raja of the kingdom of Bhawal.

Cast of Characters

Ramendranarayan Roy	the second prince of Bhawal, known as the mejo kumar
Bibhavati	his first wife, the mejo rani
Dhara	his second wife
Rani Bilasmoni	his mother
Rani Satyabhama	his grandmother
Elokeshi	his mistress
Ranendranarayan Roy	his elder brother, the baro kumar
Rabindranarayan Roy	his younger brother, the chhoto kumar
Sarajubala	Ranendranarayan's wife, the baro rani
Anandakumari	Rabindranarayan's wife, the chhoto rani
Indumayi	Ramendranarayan's eldest sister, the bara rajkumari
Jyotirmayi	Ramendranarayan's second sister, the mejo rajkumari
Tarinmayi	Ramendranarayan's youngest sister, the chhoto rajkumari
Pataki	Sarajubala's adopted son
Ramnarayan	Ananda kumari's adopted son

Satyendranath Banerjee	Bibhavati's brother
Dr Mahim Dasgupta	the royal physician of Bhawal
Ashutosh Dasgupta	his nephew and Satyendranath's friend
Colonel J. T. Calvert	civil surgeon of Darjeeling
Dr Prankrishna Acharya	eminent doctor of Kolkata
Colonel S.P. Sarbadhikari	eminent doctor of Kolkata
Mukunda Guin	an official in Ramendranarayan's retinue
F. W. Needham	District Collector of Dhaka
J. H. Lindsay	manager of the Bhawal estate
W. M. Crawford	District Magistrate of Darjeeling
Guru Darshandas	head of a band of ascetics
Dharamdas	a senior member of the band
Benoy Chandra Chatterjee	lawyer for the plaintiff
Amiyanath Chaudhuri	lawyer for the defendant
Pannalal Basu	First Additional Judge of Dhaka
Charu Chandra Biswas	a judge of the Calcutta High Court
Sir Leonard Costello	a judge of the Calcutta High Court
Ronald Francis Lodge	a judge of the Calcutta High Court
Kumudini	Bibhavati's personal maid
Chintamoni	Ananda kumari's personal maid
Kunja	the mejo kumar's valet
Kashinath Hazra	a tenant of the Bhawal estate
Taufique Ali	a tenant of the Bhawal estate

PART ONE

1

The Sannyasi

January 1921

IT WAS A RAW, BLUSTERY MORNING IN LATE JANUARY. A SMALL knot of people could be seen standing near the Buckland Bund, an embankment on the Buriganga river. The river, which swirled and foamed along the edges of the city of Dhaka, was especially turbulent this winter.

All eyes were fixed on a man, a stranger to these parts. He had been sitting cross-legged on the Bund, gazing into the distance day and night, for the past three months, impervious to the cold gusts of wind and spray that rose from the agitated waters below. There was something odd about his appearance. He could be a Bengali, the locals surmised, judging by the shape of his face with its somewhat square jawline, wide nose and high cheekbones. His body was covered with ash but the patches that were visible were as fair as a European's and his eyes, hooded by dark, heavy lids, a greenish brown. Masses of tawny hair fell in dreadlocks down his sturdy back and shoulders and a matted beard almost touched his navel. A tattoo—a word in some strange language—could be seen on his right arm. He was naked except for the strip of coarse orange cloth that covered his genitals. The men standing around stared at him with unabashed curiosity and exchanged glances. Once in a while someone would fling a question at him. They had been doing so from the first day they saw him sitting on the Bund.

'Who are you? Why are you here?' A middle-aged man in a silk lungi and woollen vest asked in a stern voice.

'*Main Bangla nahin jaanta.*' The stranger's lower lip twisted to the right as he answered in Hindi.

A barrage of questions followed in a Hindi thickly accented with Bengali.

'Where have you come from?'

'*Bahut door se.*'

'What are you doing here?'

'Nothing. Just sitting.'

'That we can see. But why here?'

'No reason. I just … just came here …'

'Are you a sannyasi?'

'Yes. I'm a roaming sadhu.'

'You look quite young. Must be in your mid-thirties. Am I right?'

The stranger shrugged his heavy shoulders and turned his eyes northwards on a massive structure looming in the distance. It was the zamindar's mansion locally known as the Rajbari. The zamindars of Bhawal were rich and powerful beyond ordinary landowners and had been dignified by the title of Raja. Their sons were addressed as kumar, each according to his position in the hierarchy.

The man in the lungi moved aside. Another, an elderly gentleman in a dhuti and shawl, took his place.

'You are too young to abandon the world. When did you become a sannyasi?' The old man leaned forward and examined the stranger's face and head closely. There was a puzzled look in his eyes.

'I ran away from home in my youth and joined a group of holy men.'

'How long ago was that?'

'I don't remember.'

'Where did they take you?'

'To the mountains. I spent many years there.'

The old man nodded. But the answer didn't seem to satisfy him. The crowd ebbed, melted and swelled once more. Others took up the interrogation.

'Do you have parents?'

'No.'

'Are you married?'

The man, calm and unruffled all this while, stiffened at this question. As though alerted to some hidden hostility. He had a prominent Adam's apple which jumped up and down his throat.

'Um …' he hesitated, 'yes … n-no. Yes. I had a wife … once.'

'You left her too?

'Yes.'

'Why do you keep looking at the Rajbari?'

'No reason.' The answer came pat as though he had prepared for the question. 'There's nothing else to see …'

The men walked away and stood a little apart. They exchanged meaningful looks and nudged and whispered. Snatches of their conversation came floating through the air.

'Exactly like the mejo kumar. The same height and build. The same small hands and feet. Even the tiny wart on the lower lid of the right eye. What do you think, Taufique?' The elderly gentleman turned to the man in the lungi.

'Yes, indeed, Kashi kaka. I never did believe the story.'

'You think anyone does?'

'I don't know about the family. The subjects certainly don't. Not one.'

'The man seems to be about thirty-five or thirty-six. Exactly the age the mejo kumar would have been today. Have you noticed the way he sits? Hunched forward like a bull.'

'And his complexion! What man other than a royal could be *that* fair? His body is covered with ashes but I noticed his hands and feet.

Particularly the feet. Rough and scaly but shell pink. Like new milk with a drop of vermilion mixed in it.'

'The colour of his eyes? And the tiny angles sticking out from the tops of his ears? The resemblance is uncanny. The mejo kumar too had …'

'There are marks on his back and legs. And tiny patches on the scalp in between the dreadlocks. I looked at them closely …'

'Yes, I noticed them too. The mejo kumar's body was ridden with syphilis when he was sent to Darjeeling. These must be the scars.'

'He seemed a bit rattled when I asked if he was married.'

'He did indeed. He couldn't decide what to say.'

'He *is* the mejo kumar,' a chorus of voices joined in. 'The story we have been told is bunkum.'

'Concocted by the mejo rani and her brother.'

'Without a doubt. Without a doubt.'

'Why do you think they did it?'

'Who knows? They must have had their reasons.'

'Mark my words, brothers,' an old man wearing a skull cap observed darkly, 'this man is pretending to be a sadhu, when he is in fact the mejo kumar – the second prince of the royal family. Now that both his brothers are dead, he is the sole heir of the estate. The real ruler. If I'm proved wrong, I'll never venture another opinion as long as I live.' He moved his head solemnly from side to side.

2

The Three Kumars of Jaidevpur

RAJA RAJENDRANARAYAN ROY, THOUGH THE ONLY SON AND SOLE HEIR to his father Raja Kalinarayan Roy's vast properties and title, had not been indulged and pampered as many other scions of great families were at the time. Reared in the shadow of a wise mother, he grew up to be a replica of his father – hard-working, disciplined and morally upright. But the same could not be said of his sons Ranendranarayan, Ramendranarayan and Rabindranarayan. One reason for this could be that Rajendranarayan had died early – before turning forty. Without paternal guidance and control, the boys—still in their adolescence—lost sight of the honourable path of their ancestors and allowed their baser instincts to take over. In this they were encouraged by their mother Rani Bilasmoni's attitude. Their tutors, some of them European, complained to the Rajmata that the kumars were imbibing the wrong influences and picking up bad habits. They were inattentive to their studies and dismissive of the moral training that was being imparted to them. But Bilasmoni, lacking the sagacity of her mother-in-law, brushed aside these warnings. She believed that while education was essential for boys from the middle class who were constrained to earn a livelihood, it was of little value to the heirs of the rich and powerful. She told the tutors that her sons, being poor fatherless boys, should not be taxed with rigorous discipline and too much study. In any case, they would inherit so much wealth; they need not trouble themselves with any occupation other than enjoying it. Thus, out of excessive motherly love, she allowed them to grow up in sloth and ignorance.

After Rajendranarayan's death, his successors being minors, the zamindari was taken over by the Court of Wards, the government department responsible for taking care of improperly managed estates. However, after a few years, on the boys attaining maturity, it was returned to the family. But not without a lot of effort on Rani Bilasmoni's part and considerable procrastination from the other side. The law of primogeniture not being prevalent in Bengal, all three brothers got equal shares and became joint owners of the estate. The annual rent collected was six lakhs and fifty thousand rupees – an enormous sum for the time. The Rajbari, built in Kalinarayan's time and designed by a famous European architect, was a palatial mansion with 365 rooms and so many halls, galleries, staircases and terraces that even the members of the family often lost count. It even had its own temple, a magnificent structure of carved stone, and its own cremation ground on the riverbank. The palace teemed with people. The largest and most luxurious apartments on the ground floor were occupied by the kumars. Their wives Sarajubala, Bibhavati and Anandakumari lived in their own wings on the first floor with a retinue of maids. Unlike their predecessors, the kumars never went out on inspections of the villages or met officials of the estate. They spent most of their time holding court in their own durbar halls, surrounded by cronies and sycophants. Rajendranarayan's married daughters Indumayi, Jyotirmayi and Tarinmayi, like other daughters of the rich, also lived in the palace with their husbands and children. The rest of the palace was filled with relatives close and distant, friends, hangers-on, toadies and servants.

Over this vast household the dowager queen Rani Bilasmoni reigned supreme. Her mother-in-law Satyabhama Debi, though still alive, had withdrawn from the world and spent almost all her time in the temple among her many gods and goddesses. Bilasmoni could clearly see her sons for what they were – idle, weak and dissolute. But that caused her no worry. Living up to her name, she loved her life of luxurious ease and revelled in the glory and power of her position as Rajmata. Her sons obeyed her. Her daughters-in-law feared her. If there was anything she regretted in life, it wasn't even her early widowhood. It was the fact that all her three sons were childless. For which, of course, she put the entire onus on her daughters-in-law.

Of her sons, the second, the mejo kumar, was the least like his ancestors. Apart from attending the annual *punyaha* ceremonies when tenants would pay *nazar*, the first instalment of the annual rent, he took absolutely no interest in the zamindari, preferring to leave everything in the hands of his eldest brother and officials of the estate. On these occasions the two younger princes would stand dressed in royal robes, on either side of the baro kumar, under a silver canopy held over their heads by armed guards, enjoying the attention paid by loyal subjects who prostrated themselves at their feet and sought their blessings. Apart from such symbolic gestures, the rest of the second prince's time and energy went in the pursuit of entertainment. A keen hunter, he sought out the most dangerous animals and went for the kill. He was successful, too, most of the time and, by the age of twenty, had earned a reputation for himself as an intrepid tiger stalker and shooter. Unlike his eldest brother, who was periodically examined for complaints caused by excessive drinking, Ramendranarayan was not an alcoholic.

But he had a worse affliction – an excessive fondness for women. He started keeping mistresses from his teenage years. One of them, a dancer named Elokeshi, actually lived with him in his apartments. This was unprecedented and created a major scandal in the kingdom. His infatuation with her lasted well into his marriage with Bibhavati, a beautiful, sensitive girl of thirteen with far more education than her husband. It was only later, at the insistence of his mother, that he removed Elokeshi to a house in Dhaka. But he visited her regularly.

Elokeshi was the first in a line of mistresses, among them the famous courtesan and professional singer Malika-jaan. On one of his trips to Kolkata he met an Anglo-Indian woman, a cabaret dancer, and was completely besotted by her. However, the affair didn't last long. She was a gold digger and as soon as she had extracted as much money and expensive jewellery as she could, she left him for another man.

Music and dance were Ramendranarayan's passion. While in Jaidevpur, he surrounded himself with singing and dancing girls procured for him by the band of faithful sycophants he nurtured. When satiated with such pleasures, he made his way out of the Rajbari, in the dark of night, to the dwellings of the lowest of the low. He found the women of the scavenger and tanner castes a refreshing change from the simpering prostitutes his toadies brought. They were less obsequious, high-spirited, impudent and quick-tongued. And many of them were beautiful with surprisingly fair complexions bestowed on them by members of the ruling class through sexual intimacy with their foremothers. As a result of such interactions in his adolescence, the mejo kumar had acquired a malady associated with promiscuous living. He suffered from numerous skin afflictions which would later be diagnosed as syphilis.

3

The Story Nobody Believed

IN 1909, WHEN OUR STORY BEGINS, THE ELDEST KUMAR WAS TWENTY-seven years old, the second twenty-five and the youngest twenty-two. Rani Bilasmoni had died two years ago, and whatever little control she had exerted on her sons had gone with her. The three princes were displaying a degree of recklessness that disturbed all their well-wishers, their three sisters in particular.

In February the same year, the princes went to Kolkata to consult specialists. The baro kumar had a chronic heart condition brought on by excessive drinking. The mejo kumar's health had been troubling him for the last three years. His syphilis had reached an alarming stage. Ulcers had broken out on his back, arms and legs. Colonel Sarbadhikari, a specialist in venereal diseases, treated him and he responded well. As a follow-up measure, the doctor advised a change of environment. A trip to the hills, perhaps, where the unpolluted air and pristine water of mountain streams would boost his immunity and help him fight the infection better. The Bhawal family physician, Dr Mahim Dasgupta, endorsed this view wholeheartedly. Seeking an audience with the eldest princess Indumayi, who had taken her mother's position as Head of the Royal Household, he made his opinion known to her. Indumayi considered it and asked, 'Where do you propose to send him, daktar babu?'

'To Darjeeling.'

'Will you accompany him?'

'I'm afraid not. There are some serious patients in Dhaka and Jaidevpur whom I cannot leave at present. But I will send my nephew Ashutosh. Ashu has recently obtained his licentiate certificate and will be able to give the patient all the medical care he requires. The prince's condition is not serious. He just needs a change of air.'

On Indumayi giving her permission, the mejo kumar's brother-in-law, Satyendranath Banerjee, offered to make the arrangements. He made a scouting visit to Darjeeling, then a popular health resort for the rich, identified a house and took it on rent for six months. Plans and schedules for the trip followed. It was decided that Bibhavati would accompany her husband and her brother. A retinue of twenty-one persons comprising officials of the estate, servants, guards, gardeners, cooks and maids would be sent ahead to get the place cleaned up and make all the arrangements necessary for the patient's comfort.

The Bhawals were conservative and usually insisted that some older women of the family accompany a young daughter or daughter-in-law. Surprisingly therefore, Indumayi allowed Bibhavati to join her husband who would be travelling with a party consisting solely of male members and servants. She had suggested at first that her second sister Jyotirmayi be taken along as an escort to her young sister-in-law. However, as Satyendranath explained, the house, though very large by Darjeeling standards, fell pitifully short of royal expectations and there was no way that space could be found for the second rajkumari and her retinue.

The first two weeks of Ramendranarayan's stay in Darjeeling passed uneventfully. From the reports that came, it seemed as though he was improving from the healthier climate and disciplined lifestyle enforced on him by his wife and his doctor. Nourishing meals, sufficient hours of sleep and regular medication were aiding the recovery. Then, on the sixth of May, a member of the prince's retinue sent a telegram to the baro kumar, informing him of a sudden decline in his brother's health. However, the following morning, on the seventh of May, another telegram arrived with the reassuring news that the pain and fever had abated and there was no cause for alarm. But close on the heels of the earlier communication, just as his sisters and brothers were sighing in relief, yet another arrived carrying the shocking message: *Kumar seriously ill. Frequent watery motions with blood. Come sharp.*

Ranendranarayan held a family consultation. All the members were of the opinion that leaving the mejo kumar in the hills, in the sole care of Dr Ashutosh Dasgupta, was not a good option. It was decided that Rabindranarayan would proceed to Darjeeling by the first train the next day and bring his brother back to Bhawal. Ranendranarayan would, in the meantime, send for specialists from Kolkata to assess the situation and suggest a better line of treatment.

But even as the chhoto kumar was making his way to the railway station the next morning, his phaeton was stopped by an official from the post office waving a telegram. On being asked to open it, the man did so and read out the devastating news. The mejo kumar had died the previous night and the body had been cremated. Dazed with shock, Rabindranarayan returned to the palace and handed the telegram to his eldest brother.

The news spread as quickly as a forest fire and, within minutes, the kingdom was plunged in mourning. Inside the palace, wails and lamentations rose to the sky. And at the *deuri*, the great gates of the Rajbari, men and women huddled in knots, their faces pale and anxious. The mejo kumar, for all his wild ways, had been popular with his subjects. He had a ready smile and a witty tongue and, unlike his parsimonious brothers, was generous with his money. Tell him any tale of woe and he would be sure to dip his hand in his pocket and come up with a fistful of notes and coins. And he always came to their rescue in times of distress. Once he had seen a British official harassing some villagers and, pulling out a gun, he had chased the man away, to the delight of the gathered crowd. Hundreds of bewildered eyes asked the same question. How could the life of a young man as big and burly and intrepid as the mejo kumar be snuffed out in a few hours? He had been ill, it was true, but not ill enough to die. Besides, he was recovering, wasn't he? What happened, all of a sudden?

Within and without the palace a tiny flame of hope still burned. So many contradictory messages had arrived in the last two days. Who knew but another would come with the news that the earlier one contained erroneous information sent in haste? A telegram assuring everyone that the prince was alive and well ...

Sadly, it didn't take long for the glimmer of hope to die. Three days later the party from Darjeeling returned, weary and travel-stained. A fainting Bibhavati was carried into her apartments by her brother and maids. The doctor shuffled in, head bowed, face dark with anxiety and guilt. The servants stood around as though turned to stone.

The customary rituals were carried out from the very next day. Bibhavati was taken to the river by the palace widows. Her conch bangles were broken on the stone steps of the ghat, the sindoor rubbed off her brow and parting, her jewellery removed, and the iron hoop of wifehood slipped off her wrist and thrown into the water. She returned to the palace, wrapped in a white *thaan*, looking like a caricature of her former self.

The *ashouch* followed – a period of mandatory mourning during which the widow and close members of the family were required to purify themselves through privation and abstinence. Then, on the eleventh day since the mejo kumar's death, came the *shraddha*, the rituals of which would ease the spirit out of the earth and send it winging towards heaven. It was to be an elaborate affair held in the *naat mandir*, the immense courtyard adjoining the temple, with three priests conducting it and thousands of subjects in attendance. Four healthy bulls, procured for the *brishotsarga*, stood tied to their posts snorting with impatience, tossing heads streaked with sindoor and stamping hooves adorned with anklets. They waited for the mantras which would spell their release. Wooden barrels filled with coins and stacks of dhutis, saris and shawls were kept ready for distribution to brahmins and the poor.

Two days before the ceremony the head priest of the temple, Kaliprasanna Bhattacharya, came to the palace and sought audience with Indumayi and Ranendranarayan. 'I come to you with a proposal, Baro Kumar,' he addressed the latter, a worried expression in his eyes. 'I feel that the burning of a *kusaputtalika* should precede the rituals of the shraddha. I've come to seek your permission.'

'What's a kusaputtalika?' Ranendranarayan's brows came together.

'It's an effigy of the dead person made of dried grass. A mock cremation you might call it.'

'But why must such a thing be done?'

'Because of the rumours.'

'What rumours?'

'Doubts are being cast on the validity of the cremation in Darjeeling. A large number of people are of the opinion that it was performed in haste without due regard to detail. Some are even saying that there was no cremation at all. Such talk is rife in all the villages of Bhawal. Even I have heard—'

'Who is spreading these rumours?'

'From what I hear,' the old man let out a discreet cough, 'they have originated from the Rajbari itself. From the servants' wing.'

'But … who … who would say such a thing?' Ranendranarayan spluttered in disbelief. 'And what is being said? I mean what, precisely?'

'From what I've heard, the servants who accompanied the mejo kumar have come back with some strange stories. Two, in particular, are doing the rounds. One of them is that his death was not a natural one. He was poisoned.'

'Who has said this?'

'A palace orderly named Sharif Khan. His story is that on the evening of the mejo kumar's death, he was sent for by Ashutosh Dasgupta and instructed to move the sick man's bed from its place by the window to an adjacent wall. "Clouds are gathering in the sky and a cold wind is blowing," the doctor had explained. "I don't want my patient to catch a chill." As he was moving the bed, Sharif Khan says, the prince sat up, retched violently, and vomited. Some of the vomit fell on the orderly's shirt. Later, when he tried to wash it off, he found the material giving way in his hands. The vomit was so corrosive it made a big hole where it had fallen.'

Ranendranarayan's face turned white. 'And the other ...?' he asked in a whisper.

'The second rumour is even more worrying. And more persistent. Not one; several servants who had accompanied the prince to Darjeeling are saying that the kumar's body was taken to the cremation ground but the rites were not performed. Apparently a terrible storm had broken out that night, increasing in intensity just as the pall bearers were entering the *samsan*. Taken by surprise at the sudden onslaught of rain and hail, they had left the pallet on the ground and run off in search of shelter. Returning a couple of hours later, they had carried out the cremation. This was their version. It was accepted by the mejo rani and her brother. But some contradictions in their separate accounts sparked off doubts among the staff who, for some reason, have come up with another. Which is that on their return, the pall bearers had found the pallet lying where they had left it. But it was empty. The corpse had vanished. The four men had searched for a while then, setting the vacant pyre alight, come back to the house and informed the family that the cremation was over. But what had actually happened was that the body had been dragged away by jackals during the time that it was left unattended. Afraid of the repercussions that would follow, the pall bearers were claiming that they had completed the work entrusted to them, spinning a web of lies, so inconsistent that even a fool would see through it. Members of the prince's retinue are saying that they had kept their opinion to themselves at the time. But after their return to Jaidevpur, they've opened their mouths. Today the servants' wing is humming with gossip and speculation. I'm surprised that you have no knowledge of what is going on under your own roof.'

'Nothing of the sort has come to my ears,' the baro kumar murmured in a puzzled voice. 'You say you've heard these rumours. But do you believe them?'

'I haven't formed an opinion as yet. But one or two things do strike me as strange. Why was the body sent to the burning ghat the same night? That too, a windy, blustery night in the middle of a raging storm? And why were the pall bearers not accompanied by members of the family? Is this the way a prince is cremated? Do you understand my predicament, Baro Kumar? How can I perform the shraddha of a man whose very cremation is in doubt? The practice of burning a kusaputtalika has existed for centuries. It was advocated by our ancestors for precisely such cases. It is the only way out.'

'No.' Indumayi now spoke up, waving her hand in dismissal of the argument. Her face was very pale but her voice was firm. 'While what you have just told us is very disturbing, I refuse to equate my brother, a prince of the realm, with a grass doll. It is demeaning not only to his memory but to the prestige of the Rajbari. Burning a kusaputtalika is tantamount to accepting the hearsay, giving it credibility. What message would it send out? Wouldn't we be admitting before the world that we were lax and inept? That we did not value our prince enough to even give him a proper cremation? Let people say whatever they wish. We may or may not believe the rumours, but we will not respond. We will go along with the previous arrangements and give the mejo kumar a shraddha worthy of a prince of Bhawal.'

'But consider this—'

'No, thakurmoshai. My mind is made up. We will deny these reports and so will you.' She drew a deep breath and turned to her brother, 'What do you say, Baro khoka?'

'I agree. Giving ear to gossip is risky for people in our position.

Loose talk like this will not die out with the burning of a kusaputtalika. In fact, it may get aggravated and other complications might follow. We must proceed with the utmost care.'

Indumayi sighed. She looked at the priest and said, 'If at all anything more has to be done, let it be a grand *yagna* to purify the household. There is rot here. Evil. I sense it lurking within the walls of the palace though I cannot put a finger on it. I've had this strange sensation ever since Mejo fell ill. Cleanse the Rajbari with the power of all the rites and mantras you know and bring it back to the state of pristine purity of my mother's time.'

After the shradhha was over and the household had returned to its normal routine, Indumayi sent for Bibhavati and her brother and demanded a full account of what had transpired. But her enquiry yielded no tangible result. Bibhavati burst into tears the moment she came into her presence. The few broken words she uttered, between spasms of shivering and sobbing, only conveyed her shock and bewilderment at the cruel twist of fate that had turned her from a queen to a beggar woman. Her brother's account was more coherent. In a steady, unfaltering voice, he repeated several times that every possible care had been taken. 'Believe me, Indu didi,' he appealed, using the familiar term rather than the formal one. '*Bonai* babu's health was improving. His appetite was better after the first two weeks and he was able to leave his bed and sit in the garden for short spells. Then, suddenly, from who knows where, he caught an infection which, I'm told, is common in the hills. He started purging and vomiting and a high fever racked his body. The doctor gave him medicine and he seemed to rally on the second day. But on the third day he succumbed. His death was so sudden that it left the entire household numb with shock. I am still reeling from the blow.'

Indumayi looked him sternly in the eye. 'You know that I will not demean myself by questioning the servants. But you are aware of the rumours, are you not? What do you have to say?'

'What can I say?' A hint of belligerence came into Satyendranath's voice. Fixing his large, slightly bloodshot eyes on Indumayi's face, he said, 'Rumours are spread by people who have nothing better to do. Why should I stoop to even offer a defence? My beloved sister has lost her husband and an entire way of life. She is struggling to come to terms with a terrible tragedy. What should be my first concern? To help her regain her health and calm her wounded spirit? Or respond to idle gossip and speculation?'

'But you must admit that performing the cremation the same night, a wild, stormy night, was unnecessary. You could have waited till morning.'

'No, I couldn't. The death occurred at midnight and the body started decomposing within minutes. The sheets were covered with blood and pus from the oozing sores and the whole room was reeking. No one would want to touch the remains if we waited till morning. Naturally I thought it best—'

The blood left Indumayi's face at these words. Even her lips turned white. Her fingers clutched the arm of the chair on which she was sitting so tight that her knuckles stood out like sharp pieces of stone. An unearthly silence descended. It was broken by a low, grating whisper, 'Why did none of you accompany the pall bearers? Why did you send my brother, a prince of the realm, alone …?'

Satyendranath seemed taken aback. Both by the words and the voice – so unlike Indumayi's usual imperious one. He thought for a minute, then decided to adopt a tone of confrontation. 'Who could have gone?' he demanded. 'The doctor and I were both preoccupied with Bibhu. She had worked herself up to a shocking state. One fainting spell followed another. And in between, the moment she regained consciousness, she would run to the window and try to jump down to the ground. We were afraid that she would kill herself if left unattended for even a minute.' He paused for a few seconds and continued mournfully, 'I requested some of the older retainers to go but no one was ready to venture out. I can't blame them. It was bitterly cold that night with a dense fog, rain and hail. Visibility was zero. One false step and a man could be flung headlong down a precipice. Some pleaded sickness and some said they were afraid of the mejo kumar's ghost.' Taking a deep breath, Satyendranath went on, 'Believe me, Indu didi. I am as shattered by what happened as any of you. I can't eat. I can't sleep. I feel overwhelmed with guilt even though I know there's no basis for it.'

At the same time that his sister was questioning Bibhavati and her brother, Ranendranarayan was conducting his own interrogation. Sending for Ashutosh Dasgupta, he accused the doctor of misconduct and breach of faith. 'We trusted you,' he said solemnly. 'We sent the prince to Darjeeling under your guardianship. But it seems as though our trust was misplaced. The kingdom is rife with all kinds of rumours. But even if we disregard them, even if we give you the benefit of doubt, the best that can be said of you is that you were careless and incompetent. That you are unworthy of the degree you hold.'

But the young doctor was totally unfazed. To all Ranendranarayan's questions and allegations he offered a single sentence in reply. *He had followed the rulebook*. Every decision he had taken was in scrupulous adherence with the education he had received as a medical student. He went on to explain that even though he was not sure of how the mejo kumar caught the infection, he had treated it with all the knowledge at his command. Not even his greatest enemy could fault him for negligence and inconsistency. But sometimes there are unknown factors at work baffling even to the best, most experienced doctors. There might be something he had missed, something he hadn't understood. But it was unfair to indict him for it ...

The *yagna* performed by Kaliprasanna Bhattacharya did not yield the desired result. At least not the result Indumayi had hoped for. If anything, the shadow of evil she had sensed earlier deepened and grew more menacing. And slowly, very slowly, she identified the source. It emanated from the mejo rani's brother.

Satyendranath was a frequent visitor to Jaidevpur. He came

whenever his sister sent for him, which was often. The members of the Rajbari liked him and extended a welcome and hospitality far beyond that offered to any other guest. He got along well with them and made himself useful in many ways. In consequence, he was not only loved and appreciated, but treated like a member of the household.

However, all that was in the past. Ramendranarayan was dead. Yet month after month went by and the guest made no effort to return to his family in Kolkata. He lingered on, enjoying the luxuries of the palace. And gradually a change came over him. He started behaving as though the lifestyle he was enjoying was his by right. He became arrogant and demanding. He even began meddling in the affairs of state, raising questions on matters which were none of his concern. His behaviour became objectionable in another way. Brother and sister withdrew from all the other members of the family and set up a strange routine for themselves. Every morning, on waking, Satyendranath entered Bibhavati's rooms and the two remained locked in all day until late into the night. Satyendranath emerged for one brief period for a luxurious massage and bath given him by the palace servants, and then went back. All his meals were served to him in the mejo rani's apartment. Bibhavati made no appearance outside it at all. Such behaviour was bound to attract attention and set tongues wagging.

Indumayi sent for her two other sisters-in-law one day. 'What do you think is going on, Baro bou?' She searched Sarajubala's face with keen eyes. 'Why isn't Satya going back to Kolkata? He has a wife and children, not to forget an old mother to fend for. So many months have gone by. Why is he wasting his time in Jaidevpur?'

Sarajubala blushed and looked uncomfortable. She mumbled something but her words were inaudible. Anandakumari, however, was more forthright. 'Something *very* strange is going on, Baro thakurjhi,' she said emphatically. 'People are saying all sorts of things. Even the servants are talking about it. I overheard Bamun di ask mejo didi's maid Kumu the other day why her mistress doesn't leave her room or talk to anyone anymore and Kumu said that she is still distraught with grief and only her brother can comfort her. But people are not stupid. Everyone is whispering and sniggering behind their backs. A lot of it, I'm sure, is entering their ears but they don't seem to care at all. They shake it off like water off a duck's back.'

'Baro khoka should speak to Satya and find out his intentions. How much longer will he park himself here?'

'Your brother *did* speak with him.' Sarajubala looked around the room as though afraid of being overheard and whispered, 'He thanked him for consoling Bibhavati and helping her come to terms with her grief. Then, in a roundabout way, he asked how his family was faring without him. Satya babu replied that of course they were missing him, that his wife was urging him to return in every letter she wrote. But he couldn't abandon his sister in her hour of need. He had to look out for her since she had no one else.'

'Hmph!' Indumayi snorted in disdain.

'Your brother told him he was wrong, that *we* were her family. That we all loved her and would take the utmost care of her.'

'And what was his answer?'

'He smiled and remained silent.'

'I will have to talk to Satya myself. This is absurd. It can't be allowed to go on. Now, I want you two to do something. Go to Mejo bou's apartment this afternoon. Enquire after her health and ask in a friendly way why she is cutting herself off from the rest of the family. Tell her you miss her company. Then come back and tell me what she had to say.'

'How can we go to her apartment? Her brother is with her all the time. He might stop us.'

'He has no business to stop you. This is not his house. If he tries anything like that give him a tongue-lashing he won't forget in a hurry.'

That afternoon, after their mid-day meal, Sarajubala and

Anandakumari made their way to Bibhavati's wing. Passing through several empty halls and galleries, there was not a soul in sight, they entered the mejo rani's bed chamber. They found her lying on her back, a thin blue-veined arm flung across her eyes. Her form looked shrunken and colourless against the dazzling white sheets spread over the vast, carved bedstead on which she lay. Her thaan was crumpled and there was not a speck of gold on her person. Her lips seemed coated with wax and strands of long, tangled hair were spread out on the pillow. The two women, suddenly conscious of the rich saris and jewels they wore and of the sumptuous meal they had just eaten, pulled their *aanchal*s closer and tried to hide the gold boxes full of paan cones they carried in their hands. But they couldn't hide their faces, sleek and shining with sugar and oil, and mouths crimson with paan juice and smelling of aromatic tobacco. Satyendra sat in a chair by his sister's side. His face was bent over hers and he was murmuring something in her ears. He rose at their entrance. 'Ah!' he exclaimed, his mouth stretched in a tight smile. 'Look who's here! Our baro rani and chhoto rani have woken up to our existence at last. Did the sun rise from the west this morning? I wonder ... Stop snivelling, Bibhu. Sit up and welcome your royal guests.'

Bibhavati removed the arm from her face and sat up slowly. Her eyes were swollen and there were tearstains on her cheeks. Her torso swayed a little as she clutched the sheets with both hands. '*Na, na.*' Sarajubala hastened to her side. 'You don't have to get up.' Taking the young widow's head in her hands, she laid it gently back on the pillow. Then, in a voice of sisterly reproach, she added, 'What's wrong with you, Mejo bou? Your maids tell me that the amount you eat wouldn't fill a bird's stomach. That you send your *thala* away with most of the food untouched. You don't even allow them to give you a proper bath or comb your hair. Why are you behaving like this? I recall the day you came to this house as a bride. You were so plump and fair and pretty. Just like a *mem putul*! Even when you returned from Darjeeling you looked better than you do now.'

'Ah, Didi!' A shiver passed over Bibhavati's frame and fresh tears rolled down her cheeks.

'What "Ah, Didi"?' Anandakumari's penetrating voice cut into Bibhavati's whimpering one like a knife. 'Can you deny that you aren't eating enough? That you are keeping yourself locked away in this dark room? You've turned so thin and frail in these few days it seems as though a puff of wind can blow you away. You don't even have the strength to sit up. Have you glanced into the mirror lately? You can easily pass for the *shaankchunni* from the neem tree that village women frighten their children with. Only the other day …'

'The other day you speak of was a lifetime ago, sister. I'm not the same woman …'

'Why not?' Sarajubala stroked the younger woman's hair and murmured gently, 'Because you've lost your husband? Is that your fault?'

'It must be. Otherwise why is it only I …?'

'Life and death are in God's hands. We *have* to accept whatever he deems fit to send us. But does submitting to His will mean torturing oneself? Yet that is exactly what you are doing. Punishing yourself for something over which you had no control. You've withdrawn from everyone as though your presence is a pestilence. Why? Is a widow a leper? Come back to us, Mejo bou. Make an effort. Be your old self. Nothing has changed between us. We miss you.'

'That's easier said than done,' Satyendranath observed grimly. 'Things *have* changed for my sister. Everyone has changed towards her, including the two of you. If not, it wouldn't have taken you so long to come see her. That, too, at the baro rajkumari's command.' Then, noting the look of surprise in the eyes of the visitors, he added, 'I know what goes on in the palace. I know everything. Bibhavati has lost her place in the family and all the prestige that came with it. She is nothing but an inauspicious widow whom everyone wants to get rid of. You are keeping quiet about it, even shedding crocodile tears over her fate. But you're all plotting and planning to throw her out.

And it will happen any day now. She'll be made to leave the palace. The sooner she understands the reality of her situation the better it is for her.'

Leave the palace! The three women looked up, startled. Bibhavati turned a pair of stricken eyes first on her brother, then her sisters-in-law. Sarajubala, aghast at the words, stared back at her. Anandakumari opened her mouth to contradict Satyendranath but, too shocked to utter another word, shut it again with a snap. There didn't seem to be anything more to say. Furious at the way they had been treated, the two made their way, red-faced, out of the room. Going straight to their sister-in-law's apartments, they reported the conversation they had had with Bibhavati and her brother.

'So that's what he does all day!' Indumayi muttered grimly. 'Locks himself up with his sister in this unseemly way only to put such ideas in her head. Well, he'll have to reckon with me. I'll teach him what's what. If anyone has to leave the palace, it is him.'

'But why do you think he's doing this?' Sarajubala asked in a wondering voice. 'What has he to gain?'

'Time will tell,' Anandakumari answered, her lips tight with suspicion. 'Satya babu and his kind are like jackals. They hide in the shadows all day, quiet as lambs. But they turn into deadly predators when they come out at night.'

Indumayi planned to send for him the next day, to accost him and ask for an explanation. But she was saved the trouble. Satyendranath went to the baro kumar's wing the same evening. 'A piece of news has come to my ears,' he said abruptly, 'and, needless to say, it has disturbed me a good deal.'

'What news?' Ranendranath looked up with a frown.

'You've instructed your lawyers to draw up a deed that will exclude my sister from the management of her share of the estate in return for a monthly allowance. Which, in effect, means that you are depriving her of her inheritance.'

'Nonsense. I've given no such instruction. The mejo rani's

position in the kingdom of Bhawal is unassailable. She is still in shock and that is why we are not troubling her with official nitty-gritty. She will carry out her duties and obligations to the estate, in her husband's absence, as the widows of the family have always done, and will be accorded the same dignity and status. But she must get over her grief first. And here, Satya babu,' Ranendranath looked straight into his visitor's eyes, 'I feel that far from helping her to do so, you are encouraging, even urging her, to protract it. She has been an integral part of this family for seven years. Why does she suddenly feel she has no friends here? Why does she keep herself locked up in her room day and night? Why does she communicate only with you? It isn't natural. Everyone is saying so.'

Satyendranath's heavy, florid face turned white with shock. He had come in a combative mood, to hurl accusations and shame the prince into acknowledging his guilt. He was totally unprepared for such an attack. More than his words, it was the snide smile on the baro kumar's lips that devastated him. It expressed, in unequivocal terms, the depths to which he had fallen in his host's esteem.

'Are you ... are you saying ...? What are you saying? That I ... I ...' he stammered, clutching wildly at the air, trying to come up with some, any, reply.

'I know you have informers among the servants,' Ranendranath cut in smoothly. 'You bribe and coerce them into bringing you all kinds of news. But I have my sources too. And they are far more reliable than yours. My officials tell me that you have started meddling in the affairs of the estate. That you ask probing questions and harangue them when they don't give you the answers you want. This kind of behaviour from an outsider is unacceptable.' Raising his hand, he stopped Satyendranath from bursting into denial. 'Another thing,' he went on inexorably, 'we, that is the baro rajkumari and I, have been meaning to talk to you about your prolonged stay in Jaidevpur. Four months have passed since the mejo kumar's death. Yet you make no move to return to Kolkata. You say you are here for your sister's sake. But is your sister your only responsibility? Don't your wife and children deserve some attention?'

Satyendranath couldn't believe his ears. The muscles of his face went slack. His jowls shook and beads of sweat broke out on his forehead. He looked as though he was about to have a heart attack. 'You don't want me here,' he shouted angrily and rose to his feet. 'Why don't you say so outright? Why humiliate and vilify me? I will do what you want. I will leave the palace tomorrow. But I'll take my sister with me. She isn't safe here with depraved, dishonourable people like you.' He stormed out of the room.

Satyendranath left a few days later. But Bibhavati didn't go with him. It was not from lack of persuasion on his part, so her serving women said. He had spent hours trying to make her leave. But though she had wept and trembled, she had resisted.

A couple of months went by. News of Satyendranath kept coming from time to time. He had moved his family from Kolkata to Dhaka. He was living there now in a rented house about twelve miles away from the Rajbari. Pretending to keep a physical distance from his sister, he came to the Rajbari rarely these days and stayed for only a few hours. Instead, he was bombarding her with letters. It was obvious that he was putting pressure on her to leave the palace and come home to her mother and brother. But she didn't seem ready to do so. At least not yet. A tense, uneasy calm followed.

Then, in November, six months after the mejo kumar's passing, the blow fell. Bibhavati sent her brothers-in-law a legal notice stating that she had appointed her brother Satyendranath Banerjee as her manager and agent. Another one came on its heels. This was from Satyendranath himself demanding thirty thousand rupees on her behalf, the value of a life insurance policy the estate had bought in the mejo kumar's name in March that year.

But that was not all. A few days later Satyendranath sent another legal notice. The mejo rani, it stated, was no longer interested in residing in the palace or retaining contact with any of its members.

She was relinquishing her title as well as her share of the estate in return for a one-time payment of thirty-five thousand rupees and a monthly allowance of eleven hundred rupees.

Bibhavati left the palace as soon as the legal papers were signed. Her brother received the money on her behalf and promptly set about spending it. He bought a fine new house on Lansdowne Road, the most fashionable quarter of Kolkata, and moved in with his family including his mother and sister. With the rest he bought company bonds in his own name.

After Bibhavati's departure, dark days descended on the royal family. In September 1910, Ranendranarayan died suddenly after a brief illness. Eight months later, in April 1911, the mejo rani received a letter from the British manager of the zamindari, Mr F. W. Needham, informing her that her share of the estate was being taken over by the Court of Wards. The excuse offered was her prolonged absence from Bhawal. A month later it was the chhoto kumar's turn. This time even a pretext was deemed unnecessary. Worse followed. In May 1912, the baro rani's share was appropriated and with it the entire estate came under the jurisdiction of the British government. The blow hit Rabindranarayan so hard he developed heart trouble and died a year later in September 1913. With his death, the Bhawal glory, faint and flickering in the last four years, was totally extinguished. The premier zamindar family of Bengal had lost all its men. Only a bunch of widows remained. The ancient dowager, Rani Satyabhama Debi, retreated more and more into the shadows of her gods and goddesses. And the three ranis, young childless widows, were robbed of all their rights. The mejo rani had abandoned the palace long ago. It was time now for the other two. Both left Bhawal to settle down in Kolkata and, over the next few years, adopted a boy each, clearly with the hope of getting him declared as the heir.

By 1915, the Court of Wards and the Board of Revenue had taken over the management of the entire estate. But a few years later, in 1919, the British government in India took a curious decision.

To everyone's surprise, it endorsed the youngest rani's adoption. An *abhisekh* ceremony was held in which the Earl of Ronaldshay, then Governor of Bengal, anointed Anandakumari's adopted son Ramnarayan. Though nothing was spelled out, it was everyone's guess that the message being sent out was that *he* would be the future Raja of Bhawal.

The whole of Bengal was mystified. An action like this ran totally contrary to the avowed policy of the white rulers with regard to the Bhawal estate. Was this a public relations ploy to appease a section of the family? Or was it a subtle manoeuvre to stem the rising tide of nationalistic sentiment? Or was it aimed at drowning the voice of an increasingly vocal Indian press which wasn't shying away from denouncing the colonial government in the most strident terms for its injustice to a royal family already plagued by misfortune?

But despite all the upheavals in the kingdom, the grapevine of rumour and speculation started by the palace servants did not die out. If anything, it stretched longer and took in more twists and turns. Now it wasn't only a question of the mejo kumar's body not being properly cremated. Rumour ran rife that he hadn't died at all. It was strengthened with a stranger's arrival in Jaidevpur. The man claimed that he had seen a Bengali youth, from an obviously wealthy background, in the company of some mendicants in a pilgrimage spot somewhere up North. He had got into conversation with one of them and been told that the young man had been found in a forest near Darjeeling some years ago. On being asked if he would like to become an ascetic and join them, he had agreed and had been with them ever since.

The stranger's claim rocked the kingdom. The Rajbari, hitherto mute and unresponsive to all gossip and speculation, sprang into action. Messengers were sent to as many places of pilgrimage as possible in the north of India. From Kashi, Gaya, Mathura, Vrindavan and Kedar–Badri to obscure ones hidden in the small hamlets of the Himalayan foothills. The reports that came contradicted one another.

Hopes were raised and dashed. But many members of the Rajbari clung to their belief that the mejo kumar was alive.

One of the believers was his grandmother, the dowager Rani Satyabhama. She came out of her self-imposed exile within the walls of the temple and took a pro-active step. She wrote a letter to the Maharaja of Bardhaman, who had been present in Darjeeling at the time of the mejo kumar's supposed death and cremation, asking him if he could confirm the demise. The maharaja wrote back to say that it was a long time ago and he couldn't provide any specific information. However, he did remember hearing something of the sort and sending gangajal and tulsi leaves to the bereaved widow.

Five years went by. The rumours persisted even though nothing was proven. More than the Rajbari, the subjects were willing to believe that the mejo kumar was alive. With no titular head governing them, and only a nebulous hint of a future puppet ruler floating in the air, they felt lost and abandoned.

And then, just when the time was ripe for a genuine claimant to surface, the mendicant appeared on the Bund ...

4

Jyotirmayi Debi

Jaidevpur
April 1921

EVERYONE SAYS THAT MY SON BUDDHU HAS MUSTARD SEEDS UNDER HIS feet. He is very restless and can't stay in one place for more than a few hours. He roams around the estate all day poking his nose in everyone's business and is, in consequence, the chief provider of information for the members of the Rajbari. Not all the news he picks up is authentic. A lot of it is gossip and loose talk. My grandmother Rani Satyabhama Debi loves to joke about it. 'Narad! Narad!' she calls out whenever he appears before her, bursting with something new to tell her. But, in all fairness, he isn't always the harbinger of evil tidings. Or fake information. Occasionally he does bring news that is both good and true.

When the sannyasi appeared on the Bund, three months ago, Buddhu was the first from the Rajbari to check him out. Though the man looked somewhat like his uncle, Buddhu said, he was by no means the mejo kumar of Bhawal. 'I introduced myself to him as his nephew Buddhu, but the face he turned to me was as blank as stone. I also tried to tell him how shocked and miserable we were when we received the news of his death. How, though very young at that time, I remember the way the whole palace went into mourning. Why only the palace? Everyone in the kingdom. But he didn't seem to understand a word I was saying. He is clearly from the North and speaks and understands only Hindi.'

Later it was Buddhu who brought the news that the sannyasi had been sent for by Saradaprasad Roychoudhury, zamindar of Kasimpur to perform a *putreshthi yagna*.

'A man with hair as white as *kash* wants to invoke the gods for the boon of a male heir!' Buddhu couldn't stop laughing. 'Even after trying to impregnate six wives and heaven only knows how many other women and getting a big zero, he hasn't realized where the problem lies. But the sannyasi has refused saying he doesn't know the mantras of such a ritual.'

'Stop it, Buddhu,' I scolded. 'Don't make fun of another's misfortune. Our destinies are not in our hands. Who knows what the gods have in store for us? Durga! Durga! Preserve and keep us well and safe, *Ma go*!'

From what he heard later, the zamindar had begged and pleaded and carried the holy man off, practically by force, to his mansion in Kasimpur. Whether the putreshthi yagna had been performed or not, Buddhu could not say, but that was where the ascetic was living at present.

On hearing this, my grandmother, whom we call Rani thakurma, expressed a desire to see him. If he could abandon his position on the Bund at the behest of the zamindar of Kasimpur, why couldn't he come to her? She sent a messenger to Saradaprasad requesting him to send the sannyasi to Jaidevpur even if it was for only one day. Saradaprasad agreed. On being asked if he was a vegetarian, Saradaprasad informed us that he belonged to a sect of naga sadhus who had no food restrictions. He promised to send him with his younger brother Atulprasad the very next morning.

The Rajbari of Bhawal is a complex of buildings standing within an area of about two and a half square miles. The palace, where we had all lived together till only a few years ago, faces the river. On the other three sides are fields and forest land dotted with tiny villages.

After the death of my second brother in Darjeeling and the departure of his wife from Jaidevpur, a curse seemed to have fallen on the Rajbari. My two other brothers died, in quick succession, within the next five years. My mother, mercifully, hadn't lived to see the deaths of her sons and the disaster that overtook the family, having passed away in 1907. After her husband's death, Rabindra's wife Anandakumari followed the mejo rani's example and left Jaidevpur. She writes to me from time to time. It seems she is quite well and happy. She has adopted a little boy whom she is rearing with all the opulence and splendour befitting a true prince of the realm. Following the family tradition, she has named him Ramnarayan. Or so she says. Does she really believe that, on attaining maturity, he will become the ruler? Doesn't she realize that the investiture ceremony, conducted by Ronaldshay, was nothing but a hoax? But she was always somewhat headstrong and arrogant. Irreligious as well. I was never fond of her. Of Bibhavati, whom I liked but never understood, I have no news.

After the government had seized the estate, we were left in acutely straitened circumstances. There was so little money that we couldn't afford even a semblance of our old lifestyle. We began by shutting down half the palace, reducing the number of staff to a minimum, and giving up luxuries that we had considered necessities all our lives. Over the months, even our drastically reduced standard of living was no longer feasible, and we were forced to leave the palace. The sisters moved out first. Baro didi, the eldest of our siblings and the one who had taken our mother's place in the royal household, had to face the humiliation of moving to a house owned by her husband. Tarinmayi and I followed. I now live in a twelve-room bungalow that was part of my dowry. Tarin lives quite close to me. Both houses are located within the complex. My grandmother, a doughty dame of seventy-nine, lives with me. She visits my sisters from time to time, when she feels the need for a change.

The sannyasi came on the auspicious day of Guru Purnima. Rani thakurma and I rose at first light and went down to the river. We took our hundred and eight ritualistic dips accompanied by *suryanamaskars*, then chanted mantras invoking the blessings of our ancestral guru Sri Shraddhananda Bhatta. It was from this acclaimed saint and sage that my great-great-grandparents, Loknarayan Roy and his feisty wife Siddheswari Debi, had received *deeksha* and it is his progeny that have served as *raj purohits* of the royal temple, in an unbroken line, to this day.

Though so early, the banks were lined with supplicants and beggars who had gathered from the moment they spied the palanquin with the Bhawal crest. Rising from the river, we distributed alms before making our way back home.

I gave orders to the cooks to prepare a lavish mid-day meal. Then, after we had concluded our puja and were ready for the day, Rani thakurma and I positioned ourselves before a window facing east which provided the best view of vehicles coming in from the gate. The sadhu was expected to arrive at eleven o'clock and, punctual to the minute, Saradaprasad's motor car, shining black with brass lamps and fittings, entered the drive. But it didn't come as far as the porch. It stopped at one corner of the compound close to the banyan tree that grew a little distance away from the window at which we stood. Two liveried servants jumped out and opened the doors from both sides. A roly-poly figure in a spotless white dhuti and crimped silk shirt tumbled out of one. Though I had never seen him before, I guessed he was the zamindar's brother Atulprasad. And, out of the other, another man stepped out and started walking towards the tree at a slow, measured pace. His body was coated with ash and he was naked except for a flimsy bit of saffron cloth covering his genitals. Reaching the tree, he sat on the ground in the lotus position. But he wasn't praying or meditating. He was looking around, his neck turning this way and that, as though he felt he had been here before and was trying to recall when. But I was not impressed. *This man has no resemblance to my big, portly brother*, was my first thought. *Tall, yes, but not as tall. Besides, his frame is quite different.*

I glanced at my grandmother. Her face had a puzzled expression. Perhaps the same thought was passing through her mind. The sannyasi had wide shoulders, but they were straight as arrows unlike Mejo khoka's which had slumped a little. His neck was sturdy and upright. Mejo's neck, though strong, was habitually sunk in a roll of flesh. His torso had been fleshy with a distinct paunch. This man's chest and abdomen were as flat as boards. But his legs were somewhat like my brother's. Stocky with bulging calves and slim ankles. I couldn't see his face very well, half hidden as it was by a flaring beard and swinging dreadlocks. Rani thakurma and I exchanged glances. We shook our heads. Then, suddenly, something struck me. Something seemed familiar. The sadhu had been leaning a little to the right while walking towards the tree. *Durga! Durga!* A shiver ran down my spine and my heart started to thump. I turned to Rani thakurma. 'Wasn't that the way Mejo used to walk? I seem to remember …'

'Yes … yes,' she answered slowly. 'You're right. His body slanted somewhat to the right. Even as a boy. His right shoe always wore out before the left one.'

'He started walking like that after his accident, didn't he?'

'Yes.'

The sadhu sat where he was for a while, his companion waiting a few feet away. Then, after ten minutes or so, Atulprasad approached him and, pointing to the window at which we stood, muttered something in his ear. The man looked up, rose and walked slowly towards the main door which stood hospitably open. The servants ushered him in and brought him to the gallery on the first floor where arrangements for washing his feet had been made. A winged chair covered in red velvet had been placed in the centre. A silver basin and a jug full of gangajal stood just below it. The sannyasi needed a little prodding before he agreed to sit on the chair and place his feet in the basin. But the moment Rani thakurma knelt before him and lifted the jug he sprang to his feet and ran to the extreme end of the gallery. '*Nahin! Nahin*!' he cried shaking his head vehemently, '*Aap nahin*.'

'Why not, baba?' Rani thakurma asked in her sweet, high, sing-song voice. Her perplexed eyes followed him as he continued to shake his head. His eyes, beneath lowering eyebrows, held an expression akin to horror.

'Sadhus are God's representatives on earth,' I added my pleas to hers. 'It is our duty to show them respect and reverence. You are in our house. Allow us to serve you.' But he wouldn't budge from his place. Every time someone went near him, he moved further and further away. After a long time and a lot of coaxing and cajoling, he sat on the chair and allowed a maid to pour water on his feet.

'Where do you come from, baba?' Rani thakurma asked, smiling.

I had heard Buddhu say that the sadhu did not speak or understand Bengali. But he seemed to comprehend her. '*Bahut door se*,' he answered, '*Haridwar se*.'

'Is this your first visit to Bengal?'

'Hunh.' A frown appeared on his face.

Rani thakurma asked a few more questions but he shook his head in a bewildered way as though he couldn't understand a word. He continued to sit where he was for the next twenty minutes, saying nothing. But his eyes roved here and there. It rested on my face for a few minutes. He opened his mouth as if about to say something, then shut it abruptly. An uncomfortable silence followed. We were all relieved when it was broken by the arrival of the cook with the message that the mid-day meal for our guests had been served in Rani thakurma's apartment.

Two velvet asans sat, side by side, on the marble floor. Two silver thalas, ringed with bowls filled with an assortment of fish, vegetable and mutton preparations were placed before them. There were separate silver dishes with kheer, payesh and varieties of sandesh. Atulprasad performed *gandush*, the ritual offering of rice to the gods before partaking of a meal, mandated for brahmins. But the sannyasi did nothing of the sort. He didn't even wash his hands. He poured dal on his rice and, pushing aside the other vegetables, emptied the bowl of drumstick chachchori on his thala.

Rani thakurma and I exchanged glances. It seemed an odd choice for a man who said he hailed from the north where, from what we had heard, drumstick is not eaten, or if at all, rarely. He ate with relish, picking up three or four pieces at a time and chewing energetically till nothing remained but the fibres which he stacked in a neat pile on the floor. Seeing him smacking his lips, Rani thakurma asked if he would like some more. He nodded. For the first time a smile appeared on his face. I noticed how white and even his teeth were. I noticed several other things. How his index finger stuck out as he pushed balls of rice into his mouth. How his hands and feet, though cracked and dirty, were small and well formed. How his Adam's apple bobbed up and down as he ate. Exactly like Mejo khoka's …

He Ma Kali! He Ma Durga! I muttered to myself. *Give me a sign. If this man is my brother, give me a sign. Don't keep me in this terrible suspense.* I remembered Mejo's love of drumstick chachhori. We sisters used to tease him about it. We would tell him that he must have been a peasant in his earlier incarnation – so poor he couldn't afford to eat anything better than drumsticks which hang from every second tree in the villages of Bhawal. So many years have passed since those days. We have seen so many ups and downs. Yet, how could I forget? We had lived together, eaten and played together …

I don't know what happened to me. The sob I had restrained for a long time burst out of my throat with a suddenness that startled everyone. I tried to stifle the ones that followed by cramming my aanchal into my mouth. The sannyasi's eyes were on me. And now tears were streaming down his face, the drops clinging to the hairs of his rough, reddish-brown beard. I felt the muscles of my face contorting and turned it away.

Thoughts and emotions, positive and negative, washed over me in waves. Was the man my brother? Or was he an imposter? But, as my rational mind reminded me, *he has never claimed he was the mejo kumar of Bhawal. If at all, he has firmly and unwaveringly insisted that he is none other than a sadhu from the north.* When the similarities between the two men came before my eyes, I felt convinced that the sannyasi and my second brother were one and the same person. Perhaps this was self-delusion. Perhaps it sprang from my need of an anchor. Not only for myself. For the whole family … indeed the whole kingdom. We needed something, someone, to hold on to. Then, all of a sudden, the pendulum would swing in the opposite direction and I would find it hard to reconcile the dirty, naked, bearded figure with the image I carried in my mind, an image undimmed by time, of my handsome, dapper brother. Mejo was quite a dandy and always dressed in the highest fashion of the times. His dhutis had wide borders woven from gold or muga thread. Diamond buttons flashed from shirt fronts of the finest silk, crimped painstakingly with mimosa seeds by his expert valet. Emeralds, rubies and sapphires sparkled from milk-white hands. And he was such a fastidious eater! Before starting a meal, he invariably dipped his forefinger into every bowl and touched it to his mouth to assess the taste. Then, pushing away everything that didn't meet his exacting standards, he ate slowly, savouring every morsel.

I shook off the thought and turned my eyes on the sadhu. He had given over weeping and was eating with gusto. I noticed that he hadn't touched the *parshe* fish, cooked whole in a delicate broth, and the steamed *ilish* with mustard and chilli paste. He had emptied the bowl of *muitha* on his thala. Muitha was our local delicacy made from the scraped flesh of the silvery *chital* that swam in shoals over the Ganga. My heart missed a beat. *Mejo loved muitha!* But a moment later another thought struck me. The man was not a Bengali. He was, quite naturally, nervous about tackling fish bones which could stick in the throat and cause acute pain and discomfort. Muitha was a dish of boneless fish balls cooked into a delicious curry with a variety of spices.

Another thought. Why did the sadhu burst into tears when he

heard me sobbing? Were ascetics, being men of God, endowed with a special empathy? Or could it be that he was … truly was …?

I remembered with a twist of the heart that out of all my brothers, Mejo was the most sentimental and soft-hearted. He wept easily even as an adult. Suddenly a scene came before my eyes. A large, handsome, dazzling prince of the realm crying and begging his eldest sister not to send him to Darjeeling.

'It's only a boil, Baro didi!'

'Not one boil, Mejo khoka.'

'A few boils. Everyone gets them. In summer during the mango season…'

Baro didi and I had exchanged glances. The boils on his body weren't ordinary boils. They broke out when one contracted a disease called syphilis. Our family doctor, Mahim Dasgupta, had told us that.

My mind teemed with conflicting thoughts for the rest of the day. Then, towards evening, I sent for Atulprasad and requested him to let his guest stay with us for a few more days. I wanted to observe him for some more time before making up my mind. But that, Atulprasad said, was not possible. The sannyasi had expressed a wish to visit Chandranath, a shrine in Chittagong, and all arrangements had been made. He was to leave the next day.

Reports reached us, a week later, that he had returned from Chittagong and was back at his old spot on the Buckland Bund. Buddhu went to see him and managed to persuade him to come to Jaidevpur as our guest. From the first day of this second visit, friends and relatives started flocking to my house. Rumour had run rife by now that the ascetic was none other than the mejo kumar of Bhawal. The crowd swelled with each passing day and he was surrounded, at all times, by an admiring group of people. In the few months of his sojourn in our province the sannyasi seemed to have picked up the rudiments of the Bengali language. Though he still couldn't speak Bangla, he seemed to understand it and was able to respond to questions.

There were many bathing rooms in the house, but our guest continued to bathe in the river. Rising at dawn, he made his way to the Ganga, took his ritual dips, did his meditation and performed his suryanamaskars. Then, coating his body with ashes, he made his way back to the house.

I still hadn't made up my mind about him. I wanted to check his body for the marks that Mejo had carried since he was a boy. A jagged scar on his left ankle, from an injury caused when he was eleven, by a carriage wheel running over his foot. A tiger claw mark, with pink, puckered edges, on his right arm. Slight discolouration of the skin on his wrists and insteps. The scaly feet unusual in an aristocrat. I requested the sannyasi not to cover himself with ash but he refused to oblige. Then suddenly, one day, he returned from the river, his face and body scrubbed clean. I stared in amazement at the transformation. His skin gleamed, white and lustrous as a pearl. All the old marks were there including the pits caused by syphilis on his back and legs. His light eyes, the eyelids somewhat darker than the rest of his face, were Mejo khoka's eyes.

I burst into tears. My grandmother, my sister Tarinmayi and the other women present in my room, wept with me. There was no doubt left in anyone's mind that the man standing before us was the second prince of Bhawal.

A stunned silence followed. Only the sound of weeping filled the room. The sannyasi stood where he was as though rooted to the ground. His hands were clasped at his chest. The muscles of his cheeks were working. A pulse throbbed at one temple. He seemed to be struggling with conflicting emotions. I mopped my face with my aanchal and looked at him. 'You are the mejo kumar of Bhawal,' I said gently. 'Why this pretence?'

A flicker of annoyance passed over his face. 'I have told you and everyone else that I am not the one you think. I am an ascetic. I came here for a short visit and will go back soon.'

'Where will you go?' Tarinmayi asked softly.

He turned towards her. His face was impassive but there was a strange expression in his eyes. It may have been my imagination but he looked at her, I thought, the way a father looks at a long-lost daughter. With deep love and compassion.

'To Haridwar,' he answered. 'From where I came.'

Tarin's mouth quivered and her cheeks crumpled like a child's. 'If you are not my Mejo dada,' she murmured, 'why do you look at me out of his eyes?'

The sannyasi had no answer to that. He gazed at her for a while longer and turned to leave the room. I stood still, not knowing what to do. *Should I stop him or let him go?* He looked like my brother but was that enough? He said he wasn't. Who was I to contradict him? What proof did I have that he was lying?

Suddenly I felt a presence in the room. There was someone with me. I couldn't see Him in the sudden bright light that dazzled my eyes. But I knew who He was. He was my golden god, my *Madanmohan* whom I had worshipped since I was a little girl. *Follow your heart,* a deep musical voice rang in my ears. *Be guided by it. This is a moment of destiny. Grasp it. It may never come again.*

'You must declare your identity,' I called out with a suddenness that startled everyone in the room, including myself. The sannyasi turned back slowly and looked at me with puzzled eyes. But I had made up my mind. 'I will send word to the subjects that the second prince is not dead,' I announced with a firmness I didn't know I possessed. 'He is alive and in Jaidevpur. People will start gathering in a few hours. You must meet them and tell them who you truly are.'

'Why are you doing this to me?' he sighed. 'Let me go my way.'

'No. Hear me out, Mejo. I swear on all the deities in the royal temple that I will go on a fast unto death. Neither food nor drink will pass through my lips till you come out with the truth.'

5

Taufique Ali

Kankrajoli Village, Bhawal
May 1921

AT LAST THE RAJBARI HAS WOKEN UP TO THE FACT THAT THE SANNYASI is the mejo kumar. We, the subjects, had recognized him months ago and told the royal family but they had ignored us and maintained a strange, mysterious silence. It was only recently that Rajkumari Jyotirmayi Debi invited him to her house. It took two visits for her to make up her mind and acknowledge him as her brother. Yesterday she sent her son Jaladkumar, known as Buddhu babu by the common people, to spread word in the villages that all the marks the mejo kumar of Bhawal carried on his body had been found on the sannyasi's. It is now twelve years, almost to the date, that the supposed death in Darjeeling had taken place.

The local grapevine got busy and within a couple of hours people started gathering outside the second Rajkumari's house. By afternoon the crowd had swelled to over a thousand. Men, women and children pushed and shoved for the best positions and talked in high, excited voices.

Suddenly a hush fell on the assembly. Even the babies on their mothers' hips stopped crying and looked on with big, round eyes.

The sannyasi was standing on the balcony above us. His hands were raised as though in blessing.

And now a voice rose from the crowd. 'What is your name?'

It took a few moments for the answer to come but, when it did, it came in a rich, booming voice, quite unlike the sannyasi's soft, gentle one.

'Ramendranarayan Roy.'

'What is your father's name?'

'Raja Rajendranarayan Roy.'

'Your mother's name?'

'Rani Bilasmoni Debi.'

There was a stunned silence. People stared at one another, speechless, as though a lock had been clamped on every tongue. Suddenly a little old woman with a hump pushed her way to the front.

'Everyone knows the names of the late Raja and Rani,' she cried in a shrill, quavering voice. 'What was your milk mother's name? The one who nursed you at her breast and took care of you through your infancy?'

'Aloka.'

The woman burst into a loud fit of sobs. '*O re amaar sona re! O re amaar Raja baba!*' she cried. 'You remember me! After all these years!'

Tears gushed into the sannyasi's eyes. 'Dhai Ma,' he muttered. A sad little smile appeared on his lips.

I had come early and found a place right in front. I could see and hear him clearly.

And now the people went delirious with delight. '*Jai! Jai!*' they cried. '*Mejo kumar er jai!*' The men laughed and slapped each other on the back. Women began ululating. The sannyasi raised his hands trying to calm the frenzied mob. Then, as though unable to cope with the hysteria his words had set off, his knees gave way. He fainted and fell to the floor. Rajkumari Jyotirmayi Debi and the other women watching the scene, from behind screens set up on the balcony, ran towards him. They fanned him, sprinkled rose water on his face and called out to the servants who rushed in and carried him into the house. The people, who had kept control of themselves until now, surged towards the main door as though blown by an unruly wind. I was carried along with the crowd. But we were stopped from entering the house by armed guards.

6

Excerpts from a Letter Written by F. W. Needham, Manager of the Bhawal Estate, to J. H. Lindsay, Collector and District Magistrate of Dhaka

My dear Lindsay,

A very curious and extraordinary thing is happening here which has created a tremendous sensation throughout the Estate and outside.

About five months ago a fair-complexioned mendicant came to Dacca, it is reported, from Hardwar, and stayed on the riverside ... During his stay ... he was taken to the house of Srj Jyotirmoyee Debi. Srj Jyotirmoyee Debi began to shed tears, finding in the sadhu some likeness of her late 2nd brother ... and the sadhu too burst into tears ... He was questioned by the inmates of the house as to who he really was but, without giving any answers he left abruptly for Dacca. For a few days nothing was heard of the sadhu.

A week ago, the sadhu was again brought to the house of Srj Jyotirmoyee Debi ... On seeing the sadhu, who is here now, an impression has been made upon the minds of the people who are visiting him in hundreds that he is the late

2nd Kumar. Tenants from different parts of the estate, and also outsiders, are daily coming in large numbers and giving out that he is the 2nd kumar. His presence has created a great sensation in the locality.

Last evening the sadhu, being questioned and hard pressed by several hundreds of tenants, at last gave out that his name is Ramendra N. Roy and his father's name was Rajendra N. Roy and his nurse was Aloka Dhai. After this the sadhu fainted and the numerous people present began to utter 'Hullu-dhani' and 'Jay-dhani'. All the people who were present at the time were convinced that he was no other than the 2nd kumar and the tenants gave out that, even if the estate would not accept him, they would stand by and maintain his position. Under the circumstances, a sifting enquiry about the sadhu is urgently needed. From morning, crowds of people have been flocking to see the sadhu, and the excitement and sensation is so great that the matter may take a serious turn unless necessary steps are taken promptly.

I am awaiting your instructions in the matter ...

7

Letter to the Editor, *The Englishman*, Calcutta

Sir, you published on Saturday morning a report sent by the *Associated Press* from Dacca under the heading "Dacca Sensation" to the effect that a person has suddenly appeared who claims to be the Second Kumar of Bhowal, who died twelve years ago.

The late Kumar was attended in his last illness by Lieutenant–Colonel Calvert, the then Civil Surgeon of Darjeeling and the death certificate was given by Mr Crawford, Deputy Commissioner of Darjeeling.

I was personally present at the time of the death of the late lamented Kumar and attended the funeral service along with numerous friends and relatives of the deceased who were then present in Darjeeling. The Rani of Bhowal, the widow of the Second Kumar, who is my sister, is still alive. Yours etc., S. N. Banerjee.

8

Kashinath Hazra

Kankrajoli Village, Bhawal
May 1921

A BAD BOUT OF LUMBAGO THREW ME TOTALLY OUT OF COMMISSION, keeping me confined to my bed for three whole days. As luck would have it, this happened just around the time the sannyasi admitted that he was indeed the second prince. Though I was not present at the gathering where he disclosed his identity, I heard about it, down to the last detail, from my neighbours Taufique Ali and Saidul Islam, and my nephew Satinath. Satinath is doing his BSc from Jagannath College in Dhaka and is here for the summer break. Between the three they kept me abreast of all the recent developments.

As soon as I felt strong enough, I set off on the three-quarter mile walk to the second Rajkumari's house. Upon reaching, I found the main hall so crammed with people that some were spilling out onto the veranda and porch. I managed to squeeze my way through and find a place to stand right at the back from where I got a good view.

I was amazed at what I saw. Caste, class, gender and religion were completely forgotten. Men and women, Hindu and Muslim, brahmin and shudra, rich and poor, were sitting huddled together looking up with rapt faces at the sadhu who sat in a winged chair at one end of the hall. He had dispensed with the appearance of a mendicant. He had washed off the ash from his face and body, shaved his beard, and was dressed in a sparkling white dhuti and *piran* made of fine *addi*. He had retained his dreadlocks. But they looked clean and oiled. He had shed all pretence by now and was conversing with the people in easy Bengali. He answered questions and wept at shared memories. I stood watching the scene for a long time. Then, when my back started hurting, I left and made my way back home.

In the evening I went to Bhabeswar Bhaduri's house. Bhadurimoshai is the headman of our village and an influential member of the district panchayat. I gave him an account of what I had seen and heard.

Bhadurimoshai heard me out, wagged his large white head and said, 'I haven't been to the Rajkumari's house myself, but I've heard everything from Dhanapati Daroga who came to see me yesterday. He gave me all the details. He said he had information that a big meeting is being planned, for Sunday, the fourteenth of May, in front of the Rajbari. It is to be an open meeting with talukdars, panchayat members and tenants from every village of Bhawal attending. A resolution will be passed to the effect that the entire tenantry of the kingdom of Bhawal acknowledges and accepts the sannyasi as the mejo kumar.'

The old man smiled wryly and added, 'He asked me if I would attend the meeting. I sensed some embarrassment in the question. Being an official of the British government, it is a difficult situation for him. He is torn between two loyalties. The royal family and his white masters. I told him I would. Then Dhanapati shared an extraordinary piece of news. He said that Mr Needham had written a letter to the DM of Dhaka apprising him of the latest developments in Bhawal and asking for instructions. A copy of the letter had been forwarded to the mejo rani at her Kolkata address. But, strange to say, a good five days have passed but there has been no response from her. I was shocked to hear this. A woman whose husband was said to have died has come back to life, and she shows no interest. No curiosity even!'

'She's probably convinced that the sannyasi is an imposter,' I suggested.

'Even if that is so, what would any other woman have done? Wouldn't she have come rushing to Jaidevpur to check him out? This total silence from her side is very peculiar.'

The police's information was correct. An open meeting was held outside the Rajbari on the 14th of May. On that day, streams of people started arriving in Jaidevpur from morning onwards. They came from far and near, some even from places as distant as Munshiganj and Mymensingh. The railway company had to run special trains to accommodate the crush. Even then, people could be seen sitting on the roofs of trains and hanging from the footboards. Those who hadn't been able to manage even that came walking the whole way. By late afternoon the crowd in front of the Rajbari had swelled to several thousands. A dais had been set up in front with a row of chairs for the important men of the district.

Adinath Chakrabarty, a prominent talukdar of Bhawal, began the meeting with a recounting of all the information released by the Rajbari from the time of the second kumar's departure for Darjeeling till the present day. He went over the kumar's illness, his supposed death and cremation, the grand shraddha, the rumours spread by the servants who had accompanied the royal party and the recent appearance of the sadhu. He said that, though most of the mejo kumar's relatives had endorsed the sadhu's claim after questioning him and checking for marks on his body, there were some who were resisting the idea or maintaining a mysterious silence. Clearly for some vested interests of their own. However, to his knowledge, all the talukdars and tenants of the Bhawal estate were united in their conviction that the sannyasi was their beloved mejo kumar. They should now come forward and pledge their support in public. He asked for a show of hands. Every hand went up. He now invited anyone who doubted the veracity of the sadhu to proclaim his dissent openly. Not a murmur rose from the crowd.

Next a resolution was drafted and moved. Purnachandra Chatterjee, another important talukdar of Bhawal, read out the text to the assembled tenants:

We the subjects of the kingdom of Bhawal are of the firm conviction that the sannyasi is none other than Ramendranarayan Roy, second son of Raja Rajendranarayan Roy. Furthermore, we accept and acknowledge him as the legal heir to the said Raja Rajendranarayan Roy, erstwhile ruler of Bhawal.

The resolution was passed unanimously. It was decided that copies would be sent to the Governor, the Board of Revenue, the Divisional Commissioner and the District Magistrate.

Now Adinath Chakrabarty rose and addressed the audience.

'Friends,' there was a break in his voice as he spoke, 'it is our great good fortune that the second prince of the kingdom of Bhawal is here in Jaidevpur today. Let us all rejoice that after so many years of doubt and despair, God has seen fit to send us our rightful ruler.'

'*Jai! Madhyam kumar er jai!*' A burst of applause broke out loud as a clap of thunder. '*Jai Raja Ramendranarayan Roy er jai!*' Men shouted and embraced each other, women ululated and blew conches, and children shrieked with fear. The rest of Adinath Chakrabarty's speech was lost in the tumult.

In the excitement of the moment, no one noticed that the sky had darkened and a *kalbaishakhi* storm, usual at this time of the year, was about to break. It came on so suddenly that it caught everyone unawares. Lightning streaked across the sky like flaming snakes with forked tongues. Thunder crashed with a deafening boom and the swishing of giant palms filled the air. Blinded by the fierce gusts of dust-laden wind, and eager to escape the lash of stinging rain and leaves torn from the trees that surrounded the Rajbari, the gathering dispersed in minutes. People rose hastily to their feet and fled in different directions.

Old age and lumbago made me slower than the rest and I was one of the last to leave the place. As I hobbled across the compound, a strange sound came to my ears. It was deep and sonorous, rising above all the others. I glanced in the direction from where it had come. And now, my eyes beheld a scene I will never forget in my life. An elephant, enormous as a mass of cloud, stood near the dais. Its front legs were raised, its trunk lifted in an arc high in the air, like a trumpet. I recognized it. As boys, we often played outside the royal stables which housed forty horses and twenty elephants. This was Phoolmala, the mejo kumar's favourite. The stormy air resonated with the creature's cry – a cry of joy. And on her back, the sannyasi sat in the pouring rain. Back upright, shoulders straight, head held high, dreadlocks blowing about his face in the unruly wind. Master and animal knew each other, recognized one another. The two forms blended into one, like a magnificent piece of sculpture. This man was no longer the sadhu who had sat, tense and timorous, on the Buckland Bund, fending uncomfortable questions. He was a regal, stately figure. The mejo kumar had declared his identity and resumed the posture that had been his through life …

The Bhawal Talukdar and Praja Samiti was formed a few days later. Its purpose was to collect funds and establish the mejo kumar in his rightful position through due process of law. In the association's first meeting it was decided that the sannyasi, accompanied by two lawyers, would be taken to the house of the District Magistrate and Collector where he would stake his claim as the lawful ruler of Bhawal.

9

J. H. Lindsay's Report

Dhaka
7 June 1921

The sadhu came today at about 11 a.m. with Babu Sarat Ch. Chakrabartti, Babu Peari Lal Ghosh and, I think, the Kasimpur manager. He said he wants some arrangement made about his estate so that the tenants could be benefited. I explained that the Board of Revenue must hold him not to be the Second Kumar as they have carried out the work of the estate on that assumption for many years. I said he could prove his identity in court in a suit or if he preferred to produce his evidence before me, I was willing to record it. He agreed to the latter procedure, and the pleaders said they would file a petition tomorrow for such an enquiry. They asked that the Board might pay the expenses and I replied that if they put in a petition to that effect, I would get orders on it.

In reply to my questions the sadhu (Second Kumar) told me that he had been ill for 2–4 days ... before he lost consciousness in Darjeeling ... that he recovered his senses ... in the presence of one sadhu who has since been his

> Guru, that the sadhu said he had been senseless for 3–4 days, that the sadhu told him that he had found him lying on the ground as if he had been thrown there and that his body was wet with rain as it had been raining before he found him, that the sadhu did not say whether he found him in the day or at night. The sadhu appeared to be an up-country man with beautifully clear skin with no sign of syphilis.

Five days later the following public notice was issued in Bengali:

> All the tenants of the Bhawal estate are hereby informed that the Board of Revenue has got conclusive proof that the dead body of the second kumar of Bhawal was burnt to ashes in the town of Darjeeling twelve years ago. It follows therefore that the sadhu who is calling himself the second kumar is an imposter. Anyone who will pay him rent or subscriptions will do so at his own risk.

10

Bibhavati Debi

Kolkata
May 1921

THE LETTER ARRIVED YESTERDAY. DADA BROUGHT IT TO ME. 'HERE,' he said, handing me a slim brown envelope with the words 'On His Majesty's Service' printed on it in bold, black letters. I knew what it was. I had received missives like this one over a decade ago from Mr Needham, the manager of the Bhawal estate. I was a bit puzzled by the address: Mrs Bibhavati Roy, C/O Mr Satyendranath Banerjee, 19 Lansdowne Road, Kolkata.

Mrs Bibhavati Roy? Letters from him were always addressed to the 2nd Rani of Bhowal, Rajbari, Jaidevpur. My confusion lasted only a few seconds. I remembered that, soon after my husband's death, I had relinquished my title together with all my rights for a sum of 35,000 rupees and a monthly allowance. Dada had bought this house with some of the money and filled it with expensive furniture, paintings and objects of art bought from English auction houses. Ma had been against it. 'It is Bibhu's money,' she had reminded him. 'It should be kept in the bank in her name to use when she needs it. She is a childless widow. Who will look after her in her old age?'

'I will. Who else?' Dada had avoided looking at Ma.

'You won't be around forever.'

'In my absence my sons will do the needful.'

'You can't be sure of that.'

'I *am* sure.' Dada's face had turned red and angry. 'Besides, don't forget that she is used to every kind of royal comfort. Shouldn't we provide her with at least a semblance of what she has left behind? Can we keep her in the way we live now? In this dump?'

A bitter argument followed. My mother was a woman of great personality and could handle my brother's belligerence without turning a hair.

'There was no need to make her leave the palace in the first place,' she said grimly.

'There was every need. They hated her. They would have poisoned her.'

'Nonsense.'

'How do you know it's nonsense?'

'Because I know you.'

The argument would have gone on had I not intervened. 'Let it be, Ma,' I said, drawing my mother away. 'I came back to you and Dada of my own free will. No one forced me.'

I said that to preserve the peace though in my heart of hearts I knew it wasn't true …

'What's the matter?' Dada made a gesture of impatience. 'Don't you want to read the letter?'

'Of course.' I said meekly, rising to my feet. 'I'll just fetch the paper knife.'

'There's no need. I've opened it.'

I turned the envelope over in my hands. There was a hairline slit at one end, so neat and even that I hadn't noticed it. I put my thumb and forefinger through it and pulled out two sheets of paper. It was the copy of a report submitted by Mr Needham to the District Magistrate of Dhaka.

I felt my face flame as I went through the contents. My hands and feet went cold. My mouth turned dry and my heart started thumping like a ball of lead against my rib cage. I am subject to such sensations when I'm stressed, when I know that some hard decision is expected of me. The doctor in Jaidevpur had diagnosed these feelings as panic attacks that happened to people with a persistent anaemic condition like mine. He had given me medicines and advised me to stop running away from my problems. To start taking the bull by the horns. It would be difficult at first, he said, but the nervousness and hesitation would pass eventually. It didn't matter if I took some wrong decisions. Everyone did, from time to time. The very knowledge that I had taken a stand would give me strength and confidence. He told me to remind myself, at all times, that I wasn't a nobody. I was the mejo rani of Bhawal.

But I couldn't follow his advice. Not for a long time. I preferred evading issues to confronting them. It was so much easier.

'What do I do now?' I turned to my brother, my voice a whisper.

'Nothing. I will do whatever needs to be done.' Then, seeing the distress in my face, Dada put his hand on my head and continued gently, 'No need to worry, Bibhu. Your Dada is here to look after you. Remember that I love you above everyone else. Even my own children.'

I nodded. It was true. Dada had always loved me best. As a boy, he had saved his tiffin money and bought me dolls and toys. And even after I got married, he continued to pamper me. He slipped away from Kolkata and came to visit me at the palace whenever he could, bringing with him things I loved. A storybook, the latest issue of *Sandesh* or *Mukul*, sheets of dried mango pulp and jars of tamarind pickle pilfered from Baro Mami's larder. I had to hide them from my royal sisters-in-law, knowing they would laugh at the gifts and call them cheap and tacky …

Dada's love for me was fierce and possessive. It manifested itself in strange ways. It took forms which thrilled and excited me and frightened me at the same time. He treated me like an expensive doll, which had to be preserved in a glass case, to be cherished and lavished with care. Only by him. No one else. He expected absolute obedience in return for his love, a loyalty that bordered on slavish devotion. The slightest murmur of dissent on my part would shatter the glass. It was that fragile.

We had never been rich. My father was an advocate in the Calcutta High Court with a moderate income that ensured the best education for his children, a roof over their heads and plenty of good, nourishing food. Clothes were bought strictly according to requirement. Nothing more. No extravagance or indulgence. My mother, Phulkumari Debi, was an educated woman from an enlightened, upper middle-class family of Uttarpara. Her father and brothers had been active participants in the campaign for women's liberation spearheaded by the Bengal Renaissance. My mother wore her sari in the Pirali style, did not observe purdah and brought up her daughters to think themselves equal to men.

My father died when I was so little that I can barely recollect what he looked like. He couldn't have been more than thirty-five or thirty-six. It was a terrible time for my mother. Left with no income, a young son appearing for his matriculation examination and two unmarried daughters, she must have seen nothing but darkness in front of her. But she was a woman of great strength and presence of mind and did not break down. She sold her house and furniture and kept the money in the bank. Her jewellery, she put aside. It would come of use when her daughters got married. So, when her brothers came to take her away, she did not go empty-handed. She had a stock of gold and a small income from the interest from her bank account.

My uncles and aunts were kind to us, and we were quite happy living with them. In fact, the only home I remember from my childhood was the one in Uttarpara.

My uncles sent my brother to college and found surprisingly good matches for us girls at the appropriate time. This, as everyone said, was because we were both exceptionally beautiful and talented. We had studied in missionary schools and could read, write and speak English with a degree of fluency quite unusual for the time. In addition, we had been taught nursing, elocution, painting and fine embroidery.

My sister, Molina, was married into the family of Kanti Mukherjee, the Dewan of Jaipur. His was a household name known through the length and breadth of Bengal and his meteoric rise to wealth and power was the pride and glory of her people. Fathers held him up as a role model to jobless, stay-at-home sons.

His story was, indeed, made up of the stuff of legend. A penniless graduate, unable to find employment, he travelled from an obscure village of Bengal to distant parts of the country in search of a job. In the course of his wanderings, he happened to reach the court of Sawai Madho Singh, ruler of Jaipur. Sawai Madho Singh was looking for just such a young man to tutor his sons. Intelligent, zealous, disciplined and high-principled – qualities he wished to inculcate in his heirs. Over the years, Kanti babu proved himself to be not only a brilliant tutor but an astute administrator. His understanding of politics and affairs of state and his knowledge of English propelled him to the highest position in the official hierarchy. He became Dewan and Advisor to the Maharaja.

Didi went away to live in Jaipur, one of the fascinating desert kingdoms of Rajputana we had only heard and read about in ballads and folktales. When my turn came, my uncles, everyone thought, did even better. At the age of thirteen, I was wed to the second son of Raja Rajendranarayan Roy, the fabulously wealthy zamindar of Bhawal, and received the exalted title of Mejo Rani. Looking back, I wonder at the choice they made. They had educated me so well! Yet the man they were marrying me to was almost illiterate. He could read and write a little Bangla and could sign his name in English. That was all. I suppose they were tempted by the wealth and prestige of the family. Friends and relatives marvelled at our mother's luck in being able to procure two such extraordinary sons-in-law. My uncles were thrilled by the success of their missions and my mother was overwhelmed with gratitude.

Only I knew what it was to be a queen and live in a palace. I learned what my life would be the hard way from the moment I arrived in Jaidevpur.

I got my first glimpse of the Rajbari, which was to be my home for seven years, two days after the wedding. Exhausted by the long journey, first by train from Kolkata, then over the Ganga by boat and finally bundled into a palki, I had fallen asleep when a burst of fireworks, sounds of yelling and whooping, ululation and blowing of conch shells jolted me awake. 'Look,' my new husband nudged me with his elbow, 'we have arrived. The Rajbari is there, right in front of you.' This was the first time I heard him speak a full sentence. He had a strange accent. For a moment I wondered if he suffered from a speech difficulty. Then I remembered my uncles saying that folk living on the other side of the Ganga spoke differently from us.

I opened my eyes with difficulty. The sun had set, and the shadows of dusk were closing around us. A colossal structure loomed a little distance away. Though blazing with light from thousands of lamps, there was something ominous and eerie about it. I felt a wave of panic pass over me.

'How can I live in such a big house?' I muttered. 'I'll lose my way ...'

'Ha! Ha! Ha!' A low laugh came from the form sitting by my side. 'You'll get used to it. Besides, you'll never have to step out of your room alone. There'll always be someone with you.'

His words and laughter struck terror into my soul, I don't know why. A trickle of ice water crept down my spine. My hands and feet grew cold. I looked frantically this way and that. The road was lined on both sides with people hollering and shouting. I couldn't make out what they were saying at first, then the words '*Jai Mejo Kumar er jai! Jai Mejo Rani ma'r jai!*' came to my ears. In one of the lulls between the shouts another voice, a single one called out, 'Could we have a glimpse of the bride's face? We've heard she's very beautiful!' A roar of laughter followed. 'Yes, yes,' some other voices took over, 'We want to see the bride.'

'*Hato! Hato!*' The palki-bearers swung their lathis at the crowd. 'Make way!' They pushed ahead and resumed their endless, whining monotone: '*Hu-hum-na, hu-hum-na.*'

My memory of what happened next is shadowy, indistinct. Jumbled images and sensations crowd into my mind when I try to remember. Being lifted out of the palki by an obese woman with huge breasts, the soft warmth of which permeates my newly budding ones. The arms that hold me are the size of bolsters, smooth as silk, dazzling white, and weighed down with bangles.

Another scene. I am surrounded by strange veiled figures, glittering with gold and gems, in the semi-gloom of what seems to be an enormous courtyard. They pounce on me by turns, make me open my mouth, close my eyes, take a step forward, move back, hold this, let go of that. Images follow in quick succession. Being whisked away to a huge room whose ceiling seems to reach the sky. Being bathed and dressed by maids in new finery, my head bobbing on my chest in exhaustion. *Kheer mudki* being pushed into my mouth with plump fingers, nails knocking against my teeth, making me want to puke. Finally, mercifully, someone parts the curtain of jasmine flowers that hangs around a vast bedstead and pushes me in. Whereupon I promptly fall asleep.

Several hours later, I don't know how many, the bridegroom comes into the room and wakes me up. He slips a ring on my finger and places a heavy box on my lap. 'Go back to sleep,' he says kindly. 'You are tired.' The box slides away as my head hits the pillow.

I see it the next morning. It is a beautifully carved mahogany case full of dolls. Several hours later, the same day, I see him again. Properly, for the first time. He had been a faceless form so far. A dim shape sitting by my side through the rituals. I had felt his hands, cool and moist on mine, when he slipped the ring, a huge diamond flashing blue fire, on my finger. But I hadn't seen his face. My eyes were half-shut and my senses blurred …

At noon I was taken to my mother-in-law's apartments for the *bhaat kapad* ceremony. I watched her furtively from behind my veil as I stooped to touch her feet. She was in her early forties, tall with a very fair complexion, a finely cut face and a stately form wrapped in white garad silk. She wore no ornaments barring a gold chain, thick as a garland of *jui* buds, which fell to her navel. She sat on a vast, carved chair with a younger woman beside her, a woman fair like her but not as beautiful. Rather square and stocky. But she had tremendous personality. A regal aura. As though a voice unheard, emanating from her presence, was announcing to all those who stood around her, *I'm a true princess. I know it. And others had better do so.* A jamdani sari was draped over her arm. Crimson as the heart of a ruby, diaphanous as gossamer, and woven over with hundreds of golden birds of different shapes and sizes. It was the most beautiful sari I had seen in my life. I heard, later, that it had been ordered specially for the ritual and had taken the royal weavers ten months to weave. I didn't throw it away even after it became unwearable. I have kept it, to this day, wrapped in a piece of muslin at the bottom of my trunk. It falls to bits whenever I touch it. But the colour glows, rich and vibrant as ever, and the gold is untarnished.

'Send for the mejo kumar,' my mother-in-law commanded as one of the maids led me to a velvet asan in the centre of the vast room. 'And tell Bamun di to prepare the *Raniswari* thala and bring it.'

Presently an elderly woman came in holding a huge gold thala with both hands. It had a beautifully carved scalloped edge. Surrounding the mound of rice in the centre were at least twenty gold bowls filled with curried mutton, fish and eggs, vegetables and greens, relishes and preserves, curds, *payesh* and sweets. The mejo kumar walked in a few minutes later, looking very natty in a brocade coat with a row of diamond buttons running down his chest. Ropes of pearls hung from his neck. I thought him quite handsome. He threw a quizzical glance around the room, laughed, and turning to the lady standing by his mother's side, said, 'Here I am. What am I supposed to do? Your wish is my command, Princess Baro Didi.'

'Stop your nonsense, Mejo.' His sister, whom I was instructed to call Baro thakurjhi, handed him the sari and said, 'Drape this around the bride's shoulders. Then take the thala from Bamun di and give it to her with the words, *Aaj theke tomar bhaat kapad er bhaar nilam* (From this day onwards I take the responsibility of feeding and clothing you).'

He grimaced and muttered, 'Do I *have* to say this?'

'Yes, you do.'

He placed the sari in my lap, then taking the thala from Bamun di, handed it to me. I managed to hold it for a few seconds but it was so heavy that it wobbled and would have fallen had he not put out his hands, quick as a flash, and caught it.

'Say the words,' a woman in the room prompted.

'From this day onwards, I take the responsibility of looking after all your needs,' he said, setting the thala down in front of me.

'Say "*bhaat kapad er bhaar*".'

He shook his head and walked out of the room. I was glad he hadn't uttered the words. They were so crude. 'All your needs' sounded much more civilized. My heart lifted a little. I turned to my youngest sister-in-law, Tarinmayi, who sat next to me, and smiled. She smiled back and, picking up a piece of fish from one of the bowls, bit into it with gusto.

'*Chhi! Chhi! Chhi!* You greedy girl.' Baro thakurjhi scolded. 'Get up at once and let the new bride eat in peace.'

'No. No,' I said hastily. 'Let her stay. I can't eat so much.'

'That's not the point.' My mother-in-law, addressing me for the first time, treated me to a little lecture. 'You aren't living in the middle-class household of your uncles anymore. You are a royal bride. You don't have to worry about what's left on your thala. Just eat what you want and leave the rest.'

'Do you always eat out of gold vessels?' I asked Tarinmayi, curiously, some days later. We were about the same age and had become friends. Though married, she hadn't gone away to her husband's home. He had come to hers.

'Not always,' she had replied. 'There's a vault full of gold and jewels running from one end of Ma's bedchamber to another. It's bricked over and whitewashed so neatly, no one can guess what lies behind it. Only two trusted maids, Dakshabala and Kadam, know the location. And Ma and the royal mason of course. The wall is broken just before special occasions like weddings, funerals and rice and thread ceremonies. Daksha and Kadam take out the necessary vessels, watch them like hawks all through the celebrations, and put them back when the event is over. After which the wall is built up again.'

'What if someone passes by your mother's room and sees the broken wall?'

'No one is allowed to enter Ma's bedchamber. She locks the door and keeps the key tied to her aanchal.'

The wedding celebrations lasted a whole month. There were fireworks every evening, followed by a cultural programme in the temple courtyard. Men, women and children from the surrounding villages attended in huge numbers, sitting in designated areas. I envied the women their freedom. We had to sit squashed together, behind latticed screens.

The performances went on till late into the night. Theatre and *jatra* parties, in fierce competition for the hundred-rupee prize declared by the baro kumar, bent over backwards to put in their best. *Kirtaniyas*, male and female, came from Nabadweep and Halishahar and *khemtawalis* from Dhaka and Kolkata flaunted their voluptuous bodies in shameless gestures. Thumri and dhrupad singers were invited from areas as far flung as Agra and Benares. There was local talent as well. Kathak thakurs sang the *Agomoni* and narrated the legend of *Manasa Mangal*, delighting the hearts of the elderly. Bauls strummed ektaras and went round and round, with bells on their feet, singing compositions by Lalan Fakir and Duddu Shah. I could make no meaning of the words and found the tunes boring and monotonous. What I loved and looked forward to was the lively jhumur dancing and the soulful strains of *bhatiali*, the song of the lone boatman, which brought tears to my eyes and made me long for my mother.

After all the excitement was over and ordinary living resumed, I tried to resolve some of the issues that disturbed me about my life in the Rajbari. The daily routine of being massaged, bathed and dressed by serving women, that had been so irksome and embarrassing in the beginning, became more acceptable as each day passed. I even got used to being swathed in heavy saris and jewels, day and night, and the long *ghumta* which my personal maid Kumudini fixed to my *khonpa* with diamond clasps and pulled firmly down whenever I left my rooms. Eating out of a thala with enough food on it to feed ten people ceased to bother my conscience after a while. But my appetite began to fade. A time came when the sight of food made me nauseous. I started losing weight and my complexion changed from pomegranate pink to the colour of chalk.

What I couldn't get used to was my husband's absence from my life. I liked his handsome face and quizzical smile. I liked the way he had patted my head on our wedding night and said, 'Go to sleep. You are tired.' I missed him. I wanted him. The three kumars had apartments opening out onto an immense courtyard on the ground floor. The *andarmahal* or women's wing was on the first floor, where each rani had her own suite of lavishly appointed rooms. Curious to know what the princes did all day, I would sneak out and stand in the gallery whenever I could. The deep verandas on three sides of the courtyard, were furnished with English sofas, Persian carpets and carved mahogany stands with porcelain fairies holding lamps in their hands. Sometimes a door to one of the apartments was left open and sounds of singing, dancing and drunken laughter came to my ears. I would unlatch the shutters, lean over the railing and strain my eyes to see what was going on. Till Kumu spied me, pushed the ghumta down my head, and dragged me away.

'Tch! Tch!' she would click her tongue in annoyance. 'You mustn't stand in the gallery, Mejo Rani. Someone may see you.'

'What if they do? How can I stay cooped up in one place day and night?'

'Ranis are supposed to live like that. If word of this reaches your mother-in-law's ears, she'll be furious. And I'll lose my job.'

'Why do the kumars stay downstairs all day?'

'That's the way it is in royal families. Wives see their husbands only at night.'

But that was the problem. I didn't see my husband at all. Not even at night. Tarinmayi prattled all day long about the sweet words her husband murmured in her ears when he came to her and the shocking things he did. I've seen the baro kumar coming to his wife's apartments, which were next to mine, with my own eyes. He was so drunk at times that his feet tottered and he had to be supported by servants. But he came. And my husband? Barring that one night of the *phul sajya*, the flower bed ceremony, when he had brought the ring and the box of dolls, he stayed away. I slept alone on dazzling white silk sheets in the vast bridal bed. The strange thing was that no one in the household noticed this or tried to remedy the situation. It seemed as though they felt they had done enough for me by providing two maids who slept on the floor and were on call if I felt frightened.

One morning, as Tarin and I were playing with our dolls, she asked me, 'Why do you look so sad, Mejo boudidi? Are you missing your mother?' I turned my head to hide my trembling lips and stinging eyes. I missed my mother of course, but how could I tell her that everything about my new home depressed me. I felt trapped in the rooms in which I was constrained to live. The heavy velvet drapes keeping out the sun and wind, the massive carved furniture and life-size marble statues gleaming eerily out of the semi-gloom, made me claustrophobic. The huge gilt-edged paintings of foreign men and women with white faces and strange-looking clothes, peering at me with malevolent eyes, frightened me. I had never felt so lonely and alienated as I did now.

'You poor thing.' Tarin wiped the tears away and, putting her arms around me, said ruefully, 'You should have been born a princess. Then you could have lived with your mother. Tch! Tch! Don't cry. See …' She put a blue-eyed doll wearing a lace dress in my lap. 'She's my favourite but I'll give her to you. That's because you're missing your mother.'

'What's her name?' I muttered. I had many dolls and didn't need any more. But I didn't want to hurt her feelings.

'I wanted to call her Chitralekha. But Mejo dada, who gave her to me, said it was a silly name for a *mem putul*. He told me to call her Rosemary.'

'Does your Mejo dada love you?'

'Very much. Don't worry. He'll love you too.'

'Why doesn't he come to the andarmahal?' The words burst out of me before I could stop them.

'He doesn't?' Tarinmayi's mouth went round with surprise. Her eyes stared into mine.

'No. Never. Not even at night.'

She was silent for a few minutes. Then her plump, pink face grew red and angry. 'It's all that *mukhpuri* Elokeshi's doing,' she cried out in the voice and intonation of a middle-aged housewife. 'She won't let go of him for a minute.'

'Who's Elokeshi?'

'A woman Mejo dada brought from Chandni Ghat. She lives in his apartment. He's completely besotted by her.'

I felt the blood draining from my face. I wasn't a child. I was fourteen years old and knew what that meant.

Tarin saw the anguish in my eyes and added quickly, 'Don't worry. She'll be gone soon. I overheard Ma telling Baro didi that it was time Mejo dada gave her up. "It doesn't look good," Ma said. "Especially now that he's married. What will the new bride think?" Baro didi shook her head and said, "He won't give her up in a hurry." To which Ma retorted, "Then he should keep her in another house. That's the least he can do. Never in the history of this family has a mistress been kept in the palace. It's disgraceful. I shall speak to him about it." Believe me, Mejo bou, I heard her say this with my own ears.'

Turning my averted face towards hers, she said, '*Ebaar ektu hansho tho.* You have such lovely teeth and you look so beautiful when you smile.' Then, as my lips parted in a watery smile, she snuggled up to me and said, 'That's my sweet Mejo boudidi. Now forget Elokeshi and tell me a story.'

Elokeshi was removed from the Rajbari, eventually. Tarinmayi brought me the news. 'Mejo dada has sent her away,' she cried, grinning from ear to ear. 'He has bought her a house in Dhaka and settled her in with a retinue of servants. His valet Kunja told my maid Giri that she had protested a lot, but he wouldn't listen. Good riddance! Aren't you happy, Mejo boudidi?'

I *was* happy for a few days. But I realized quite quickly that my destiny hadn't changed. My husband came to my rooms once or twice a month under pressure, I'm sure, from his mother and sister. He was kind to me and brought me presents but I don't think he liked me much. He did whatever was expected of him. But his lovemaking was hurried and passionless and gave me no pleasure. And he always left before I awoke.

With the passing years my loneliness deepened into melancholia. My unfulfilled body grew starkly thin and my soul remained parched and arid.

Things were made worse by my mother-in-law's constant probing. She never blamed me or uttered a harsh word. All she did was ask questions and offer advice. *Was the mejo kumar neglecting me? Was he not coming into my rooms often enough? Wasn't it strange that a beautiful and well brought up girl like me couldn't hold her husband's affections? Did I think I could try harder? It was time, was it not, that the kingdom of Bhawal got an heir? After the baro rani's two miscarriages and the loss of her only living child, she had given up all expectations from her eldest daughter-in-law. She was pinning her hopes on me. So were the subjects.* Counselling sessions followed, replete with tips, veiled hints and, what she considered, useful suggestions. My sister-in-law, Princess Indumayi, was more understanding. 'Go, Mejo bou,' she would say to me, interrupting her mother in full flow. 'Go get some rest. You look peaky.' Once or twice, I heard her whisper fiercely as I left the room, 'Stop it, Ma. What's the use of harassing the poor girl? You know your son. Why don't you speak to him instead?'

But my mother-in-law wouldn't give up. She sent for me at least once a week and said the same things over and over again. As time went by, I came to dread her summons and started evading her by pretending to be sick. Gradually pretence turned into reality. I became truly sick. I lay in bed all day, wan and listless, weeping into my pillow. I had no energy, no appetite, and was desperately lonesome. The mejo kumar turned my poor health to his advantage and reduced his nightly visits. Even Tarinmayi lost interest in me. My brother-in-law Rabindra had been wed the previous autumn and the new bride Anandakumari, a sprightly, quick-tongued girl, had taken my place in her affections.

It was Bara thakurjhi who first noticed the severity of my condition and suggested that the family physician, Mahim Dasgupta, be sent for. Kumu brought me the news. My mother-in-law, apparently, had demurred a bit. It was unseemly, she told her daughter, for a male doctor to attend to a royal female. He would have to see her face, hear her voice, and perhaps, even touch her. It went against the tradition of the Rajbari. But Bara thakurjhi insisted. Times had changed, she argued, and our ways of living had to be modified from time to time. It was foolish to cling to medieval traditions in a matter of life and death.

'When she first came to the palace,' she reminded her mother, 'Mejo bou was as plump and healthy as Tarin. And look at her now!

Don't forget that she has a mother and brother in Kolkata to whom we are answerable if anything untoward happens.'

She won the argument as always and Dr Mahim Dasgupta was asked to pay a visit. He examined me carefully, clicking his tongue in annoyance at my condition. Diagnosing my ailment as acute anaemia, he prescribed a diet rich in minerals and iron. Lots of milk and eggs, fruits like apples, oranges, grapes, dates and pomegranates, soups made of *magur* and *singi* fish, and green leafy vegetables cooked lightly with very little oil and spices. But I was horrified at two other suggestions he made. A piece of raw liver, eaten every morning on an empty stomach, worked wonders in cases like mine, he said, as did the broth obtained from boiling a sheep's trotters. The next day he sent bottles of pills, red wine and tonics which Kumu was instructed to bring to me at the appointed times without fail. However, despite the care lavished on me, and though the new diet suited me better than the oily, heavily spiced royal dishes I had been made to eat so far, my condition improved only marginally.

But, here, I must make a confession. I poured the trotters broth down the drain every day, and threw the raw liver, ground to a paste with salt, tomatoes and coriander leaves, out of the widow where stray dogs and cats polished it off in minutes.

As I said, my health improved a little, but my heart was heavy and my mind in constant turmoil. Gradually, the craving for my husband's company faded and I developed a curious sense of disconnect. With him, the palace, and my life as a queen. I longed to go back to the simple comfort of my mother's home and the only thing that sustained me during those bleak years was the thought of my brother's love. I yearned and looked forward to his visits. He came often, at least once every two or three months, and stayed for several weeks. He had cleared his law exams and had started frequenting the lower courts of Kolkata. But his efforts weren't yielding much result. To build up a worthwhile legal career, one needed backing and capital. Dada had neither. He was now thinking of quitting the law and securing a job that was respectable and brought an adequate income at the same time. Looking to his royal relations to help him, he spent week after week in Jaidevpur trying to persuade the baro kumar to use his influence with the sahebs and set him up as a government official in Shillong. The baro kumar had his constraints, I suppose, and it hadn't happened so far. But Dada wouldn't give up.

It was Dada who took back the news of my husband's neglect and my failing health to Kolkata. Ma and Didi were so worried they wrote me long letters full of instructions and advice. Didi, who was married into a feudal family like mine, understood my predicament but disapproved of the way I was handling it. She wrote:

> I hear that you are behaving like an idiot and neglecting your health most shamefully. What's wrong with you? You used to be such a smart, intelligent girl! Now, it seems you have no idea of what is good for you. You should try to please Ramendra and keep him happy with sweet smiles and sweet words. You should also dress in a manner he likes. Be as close to him, as dear to him as possible. Insist on sleeping next to him even when he is in his own apartments. And, above all, keep in good health. No man likes a faded, sickly wife. In short, dear sister, it is our husbands' love that brings supreme happiness in our lives. And guiding their affections towards us should be looked upon as a pleasure and duty.

Ma's response was more emotional. Pouring her heart out in an unrestrained flood, she wrote several letters:

> My darling Bibhu,
>
> I am in great anxiety because of your disease. I have read a great deal about it and it appears that whoever falls victim to it loses his/her memory altogether. I also found

out that, apart from taking nourishing food and exercise the patient has to remain cheerful, at all times. In my experience nothing braces and cheers the mind as much as music. Speak to your mother-in-law and ask her to engage a lady tutor to teach you to sing and play the harmonium ...

Bibhu, my jewel,

Daktar babu has asked you to take four ounces of raw liver every morning and evening. From what I hear, arrangements have been made to bring it to you in as appetizing a form as possible. With lemon juice, tomatoes and coriander leaves. But who can help you if you throw it away? Don't be so foolish, my darling child. All you need to do is pinch your nose tight and swallow it in a couple of gulps. Keep a paan handy and pop it into your mouth immediately afterwards. I understand your distaste in consuming the stuff. But how else will you make up the quantity of blood you have lost? I don't want to listen to any excuses or objections. Just take it. Mellins Food mixed with milk provides very good nourishment. Drink one glass at least three or four times a day. Another thing. Check your temperature two or three times every day. Keep a thermometer handy ...

In another letter she addressed the problem I was facing with my husband.

Darling Bibhu,

You write that your heart pines and wanders because there is no one in the house with whom you can share your thoughts and feelings. But do you not see Ramendra often enough and talk to him at length? I know that in your family, meeting one's husband during the day and pouring out one's troubles in his ears is considered shameless conduct

> in a daughter-in-law. But, in my judgement, there is nothing wrong or immodest in it. If husband and wife are together, both feel happy and relaxed and their love for each other is heightened. So, from now on, you must make sure that Ramendra spends several hours with you during the day ...

Ma did not approve of Dada's frequent visits. No self-respecting man, she felt, would park himself in his sister's husband's house for such long stretches. She wrote him angry letters remonstrating with him for wasting his time in the Rajbari ...

Come back home – and don't try to fool me with flimsy excuses, she wrote, over and over again, *I can stand everything, but I cannot stand anyone fooling me. I am not as stupid and ignorant as you think I am. I can see through all your pretences. Every time you go to Jaidevpur you don't feel inclined to come back. But how will you secure a livelihood if you idle your time away sitting by your sister's side and holding her hand? She has grown up now and can take care of herself. Leave her alone, for God's sake. Don't you know my position here? Have you no idea of how exasperated I feel by the taunts and ridicule I have to suffer on your behalf ...*

Dada showed me the letters every time they came and, shaking his head sadly, said that he had no option but to leave for Kolkata at once. But I clung to his arm and begged him not to go. I would feel so lonely. So bereft. I said I would write to Ma and implore her to let him stay a few more weeks. I understood Ma's predicament. My uncles had looked after her when she was a young, helpless widow. But she wasn't young and helpless anymore. Her daughters were well married, and her son had cleared his law examination. There was a general expectation that she would leave the protecting umbrella her brothers had provided all these years and start fending for herself. I don't know who taunted and ridiculed her. Not my uncles and their wives surely. They weren't the type. Perhaps their sons and daughters-in-law. Or some distant relations. Perhaps it was all in my mother's mind. She was too self-respecting a woman to live on charity one moment longer than necessary. She realized that it was time for her to move away from the house in Uttarpara and strike out on her own. But she couldn't do it without her son's help. Hence her anger and frustration.

The members of the royal family, and this I must say in all honesty, were very kind to my brother. My sisters-in-law, seeing how much better I felt when he was around, encouraged him to stay. So did my mother-in-law. And gradually he started taking on various responsibilities. Such as providing the baro kumar with legal advice, counselling my husband when he behaved in too wayward a fashion and rushing off to Dhaka to procure tonics and medicines not available in Jaidevpur.

I wrote to Ma saying that Dada was not wasting his time here. He was looking for a job and the royal family was helping him. This, of course, I did not know for certain. I believed what he told me. That the baro kumar had drawn up a list of British officers and was arranging meetings with them. *My in-laws are very fond of him and treat him, not like a guest, but a member of the family*, I wrote. *Don't worry. He'll go back as soon as the baro kumar finds him an opening. Besides, your son-in-law hasn't been keeping well for the last few months. He needs to be taken to Kolkata for treatment. Dada will be travelling with him. You will see your son soon ...*

But Ma was not convinced. She didn't seem to believe a word. On the contrary, she lashed out at me in a letter which filled me with guilt and shame.

> That scoundrel has stopped writing to me. I have no idea what he is doing in your house for so long. Can't you understand how anxious I am for him? And you, too, for that matter? You're not a fool. You know very well why I disapprove of his frequent trips to Jaidevpur. Tell him that he needn't look for employment anymore. His excuse of meeting sahebs is

nothing but a pretence. I can't stand this hypocrisy anymore. If this is the way he is trying to get a job, he will never get one in his life. Send that worthless fellow home as soon as you can.

As for the excuse that he has taken on the responsibility of bringing Ramendra to Kolkata for treatment, I haven't heard anything so foolish in my life. If your husband has been ill for months, what were you doing all this time? Why didn't your clever brother, who has been kicking his heels in Jaidevpur for so long, have the bright idea of bringing him here earlier? Now that I want him back, you offer the pretext of his having to accompany Ramendra to Kolkata. If you were serious, you could have taken this decision long ago. I'm so disgusted I feel like committing suicide. I shall have to do so before long. I shall have to atone for the sin of bearing such a son in my womb ...

Ma's letters alarmed me. She sounded desperate. I feared that if we didn't obey her, she might be driven to take the next step. She might write to Princess Indumayi who, after her mother's death, had donned the mantle of Head of the Royal Household and urge her to send her son back. If such a thing were to happen, my position in the Rajbari would be severely jeopardized and Dada would find himself in an extremely embarrassing situation. He realized that he had to act swiftly and laid his plans.

It wasn't only the mejo kumar who needed specialized medical advice. The baro kumar was suffering from the ill effects of alcoholic excess and his heart had shown signs of damage. Seeking an audience with the eldest princess, Dada proposed to take them both to Kolkata and arrange consultations with top specialists. He also sought her permission to take me along.

'Bibhu is my mother's youngest child and the apple of her eye,' he told her. 'Ma is missing her a lot. She also worries about her and keeps begging her to come to Kolkata, if only for a few days, in every letter she writes. Besides, Bibhu has been in delicate health for quite some time now. A change of scene might do her good.'

Princess Indumayi agreed and suggested that since the baro rani hadn't visited her family for many years now, she should be included in the party. There was a condition, though. We would stay with our husbands in the mansions owned by the Bhawals in Kolkata. We could visit our parents as often as we wished but would not spend a single night under their roofs. Dada was disappointed but, realizing that this was the norm in my husband's family, he thanked her for her kindness and started organizing the visit. At the last moment, Anandakumari clamoured to be taken along and she and her husband were given permission to join us. In early December 1908, all three princes of Bhawal and their wives set off for Kolkata.

It was on this trip that I met Dada's wife for the first time. He had got married two years ago but, even though everyone from the Rajbari had been invited to the wedding, no one had attended. Baro thakurjhi had sent presents – a pearl and ruby sitahaar, two jamdani saris, a hand mirror set in a carved silver frame, alta and sindoor in gold containers and a crystal vial of attar.

The bride's name was Sandhyarani. She was a slim, shy girl of fifteen with nothing much to her face and figure. Except for her eyes. She had wonderful eyes. Large, liquid, deeply lashed, they looked out on the world with a direct, trusting gaze. They held a world of innocence. For some reason I couldn't look into those eyes. They made me uncomfortable and have done so ever since. I cringe before them to this day.

Ma was overjoyed on seeing me, though she felt saddened at the thought that I wouldn't be staying in Uttarpara. However, she made the most of the few hours I spent with her three or four times a week. She petted and pampered me. She oiled my hair, combed out the tangles and put it up in an elaborate *khonpa* framed by a gold *berha* and studded with jewelled pins. She scrubbed my face and arms with cream and flour, showering me with kisses all the while, just as though I were the same little girl who had been snatched from her arms six years ago.

And the meals she served brought back my childhood in a way I had never imagined possible. She was a wonderful cook with magic in her touch. She could turn out the most delectable dishes from the simplest of ingredients. She remembered all my favourite foods and cooked them with her own hands. Succulent crab curry, duck's eggs in a rich red gravy with peas and new potatoes, tiddlers in a sweet and tart sauce, *puin* greens with shrimps, fat wedges of ilish fried to a golden crispness and served sizzling hot straight from the wok. And as the old, familiar, delicious odours wafted into my nostrils, my appetite returned. Flinging caution and the doctor's advice to the winds, I gorged on everything that was set before me. My aunts did their bit by bringing out their best pickles, preserved ginger and *amloki*, sheets of dried mango, coconut balls and crunchy sesame slabs.

Between the indulging and cosseting, Ma asked me a number of leading questions about my life in general and my relationship with my husband in particular. I tried to fob her off with evasive replies. She was surprised by my reticence and tried to probe deeper. But I wouldn't let her. I realized that she felt a bit hurt. But how could I bring myself to tell her about my husband's continued infidelity? Elokeshi was out of the picture. But other women had taken her place in an unbroken line. From the palace gossip that came to my ears I knew that a famous singer called Malika jaan was one and an Anglo-Indian cabaret dancer, who went by the name of Dora Gibbons, another.

Ma expected me to confide in her but how could I do so without breaking her heart and carrying the guilt for it all my life? Worse, how could I confess that, over the past seven years, my love and yearning for my husband had died a natural death and I was as indifferent to him as he was to me. How could I tell her that on the occasions when he did come to my bed – they were fairly frequent now – I turned myself into a block of ice? That his kisses and caresses stirred me not at all. I submitted to them wordlessly, seeing nothing, feeling nothing. How could I tell her that I heaved a sigh of relief when I woke up in the morning and found him gone? My sister-in-law Sarajubala once asked me, with a secretive smile, why I always looked so strained and tired in the mornings following the mejo kumar's visits.

'You look pale. There are deep shadows under your eyes and your lips are bone dry. What went on last night? Did Mejo thakurpo wear you out with his ardour? Keep you awake all night?'

'Not at all. I slept the sleep of the dead.'

The smile faded. She was puzzled. 'What do you mean?' she murmured, 'I don't understand you.'

'You would,' I answered, 'if you felt as I do. A log of wood or a corpse pretending to be alive.'

Although it lasted only a little more than three months, my visit to Kolkata did me a lot of good. My aches and pains lessened. I put on some weight and colour crept back into my cheeks. My hair, which had started falling out in handfuls, grew back again. By the time we left for Jaidevpur, I began to look and feel almost like my old self.

The princes, too, benefited from the visit. They had both been very ill when they first came. The doctors who examined the baro kumar were unanimous in their opinion that he was suffering from an enlarged heart and that, unless he took the utmost care, he hadn't long to live. He had to give up all manner of excitement, alcohol and rich food, and live a life of great discipline and restraint.

As for my husband, the ulcers which had first broken out on his back had spread to other parts of his body by the time the Kolkata doctors examined him. His condition was so bad that he had to keep his legs and arms swathed in bandages all the time. Colonel S. P. Sarbadhikari, top specialist in venereal diseases, confirmed the report of Dr Mahim Dasgupta that the mejo kumar was suffering from syphilis and that it had reached an alarming stage. Treatment was started at once and the patient responded well. By the end of February, he had benefited so greatly from Colonel Sarbadhikari's injections, medicines, balms and salves that he was given permission to return. But with a caveat. He was on no account to spend the summer in Bhawal. His limbs hadn't recovered their full strength and his digestion was still weak. He was to proceed to the hills as soon as possible and live a reclusive life, resting as much as possible, breathing fresh air and eating healthy, nourishing food. Care must be taken to ensure that he wasn't stressed or worried at any time. The choice of place was either Mussourie or Darjeeling.

The mejo kumar was extremely reluctant to obey this part of the doctor's advice. He begged him to reconsider but Colonel Sarbadhikari was adamant. He had recovered from the worst of the onslaught, the doctor told him, but his condition was still very fragile, and he needed a spell of convalescence in the cool, fresh air of the mountains.

A few days before we left for Jaidevpur, Dada walked into the room where the mejo kumar sat resting after lunch. I sat a little distance away, by the window, embroidering a *kantha* for Sandhya rani who was expecting her second child. I could hear the hum of their voices but concentrating as I was on my work, I didn't pay attention. Suddenly I heard Dada say something that startled me.

'Have you ever thought of buying an insurance policy, Bonai babu?'

'What is an insurance policy?'

'It's a scheme floated by a British company. They sell insurance, which means they invite clients to pay a small sum of money annually and get a very large amount in case of death …'

'But I am not dying, am I? I am fully cured. That's what the doctor said.' The prince's eyes were wide with surprise.

'Of course … you aren't dying. God willing, you will live a hundred years. Buying insurance is just a way of getting some extra money in case something untoward happens. Like an accident, for instance. Many wealthy men are insuring their lives these days. The premium is so little, one hardly notices it. But the amount their next of kin receive, in case of death, is huge.'

'I understand. You are worried about Bibhavati. Let me assure you that if something happens to me, she will be well looked after. My brothers will see to that.'

'I know it, Bonai babu. Bibhu will want for nothing. But some extra money is always welcome, isn't it? However, it was only a suggestion. Since you are already in Kolkata, I thought … But it is entirely your call. Do what you think is right.'

'Hmm. I see your point. It is a new-fangled notion but there's no harm in it. The estate will pay the premium from my share of the rents. I shall instruct Mukunda babu …'

'There's no hurry. Think about it for a day or two then decide.'

'No, no. Go ahead with the formalities. What do I need to do?'

'Nothing much. Just one visit to the office of the Oriental Insurance Company in Mangoe Lane. A doctor will examine you to check if you have a terminal illness like cancer or tuberculosis and record your height, weight and other distinguishing marks. Then you'll have to sign some forms. That's it.'

The next evening Dada informed me that the mejo kumar had insured his life for thirty thousand rupees and I was the nominee.

On our return to Jaidevpur, Mahim Dasgupta was told about Colonel Sarbadhikari's advice. He endorsed it wholeheartedly. Mussourie was too far away, he said. Darjeeling was the better option. Dada offered to go to Darjeeling and look for a suitable house. Mukunda Guin, the mejo kumar's secretary, accompanied him. A house was chosen and taken on rent for six months. The members of the royal family, relieved to hear that he would be accompanying his brother-in-law and staying with him through the trip, were happy to leave all the arrangements in his hands.

I was a bit surprised when Dada informed me that the date of the mejo kumar's departure to the hills had been fixed for the 18th of April.

'Isn't that too soon?' I asked. 'He hasn't recovered fully from his journey from Kolkata. Shouldn't he recuperate a bit more before undertaking another?'

'He'll get all the recuperation he needs in Darjeeling. There'll be nothing else for him to do there but rest. Besides, the hot weather has started setting in. Better we leave Jaidevpur before it turns into a bowl of steam.'

'We?'

'Yes. We. You are going with us.'

'How is that possible? Baro thakurjhi will never agree.'

'She has agreed already. She wanted me to take Jyotirmayi didi along, but I told her that the house I've found, though large by Darjeeling standards, wouldn't accommodate the second princess and her retinue.'

'So … then? Who will be my chaperone?'

'You won't need a chaperone. I, your older brother, will be with you at all times. And your maids will take care of your personal needs.'

'How many people are going?'

'We'll be twenty-five in all, including the doctor.'

'Mahim babu?' My face brightened at the thought of the tall, stooping, kindly doctor, whose presence was such a comfort, accompanying us.

'Not Mahim babu. One of his patients is in a critical condition and he cannot leave him. He suggested we take his nephew Ashutosh along. Ashutosh, though young, is a certified medical practitioner and helps his uncle with some of his cases. Indu didi sends for him whenever the servants fall ill.'

My heart sank. I had seen Ashutosh several times. He was a friend of Dada's. They were more or less of the same age and, being non-royals in a royal environment, bonded well. Dada tried to keep it hidden but the two were drinking buddies. I knew that. They were also fond of racing. Dada lost money frequently, not big amounts, and fell into debt. Sometimes I managed to help him out. Sometimes I didn't.

Ashutosh was tall, fair and good-looking. He was my brother's friend and Mahim babu's nephew. I looked upon Mahim babu as a father. But I just couldn't take to Ashutosh. There was something about him that gave me goose bumps. Even through my veil I had seen his eyes raking my form.

'Why do I have to go?' I mumbled. 'I'll only be in the way.'

'No. You won't. Ramendra will be happier with you beside him. Your presence will quicken his recovery. Besides, you've been ill too. The clean air and the peace and tranquillity will do you a world of good ...'

The house Dada had rented was called 'Step Aside'. Built in 1876, it had belonged to a wealthy Scottish tea planter named Archibald Aird. Mr Aird had lived in it with a large retinue of servants till his death nine years ago, after which it had passed to his only surviving offspring. The present owner, Mrs Penelope Dawson, had married an English stockbroker and lived in London. She had come to Darjeeling to attend her father's funeral and settle his estate. But she hadn't disposed of Step Aside. She had requested her father's missionary friend, Reverend William Jarvis, to keep an eye on the house and grounds. She sent him a regular sum for its upkeep and came and stayed in it whenever she felt homesick for Darjeeling, where she had been born and spent her childhood. The rest of the time it was kept locked or given out on rent.

I was somewhat puzzled by Dada's choice of the place in which we were to live for the next six months. Step Aside, I gathered, was a beautiful property set high among the mountains from which, on clear afternoons, one got a stunning view of the Kanchenjunga peak in all its white and golden glory. But the location was remote, quite a few miles away from the nearest human habitation.

Driving out of the station, in the two cars Dada had rented, we entered a quaint jumble of cobbled streets with shops and houses perched crookedly on the hill slopes. Narrow pavements, slippery with patches of melting snow, were strewn with carts full of fruit, vegetables, live chickens in bamboo cages, and tea packed in paper bags. The air was damp and chilly and smelled of rotting fruit and urine. Dada wrinkled his nose. 'This is the native quarter of Darjeeling,' he said. 'The locals live here.'

'And the sahebs' quarter?' I asked.

'There's no such thing. Government servants and professionals live in fine houses on the highroad which is called the Mall. Wealthier men such as tea planters and timber merchants have bought up huge tracts of land, often a whole slope, and built imposing mansions high on the hills. We shall be living in one of those.'

I looked out of the window taking in the scene outside with amazed eyes. It must have been a special day for there seemed to be a lot of people headed somewhere. Men in threadbare sweaters and filthy caps ambled down the streets smoking *biris* and chewing betel. Middle-aged women carrying baskets full of eggs, chickens and pumpkins on their heads and occasionally leading a goat by a string, and young women with snot-nosed babies on their backs, followed the men. One or two European tourists, swathed in greatcoats and mufflers, could be seen standing outside the shops. There was very little traffic. A few cars and buggies rolled by slowly, desultorily, as though they weren't bound for any particular destination.

'Where are all these people going?' Dada asked the driver of the car.

'To the Mahakali temple of Chourasta. It is Baishakhi Ashtami today. An auspicious day. Kali is a most benevolent deity and has a large number of worshippers. The devotees ask for boons and sacrifice goats and chickens to the goddess when she grants them. Those who can't afford livestock offer eggs or pumpkins.'

I stared out of the window, taking in the scene. The arrogant idle men striding along spitting and smoking biris. The women with burdens on their heads and backs, gnarled hands and sad eyes. The half-naked malnourished children. My heart sank. *Not a nice place!* I thought. *Yet, for whatever it is worth, this is where people live. There are houses here and shops and hotels. This is where we'll find help if we are in trouble.*

I communicated my fears to my brother as we made our way to Step Aside, the car winding slowly up the mountains, loop after loop, through stretches of dense virgin forest.

'How much further do we have to go?' I muttered uncomfortably. 'We've come so far away from town already. To whom shall we turn if we need help? There doesn't seem to be a soul in sight.'

'Don't be ridiculous,' Dada answered acidly. 'What help can we possibly need? We have a doctor with us. We have servants, maids, cooks and other menials to look after us. We have guards to protect us and cars to send to the town if anything is required. Stop bothering your head with silly thoughts. Leave it all to me.'

For all my doubts, I must confess that I fell in love with the house the moment I saw it. It was a large, rambling stone mansion, standing at various levels on two and a half acres of the greenest mountain slope my eyes had ever beheld. It had four entrances and several flights of steps leading to different parts of the house, terraces and gardens. The gardens were laid out in typical English style with smooth lawns and meticulously weeded borders which, in this season, were alive with promise. Soon they would be filled with a profusion of flowers. A beautiful conservatory ran all along the back of the house. On fine days its glass walls trapped the sun's light in great golden beams. Geraniums, freesias, camellias and varieties of exotic orchids swung from the rafters, trailed along the walls and sprang from marble pots on the ground. I loved this place, warm and full of sweet scents, and spent many wet afternoons curled up with a book on the sagging velvet sofas which lined the walls.

Step Aside had a library full of dusty tomes. Law books, plantation records, religious texts and musty files stacked with old bills and receipts had lain on the shelves for who knows how long. However, a diligent search revealed some old English classics, gilt-edged and bound in cracked leather. I found *Ivanhoe*, *Robinson Crusoe*, *Pilgrim's Progress*, *Jane Eyre*, *Vanity Fair*, *David Copperfield*, *Hard Times*, *Barchester Towers*, *Scenes of Clerical Life* and *Silas Marner* as well as a stack of old hunting magazines and copies of *Punch*. I had been a voracious reader as a girl. Unfortunately, that pleasure was taken away from me the moment I stepped into the Rajbari. My mother-in-law believed that women who read books were liable to become widows. Dada managed to smuggle in some books from time to time which I read with guilty delight in the privacy of my bedroom, making haste to hide them under the mattress when anyone came near. Now I was free to read whenever and as much as I liked. Hugging my secret hoard, I rediscovered my childhood in a way I had never imagined possible. It was a glorious feeling.

But what I loved best were my rambles in the orchards that sloped down to a rivulet at the extreme edge of the property. Springing from somewhere deep in the misty purple mountains, it leaped and frothed over cliffs and mossy stones and meandered in and out of the trees. Above and around the sparkling water, apple, plum and cherry branches, foaming with blossom, spread out like white and pink lace against a blue and silver sky. Below the aged trunks were patches of short tufty grass spiked with crocus, narcissus, iris and scylla. The sight never failed to send a thrill through me. These were trees and flowers I had never seen yet recognized instantly from the pictures in the illustrated English books I had read in my childhood. I knew that, as spring passed into summer and the days lengthened, the grass would grow tall, rich and sappy and more and more flowers would appear. Kingcups and daisies, cowslips and speedwells, foxgloves and swelling cushions of pink and yellow primroses. The climate of Darjeeling was like that of England, cold and rainy, and its verdure had much in common.

For the first time, in the seven years of my married life, I was happy. The loneliness and anxiety, the diffidence and lack of self-worth that had weighed me down ever since I stepped into the Rajbari, melted away. A great calm descended on my soul. I breathed in great gulps of sharp, icy air. I let the sun's mellow warmth play on my limbs. There was a spring in my step, a smile on my lips, as I wandered about the wooded slopes and by the edge of the stream. I felt as free as a bird.

Another odd thing happened. The apathy and dislike I had felt for my husband, over the last few years, disappeared. Concern and a sense of responsibility took their place. I realized now, as never before, that he was a sick, lonely man and had been so for a long time. Immersed in my own grievances, I hadn't noticed. It's a funny thing to say but I was convinced that he went to other women as a matter of habit. Not because he wanted to. Because, in some strange way, he felt he owed it to them. But *I* was the one on whom he depended. *I* was the one he truly loved.

In the last one year he had turned to me, again and again, for sympathy and understanding and I hadn't responded. His clumsy efforts at love-making were his way of reaching out to me. They were a call for help. But I had resisted him. I had let him down.

Now, more than ever, he needed me. Not for his material comfort. There were enough servants to take care of that. It seemed to me that, having left his blood relations behind, he was clinging to me as the only one he could call his own; the only one he could trust. I saw his eyes light up and the muscles of his face relax whenever I drew near. He grumbled that I wasn't spending enough time with him. And when we were together, he was reluctant to let go of me. He seemed afraid. Of what or whom, precisely, I couldn't say. But my presence reassured him. Made him feel safe. Of that, I was sure.

The only fly in the honey pot of my happiness was Ashutosh. I had always been a little wary of him. Now, living under the same roof, my discomfort turned to active dislike. I got the feeling that he was stalking me. He would appear suddenly in the garden, the conservatory or one of the rooms in which I would be resting, reading or arranging flowers and try to engage me in conversation. I gave short, cryptic replies to his questions, making my annoyance quite clear. But he wouldn't take the hint. In desperation I begged Dada to intervene. But, to my surprise, instead of being concerned, he turned on me.

'The Rajbari's primitive ways have got to you, Bibhu,' he said. 'You've forgotten who you really are. A Kolkata girl from an enlightened family, educated in a convent. Why should you feel upset when a man speaks to you? That, too, a doctor who is taking care of your husband?'

'I don't trust him.' I muttered rebelliously. 'There's something about him that frightens me.'

'Don't be absurd. What harm can he do?'

I was convinced that the mejo kumar did not trust him either. Whenever Ashutosh came near him with his medical bag, his limbs stiffened. His face turned pale. He clutched my hand and wouldn't let go even when I struggled to free myself. Sometimes he looked into my face with a plea in his eyes. 'Don't leave me,' they seemed to say. 'I am alone, quite alone, in these alien surroundings.'

I even heard him remonstrate with the doctor once or twice. 'You give me too many medicines and too many injections, Ashutosh. I'm not sure they are helping me. Mahim babu never gave me any injections.'

'But the Kolkata doctor did, didn't he?'

'Yes. But not as many as you do.'

Ashutosh was unfazed. He went on to assure his patient that the medical care he was getting was the best for him. And it seemed as though he was right. He and Dada held consultations with Colonel Calvert, the civil surgeon from Darjeeling who was summoned from time to time, and they seemed to agree on the line of treatment to be given.

After our arrival, the kumar spent the first two days in his rooms, on the first floor, recovering from the fatigue of the journey. Lying in bed for hours together, he looked out of the window at the snow-capped mountains and shimmering sky, with contemplative eyes. He seemed very thoughtful and spoke little. Then, on the third morning, he sat up in bed and swung his feet over the edge. 'It's going to be a fine day,' he said. 'I'll go down and sit in the garden.' Waving away the breakfast that had been brought up for him – fruit juice, rolled oats cooked in milk, toast and soft-boiled eggs – he asked for *luchi* and *halua*. Dada and Ashutosh exchanged glances.

'No, no. Not ...' Before Ashutosh could finish his sentence, I heard my own voice cut into his. 'Certainly,' I said, smiling at my husband. 'If that is what you wish.' Then, turning to the maid who had brought in the tray, I said, 'Take it back. And tell the cook to fry hot luchis, nice and light, and make some *suji'r halua* with plenty of almonds and raisins just as the mejo kumar likes it.'

I felt, rather than saw, two pairs of shocked eyes fixed on my face. And, indeed, I was as taken aback by my words as they were. Not only the words. The way they had been said. How cool and curt my voice had sounded. How different from my usual timid, tentative one. My heart beats quickened. But not with fear. I remembered Dr Mahim Dasgupta's advice. 'Assert yourself. Take decisions. Even if you regret them later. Always remember that you are no ordinary woman. You are a queen of Bhawal.'

Well, I had asserted myself. I had shown Dada and Ashutosh that I wasn't afraid of them. I saw them staring at each other in dismay. Triumph surged through me. They had lost their power.

The kumar was wheeled out into the garden where he spent the whole day sitting in the dappled sunshine under a huge cedar tree, his golden retriever running around him, fetching the ball he threw and nuzzling and licking his feet. A whole week went by. I revelled in my newly found confidence. The days were fine, and I started taking my husband for short walks. I insisted on giving him the food he liked.

He was eating with relish. The strained look left his face and colour returned to his cheeks. The low fever that wouldn't leave him for the last six months, abated. The only symptom he still had were the boils on his legs. But even those had started drying and shrinking. He was getting better and more cheerful by the day ...

Except when he was given his injections. His face would contort painfully then and his eyes glaze over with helplessness. He would beg me and Dada to stop Ashutosh, insisting that he didn't need injections, that they were unpleasant and not helping him. It saddened me to see the imperious royal and intrepid tiger hunter reduced to begging and pleading. But we didn't listen to his pleas. Instead, we told him that they were necessary. 'It's only a tiny prick,' I said. 'Just be a little patient and you'll be completely cured.' I was convinced that it was the medical treatment which had brought about the change ...

Then, in the middle of our third week in Darjeeling, he woke up one night with excruciating pains in his stomach. I was sleeping in my apartments – they adjoined his – when I felt Kumu's hand at my shoulder shaking me awake. 'Mejo Rani! Mejo Rani!' her voice sobbed. 'Kunja was here just now. The mejo kumar is very sick. He is asking for you.'

Rubbing the sleep from my eyes, I ran to his bedroom. I found him tossing and turning on the sheets, writhing in agony, the force of the spasms propelling him into a sitting position, then pushing him down again. I leaned over him. His eyes were stark and staring and there was froth at one corner of his mouth. 'The injection ...' he muttered feebly. 'I told you, Bibha ... the injection ... something wrong...' His voice trailed away.

I turned to Ashutosh who stood, black bag in hand, on the other side of the bed like a statue.

'What's wrong with my husband?' I demanded, my eyes burning into his. 'He was perfectly well yesterday. Where's Dada?'

As though in response, Dada came running into the room. A

glance at the patient and his heavy, florid face fell. His eyes shifted uneasily from the man on the bed to the doctor, 'Do something, Ashutosh,' he whispered urgently. 'For God's sake, do something.'

At his voice the statue came to life. Opening his bag with shaking hands, Ashutosh drew out a phial containing a shell pink translucent liquid which he poured down the patient's throat.

'What happened?' Dada asked in a bewildered voice. 'He was so much better! And why is there froth on his lips?'

Ashutosh had collected himself by now. He shut his bag and said calmly, 'It isn't froth. It's just a bit of spit that spilled out of his mouth when he was gnashing his teeth with pain.'

'But why does he have so much pain? What's wrong with him?' I asked, my voice sharp and disbelieving.

'I don't know,' Ashutosh replied, looking at me with deadpan eyes. I found neither concern nor sympathy in them. 'It could be stones in the gall bladder. It could be simple indigestion. I've given him something to stop the spasms and put him to sleep. He should feel better soon.'

Turning to Dada, he said, 'I'll consult my medical books and find out why such a thing happened. I'll also send a telegram to my uncle and ask for his advice.'

Ignoring him completely, I turned to my husband's secretary, Mukunda Guin, who stood at the door with the other retainers. 'The Rajbari must be informed at once,' I told him grimly. 'Take one of the cars and set off for the post office as early as you can tomorrow morning. Preferably before dawn. Send the baro kumar an urgent telegram telling him to come at once and take charge.' Then, fixing my eyes on Dada's face, I said, 'I don't wish to keep my husband here any longer. We will catch the Darjeeling mail as soon as the baro kumar arrives and proceed to Kolkata where Dr Sarbadhikari can take a look at him.'

'Tch! Tch!' Dada clicked his tongue. 'There's no need to panic, Bibhu. See ... the pain seems to be ebbing already and the kumar is falling asleep. Go back to your room and we'll discuss what's to be done tomorrow. Try to get some sleep.' He placed a hand on my head and stroked it gently. But, for the first time, his touch left me cold. I had had enough of his control and caresses. Jerking my head away, I turned my eyes once more on the servants and officials still standing at the door. 'I want the telegram sent first thing tomorrow morning, Mukunda babu,' I repeated. Ignoring Dada's advice about going back to sleep, I went and sat by my husband's bed. I wiped the sweat from his face and neck with my aanchal and ran my fingers through his hair and over his forehead.

He woke late the next morning. Around nine o'clock. Opening his eyes, he saw me and smiled.

'Were you with me all night?'

'Yes.'

'Why? Oh yes … of course … I remember. I was in a lot of pain and had sent Kunja for you.'

'How do you feel now?'

'Better. I slept really well.' He glanced out of the window and added, 'It's a beautiful morning. I'll get ready and go down. Send Kunja to me, will you?'

'Do you really feel well enough to go down?'

'Of course.' Taking the hand that was still stroking his forehead, he squeezed it gently. 'You're a good wife, Bibha,' he said, 'the best a man can have. But go now. Try to get some sleep. You look tired to death.'

I found Kunja sitting on the floor, back resting against the wall, just outside the door. I gave him his master's message and entered my apartments. But I didn't go to bed. I went to the bathing room, filled the tub and stepped in. The water stung my skin, it was terribly cold. I spent the next half hour soaping and scrubbing myself from head to foot so hard my limbs and scalp tingled and turned red. Then, watching the soapy water drain away, I felt cleansed. As though something unseen but vile was leaving me.

'Mejo Rani! Mejo Rani!' Kumu was outside banging the door frantically. 'Why are you bathing by yourself? That, too, in cold water before an oil massage? You'll catch your death! Why didn't you send for me? Open the door and let me help you.'

I opened the door. I let Kumu wipe my limbs and dry and comb my hair. I let her drape a fresh sari around me and put sindoor in my parting and alta on my feet. Then I walked out of the house and into the garden.

The mejo kumar was eating his breakfast under the cedar tree. Poached eggs, toast with butter and marmalade, fruits, fresh juice and milk. A tray stood on a table beside him set with fragrant Darjeeling brew and milk and sugar in silver pots. There were two Dresden cups on the tray, egg-shell fine, with a beautiful pink and blue design. He looked up at me and smiled. 'Come, join me,' he said. 'Have a cup of tea. *O re Kunja!* Go to the kitchen and tell the cook to send the mejo rani's breakfast to the garden. She'll have it with me here.'

We spent the whole morning sitting in the sun, chatting and playing with the dog. The mejo kumar seemed quite cheerful and regaled me with anecdotes from the past. I knew that he was a good sportsman, but no one had told me that he had won the Viceroy's Cup for being the best equestrian of the year in 1907. Or that he had challenged Nawab Salimullah to a *tum tum* race on the Dhaka race-course and won the wager amount of one thousand rupees.

'It caused quite a sensation, Bibha,' he grinned. 'A kumar of Bhawal getting the better of the Nawab of Dhaka, the biggest zamindar in the district. It was a big feather in Bhawal's cap.' His face was radiant with remembered glory.

'Why didn't you tell me all this before? Why didn't you share your thoughts with me? I longed and longed to be a true wife and companion to you. But you never ...'

'The truth is,' he smiled sheepishly, 'I couldn't think of you as a wife. I didn't want to marry you. You were too young.'

'I wasn't too young. All girls are married by thirteen.'

'You were Tarinmayi's age. I love Taru more like a daughter than a sister. I've done so ever since I saw her first, lying by Ma's side, in the birthing room. Looking at the tiny, crumpled, pink face, my heart filled with love of a kind I'd never felt before. I used to see you together, playing with your dolls. It made me feel odd and awkward. That's why I avoided you ...'

Towards noon, a mist rose from the valley and shrouded the mountains. The sky darkened and the wind turned cold and gusty. 'We should go in now,' I said. 'It might start raining any moment.'

'Yes,' he agreed. 'I'll go up to my rooms and rest a bit before lunch. You, too, should catch up on your sleep.'

I didn't want to go into the house. I didn't want to encounter Dada or Ashutosh. I went around the back and sneaked into the conservatory. I found *Barchester Towers*, the book I was reading the day before, lying on the sofa. Burrowing my head in the silk cushions, I opened it. But I couldn't read a line. Suddenly I felt intensely tired. My eyes burned from lack of sleep. I don't know when the lids fell, and the book slipped from my hands and dropped to the floor. I don't know how long I slept. I was awakened by a gentle hand on my head. 'Poor little Bibhu.' I heard Dada's voice in my ear. 'What a night you've had. Come. Wash your face and have some lunch. We're waiting for you.'

'Has the mejo kumar come down again?' I sat up and rubbed the sleep from my eyes. They still burned like live coals.

'No. I had his meal sent up to his apartments. He shouldn't exert himself too much. Especially after last night's episode. I advised him to sit, all snug and cosy, before the fire in his sitting room and eat.'

'Then who's "we"?'

'Ashutosh and I ...'

'I'm not hungry.' I sank down on the cushions once more. 'I'll eat later.'

'Come, come. Don't be so hard on the poor boy. He's feeling guilty enough as it is. Besides, how will sulking and refusing food help? You'll only make yourself sick. Don't forget that you need to conserve your strength for your husband's sake. You came here to keep him company and ensure that he is happy and cheerful. Come on, eat something, then go back to sleep.'

What he said seemed reasonable. I rose and went into the house.

The afternoon turned dark and dreary. Rain dripped in a steady, persistent patter on the glass roof of the conservatory. The walls had misted over. I cleared a patch with my fingers and looked out. The gardens and mountains had disappeared. A thick grey fog covered everything. There was no way I could go out and enjoy a ramble in the woods. Sighing, I came back to the sofa. I tried to read but couldn't concentrate. I couldn't sleep either. I tossed and turned for a while and then, flinging the book away, I rose to my feet. Not knowing what else to do, I ran into the house through the driving rain. Damp and chilled to the bone as a result, I made my way to the kumar's apartments.

I found him in his sitting room, sprawled in a planter's chair by a cheerful fire. He looked up at my entrance. His eyes lit up.

'Good of you to come,' he said briefly.

He seemed to have recovered completely from the previous night's incident. We chatted and played cards. He sang snatches from his favourite songs. He had a fine baritone and excellent sense of tone and rhythm.

Tea was brought up at four-thirty, along with dishes full of cauliflower *singarhas*, hot from the wok, and *khasta gaja*. I loved khasta gaja. Those golden-brown squares of fried pastry dripping with syrup were amazing sweets. They had hundreds of crisp layers but melted in the mouth after the first crunch. I was ravenous, all of a sudden, and ate heartily.

Halfway through the meal Dada came up. 'Oh! You're here,' he exclaimed, looking at me with puzzled eyes. 'I've been looking for you everywhere.'

'Come, Shala babu.' The kumar pointed to a chair. 'Join us for a cup of tea.'

Dada had barely taken his first sip when Ashutosh walked into the room. My husband was a bit put out but didn't show it. 'I hope you don't have a syringe with you,' he said with a smile.

'No, no. Just checking.' Ashutosh smiled back. 'You gave us a real fright last night.' He was talking to his patient, but I could feel his eyes, under half-closed lids, on me.

I stiffened. I found his smile, as I did everything else about him, sinister. But, as Dada said, it might have been my imagination. I rose to leave the room but the kumar wouldn't let me.

'Come, come,' he said, 'there's no need to be so proper. We aren't in the Rajbari.'

He was very cheerful for the rest of the evening. He ate little himself but plied his visitors with tea and snacks and shared his plans for all the outings and sight-seeing he meant to do as soon as he felt better. 'We'll go for a picnic to Jaldapara forest one day. And for excursions to Kalimpong and Kalijhora. And one weekend I intend to go riding to Sandakphu to see the Sleeping Buddha. With the onset of summer, the rhododendrons will start blooming. It's an amazing sight, Bibha!' He turned to me with shining eyes, 'Thousands of them lining the bridle paths. So many colours and sizes. From the tiniest, most delicate shell pink blooms to giant monstrosities flaming like tongues of fire! We'll go together. We'll order a horse from Darjeeling and ride into the heart of the mountains.' Glancing at Dada and Ashutosh, he added, 'You can come, too, if you like.'

No one responded. He seemed a bit flummoxed at our lack of enthusiasm. Scanning the three faces before him one by one, he asked, 'Why do you look at me with such mournful eyes? What's wrong? Am I dying?' He looked directly at Ashutosh and said, 'Tell me the truth. Summer is a long way off. Three to four weeks at least. Won't I recover completely by then?'

'Y-e-s, yes,' Ashutosh muttered. 'Yes, of course, you will.'

'Then?' He turned his gaze on me.

'I don't know how to ride.' I said feebly.

'You don't need to. You will sit behind me, side-saddle, though it would be better and safer to sit astride. But you'll have to wear breeches for that. Are you ready to wear breeches?'

'Certainly not.'

Now, he turned to Dada and said, 'Something's the matter. What is it?'

Dada hemmed and hawed a bit then said in a rush. 'Bibha insisted on sending a telegram to the baro kumar, informing him about last night and urging him to come to Darjeeling at once.'

'Why?' My husband looked at me with astonished eyes.

'She doesn't want to keep you here any longer,' Dada answered for me. 'She feels we should proceed to Kolkata as soon as the baro kumar arrives.'

'Why Kolkata?'

'She wants Colonel Sarbadhikari to examine you.'

'But he has examined me over and over again. That, too, barely a month ago. It was on his advice that I came to Darjeeling.'

'That's what I told her. Besides, we've paid advance rent for the next six months. We've also stocked masses of provisions. All that money and effort will be wasted.'

'Why, Bibha ...?' My husband turned his eyes – large, innocent, trusting – on my face.'

A hot flush rose from my neck and spread to my cheeks. 'Last night's incident frightened me,' I mumbled. 'You were in so much pain.'

'But I feel fine now.' Turning to Ashutosh, he said, 'Your medicine was very good. It brought me a lot of relief. But why do you think such a thing happened?'

'There could be hundreds of reasons. Your liver, kidneys, pancreas, gall bladder, intestines … anything could be affected. On the other hand, it could be simple indigestion. It is a classic case of GOK.'

'What's GOK?'

'God only knows.'

The three men burst out laughing.

'Send another telegram to the Rajbari tomorrow morning,' the mejo kumar said, leaning back in his chair. 'Inform them that I'm perfectly fine. There's no need for Dada to come post haste to Darjeeling. He isn't in the best of health himself.'

After the two had left, he turned to me and said gently, 'Don't be afraid, Bibha. I didn't want to come to Darjeeling, but now that I'm here I realize what a good idea it was. I feel so much better. You are happy here too, I know.'

'Yes,' I said, 'I love it here. I feel much better too. Only—'

'What is it? Tell me.'

'I'm not very sure of Ashutosh. Not sure of him as a doctor … I mean. He's young and inexperienced. As for Colonel Calvert, his attitude seems very offhand and casual to me. I would be happier if you were in the care of Dr Sarbadhikari.'

'That's not possible.' He thought for a while, then an idea struck him. 'I'll tell Mukunda to send a telegram to Mahim babu in my name, requesting him to come to Darjeeling. The critical patient for whom he had stayed behind, three weeks ago, must have recovered by now. Or died. We'll both feel much better with him around.'

'Wonderful!' I cried. 'We'll send Ashutosh back to Jaidevpur. If Mahim babu comes here he'll be needed there. We'll send Dada away too. Ma is very annoyed with him for spending so much time with us. Particularly now that he has a family. "Why don't you tell him to go home?" she writes in every letter. She's annoyed with me too. "Your brother has no sense of responsibility," she reminds me over and over again. "But you do. Or you should. What sort of man leaves his wife and children to hang around his sister? Bouma is quiet and gentle. She doesn't complain. But how does she feel? Aren't you a wife? Don't you know?" I was angry with Ma at first for blaming me, but then I thought …'

'Your mother is right. He should go back to his family. I'll have a talk with him tomorrow.'

'They should both go back. With Mahim babu here we won't need anyone else …'

Next morning, a Saturday, dawned golden bright. Stepping out of bed I went to the window, pushed up the sash and leaned out. Yesterday's rain had cleared the fog and mist and there, before my eyes, stood the mighty Kanchenjunga. Rising from the rest of the range, it glittered like a gigantic cone of ice. A rush of damp air carrying the scent of tiny wild daffodils, growing in drifts along the lower slopes, blew against my face. The soughing of pines above my head made music in my ears. A tremendous happiness, such as I hadn't known in years, suffused my soul. The lively tune of an old English ditty that Didi and I had been taught in school kept running in my head and I hummed snatches from it:

Early one morning/ Just as the sun was rising/ I heard a maid sing/ in the valley below.

O don't deceive me/ O never leave me/ How could you use/ A poor maiden so?

'You seem very happy this morning, Mejo Rani,' Kumu said with a smile as she got me ready for the day. 'I've never heard you sing before.'

'Would I be allowed to sing in the Rajbari? You'd be the first one to stop me.'

Still humming, I made my way through the French windows of the drawing room, down the short flight of steps that led to the terrace where the mejo kumar was sitting. I passed Dada on the way. He was coming up as I went down. I don't know what my husband had said to him or, indeed, if he had said anything at all. But I saw, or thought I saw, a shadow on his face. I smiled at him but did not stop to talk. I had no intention of starting a conversation and giving him the opportunity to change my mind with sweet words and pats on the head. As I sped past, I saw him turn to look at me with bewildered eyes. As though his world, a world he had believed in all his life, had suddenly turned upside down.

I spent the morning with the kumar. Then, after lunch when he had retired to his rooms for a rest, I went out for my afternoon ramble in the orchard. Yesterday's wind and rain had lashed at the trees, stripping the boughs of their blossoms, and I found myself walking on a carpet of pink and white petals. The sight of the denuded trees saddened me till, looking closely, I saw something that made my heart leap up with joy. The stark branches, silhouetted against the sky like black lace, were dappled with patches of velvety lime-green nodules that would burst into foliage in a few weeks. Minute balls, tinier than mustard seeds, hung in clusters from the bare twigs. The trees had started fruiting. Summer wasn't far away.

I made a resolution. I would go to Sandakphu with my husband. But not sitting behind him. I would ride by his side on a horse of my own. I could see it before my eyes. A milk-white mare with gentle eyes and quivering ears. And, to hell with the proprieties, I would wear breeches. Not only Sandakphu. We would ride together wherever our fancy took us. Over hills and dales, through forests of pine and spruce and by the banks of the Teesta which went winding like a silver ribbon in and out of the mountains. As soon as I got back, this evening, I would request the mejo kumar to send for a horse and trainer from Darjeeling. He wouldn't refuse. I was sure of that …

That night the pains came back again. Accompanied, this time, with vomiting and bloody flux. Summoned at first light, I rushed to my husband's room to find Dada and Ashutosh leaning over the bed on which he was tossing and turning, groaning helplessly, *Ma! Ma go! E ki asajhya kashto! Aar to paari na … Ma amar!* (O Mother! This suffering is excruciating. I can't bear it anymore. O my mother!) I ran to his side and placed a hand on his brow. It was burning.

'What is this?' I glared at Ashutosh. 'What have you done to him now?'

'What has *he* done?' Dada answered for Ashutosh, his voice rough and angry. 'It seems to be a case of hill diarrhoea. Quite a common ailment in these parts. Don't worry. He has been given medicines. He should get better soon.'

But he didn't get better. The fever rose higher and higher and the purging and vomiting got more virulent. The three of us sat like statues, watching him, not leaving the room for even a minute. Every now and then Ashutosh poured something down his throat or stabbed a needle into his arm. But nothing seemed to be helping.

Morning dawned and passed into noon. And now a shadow fell on the day which had begun in a burst of sunshine. A huge bank of clouds, dark and ominous, rose from the hills and covered the sun. Violent gusts of wind tore at the trees outside the window, rattling the glass panes till it seemed they would shatter with the impact. Then the rain came. Torrential rain accompanied by hailstones, the size of wood apples, beat against the walls so noisily that we could hardly hear one another.

'We had better move the bed away from the window,' Ashutosh said.

Sending for a couple of servants, he ordered them to shift the patient's bed to the opposite wall of the room. Whether it was from the movement or whatever the reason, a tremendous fit of retching and vomiting seized the kumar. And this time it went on and on. It just wouldn't stop.

I looked at Dada with eyes that had turned to stone. I should have shrieked. I should have cursed and vilified him. I should have gathered all the members of the household and, in their presence, charged the two with murder. But not a sound emerged from my throat. My mind and body felt numb.

'A telegram must be despatched to Jaidevpur at once.' Dada's voice cut across my swimming senses like the swish of a knife. Sending for Mukunda Guin, he dictated the text: *Kumar seriously ill. Frequent watery motions with blood. Come sharp.*

'Send this to Bhawal at the earliest,' he said. 'And bring the civil surgeon with you. Take the big car. It goes faster.'

'In such inclement weather?' Mukunda babu looked horrified. 'It's raining cats and dogs. And the gale is blowing harder than a cyclone. So many trees in the garden have been uprooted. Go to the window and take a look.'

'I know,' Dada answered. 'But it's a matter of life and death. You'll have to take the risk.'

Mukunda babu's plump, pock-marked face turned sullen. He set his lips in a thin line and said, 'You should have thought of this in the morning, Satya babu. When the day was fine. It's extremely dangerous now. There's barely any visibility and the mountain paths are slippery with mud and slush.'

'The driver is a hill man. He has driven over this terrain for years. Don't be afraid. He will take you to the town and bring you back safely.'

Mukunda babu sighed and gave in. 'I have eaten my master's salt for seven years,' he said. 'Now, if indeed it is a question of his survival, I must go, I suppose. But there's no chance of bringing Colonel Calvert back with me. He'll never leave his cosy fireside on a Sunday and rush out in a storm.'

'Tell him that the patient is the second prince of Bhawal and that it's a matter of life and death.'

Hours passed. We sat around the bed, watching each other with stealthy eyes. The squall gained in intensity. The shadows of dusk deepened and what little light was left in the sky faded. Servants brought up lighted candles and hurricane lamps. They filled the room with smoke and dancing shadows but the flames, wavering in the wind, shed little light.

There was a brief lull around eight o'clock. Hope surged in my breast. *The weather is changing,* I thought. *Colonel Calvert will be on his way by now. He'll do something. He'll save my husband.* From what I had heard, the civil surgeon wasn't the best type of Englishman in India. He held Indians in deep contempt and avoided paying visits to native patients unless they were wealthy and powerful. And then he would overcharge them with brazen impunity and humiliate them into the bargain with barbed comments on the lack of sanitation and hygiene in their living conditions. But he had the reputation of being a very good doctor and I clung to that fact as to a lifeline. Besides, he had been perfectly cordial to us on the few occasions he had come to Step Aside.

Within half an hour, the storm returned with renewed fury. The gale whistled and shrieked around the house, crashing against trees and tearing them down. Rain swept in through the window crevices and pooled on the floor. A sound of shattering glass came to my ears, from where I could not say. I glanced at my husband. It seemed to me that the threshing of his limbs had lessened and his frantic cries of pain had turned to moans. They were growing fainter and fainter. Was this a good sign? I glanced at Ashutosh but his face was set in stone …

The kumar died at midnight. I know the exact moment he stopped breathing because I stopped breathing too. There was an unseen hand at my throat, a hard, harsh hand, squeezing all the air out of my lungs. 'I'm choking!' I shrieked. 'I can't breathe. I need some air.' Rushing to the window, I threw up the sash and leaned out into the pouring rain. Within seconds, Dada was by my side. 'What are you doing?' he cried pulling me away. 'Have you gone mad?' I fought and struggled but my strength was nothing against his.

And now a terrible chill shot through my veins like a streak of lightning, and reached my head. A spot of black mist swirled before my eyes. It was growing larger every second. It was swallowing me up. I felt my body grow limp and crumple against my brother's chest.

You've won, Dada. That was my last thought before I fainted. *I've lost. My life was a brief spring idyll. Seized one moment, surrendered in another. The long, glorious summer that I thought lay ahead of me was only a dream …*

The next six months are hidden from my memory by a layer of fog, thick and heavy as velvet. Sounds, sensations and images prick the shroud from time to time. A train rushing through the night across a burning plain. A bowed, motionless form standing on the bank of a flowing river, surrounded by veiled women in widow's white. A wasted body, still as a corpse, lying on a vast bed in a darkened room. A whispering voice in my ear, soft, sweet and deadly … *Come away, Bibhu. Sign this paper and be rid of this obnoxious life forever. Ma and I will take care of you. You know how much I love you.*

I try to resist. I turn my head away. I try to shut out the voice. But I am weak. All my defences crumble against the power of that voice. Gentle. Persistent. Inexorable.

Then, one day, I sit up and reach for the pen that is held out to me. I sign on the dotted line. My head swims and falls back on the pillow. I close my eyes in weariness. But not before I've seen the gleam in the other pair of eyes. The ones that are watching me like a hawk.

11

Indumayi Debi

Jaidevpur
May 1921

I WENT TO SEE THE SANNYASI LAST WEEK. NOT OUT OF CONVICTION OR curiosity. My intention was to interrogate him so thoroughly that he would stand exposed for the fraud he was. A man who had died and been cremated, resurrects himself after twelve years and claims his rightful position as heir to the estate. Could anything be more ridiculous?

Unlike my sisters I hadn't allowed myself to get caught up in the frenzy surrounding the appearance of the sadhu. I had kept myself aloof from all the politics and speculation. For one thing, I was convinced he was an imposter. For another, I didn't have the physical or mental strength to take a position. I had been suffering from a heart complaint for many years. It is a family ailment. My father and grandfather had it. And both my brothers, the baro and chhoto kumar. All four died of it. I will too, Mahim babu has warned me, if I allow myself to get excited or agitated. But how can I stop these feelings? My present precarious condition is the result, I'm convinced, of the misfortunes that fell on the family after my second brother's death.

Why then did I make the journey to my sister's house? Why did

I agree to check the stranger out? The truth is that my grandmother, Rani Satyabhama Debi, sent a messenger with a letter for me in which she said that it was my duty to do so. The British government, she wrote, regarded me as the representative of the royal family and my opinion in the matter was important. I didn't agree with her but I could not disobey. She is the eldest member of the royal family and we have been taught to respect her wishes.

My sister Jyotirmayi's opinion matters little to me. She is the most credulous human being I know. She'll believe anything and everything. Especially if it comes from yogis and ascetics. She spends half her day in her prayer room, wrapped in a *namabali*, and the other half in consorting with self-styled seers and astrologers with whom she fills her house. Rani thakurma is exactly like her. Or rather, Jyotirmayi is exactly like Rani thakurma. That's why they get along so well. As for Tarinmayi, she never grew up. She is intelligent and well educated. She reads the newspapers every day and keeps herself abreast of everything that is happening in the country. But, at heart, she is still as innocent and gullible as the giggly little girl who ran after her older siblings, begging them to tell her stories and wheedling dolls and toys out of them.

Rani thakurma had expressed surprise at the utter indifference shown by my sisters-in-law at this new development. I was surprised too. Particularly at Sarajubala. I had expected her to reach out to us with some reaction, whatever it might be. Out of all my sisters-in-law, Sarajubala is my favourite. She's wonderfully kind and considerate. She had a hard time with Baro khoka's excessive drinking, but she never complained or created a scene. Her face was always serene, her voice gentle and the smile never left her lips. That could be because she came from a similar background. She knew and accepted the fact that scions of wealthy, feudal families disregard their wives and insist on having their own way in all matters.

The fourth daughter of Surendranath Matilal, of the famous Matilal family of Boubazar, Sarajubala was betrothed to my brother in infancy. Her father, a reputed lawyer of the Calcutta High Court, had a huge client base which included my father Raja Rajendranarayan Roy. Babamoshai had great respect for Surendranath Matilal and trusted him in all legal matters. They were personal friends too. To cement the bond between them they agreed to wed their children Sarajubala and Ranendranath. A grand betrothal ceremony was arranged. However, both being children at the time, Saraju was five and Ranendra ten, the wedding was postponed indefinitely. It took place eight years later. But Babamoshai hadn't lived to welcome Sarajubala as his daughter-in-law. He had died a few years earlier.

Babamoshai was a wonderful father. He was one of the busiest men I've known. Despite his ill health, he travelled extensively through the estate, taking care of every detail personally. He also went to Dhaka and Kolkata every month to attend to his legal affairs. Yet he managed to find time to gather his children around him and regale them with tales from the Mahabharat and Ramayan and comic anecdotes of the great babus of Kolkata. It was from him that we had heard of the Dattas of Hatkhola who spent all their time flying pigeons while the zamindari was falling to rack and ruin. Of the Sheels who squandered thousands of rupees on the wedding of the first lady's favourite cat. Of the Tagores of Jorasanko and the Matilals of Boubazar.

Bishwanath Matilal was one of the great babus of Kolkata. Sarajubala's great grandfather and the founder of the Matilal fortunes, he, like many of his peers, had amassed his fabulous wealth by trading in the cheapest of commodities, one found in the kitchens of the poorest of the poor. Salt.

In the early years of John Company's rule, English ships had carried away India's gold, gems, ivory and spices and returned empty since Britain had nothing of her own to sell in India. Tossed about on the waves like egg shells, they ran the constant risk of capsizing when the seas got rough. Until someone came up with a bright idea. Why not weigh them down with salt? It would serve a double purpose.

The ships would be secure against storms and tempests and the salt could be sold at a premium in the Kolkata markets. It did not matter one whit that India had plenty of salt of her own. With favourable laws and the active connivance of native agents, it was perfectly possible to push indigenous traders out of business. Over the years many such agents bought up large shares and formed partnerships with their British masters. Of these, Bishwanath Matilal was the most successful and the market owned by him, Boubazar, became the chief trading centre of Kolkata.

Sarajubala's father, Surendranath Matilal, had two wives and eleven children. Six sons and five daughters. All the girls were beautiful and, thanks to their father's wealth and contacts, were married into illustrious families. Sarajubala's second sister, Rani, was the daughter-in-law of the Raja of Uttarpara and her youngest was wed to a prince of the kingdom of Ula.

After Baro khoka's death, Sarajubala had tried living in one wing of the palace with a small retinue of old retainers. However, she couldn't do so for long. After some years she moved to Kolkata, first to her paternal home in Boubazar, then to a house owned by her husband in Ripon Street. Having no issue of her own, she adopted the son of a distant relative of hers. The boy's name is Pataki Matilal. But she didn't abandon her servants. She took them with her and looks after them and their families to this day. She sends the boys to school and college, helps them to find employment and marries off the girls at an appropriate age. On herself she spends very little.

I never had much love for Bibhavati and Anandakumari and no expectations from them. But their frozen silence on the subject of the sadhu's claim is extraordinary, to say the least. Particularly Bibhavati's ...

It is true that the circumstances surrounding my second brother's death are cloaked in mystery. Much of it doesn't add up. There was a lot of gossip and speculation at the time. And it never died down. To this day, rumours raise their heads from time to time. Someone or the other claims, or knows someone who claims to have seen the mejo kumar by some holy river or in some obscure ashram in the mountains. But I turn a deaf ear to all such nonsense. Even at the time the tragedy took place, even when we were devastated with shock and grief, the baro kumar and I had taken a decision. We would let sleeping dogs lie. Probing the matter would be dangerous. Who knew what undesirable facts would come to light?

However, we did send for Mukunda Guin and question him. 'You were the mejo kumar's secretary,' I told him sternly. 'It was your duty to bring the prince back to Jaidevpur where he could be given a cremation befitting his rank. Why wasn't that done?'

'I wasn't there.' A visibly distraught Mukunda Guin wrung his hands and looked at me with fearful eyes.

'Where were you?'

'Satya babu sent for me at five o'clock that evening. He told me to drive to town, despatch a telegram to Jaidevpur, and bring the civil surgeon back with me. There was a terrible storm raging that day. Visibility was poor and the road was blocked in places with hailstones and branches torn from the trees. The driver and I had to stop the car after every hundred yards, get out in the pouring rain and clear the debris, before we could start again. The journey, which normally takes one and a half hours, took five. It was a miracle that we reached at all. The gale was so strong that the car could have been blown over a precipice more than once.'

'Why did you have to venture out in such foul weather? Why wasn't the civil surgeon given a call earlier?'

'I have no answer to that, Baro Rajkumari. Satya babu took all the decisions. The post office had closed by the time we got there. Fortunately, the driver knew where the postmaster lived. The poor man was fast asleep. We woke him up, made him open the post office and send the telegram. But there was no question of returning that night. The driver flatly refused to take the car back and I couldn't blame him. We checked into a cheap hotel and spent the night shivering in wet clothes on lumpy, bug-infested mattresses. I could feel a fever coming on but I could do nothing about it. Next morning, after the storm had abated, we set off, taking the civil surgeon with us. But by the time we reached Step Aside, everything was over. The kumar had died during the night and been cremated.'

'Do you mean to tell us that Colonel Calvert gave a death certificate without seeing the body?' Ranendra's voice was incredulous. 'Besides, the certificate was endorsed by the Collector.'

'I don't know anything about that. I've told you what I know. The mejo kumar was dead and cremated by the time we reached Step Aside.'

'How could Colonel Calvert do such a thing?' The baro kumar looked at me as he asked the question, but it was Mukunda babu who answered him. 'I have no idea,' he said. 'I took him to the drawing room where Satya babu and Ashutosh daktar were sitting. I was shivering so violently with shock and fever that I excused myself and left immediately afterwards. I don't know what went on, after that, between the three.'

'You say it was a wild, stormy night.' My eyes held his with a piercing glance. Unlike Mejo khoka, I didn't trust the man. 'How was Satya babu able to get hold of pall bearers?'

His eyes fell before mine and he scraped the floor with his toes as he stammered a reply. 'I … I wasn't there so I c-can't say for sure. From … from what I've heard, the men who carried the mejo kumar's body weren't regular pall bearers. They were Bhu-bhutiya brahmins from the glen just below the hill. And they didn't take him to the crematorium in Darjeeling. They cremated him in their own village. Some even say they abandoned the body and jackals dragged it away. But … but that is hearsay. I can't vouch for it.'

'What do we do now?' I asked Ranendra after Mukunda babu had left.

'What can we do?'

'We must sue Colonel Calvert for unethical behaviour. We must send him a legal notice at once.'

Ranendra shook his head. 'It would be a futile exercise. Don't forget that he is a white man. And the white race sticks together. The judges will exonerate him and, quite possibly, censure us for filing a false case.'

'But we can't let him get away so easily.'

'We have no choice. He has the might of the British government in India on his side. And his co-conspirators will stand by him. What do *we* have? Only the word of a minor palace official. That, too, an old man who, by his own admission, was sick and distraught at the time. Besides, we know Mukunda babu's nature. He is weak and faint-hearted. He has also been known to lie on occasion. He'll never be able to hold his own in the witness box. Especially when questioned by an English lawyer. What is to prevent him from changing his story in court and denying everything he has told us?'

My blood boiled with fury at our helplessness. I felt like screaming and cursing. But I controlled myself and said, 'We will throw the two scoundrels out. Vipers we have nursed in our bosoms all these years. You must take care of Satya. And I'll make sure Ashutosh never dares to enter the palace again. That's the least we can do.'

'I agree. But we must proceed with caution and discretion. Inform the guards that Ashutosh is not to cross the *deuri* unless we send for him. Tell them we are in mourning and not encouraging outsiders. It is important to make sure that Mahim babu doesn't feel hurt and humiliated. I'll deal with Satya. But after some time. We mustn't act in haste.'

To lull him into a feeling of security, Ranendra allowed Satya to linger on for a few more months. Then he sent for him and told him, abruptly, that he had outstayed his welcome and must leave. Shocked and bewildered by such a summary dismissal, Satya did leave but, shameless creature that he was, he kept returning every three or four weeks and parking himself for a day or two. He told the servants that his sister's welfare was more important to him than his pride. He would shrug off the humiliation the royal family had heaped on him and comfort his sister during her difficult time.

Six months went by. Then suddenly, one day, two documents were handed over to Ranendra by one of the palace servants. Both were signed by Bibhavati. One was a legal notice stating that she had appointed her brother, Satyendranath Banerjee, as her agent. He would conduct and take care of all her affairs in the future. The other was a relinquishment deed, by which she gave up every claim to her legal inheritance, including the title of Mejo Rani, in return for a financial consideration. Brother and sister left together as soon as the formalities were concluded and the money had been deposited into Satya's hands.

They came to see me on the day of their departure. Bibhavati stooped to touch my feet but I moved back a step. 'The time for such gestures is over,' I told her coldly. 'I don't like hypocrisy.' She opened her mouth to speak but I didn't let her. 'You were never happy with us,' I continued. 'We brought you from a humble family and gave you the dignity of a queen. We took care of you through your illness. We disliked your brother's prolonged presence in the Rajbari but we not only tolerated it, we treated him like a son of the house. Only for *your* sake. You have received nothing but kindness and consideration from us. Yet you—'

Bibhavati burst into tears. Her lips trembled. Her face was pale and strained. I felt a momentary pang of sympathy. But I hardened my heart against her. She had made us suffer too much.

Her brother, however, was as belligerent as ever. 'Her husband neglected her,' he snarled. 'He kept mistresses.'

'All princes keep mistresses.' I stared him down. 'But he was never unkind to her. He was generous and gentle and compassionate.'

Bibhavati nodded. 'He was the best of husbands,' she murmured. 'I have no complaint against him or any other member of the Rajbari.

All I seek, today, is your blessing, Bara thakurjhi.' She took a step forward in another attempt to touch my feet. But I put up a hand and stopped her. 'You don't need to seek my blessing. I give it to you voluntarily. May you be happy in your brother's home. May you find the peace and contentment you craved and never found with us. But remember one thing. You have relinquished all your claims as a rani of Bhawal. And with that you have relinquished the family. From this day onwards you are nothing to us and we are nothing to you.'

These were harsh words, but they were not meant for her. They were meant for her brother's ears. I didn't want his shadow falling within miles of the Rajbari in future. But I've often thought of Bibhavati and wondered what became of her. It wasn't she who wanted to leave the palace and cut off all communication with us. I was convinced of that. It was Satya who had forced her to do so with the intention of getting hold of her money. But why couldn't she stand up to him? What stopped her? Was there more to their relationship than met the eye? Even to the most loving and trusting among us, it seemed to be of a kind somewhat unnatural between siblings. What was the nature of the power that Satya wielded over her? Why was she, a woman of twenty and a queen, a lump of putty in her brother's hands? It was inexplicable.

The palace buzzed with rumours after they left. My youngest brother's wife, Anandakumari, started them by hinting at an incestuous relationship. She said that she had seen the two in compromising situations more than once, but hadn't opened her mouth from fear of being reprimanded. But, now that the Rajbari was rid of them, it was time its members got to know the true character of their mejo rani.

She claimed she had once walked into Bibhavati's bedroom unannounced and seen her standing in front of an open window, her clothes in disarray, hair streaming down her back. Her brother stood behind her, holding her in a tight embrace. One of his hands rested on her breast, the other gripped the curve of her waist. His face was pressed into her neck. And twice she had seen them lying side by side in Bibhavati's bed, facing each other, talking in hushed whispers. Another story Anandakumari spread was that Bibhavati was pregnant when she left for Darjeeling. In fact, that was the reason her brother took her there. Had everyone forgotten how cleverly he had circumvented the proposal of the second rajkumari accompanying them? The foetus was aborted in Darjeeling with the help of Ashutosh and a local midwife. Mahim babu's nephew, she asserted, was the third member of the unholy trinity.

I had dismissed these stories with the contempt they deserved. *Anandakumari,* I had told myself, *is a petty, narrow-minded woman and jealous of her sister-in-law's beauty. Bibhavati is shy and timorous by nature. One could even call her spineless. She is intimidated by her brother. But she's not immoral. She was devoted to her husband. Disappointed in him, perhaps, but devoted. She wouldn't be unfaithful to him …*

But now, twelve years later, I found myself wondering. Could there be an element of truth in the stories Anandakumari had spread? What explains Bibhavati's strange behaviour after hearing about the sadhu's claim? The District Magistrate had written to her. He had even enclosed Mr Needham's despatch, describing the situation in Bhawal. Of how the family and tenants had accepted him as the mejo kumar. Yet she had shown no interest or even curiosity in finding out the truth. Why? Was she so happy in her brother's home that she didn't want to take the risk of becoming a wife and queen again?

These thoughts and several others passed through my head, as I sat in the phaeton, on the way to my sister's house. I relived every moment of that terrible time. The loss of all my brothers one by one. The desertion of their wives. The gradual break-up of the family. The palace turning into a shell. I had accepted it all and tried to find peace, not like Jyoti from *jap* and puja, but from within. And I had found, if not peace, at least a measure of serenity. Now, even that was being threatened by the appearance of a mendicant claiming to be the mejo kumar and my grandmother and sisters accepting him.

I sent for the man as soon as I reached Jyoti's house. I must say that his appearance startled me. The resemblance was quite uncanny. His physique was a somewhat whittled-down version of my brother's. And, except for the dreadlocks, his face was a mirror image. The same clear, fair skin, the broad nose, the slightly misty eyes. Even the tiny mole on the lower lid of his right eye. My heart beat fast. I hadn't bargained for this. But I steeled myself and asked sternly, 'Why have you come here? Why do you claim to be the heir to Bhawal when you know very well that you are not?'

'I have made no such claim. I want nothing. I have said so. Over and over again.'

I had been told that the man was from the north and his Bangla was defective. But his diction, when he spoke these words, was exactly like ours. 'It is your family and your subjects who are hailing me as their prince.' He smiled as though amused by the situation.

'You look somewhat like my late brother,' I said. 'I'll admit that. But it isn't the first time two people have been found to have similar features. I want to put an end to this pretence once and for all. I will put you through a test that will expose you for the fraud you are. Are you ready?'

'Quite ready.' The smile didn't leave his face.

'Who am I? What is my name?'

'That's easy. I was expecting you. And, even if I wasn't, I could have gathered the information from the servants. But I didn't need to. I recognized you the moment I saw you. You are Indumayi Debi, the baro rajkumari of Bhawal and my eldest sister.'

'What is that mark on your foot? I pointed to the jagged scar on his left ankle.

'I was knocked down by a phaeton when I was a boy. I was playing in the porch when I heard the horses come cantering in. I tried to run away but my foot twisted, and I fell to the ground. The front wheel went over my ankle. It should have been crushed to powder. But, quite miraculously, I escaped with a compound fracture.

It was terribly painful, and I limped for years afterwards. I still do sometimes.'

'How old were you when this happened?'

'Eleven.'

'Who was driving the carriage? And who was sitting in it?'

'Babamoshai was sitting in the phaeton. And it was being driven by ...' He paused for a few minutes. His brows came together in deep thought.

Aha! I've caught him. My heart gave a leap of triumph. *All the other information he could have collected from the servants. But who will remember a coachman's name? That, too, one who died years ago?*

'I think his name was Wali Muhammud,' the sadhu answered slowly. 'Babamoshai used to call him Oli.'

I was truly startled. *Nobody could have told him that. Besides, how would he know I'd ask him such a question?* Still, I persevered with the cross-examination. 'What did he look like?'

'Who? Babamoshai? Or Wali Muhammud?'

'The latter. Obviously.'

'Like a true Pathan. Tall and massive with a fierce beard and whiskers that curled up at the ends.'

'He had several sons. Do you remember them?'

'I remember one. He was as old as me and we used to play together. His name was Daulat.'

'Has he come to see you?'

'How can he come to see me? He was drowned in the Ganga, ages ago, trying to rescue a little boy. Both were swept away by the tide.'

I was shamed by the innocence and wonder in the eyes that looked back at me. My attempt at tripping him up had fallen flat. I felt very foolish but didn't show it.

'What else do you remember about him?' I asked.

'I remember his wedding. He was only fifteen when he was married to his cousin. Her name was Noori.'

'What was the name of our chief lathiyal?'

'Bheema Duley.'

'Do you remember anything else about him?'

'He had a fine singing voice.'

'Who was your first mistress?'

The man cringed. His face turned as white as paper. He looked up at me with shock in his eyes. As though he couldn't believe that I, his beloved eldest sister, would have the heart to shame him so cruelly. 'Elokeshi,' he murmured, then said with a tinge of exasperation, 'Why do you ask me all these questions? Why do you treat me like an accused standing in the dock? I want nothing from you. I'm ready to leave Jaidevpur this minute if you command me to. I have always loved you and obeyed you …'

Suddenly a scene came before my eyes. A plump, fair little boy tip-toeing into my room, looking this way and that. Holding out something bundled in a corner of his small gold-edged dhuti. A clutch of raw mangoes, a bunch of green tamarind, a small pile of *kamranga*. Sour fruits I craved but was forbidden to eat because I suffered from perennial colds and coughs. I felt a lump in my throat. Little Mejo! He was always the most loving and giving of my brothers. The most generous …

I swallowed the lump with difficulty. I was aware of the hurt I was causing him, but I went on doggedly, 'One last question. What happened to Dora Gibbons?'

I was startled to see the shadow on his face replaced with a broad smile. 'Nothing *happened* to her,' he said. 'She chose to run away with an Englishman. It was a great feather in her cap. As it is for all Anglo-Indian girls who manage to ensnare a white man. He agreed to the elopement, not so much for her charms I firmly believe, as for the dowry she was bringing with her. Money and jewels a foolish prince had lavished on a woman of little worth. And now,' he continued in a changed voice, a voice loaded with sarcasm, 'are you done? Will you grant me permission to leave your august presence?'

My face reddened with humiliation. But I could not blame him. I sat where I was for a long time after he left. Thoughts flew round and round my head like buzzing flies. I went over the last conversation I had had with my brother before he left for Darjeeling. I tried to remember every word he had said. Every expression on his face.

'It's only a boil, Baro didi.'

'Not one boil, Mejo khoka.'

'A few boils. Everyone gets them. In summer during the mango season—'

'These aren't ordinary boils. You know very well what they are.'

'But they are healing. Why do I have to go to Darjeeling?'

'Because the doctors say you need a change of air. Don't be a ninny, Mejo. We're not sending you to the end of the earth. It's only to a hill station right here in Bengal. And it's just for six months. They'll pass before you know it. Baro khoka and I want to see you completely recovered by the time you come back to us.'

Six months? Twelve years had passed but he hadn't come back to us. *Or had he?*

I spent the next three days and nights brooding and worrying. I knew it was bad for me. My head throbbed and my heart beat like a drum. I couldn't control the palpitations. I tried my best to make my mind go blank. But thoughts crept in like thieves in the night. What should I do? What *could* I do? Accepting the sadhu as my brother and heir to the kingdom meant fighting a prolonged legal battle with the British government. I was a sick old woman with one foot in the grave. Did I have the strength or the means to take on such a formidable adversary? Declaring him to be an imposter was the easier option. But that meant stifling the flow of love that was welling up in my heart for him. A much-loved younger brother who had suffered untold misery. All my instincts went against it …

On the morning of the fourth day, I wrote a letter to Mr Needham stating that, as the eldest member of the royal family and its representative, I was informing him that we had put the sannyasi to a long and strenuous examination and were convinced that he was, indeed, our second brother, the sole living heir to the kingdom of Bhawal.

12

Rani Satyabhama's Letter to Bibhavati

Jaidevpur
May 1921

Infinitely blessed Bibhavati Debi,

Ramendranarayan, the second son of my son Rajendranarayan, is alive. The man who came to Dhaka a little over one year ago, in the garb of a sannyasi, has been acknowledged by many tenants and bhadralok of the zamindari to be the second kumar. I have met him several times and observed him closely. In the last few days, I have seen him every day, and there is no doubt in my mind that he is my second grandson Ramendranarayan. Though I am old my sight is still good ...

You will remember the rumours that came to our ears after his alleged death. And the proposal to burn a kusaputtalika before performing his shradhha. You will also remember why it wasn't done. You have read newspaper reports and heard different versions of the story. You have not seen the man with your own eyes. It is my conviction that once you do so, all doubt left in your mind will be cleared.

I send you my affection and blessings and invite you to

come to Jaidevpur in order that the truth may be declared. Do come. See things with your own eyes and save the honour and reputation of my illustrious husband's line. By doing so you will be doing the duty expected of you according to our laws and religious practices.

Sri Satyabhama Debi

But Bibhavati did not respond to the invitation. The letter came back, by return post, to Rani Satyabhama Debi a few days later. It was unopened...

PART TWO

1

Pamphlet War

Jaidevpur
1921–1929

AFTER THE HISTORIC SCENE OUTSIDE RAJKUMARI JYOTIRMAYI DEBI'S house in which thousands of men and women heard the sadhu declare that he was the second prince, the people of Bhawal went into a frenzy. Nothing so exciting, so sensational, had happened before in this small, sleepy kingdom. A scion of the royal family had risen from the dead and returned to his people, claiming his rightful place in the hierarchy. One, moreover, who had assumed the identity of a mendicant and lived a life of penance and abstinence for a whole *yuga*, a span of twelve long years, in the caves of the mightiest mountain ranges in the world. What could be more romantic? One had read of such things in fairy tales. Never had anyone witnessed such a phenomenon in real life.

The subjects looked upon it as a sign from heaven. They had suffered extreme persecution at the hands of a corrupt foreign power which had ruthlessly turned the misfortunes of an ancient ruling family to its own advantage and let loose a wave of punitive measures against royals and subjects alike. But Bhawal's destiny was changing. The old order was coming back. Now was the time for righting all the wrongs. Now was the time for revenge. But how was it to be done?

Durgaprasad Chakrabarty, an amateur poet and member of the Association of Talukdars and Tenants, hit upon a novel method of starting the movement. He published a pamphlet, written in verse and carrying the dedication 'A Devotional Offering to the Exalted Young Sannyasi Ramendranarayan Roy'. It told the story of a king who, tortured by his conscience for his misdeeds, decides to abandon his mortal body and journey to the land of the dead. The great god Yama does not allow him entry into his realm on the ground that his time had not yet come and bids him go back to the world of the living. He does so after twelve years of penance, but not in the garb of a king. He comes wearing a loincloth and coated with ashes.

No names were taken but there wasn't a doubt in the minds of people regarding the king's identity. The story was on everyone's lips and voices became more voluble with every passing day.

Durgaprasad's pamphlet was followed by a number of publications on the subject. Some, like his, were poetic effusions veering into realms of magic and fantasy. They took the form of narrative poems, ballads and *kobi gaan* – musical debates very popular with the rural masses. Others emerged as booklets and newspaper articles. These were factual arguments addressing the two questions central to the matter. *Was the sanyasi truly the second kumar? If so, what happened in Darjeeling twelve years ago?*

The answer to the first could be provided by those persons who, after engaging in conversation with the sadhu, were convinced that he was the man they had known as the mejo kumar. The second question, obviously, had to be answered by the ascetic himself. He would have to give a logical, coherent account of how he, despite being pronounced dead and taken to the cremation ground, had managed to come back to life. Where he had lived and what he had done in the interim period and why he had decided to stake his claim after so many years.

However, none of his supporters called upon him to provide the answers. At least not publicly. Circulars, leaflets and newspaper columns took on the onerous task. *Herald*, the leading newspaper of Dhaka, reported that several zamindars of the district had met the sannyasi, heard his account, and come back convinced that he was speaking the truth. Whereupon they had banded together and sent a petition to the British government to accept him as the legitimate heir of Bhawal.

A pamphlet, drawing strength from reports in the Kolkata daily *Dainik Basumati*, about the stories being circulated in Bhawal, carried an interview with an Englishman named Edwin Fraser, a childhood friend of the second kumar. Fraser, apparently, had a strange story to tell. He had gone to Jaidevpur to check the man out, convinced that he was an imposter. He had stood at the back of the crowd watching him covertly when he heard his name.

'Edwin! Edwin!' a deep, sonorous voice had called out. 'Why do you hide yourself in the shadows like a thief? Come forward and stand before me. Tell me, to my face, that I am not your old friend, the wicked prince of Bhawal.'

Fraser had walked up to him. They had greeted each other and exchanged old memories, after which the sadhu had ordered a servant to bring a plateful of snacks and sweets. 'Tell the cook to send some roasted rice flakes sprinkled with ghee and sugar. Edwin likes his *chirhe* in the sweetened form.' Fraser had been amazed. There was no way the ascetic could have accessed this information from someone else. He had returned to Dhaka completely convinced that the man was no charlatan.

Needless to say, these reports took Bhawal by storm, emboldening the pamphleteers even further. One of them took up the matter of the alleged death and insinuated, for the first time in print, that there had been foul play. The account given out by the sannyasi was circulated. He had blacked out after the last dose of medicine was administered by Ashutosh Dasgupta. On regaining consciousness, a few days later, he had found himself in the midst of some naga sadhus. They had nursed him back to health and strength. But when they questioned him about his identity, he had no answers. He had no memory of who he was and where he came from. Not knowing where to go, he had joined the band, lived with them and gone wherever they took him. And, like them, he had had the leader Guru Darshandas's name tattooed on his arm.

This particular report was followed by an avalanche of publications openly questioning the roles played by Ashutosh Dasgupta and Satyendranath Banerjee. *What kind of medical treatment*, one pamphleteer demanded, *had been deemed necessary by the doctor for a man who had been sent to a hill station only for a change of air? And if indeed the patient's condition had deteriorated to such an extent, why hadn't Satya Banerjee sent for the renowned Dr Prankrishna Acharya who had been present in Darjeeling at the time? What, precisely, was the cause of death mentioned in the death certificate issued by Colonel Calvert?*

Another pamphlet came out with the astonishing report that Mukunda Guin, now a police inspector in Tripura, had given a statement to the effect that he had been present at his master's cremation and seen Birendra Banerjee, a clerk in the prince's retinue, performing the last rites. This piece of news shocked the readers and raised a volley of questions. *What had prompted the government to appoint a man, hitherto a minor civilian in the service of native royalty, in the Police Force? What did Mukunda Guin know about policing? Was this prestigious post a reward for services rendered? Besides, was the man speaking the truth? If he was, why had Birendra Banerjee, who was neither a relative nor a close friend of the prince, been assigned the onerous task of performing his last rites? And by whom?*

A counter campaign, steered by the government itself, ran side by side. A team, consisting of high officials from Dhaka, was set up to reach out to the public and make the government's position in the matter known. The official narrative disseminated, was the following:

The sannyasi's appearance in Jaidevpur had been engineered

by certain interested parties namely the daughters of the late Raja Rajendranarayan Roy. The three legitimate heirs had died and the poor childless widows, their lives made unbearable by the dominating behaviour of their formidable sisters-in-law, had left for their paternal homes. The princesses, having lived on royal bounty all their lives, now found themselves in straitened circumstances which could not be eased, even in the slightest measure, while the estate remained under the management of the Court of Wards. They had bided their time then, having found a man with some physical resemblance to their late second brother, had hatched a conspiracy to set the imposter up as the legal heir. They had prepared him for the part and sparked off a mass frenzy in the kingdom. Natives were instinctively drawn to romance and adventure and this was such a romantic story. Besides, the subjects had liked their royal masters. They were whimsical, oppressive and overbearing but had also been, on occasion, generous and caring. Master and subject had shared a personal bond. By contrast, the British believed in justice and fair play. They weren't ruled by impulse or swayed by irrational emotion and thus, in the eyes of the common man, they appeared somewhat cold and withdrawn. Natives were perverse creatures. They preferred their own depraved monarchy to the benign dominance of a foreign race.

Over the next few months, two rival factions emerged in Bhawal. Opinion was sharply divided. The group supporting the sadhu consisted of subjects and most of the royals. Standing in stiff opposition to them was the state government, backed by the mejo rani, her brother and some eminent natives. The British found a strong ally in one Kedarnath Chakrabarty, editor of the journal *Rayat*. Kedarnath published a number of articles in which he tried to prove that the sannyasi was a charlatan set up by the royal sisters. Certain pertinent questions were raised in his columns and inferences drawn. The mejo kumar had been dead and cremated long ago and all his property, including the insurance amount, had been transferred to his widow. No one had raised any objections at the time. Now, suddenly after twelve years, the matter was being raked up. Why? The three sons of the late Raja Rajendranarayan Roy had died without leaving any issue. But his daughters had several children each. Could it be that they were feeling thwarted and resentful at losing their way of life? The two elder princesses, Kedarnath implied, were furious and were airing their opinions freely. In their view, the government's decision to take over the estate on the excuse that the male line had become extinct, was totally motivated. Did they follow the same principle in their own country? Hadn't one of their most illustrious sovereigns been a woman? Wasn't *her* grandson the present King Emperor? So what if the three kumars had died without leaving any issue? The princesses had sons. Why couldn't one of them be sworn in as the ruler? As for their sisters-in-law, they were nothing short of traitors. Instead of adopting strays from their paternal households, should not the baro rani and chhoto rani have chosen their husband's nephews? Boys who carried royal blood in their veins?

Regarding the allegation that the body had not been cremated, Kedarnath quoted a paragraph from a letter written by Nibaran Chandra Mukherjee, a highly respected gentleman from Narayanganj to his friend Phani Bhushan Banerjee of Jaidevpur. In this, Nibaran Chandra claimed that he had been present at the late mejo kumar's cremation and had stood watching the pyre till it was reduced to ashes. He had ended the letter with the words: *I have informed the Pleader of Dacca who I believe is taking an interest in the case ... I request you not to come to any conclusion or decision with regard to this important matter without hearing from me.*

Another document produced by the British side was a letter written by Colonel Calvert in reply to a query by Mr. Lindsay regarding the medical circumstances of the death of the kumar. Dismissing the idea of foul play, Calvert wrote:

> I remember the Second kumar of Bhowal who came on a visit to Darjeeling in May, 1909. He was suffering from

> "Gallstone". His death made a considerable impression on me at the time, as I thought that had he only listened to our advice, he need not have died. On the day of his death, he was seized with a severe attack of biliary colic. An injection of morphia would have relieved him almost immediately of his pain. He refused to have any subcutaneous injection, because his mother ... had died after receiving a hypodermic injection and he attributed her death to the injection instead of to the illness which necessitated the treatment. Owing to vomiting and purging, opium by mouth and rectum was not retained. The severe pain being unrelieved, brought on collapse from which he died. I cannot now be certain if I was present at the moment of his death, but I saw him shortly before it in a state of profound collapse ... The kumar ... did not recover from the collapse and died the same night.

With this letter the British may have felt that the last thing had been said on the subject. But the pamphleteers of the pro-sannyasi camp were quick to jump into the fray. *What,* they asked, *did Calvert mean when he said that he couldn't remember if he was present at the time of the kumar's death but remembered quite clearly that he had died of a collapse? Wasn't it highly unethical for a physician to leave a patient in a state of collapse and return only to issue a death certificate? If he wasn't present at the time of death, how could he be sure that the kumar had died of the collapse and not of something else? Besides, the patient had been under the care of Colonel Sarbadhikari, an eminent doctor of Kolkata, only weeks before journeying to Darjeeling, and he had said nothing about gallstones ...*

The British side was quick to poke holes in the other's argument. Colonel Calvert, their advocates argued, was a reputed English doctor and a high official in His Majesty's Service. He didn't need a native journalist to tell him how to conduct his practice. Besides, what evidence did the sannyasi's supporters have to back their claims of death by foul play other than servants' gossip?

The two parties went at one another, hammer and tongs, the opposing narratives spreading far and wide. Beyond Bhawal to Dhaka, Barisal, Faridpur and Mymensingh. Even as far as Kolkata and its environs. To small towns and villages. Suburbs and purlieus. Over the next few months, the whole of Bengal was plunged in war. Pamphlet war.

2

Tarinmayi

Jaidevpur
January 1931

I WAS SHOCKED WHEN RANI THAKURMA'S LETTER TO MEJO BOUDIDI came back unopened. Rani thakurma hadn't learned to read and write, so I was the one who had written it in her name. I was so eager for my sister-in-law to come to Jaidevpur and identify the sannyasi as her husband that I had bent over backwards to please her. I had addressed her as 'Infinitely blessed Bibhavati Debi' and pleaded with her to save the honour and reputation of our ancient line. In normal circumstances, Rani thakurma would never have adopted such a tone of ingratiation and supplication with a mere daughter-in-law of the family. But our need was great and she hadn't objected. The return of the letter left us all gaping. Mejo boudidi, everyone had thought, was a gentle, well-behaved girl. Who could have imagined her capable of humiliating a former queen of the realm, who was also her grandmother-in-law, in such a manner?

Out of all our siblings, Baro didi and Baro dada had received the best education. Not only were they proficient in Bengali, they even had a smattering of English. Baro didi was even more knowledgeable and well informed than Baro dada. From what I have heard, our father was very proud of her and regretted the fact that she had been born a girl. Had she been a boy, he often declared, she would have made a better ruler of the kingdom than any of his sons. My two other brothers found lessons boring and had learned little despite the best efforts of their tutors.

Babamoshai had believed in educating his daughters, which was unusual for the time, and had employed teachers and governesses for us. After his death, Ma, who was against women's education, dismissed them. She encouraged us to occupy ourselves, instead, with saris and jewels and beauty treatments with herbs and potions. I was only five and had just started learning the Bengali alphabet when my father died. But, unlike my second sister Jyotirmayi, I wanted to continue with my education. Mejo didi was very devout and, under the influence of my grandmother, occupied herself with fasts and *bratas* like s*enjuti and punyi pukur* from early childhood. Unlike her I loved reading and writing. In fact, one of the reasons I liked Mejo boudidi so much was that she knew many stories. She also had books and magazines, which Satya dada smuggled into the Rajbari whenever he came, hidden under the mattress of her bed, and we read them together in secret. *Ma go, Ma!* How delightful those days were! And how life has changed since then!

After Ma dismissed my tutors, I begged Baro didi to teach me to read. Which she did on the sly, without our mother's knowledge. I made good progress and learned to read and write Bangla with ease. As I grew older, my passion for the written word grew into an obsession. I read whatever I could lay my hands upon. Every evening, after the men had left, I sent my maid to the *baarmahal* to pick up the newspapers of the day and whatever else she could find. Textbooks discarded by my brothers, official letters, obsolete records, all were grist to my mill. Seeing my avid passion for reading, my husband gave up his initial reluctance and ordered books and journals from Dhaka bookshops. He also conveyed to me all the political news he picked up from his visits to the big city.

With the passing of the years, I became quite proficient in English too. That is how, after Baro didi's death, I've became the official letter writer for the women of the family.

Baro didi died a few months after writing her letter to our estate manager J. H. Lindsay, conveying her considered opinion that the sannyasi was the mejo kumar of Bhawal. From what her servants told me, she was very disturbed and anxious afterwards. Perhaps she feared the consequences of her action. Perhaps she was not fully convinced of the sadhu's identity. Whatever the reason, she woke up one night, sweating and trembling and complaining of palpitations and excruciating pain in the chest. The doctor was sent for but, by the time he arrived, all was over. We didn't get to know of her death till the next morning.

With her passing we, Rani thakurma, Mejo didi and I, felt as though we had been cast adrift in a storm-tossed ocean without an anchor. We realized only then what a pillar of strength she had been in our lives.

Mr Lindsay took no notice of her letter. He didn't even bother to answer it. The British government conducted a partial, one-sided enquiry, after which it moved decisively against the sannyasi who, I firmly believe, is my brother. Officials were instructed to take tough action against those tenants who supported him and refused to pay rent to the government. Legal steps were taken, penalties were imposed and then the dreaded Certificate Procedure was set in motion, whereby property could be confiscated if documentary proof of ownership was not submitted. The tenants were outraged. Many of them had held lands for over a hundred years, from a time when documentation hadn't even been heard of. Support for Mejo dada became vociferous and people started openly flouting the orders. Thousands of subjects flocked to Rani thakurma every day, as to a rallying point, and begged her to intervene. She couldn't help them but was delighted at the turn of events.

The rulers were in a quandary. How was it possible to control an entire population? In their desperation they issued a formal declaration that the sadhu was an imposter and barred him from entering Jaidevpur. Mejo dada was forced to move to Dhaka. And now he made up his mind. He would confront the unfairness of the rulers with all he had at his command. *Punyaha,* a ritual symbolizing the bond between ruler and subject, was revived. A grand celebration took place for the first time since Baro dada's death. People from far and near assembled to prostrate themselves before their long-lost prince and offer him tribute. The whole of Bhawal stood with him, willing to support his claim even if it meant a headlong confrontation with the government …

Rani thakurma was highly offended by Bibhavati's action in returning her letter. She was also surprised and hurt by the apparent indifference of my two other sisters-in-law. 'What sort of women are they?' she looked at me with puzzled eyes. 'Do they have no feelings at all? No regard for the family?'

'You're right,' I answered. 'I'm as shocked as you are. Chhoto boudidi was always somewhat self-centred and callous. But Bara boudidi? She was such a good woman, so loving and giving, yet she hasn't cared to visit Jaidevpur even once and lend support to the family. As for Mejo boudidi … *Ma go, Ma!* Why have people changed so drastically?' I stared at my grandmother.

However, Rani thakurma did not give up. She, who had withdrawn from active life after Raja thakurda's death and was spending practically all her time in the palace temple, became her old imperious self again. After Mejo dada was forbidden entry into Jaidevpur, she insisted on travelling to Dhaka to be with him. Since we couldn't let her go alone, I went with her and we all stayed together in the same house. With each passing day her conviction that the ascetic was her grandson grew in intensity and, after about a month, she decided to write to the new estate manager Mr Drummond. She dictated a letter, raising certain pertinent questions. The British position being that the fullest possible enquiry had been made, proving without a doubt that the sadhu was a fraud, she wrote:

> Allow me to bring to your attention the fact that an enquiry in which close members of the family were not brought in contact with the alleged imposter cannot be deemed completed or concluded. I beg leave to point out that Rani Bibhavati Debi was never brought face to face with the sadhu and asked if she recognised him as her husband ...
>
> There have been rumours of poison being administered to my second grandson in Darjeeling and a deep mystery surrounds his supposed death and cremation. As far as my information goes, Rani Bibhavati Debi, though present in Darjeeling at the time, did not perform the last rites which, as wife of an issueless male, was her duty as decreed by our shastras. She didn't even attend the cremation. She has evidently relied on the assurance of her brother, Satyendranath Banerjee, that all the rituals were performed as per traditional norms. But we, the members of the prince's family, do not believe this. We do not trust Satyendra. He was in charge of the party which went to Darjeeling and his conduct at the time and afterwards is not free from suspicion ...
>
> I shall be obliged if you kindly supply me with a statement of the nature of the enquiry conducted and also with a copy of the evidence that has been obtained for the purpose. I wish to have it examined by a team of lawyers, preferably one from each of the six High Courts of India. These lawyers will be persons unconnected with the Bengal Court of Wards or any member of the Bhawal Raj family. I also wish to engage some honest, preferably retired, officers of the Detective Department to investigate the case ...
>
> To make sure that I am not suffering from any defect in vision, I have had my eyes examined by the civil surgeon

> of Dhaka. I enclose the certificate which is a recent one. Therefore, the fact of my recognition of the sadhu as my grandson cannot be regarded as an illusion ...

The letter was posted on the 2nd of July, 1922. But no reply has come from Mr Drummond to this date.

Those were trying times and we were all under pressure. But the thought that worried and perplexed me the most was Mejo boudidi's attitude. Her husband was keen to meet her. He was in Kolkata often these days for consultations with his lawyers and had been accepted by many members of the elite. He was invited to parties and receptions and, on one occasion, even introduced to Lord Lytton, the governor of Bengal, as the kumar of Bhawal. But the police had placed restrictions on his movements. On no account was he to be seen in the vicinity of Lansdowne Road, where Bibhavati Debi lived. If he was, he could be arrested. This was obviously on her or her brother's instructions. From what I've heard, not only did she refuse to meet him, she even made a trip to Jaidevpur and tried to instigate the subjects against him. While in Jaidevpur, she made no attempt to meet the family. This I found very odd. Even if she believed him to be a fraud, wouldn't it make sense to talk to us and, if still unconvinced, confront him and make a public declaration? What explained this rigid, uncompromising denial? Was it possible that she was afraid he was speaking the truth and that meeting him would break her defences? Defences she had carefully set up to avoid contact with her past?

But why? I know she hadn't been very happy in the Rajbari. But was her present situation all that wonderful? Apart from the fact that the lifestyle her brother was providing her in Kolkata could be nowhere near the one she had enjoyed in Jaidevpur, was she not having to undergo the rigours that custom decreed for a widow? However modern her family might be, however lenient with her, certain fasts and abstinences were mandatory. Her mother was a widow too and, from what I've heard, observed them faithfully. She could, at most, allow her daughter to drink water on *ekadasi* and wear a narrow bordered dhuti in place of a thaan. She could supplement her vegetarian meals with increased amounts of sweets, milk and ghee. But could she protect her from the stigma of widowhood? The pain, the shame, the marginalization? The scorn and pity of relatives and neighbours?

Her life, as she lived it now, could never compare with the one she would have if she accepted the return of her husband. She would recover the status of a wife and, with it, her lost honour and dignity. All the luxuries she had been used to. Moreover, she would be the consort of the ruler of Bhawal. The queen of the realm. She could even have a child. The subjects would shower her with glory. They would put her on par with the great sati, Savitri, whose extraordinary chastity had enabled her to bring her dead husband back to life. She could have had all that. Yet she wanted to keep things the way they were. Why?

Yet, her behaviour after returning from Darjeeling had been completely natural. She had been overwhelmed with grief. I remember her pale face and stricken expression. Her numerous fainting fits. The way she lay in bed dazed and lifeless for weeks together, refusing to bathe and eat. If she spoke at all it was to curse the fate that had reduced her from a queen to a beggar woman. What had happened in the interim years to change her so drastically?

Mejo dada waited nearly ten years before moving the courts. He had hoped that such an action would be unnecessary. That the overwhelming support of his cause by family, friends and subjects would force the British government to acknowledge the truth of his claim. But days passed into months, months into years, till all hope of an easy resolution was lost. Saddened and dispirited, he yielded, at last, to the promptings of his well-wishers and filed a suit in the court of the first sub-judge of Dhaka.

His plea contained an account of his illness in Darjeeling, his supposed death and cremation, his return to Jaidevpur after twelve years, and the acknowledgement of his family and subjects that he was indeed the second kumar of Bhawal. He also alleged that his wife Bibhavati Debi had denied his identity without even seeing him and that she and her brother had conspired with the collector and induced him to issue the imposter notice. The suit was filed on the 24th of April, 1930. Bibhavati Debi was the first defendant. And who was the second? *Ma go, Ma!* The second defendant was our Bara boudidi, Sarajubala Debi!

I couldn't believe my ears when I heard this. Mejo dada tells me that she had refused at first. She had appealed to the Court of Wards not to file any statement on her behalf and categorically refused to contribute to the expenses of the suit. Later, under whose influence he couldn't say, she changed her mind. The third defendant was Ramnarayan, the adopted son of my youngest sister-in-law Anandakumari, now a young man of twenty. Anandakumari herself was the fourth.

The lawyer chosen by my brother was Benoy Chandra Chatterjee, son-in-law of the eminent nationalist Surendranath Banerjee, of whom I had heard so much from Mejo boudidi. Her uncles had been freedom fighters and staunch loyalists to his cause. A student of Lincoln's Inn, London, Benoy babu had returned to India in 1905, just in time to join the Banga Bhanga Andolan, the movement against the bill for the Partition of Bengal brought in by Lord Curzon. In his early fifties now, he was at the peak of his career with a track record of brilliant defence arguments on behalf of several freedom fighters. It was natural for him to take up the cause of a native prince trying to hold his own against a tyrannical foreign power and he did so without hesitation.

The counsel for the defendants, Amiyanath Chaudhuri, of the famous Chaudhuris of Krishnanagar now settled in Kolkata, was a very different proposition. He was the youngest of six brothers, all lawyers, two of whom were married to nieces of the poet Rabindranath

Tagore of Jorasanko, the man who had spearheaded the Banga Bhanga movement by exhorting all Bengalis to come together in defence of their linguistic and cultural rights. The symbol of this brotherly bonding was the simple rakhi which he called upon all, Hindu and Muslim alike, to tie on each other's wrists. And the people responded to his call with an enthusiasm that shook the rulers. The newspapers carried reports of this extraordinary phenomenon for weeks together.

Mejo boudidi was a great admirer of Rabindranath's poetry and could recite whole poems from his *Bhagna Hriday* and *Prabhat Sangeet*. She also knew a lot about the Tagore family from the books she read and the letters she received regularly from her mother and uncles. The two Chaudhuri wives, Pratibha and Indira, she told me, had not only participated in their uncle's movement, but had also worked actively with the other women of Jorasanko. They had made thousands of rakhis and despatched them all over the country and beyond. Oddly enough, their husbands had kept themselves aloof, preferring not to muddy the waters on which they sailed their boat.

Of all the brothers, Amiyanath was the most determinedly Anglophile. This and a lot of other information about him, I gathered from *Hicky's Gazette*. He was married to Millie Bonnerjee, a daughter of the illustrious barrister W. C. Bonnerjee. Millie had been educated at the Sorbonne, in Paris, and was more foreign than Indian in temperament. Under her influence, Amiyanath had adopted an extravagantly westernized lifestyle and moved in an exclusive social set comprised of British officials and other expatriates. Approached by the Revenue Board to appear for the defence in the Bhawal case, he agreed. At any other time, he would have considered it beneath his dignity to appear in a district court. But this case was special.

I used to read all the newspapers, English and Bangla, from cover to cover, keeping my eyes peeled for any information concerning the Bhawal case. Gradually this became an obsession. It reached a point when my family members started complaining that I was neglecting all my other duties. Perhaps I was, but I was so completely sucked into the complex web of treachery, slander and intrigue that I couldn't extricate myself. Every fact that emerged read like a new issue of a popular crime novel.

Since the key defence witnesses, Colonel Calvert, J. W. Lindsay and Mr Crawford, had retired and returned to their home shores, their cross-examinations could only take place in England. For this purpose, a trusted government lawyer named Sasanka Coomar Ghose was sent out to England with the requisite papers. The expenses of travel and accommodation incurred by him were to be paid by Bibhavati Debi, it being decided by the Board of Revenue that the second lady's share would be liable for the whole cost of the declaratory suit. Strange as it may seem, she and her brother agreed to the arrangement without a murmur. On hearing this, I was assailed by the strangest sensations. My hands and feet went cold and my heart thudded in my chest.

Ma go, Ma! Was this Bibhavati the same girl who had been my brother's wife? The girl I had loved and played with? Or was she someone else? A malignant spirit, risen from a nether world, hell bent on destroying my brother?

3

District Court

Dhaka
1933

THE COURT OF THE HONOURABLE JUSTICE PANNALAL BASU WAS IN session. The trial began with the testimonies of Rani Anandakumari, Rani Sarajubala and Dr Prankrishna Acharya and was followed by a presentation of the recorded statement of Colonel J. T. Calvert.

Anandakumari, tall, fair and regal in a white silk sari and delicately embroidered cashmere shawl, looked straight into the eyes of the plaintiff and declared that he was not the mejo kumar of Bhawal. Her voice was strident and unwavering.

'I'm not seeing this man for the first time,' she continued with an arrogant lift of her head. 'I have seen him twice before. Both times I got the feeling that he was an imposter. But now, having seen him for the third time, I'm convinced. He is as unlike the mejo kumar as a sparrow is to a peacock. I have a clear memory of not only the late prince's features but his temperament and personality. They were at total variance with those of the man present here today.'

'What, in your opinion, is so different?' B. C. Chatterjee asked her. 'Can you give us some details?'

'To begin with, all three princes were well educated. They hadn't received university degrees but could read and write Bengali with ease and speak English. I have heard them conversing with the European ladies who came to the palace sometimes and had tea in our apartments. I didn't understand what was being said but I knew that the language they spoke was English. The plaintiff, by his own admission, has received little education and doesn't know a word of English. How, then, can his claim that he's the mejo kumar be taken seriously?'

'What other difference have you observed?'

'The second prince had a vibrant personality. He was high-spirited and full of fun. Always looking for excitement. This man appears dull, morose and withdrawn. Besides, it seems to me that he doesn't fully comprehend what is going on here today. Though made up to play the part, his demeanour is more like an unlettered peasant from the north than a Bengali gentleman from a royal house.'

'Were you on good terms with the second prince? Did you like him?'

'We didn't communicate with each other. He was my *bhashur*, a revered elder, and I was expected to observe purdah in his presence. But I've seen the way he treated the members of the household. His warmth and generosity even to the servants. Yes, I did like and respect him.'

'What were your feelings when you heard the rumours of his being poisoned and of not receiving a proper cremation? You must have been devastated.'

Anandakumari's face turned blank. 'I've heard nothing of the kind.'

'How can you say that?' B. C. Chatterjee's voice was incredulous. 'You were living in the Rajbari at the time. Do you mean to tell me that no rumours came to your ears? You may or may not have believed them, but how can you deny their existence?'

'I haven't heard anything.' Anandakumari's mouth was set in prim lines. Her thin lips were pressed tightly together.

'Next you'll say that your brother-in-law's death wasn't sudden. That it was expected.'

'He had been very sick. Sick people die ... don't they?' Her lips twisted in a snide smile.

'True. But he had recovered. He had only gone to Darjeeling for a change of air. The Rajbari had received reports that he was doing fine. People aren't fine one minute and dead the next. What do you make of the telegrams carrying contradictory messages that arrived from Darjeeling?'

'What contradictory messages? I am not book-learned. I can't read and write. But my husband told me that he had seen only one telegram. The one that conveyed the news of his brother's death and subsequent cremation. There were no others.'

At this point, B. C. Chatterjee reminded the defence witness that she was under oath and liable to be indicted for giving false testimony.

'Your Honour,' he said turning to the judge, 'it is clear that the witness is misleading the court and she is doing so with a specific intention. Her adopted son was recognized as the future ruler of Bhawal in an investiture ceremony conducted by some British officials some years ago. If the plaintiff wins the case, the investiture ceremony would become meaningless. Hence all the lies and fabrication.'

'Objection, Your Honour!' A. N. Chaudhuri thundered. 'Counsel is maligning the witness. She is a highborn Hindu lady from a royal house. He has no right to humiliate and intimidate her.'

B. C. Chatterjee appeared unfazed. Requesting the judge to allow him to cross-examine her further, he said that he would expose her as a woman of loose moral character, one who had been unchaste even during her husband's lifetime, and thus prove that her evidence was unreliable. 'As per Hindu law,' he added, 'such a woman would be disqualified from inheriting her husband's property, let alone be allowed to adopt a son.'

Anandakumari's face turned a fiery red. Her eyes glittered dangerously. She was about to burst into speech when the judge raised his hand and stopped her. 'That's enough, Counsel,' he told the lawyer sternly. 'I will not allow such a line of questioning. It has no relevance, whatsoever, to the case.'

Dr Prankrishna Acharya told a strange story:

'I was fast asleep on that fateful night, when the shrill ringing of the telephone woke me up. I made my way to the sitting room where the instrument was placed and picked up the receiver.

'"Dr Acharya?" A woman's voice came through the line. It was low and husky and she was breathing hard. As though she had been running …

'"Yes. Acharya here. Who is this?" I asked.

'"I'm speaking from Step Aside," the woman answered. I'm the nurse employed to take care of the mejo kumar of Bhawal. I fear he is ill. Very ill indeed. Please come at once."

'I glanced at the grandfather clock that ticked on one wall. It was 2 a.m. I shivered with cold and dismay. It had been raining heavily for the last twelve hours and the roads were unsafe. Besides, I had been in Darjeeling for only three days. The place was unfamiliar and I had no idea where Step Aside was.

'"I'm here on a holiday. I'm not taking calls," I replied.

'"You must … this once," the women urged. "My patient is on the point of death. Only you can save him."

'"Why wasn't I informed earlier?" I asked.. "It's too late now. I'll come in the morning."

'"Please don't delay, doctor," she said. "He might die any moment."

'"I'm new to Darjeeling and have no idea of the location," I told her. "Besides, it's a wild, stormy night. I can't take the risk of venturing out in such foul weather."

'"It has stopped raining," the woman pointed out. "Look out of the window and see for yourself. As for being unfamiliar with the location, please don't worry. Everyone knows where Step Aside is. Your driver will have no difficulty in finding the place."

'"Who has been treating him so far? Why don't you give *him* a call?" I insisted.

'But the woman disregarded the question. She begged some more, repeated that only I could save her patient, then disconnected the phone abruptly. I stood where I was for a long time. I couldn't decide what to do. Should I or should I not respond to the call? Looking out of the window and seeing that the storm had abated, I made up my mind. I had taken the Hippocratic oath. I had to serve the sick at all costs. Besides, the patient was the mejo kumar of Bhawal. I had met him once or twice in Kolkata and felt a sense of obligation. And, if the caller was to be trusted, it was a matter of life and death.

'I sent for my car. The woman was right. The driver knew where to go and we made our way up the mountains slowly but steadily. It might have been about four o'clock in the morning when we reached Step Aside but the sky was still pitch black. I was led to a room, dim and shadowy, in the light of a single lantern. On an ornate bedstead, a figure lay covered from head to foot in a sheet. There were several people huddled around it, conversing in soft voices. "Why is the room so dark?" I said as I walked towards the bed. "I'll need more light. Send for some more lanterns." I was about to remove the sheet when I was stopped by one of the men standing by the bed. "Please don't touch the body, doctor," he said and, plucking at my sleeve, drew me aside.'

'Do you know who he was? Did he look like a member of the family or an official of the estate?' B. C. Chatterjee asked frowning.

'I've no idea. He was well dressed and spoke with authority …' Dr Acharya was silent for a minute before continuing, 'I was extremely annoyed at the way I had been prevented from examining the patient. "How are you sure he is dead?" I asked sternly. "Has another doctor told you so?"

'"No. But he isn't breathing … he has to be dead," the man said.

'"Who are you to decide that? Let me examine him first …" I pressed.

'"No. We can't allow you to touch the body," he insisted.

'"Why not?" I asked, incredulous.

'"Because you are a Brahmo. Our scriptures do not allow a non-Hindu to touch a brahmin's corpse." I was amazed at the man's logic.

'"Why was I sent for then?" I demanded. "Where is the nurse who telephoned me? Let me speak to her."

'The men glanced at one another and kept a studied silence. I waited a while expecting her to appear any moment. But she seemed to have vanished …'

Turning to the judge, Prankrishna Acharya concluded his account, 'I walked out of the house fuming. Never in the forty years of my medical career had I been prevented from touching a patient, dead or alive, on the grounds of my religion. Had I been allowed to conduct the examination, I could have ascertained if the person was truly the kumar or someone else. If he was indeed dead or had merely fainted. And, if dead, for how many hours. I was puzzled. I couldn't make out head or tail of the matter. Why did the kumar's relatives send for me? What was their intention? Now, in hindsight, Your Honour, I have the answer. They wanted me to issue a death certificate without examining the body. Had I not walked away in a huff, they would have tried to persuade me. They might even have offered inducements …'

Sarajubala's testimony was also unexpected and left the assembly in a state of wonder. She had been listed as one of the defendants but now she made a complete somersault from her earlier position.

'I had supported Bibhavati in her denial of the sannyasi's claim, at first,' she told the court. Her eyes were frank and steady and her voice completely free of shame or guilt. 'That was because his story, it seemed to me at the time, defied logic and reason. But the moment I saw the man – he had come to see me in Kolkata three years after his arrival in Jaidevpur – I recognized him. There was no doubt in my mind that he was my brother-in-law, Ramendranarayan Roy.'

Amiyanath Chaudhuri tried to counter her argument by suggesting that her change of stance was related to the third rani's adoption of a son. He informed the court that Sarajubala had opposed the adoption in the interest of her own protegee, Pataki Matilal, and Bibhavati had supported her. The latter had, for some reason, changed her mind a few years later and joined forces with Anandakumari. Feeling hurt and betrayed, Sarajubala was taking revenge on her sister-in-law by switching sides.

Sarajubala was stout in her denial of the charge. 'The learned counsel is completely mistaken,' she said forcefully. 'Anyone who knows me will swear that I'm not the vengeful type. Nor am I overly ambitious for my adopted son. It is quite wrong to say that I opposed Anandakumari's adoption of Ramnarayan. I did nothing of the sort. If I was so inclined, I would have urged the Earl of Ronaldshay to hold the right of my son Pataki to rule Bhawal as superior to that of Ramnarayan's. He is the older of the two. But I didn't do so. The counsel for the defence is sullying my good name, Your Honour.'

'Why the volte face then? Why are you suddenly on the sannyasi's side?' A. N. Chaudhuri asked with a sly smile. 'There must be some reason.'

'I've just told you. In the beginning I thought he was fooling the family and the public. I trusted Bibhavati implicitly. What woman would turn her back on her own husband? She insisted he was a fraud and I believed her. After seeing the man, I was astonished at her reaction. I still cannot fathom why she is denying him. My acceptance of the plaintiff's claim, I repeat, is based solely on my recognition of the man. It has nothing to do with Bibhavati or Anandakumari. In fact, even my own brother Shailendra wasn't able to influence me. He had seen the sannyasi, soon after his arrival in Dhaka, and told me that he was the second kumar. But I wasn't convinced. I reserved my opinion till I had seen him for myself.'

Colonel Calvert's testimony as recorded by the eminent lawyer S. N. Mukherjee, who had examined him in England under the guidance of Sasanka Coomar Ghose, was placed before the judge.

The contents, when read out in court, came as a shock to those who remembered the document produced by the British side in 1921. The letter written to Mr Lindsay by Colonel Calvert in which he confessed that he couldn't be certain if he had been present at the time of the second prince's death. But, a decade later, he was confirming under oath that the prince had died in his presence and that he had left the house some hours afterwards.

There were other confusions and contradictions in Calvert's testimony. On being asked if he had administered any medicines, he lost his temper and said, 'I wish to protest against questions on immaterial matters which, in my opinion, only lead me or confuse me to think that I remember those small details after such a long lapse of time.' Undaunted by the witness's belligerence, S. N. Mukherjee had repeated the question and received the evasive answer, 'I don't remember now but I must have done so.'

'What medicines did you give him?' the counsel had persisted.

'I treated the condition from day to day,' Calvert had replied, 'and I can't remember now what I gave him.'

There were other things he couldn't remember. The time of death was one of them. He said that he never made notes or kept a diary and so had forgotten the precise time. On being reminded that he had specified it as 11.45 p.m. in the death certificate, he said it was possible but he had no memory of having done so. S. N. Mukherjee had pointed out the discrepancy between Calvert's present testimony and what he had written to Mr Lindsay in 1921 and called for the letter to be produced in court. But the British lawyer defending him had objected, saying that this was not an appropriate time and his view was upheld by the judge, Mr Pringle.

Now, in the court of Pannalal Basu, B. C. Chatterjee pointed out the contradictions in Colonel Calvert's testimony, expressed surprise at the unwillingness of the defence counsel in London to produce the letter he had written to Lindsay, and raised a question regarding the authenticity of the death certificate which gave out that the patient had died of gallstones and biliary colic. It was, he declared, at odds with the prescriptions, medical records and the testimonies of other witnesses. To prove his point, he called upon two experts in the field.

The first, Dr A. C. MacGilchrist had worked extensively in India and was a research scientist and clinical practitioner with outstanding credentials. He had degrees in medicine and pharmacology from London and Edinburgh, and was a member of the Royal College of Physicians, London. After a meticulous examination of Colonel Calvert's prescriptions, his considered opinion was that they were inconsistent with the treatment of biliary colic. The first one appeared to be for simple indigestion and flatulence. Another, the external application of opium, would be useless for biliary colic since none of the active ingredients would be absorbed. The third seemed to be for diarrhoea. On examining Dr Ashutosh Dasgupta's prescription, he said it contained quinine, arsenic, strychnine and two purgatives – aloin and euonymin. These could be given as a general tonic for chronic malaria and the doses were within pharmaceutical limits. But the two doctors seemed to have proceeded on different assumptions. Calvert's medicine would act as a sedative. Ashutosh Dasgupta's would disturb the stomach. It was possible that Colonel Calvert was unaware of the other doctor's intervention. But even so, it was a fact that neither line of treatment was aimed at giving relief from biliary colic.

Another medical expert called by the plaintiff's counsel was Dr Bradley, a fellow of the Royal Society of Tropical Medicine, Kolkata. He said that, given the symptoms as reported, death could have resulted from an overdose of arsenic. Twelve pills had been given for no apparent reason. It could have been, it most probably was, an accident. The case, he felt, had been muddled up in some way. Mentioning the nurse who was supposed to have had the care of the patient, as per Dr Prankrishna Acharya's testimony, and who had mysteriously disappeared since, he said he sensed something wrong somewhere. He didn't want to criticize Colonel Calvert or cast aspersions on his medical ethics, but there had definitely been some mistake on his part. An oversight or a lapse of memory …

4

Anandakumari

Dhaka
1933

YESTERDAY I STATED ON OATH, IN THE DISTRICT COURT OF DHAKA, that the plaintiff wasn't the mejo kumar of Bhawal. I did so at the request of my sister-in-law Bibhavati and her brother. No. That isn't the exact truth. It was Satya babu who had made the request. Bibhavati had maintained a studied silence. She had glanced askance at her brother from time to time but hadn't contradicted him. From which I gathered that it was her wish that he was expressing. Whatever it was, the fact that I agreed to do what they wanted surprised everyone who knows me because I've never hidden my dislike for the two. Bibhavati and I had a strained relationship from the time I came to the palace as the chhoto rani. I was envious of her beauty and she treated me as though I didn't exist. However, much water has flown down the Ganga since those first days. We have witnessed many upheavals and faced many ups and downs. We have both wept and suffered from the same sorrows in the past. From the indifference of our husbands and our inability to bear children. Not together; never together. But now the equations have changed. We both live in Kolkata and have slowly learned to see one another's point of view.

But perhaps I should start from the beginning …

I was one of four children of the *baro taraf*, Anukul Mukherjee, owner of seventy percent of the zamindari of Phoolpur and Chandipur. His brother Aghornath, the *chhoto taraf*, owned the rest. My father had two wives. His first, my mother Asrumati, was the daughter of a reputed zamindar of North Bengal. Wedded at nine, she had brought such a huge dowry of gold and silver that the family vaults weren't large enough to hold them and new ones had to be ordered from Kolkata. So I've heard my grandmother say.

She seemed to have been aptly named, for all she did was weep. At least for the entire period of her life that was known to me. She wept for her husband's neglect of her, her many miscarriages and still births and most of all, it seemed to me, for the fact that her only surviving children were both girls.

My father waited twenty years for her to give him an heir. Then, losing patience, he married Krishnamohini, the thirteen-year old daughter of his rent collector Srimanta Banerjee. Krishnamohini didn't bring any dowry. But she was very pretty, docile and suitably subservient. She was diligent in the performance of her duties as well. Within three years of marriage, she had presented my father with two lusty sons. Baba, fat and silvered with his advanced years, revelled in her youth, beauty and fecundity.

I resented her entry into our household and the favoured position she enjoyed in it. Considered too tall and thin for a girl, I envied her plump prettiness. Besides, the women of the family never tired of singing her praises or comparing her with me. She was sooo well brought up! Sooo dutiful! She took off her husband's shoes every evening on his return from his day's work, and washed his feet with her own hands. She kept many fasts and observed many religious austerities. She never raised her voice and always kept her eyes lowered to the ground. She was hard-working, good and gentle.

And I? I was rough and plain and totally lacking in every feminine virtue.

My blood boils with fury, to this day, when I remember a conversation I overheard when I was about ten years old. Why do I say *overheard*? It took place right in my presence, as though I was a stone and had no ears. No feelings.

A group of women – my mother was never invited to join them – were sitting together after their mid-day meal, chewing paan and gossiping, while maids fanned their limbs and dried their hair. Krishnamohini sat with them, dimpling demurely behind her ghumta. Prasanna Pishi, a distant cousin of my father's, caught sight of me standing behind a pillar. Throwing a stern glance in my direction, then a loving one at my stepmother, she sighed and said, '*Ma ke dekho! Ki sundari, ki labanyamayi! Aar meye jeno shukno baans!* (Look at the mother. So pretty and blooming! And the daughter? A length of dry bamboo!)'

As though I had been born from Krishnamohini's womb and ought to have looked exactly like her.

'But Prasanna,' Natun thakurma, a fat motherly woman with a broad streak of sindoor on a cloud of silver hair, was kinder, 'you'll have to admit that our Aanumoni is very fair. And her hair is long and thick.'

'She would be passable,' another great aunt swayed her tonsured head and rolled her eyes at me like a cunning old cockatoo, 'if her cheeks weren't pitted by the pox she had as a baby.'

'They'll grow fainter as she grows older and her face fills out.'

'If only she had a little more grace! Like our new bride here.' Prasanna Pishi patted Krishnamohini's head and continued, 'Two girls of more or less the same age. One as sweet and gentle as the goddess Lakshmi and the other wild as a monkey! Playing pranks all day. Climbing trees, diving into ponds, and flying kites. Is she a boy or a girl?'

'Pishi is right, Aanu.' My older sister, married a year ago, took it upon herself to lecture me. 'It's time you started behaving your age. Ma should have stopped your running about and playing with boys long ago. But—' She shrugged her shoulders and grimaced. The words she left unsaid were loaded.

This was the last straw. My face flamed and my eyes stung with angry tears. I stamped my foot and burst out, 'I'll do just as I please. Who are you to stop me? And who are you to find fault with Ma? Your own mother! Don't you have any shame?'

'How dare you?' Didi sprang to her feet and made a rush towards me.

'Stop it, both of you.' Natun thakurma hastened to make peace. 'Control yourself, Khukumoni. And you too, Aanu. Sisters should love each other. Not fight like cats and dogs.'

'That may be true, Natun Khuri,' Prasanna Pishi said, putting out an arm and drawing Didi away, 'but there was nothing wrong with what Khukumoni said. Aanu should stop behaving like a tomboy. She's ten. She'll be married in a few years. What will she do then? Isn't it time she stayed in the house and learned cooking and sewing like other girls her age?'

'She won't need to do any cooking and sewing in her husband's house.' Natun thakurma's round face beamed with smiles. 'Anukul sent for our family preceptor yesterday evening, showed him Aanu's horoscope and asked him when he would find a suitable match for her. Guru Thakur told him that it wouldn't happen soon. But he was not to worry. Though late, she would marry into an extremely wealthy family. So, you see, there's no need for her to learn any household arts. As for running wild why grudge her a little freedom? She'll be locked up in an unknown andarmahal soon enough. Let her enjoy her childhood while she can.'

Turning to me she said, 'Go child. Go and play with your friends. But stay in the shade. You don't want that milk-white skin to get burned black in the sun, do you?'

Guru Thakur's words were proved right. Four years later I was wed to the youngest son of late Raja Rajendranarayan Roy, an immensely wealthy man who had left an estate ten times the size of my father's and uncle's put together. In addition, I was given a title. I became the chhoto rani of the kingdom of Bhawal.

I accepted my new conditions. I had anticipated them. They weren't all that different from the ones followed by the women of my father's house. Except, of course, that life here was lived on a much larger and far more opulent scale. I had my own apartments on the second floor, lavishly furnished with Persian carpets, marble statues, paintings and crystal chandeliers. I had a personal maid and so many saris and jewels that I couldn't keep count of them. Yet, just before an occasion, be it a wedding or a rice or thread ceremony, or the annual Durga Puja celebrations, the royal weavers and jewellers would be summoned to my mother-in-law's apartments and the daughters and daughters-in-law of the house would be allowed to pick up as many saris and as much jewellery as they wanted.

I stood in awe of my mother-in-law and, even more, of my eldest sister-in-law, Princess Indumayi. Her word seemed to be the last one, not only for us *bou ranis*, but her brothers as well. The second princess, Jyotirmayi, was a large, squarely built woman, exceedingly plain, with a mild manner and gentle voice. She was very religious and spent a lot of her time in the palace temple. She was kind and non-interfering and we, younger women, felt comfortable with her. The youngest princess, Tarinmayi, was a bright, intelligent girl of about my age. She was book-learned, unlike me who could barely tell one letter from another. But, having lived a completely secluded life in the palace andarmahal, she had absolutely no idea of the real world. Of its guile and complexities. Her mind was as pure and innocent as a child's.

She and her second brother's wife, Bibhavati, were great friends. Bibhavati was a doe-eyed beauty with rose petal skin and silky black hair rippling to her knees. A tiny mole gleamed tantalizingly just above her upper lip. An air of melancholy clung to her face like a fine mist, giving it a mystique that was heartbreakingly beautiful. But from my first glimpse of her, the old envy and anger, the resentment and frustration I had felt when Baba brought his new bride home, began churning within me. I felt crude, plain and gawky in her presence. I thought everyone was comparing me with her. In hindsight I know that my fears were baseless, totally imagined. No one ever said a word. Yet, through the years that we lived together under one roof, I was unable to open my heart to her and she, it seems to me now, didn't have the confidence to open hers.

A few months after my wedding, I was stricken with a severe attack of jaundice. I lay, week after week, in a feverish stupor, my head throbbing like a live coal, my hands and feet as cold as ice. From the whispered conversations of the maids, I gathered that my mother-in-law was very worried about me. The royal physician, Baikuntha Kaviraj, had told her that his herbs, roots and potions were having little effect and he wasn't sure if he could save my life.

His fears, however, were ill-founded. It was a long battle but the fever abated eventually and strength returned slowly to my limbs.

I asked for a mirror on the day I was given my first proper bath. I could sense a little hesitation in my maid Chintamoni but I insisted and she obeyed. I got the shock of my life when I looked into the face that stared back at me. The pockmarks had sunk deeper into their pits and seemed to be blinking at me like malignant eyes. My hair had lost its sheen and was coming out in handfuls. I was thin, oh so thin! As gaunt and bony as a skeleton. Horror and repulsion devastated me. I felt like drumming my heels on the floor and screaming like a child. Chinta saw the expression on my face and rushed to my side. 'Don't feel so bad, Chhoto Rani,' she put her arms around me. 'You've been very ill. Everyone thought you would die. But our temple deities have saved your life. Let us all be grateful for that. What's a little loss of looks? Besides, it is only temporary. You'll be your old self in a month or two. Never fear.'

Embarrassed to show my face, I refused to leave my apartment. No one from the family, not even my husband, came to see me. Except Tarinmayi. '*Ma go, Ma!*' she would exclaim, a hand on one cheek like a middle-aged matron. 'What have you done to yourself, Chhoto boudidi? You look as pale as a ghost! That's because you lock yourself in your rooms all day and mope. Why don't you come and play with Mejo boudidi and me?'

I would see concern and compassion in her eyes and burst out crying. 'I'm too thin and ugly. And my hair is falling out. I shall soon grow bald. I can't show my face to anyone.'

'Come, come,' she would wipe the tears away from my cheeks. 'Don't be sad. All will be well. Besides, who cares what you look like? I don't and I'm sure Mejo boudidi doesn't.'

I thought of my face next to Bibhavati's and didn't want to go. I held out as long as I could and then, one day, I yielded. But their company gave me no pleasure. The two played with dolls, read books, and told each other stories. I hated dolls and didn't particularly care to listen to stories. I suggested that we play some other game. I had a pack of cards tucked away at the bottom of my trunk. I brought it out and taught them how to do the card tricks I had learned from my cousins in Chandipur. Tarinmayi was eager and quick to learn. But Bibhavati seemed listless and unable to concentrate. Looking back, I realize that the disease she suffered from in later years, had already wormed its way into her veins and started feeding on her life blood.

Gradually I introduced Tarinmayi to other, more adventurous, games. We played hopscotch on the chequered marble of the gallery, knowing fully well that it wasn't allowed. We played *Chor Police* in the darkened rooms of my apartment, banging into furniture and statues and often hurting ourselves. The risk of being caught and punished added spice to our enjoyment. And, gradually, she gave up playing with Bibhavati and became my constant companion.

My first summer in Bhawal passed. I had recovered my health in full and looked my old self. Now it was the month of Shravan. I loved the monsoon season. Not only did it offer respite from the burning heat, it also brought so much else. Cool breezes free of dust, cloudy skies, sheets of rain and masses of fragrant flowers which the palace malinis brought in every day. *Bakul, jui, bela and rajanigandha* strung into garlands which we would twine around our arms and hair. I would draw aside the brocade curtains of my apartment each morning and spend hours looking out on the landscape; shades and shades of green, stretching right to the horizon.

On the day of Bishwakarma Puja the sky was dotted with kites. So many sizes! So many colours! A wave of nostalgia swept over me. If I wasn't married, if I still lived in my father's house in Chandipur, I could have rushed out of doors with my cousins and flown kites with them. I was so good at it. Much better than any boy. I sighed and resigned myself to my fate.

But I wasn't made for resignation. After moping for a while, I had a bright idea. Sending for Chintamoni's son Golok, I tucked a four anna bit into his fat, sweating palm. 'Go to the bazaar, Golu,' I whispered, 'and fetch me two kites and rolls of string. Wear your *dolai* and hide them under it. Be careful. No one must see you. Not even your mother. We'll all be in terrible trouble if you're caught. You'll never be allowed inside the palace again and Chinta might lose her job. Do you understand? Go now. The rest of the money is yours to spend as you like.'

Golu had probably never held a four anna coin in his hands before. Face wreathed in smiles, he nodded and scampered off. And, sure enough, he returned an hour later, safe and sound with the loot.

That afternoon, Tarinmayi and I crept out to the balcony adjoining my apartment and began flying our kites. But she was hopeless at it. She giggled and pulled her string at all the wrong times. Her kite was cut off in seconds.

Tarinmayi and I, like other girls of our age, loved the chilli-hot, sweet and sour stuff sold in the local bazaar. These cheap treats, laid open to dust and flies, were strictly forbidden by my hygiene obsessed mother-in-law. My success with acquiring the kites emboldened me. I started sending Golu out to fetch us *hing guli*, *aamchoor*, acid drops, spiced gram and red-hot pickles wrapped in sal leaves. Tarinmayi was wary of eating anything at first. Her plump, rosy face looked worried. 'What if we catch an infection?' she said. 'Don't forget you had jaundice only a few months ago.'

'*Arre na, na*,' I assured her. 'Why are these things sold if no one is to eat them? Besides, what has to happen will happen. I hadn't eaten anything from the bazaar when I got the jaundice, had I? Stop worrying.'

We ate the filthy bazaar stuff, licking our fingers, teeth on edge, mouths flaming. The fear that accompanied the glee made everything taste wickedly delicious.

One day I played a dreadful prank on my sweet, innocent little sister-in-law. A prank that would change my life forever …

'Let's go to the *chile kotha* this afternoon,' I said to her. 'I have something to show you.'

'Why the chile kotha?'

'Because that's where the secret is.'

'What secret?'

'You're a silly girl, Chhoto thakurjhi. How can it be a secret if I tell you all about it?'

'You've made Golu fetch something from the bazaar. Something you're afraid to eat inside the house. What is it? Hog plums? Star-fruit slices? Black bel mush? *Kulchoor*?'

I shook my head at every guess.

'Then what? Oh! I know. It's *jhaal muri*. You said yesterday that you wanted to eat jhaal muri and onion rings from Batashi's shop. Batashi is a *dom*. We'll be in deep trouble if Ma finds out.'

'You're wrong. It isn't anything to eat. Stop asking so many questions. If you want to come, come. If not, forget about it.'

Tarinmayi's face was a study in conflicting emotions. Curiosity warring with fear. She pursed her lips and said, 'I'll come. But what if someone sees us?'

'We'll go in the afternoon when everyone is asleep. I tell you what. We won't go together. I'll go first and make sure the coast is clear.

You come up the moment the grandfather clock in the hall strikes two. Wear your simplest cotton sari and pull a ghumta over your face. Then, even if someone sees you, they'll think you're a maid. Oh! And take off your anklets before you start to climb the stairs.'

The chile kotha was a small room tucked away in a corner of the roof. No one knows why it was built in the first place or what purpose it had served. Over the years it became a dumping ground for the discarded articles of the household. Stuff that servants meant to take away with them but hadn't found the time. A bedstead with a split headboard stood in the centre. Torn mattresses and pillows with cotton oozing out of them were piled on it. There were mats coated with dust, broken chairs, cracked mirrors, rusted lamps, old shoes, and a lot of other things. The room was dim and full of shadows. Rats and spiders scuttled about on the floor.

After lunch, that afternoon, I sent Chintamoni away. 'You look tired, Chinta,' I told her kindly. 'Go have your own meal and get some rest. I'm tired too and will sleep for a while. I won't need anything till four o'clock.'

After she left, I put my plan into action. I took off my heavy sari, jacket and jewellery. I mixed talcum powder with Vaseline, and smeared the paste all over my face. I painted large circles around my eyes with kajal. Popping a handful of paan cones into my mouth, I chewed energetically, covering my lips with the thick red juice and letting it dribble down the corners. I combed my hair upwards till it formed a halo of tangles around my face.

Next, I opened my trunk and took out the sari my mother-in-law had sent for my turmeric ritual along with the other gifts. It was a dhakai muslin, snowy white, with beautifully worked red borders. I tore the borders away and draped the rest of the material around my form. It had some yellow marks on it but they wouldn't be visible in the dark. Pulling a ghumta down to my breast, I stole out my apartment and crept up the stairs. I entered the chile kotha and sat on the bedstead with my back to the door.

Tarinmayi came at two minutes past two. 'Chhoto boudidi,' she called softly, 'I'm here. Where's the secret?'

'I'll show it to you in a minute,' I said, making my voice high-pitched and nasal. 'Do you remember the time I had jaundice? When Kaviraj Moshai thought I would die?'

'Of course, I remember. It was only last year. Why are you sitting with your back to me? And why do you sound so strange?'

'Because something happened then ... something you don't know about. No one knows.'

'What happened?' Her voice shook a little.

'I died,' I whispered. 'I died and became a ghost. Look.' Turning slowly, I pulled the ghumta away from my face.

I caught a brief glimpse of huge eyes rolling in a face turned to ash. Then *A-a-a-a-n! A-a-a-a-a-n!* an agonized scream pierced my ear drums, almost tearing them apart. Before I could stop her, Tarinmayi ran across the roof and down the stairs shrieking '*Bhoot! Bhoot! Ma go Ma! Bhoot! Bhoot!*'

'*Arre! Arre!*' I ran after her. 'It's a joke. Come back, Chhoto thakurjhi. It's only a joke.' But she kept running, her body shaking with sobs, her aanchal trailing on the floor. She tripped over it, tumbled down the last four or five steps, picked herself up and ran down the gallery to her mother's wing. I didn't have the courage to follow her. I stood rooted to the ground for a few seconds, then walked in the direction of my own rooms. Dropping to the floor, I sat hugging my knees and cursing myself. Waiting for the inevitable ...

I didn't have to wait long. Within ten minutes, my mother-in-law's maids Dakshabala and Kadam burst in, pounced on me and bore me away, struggling and protesting, to where their mistress sat, her face grim, back straight as a ramrod, flanked on either side by her two older daughters.

The room was full of women and the sound of clamouring voices filled the air. The baro rani stood a little apart. She had, quite obviously, been rudely awakened from her siesta. Her eyes were stark and staring and her hair and clothes in disarray. The ghumta had slipped from her head and half the buttons of her jacket were undone. Part of a plump, white breast was in full view. She stood bare-headed and bare-breasted before her mother-in-law and was completely unaware of it.

Tarinmayi lay in her old nurse Bimbabala's arms. Bimba was stroking her head and making comforting, kissing sounds in her ears. Two maids chafed her hands and feet. Another held a glass of water to her lips, coaxing her to take a few sips. But Tarinmayi wouldn't give over weeping. She sobbed and shuddered, kept crying out '*Ma go, Ma*' and pressed her face deeper and deeper into Bimba's ample breasts. A gasp of horror rose from the assembly the moment I entered. It was followed by a hushed silence, lasting what was probably two minutes but seemed like hours. Princess Jyotirmayi was the first to break it.

'*He Ma Kali! He Ma Durga!* What a fright! What have you done to your face, Chhoto bou?' She pressed her hand on her vast bosom as though afraid her heart might jump out of her rib cage.

'Why only her face? Look at the rest of her.' Dakshabala waved a hand at me. Daksha had been Rani Bilasmoni's milk mother and had accompanied her when she first came to Bhawal as a little bride of seven. Her long years in the palace and her proximity to the mistress entitled her to a freedom of speech denied to other servants. 'Not a single ornament on her body!' she went on with her harangue. 'Not even the sadhaba's iron hoop. And draped in a thaan! Where did you get the thaan, Chhoto bourani? Did you bring it with you from your father's house? *Chhi! Chhi! Chhi!*' She touched her ears and bit her tongue.

'It isn't a thaan.' My mother-in-law's other trusted maid Kadam explained. 'It's her turmeric ritual sari. She's torn off the borders. *Ma go!* A girl is supposed to preserve her turmeric sari till the day of her death. Unless of course ...'

'Be quiet, Kadam,' Rani Bilasmoni raised an imperious hand and stemmed the flow. 'Let me deal with her. Why are you made up like this Chhoto bouma?' she asked in a voice as cold as ice. 'Are you an actress in a jatra playing the role of a *petni* hanging from a shaddock tree? Did your father run a jatra party in Chandipur? Enlighten me.'

I was quiet. What was there to say? I couldn't even raise my eyes to hers, hard and sharp as flints, leave alone speak. I stood where I was, shuffling my feet uneasily, eyes on the ground.

'When I agreed to the proposal,' she went on, 'I thought I was bringing a girl from an old and respectable family. The daughter of a zamindar, however small and petty his estate. One who had a proper upbringing and had been taught the right values. But now I see you've been taught nothing. You are as rough and ignorant as a peasant girl. You don't fit in with us.' She paused for breath, then went on. 'Reports of your wild ways, your tempers and tantrums have come to my ears before. I chose to ignore them, chiefly because I didn't want to admit that I had made a mistake. But this ... this is too much! Look at what you've done to my daughter! The shock could have killed her. She could have died of heart failure ...'

'But her heart hasn't failed,' I found my tongue at last. 'She's just frightened. I begged her to stop and listen to me. I wanted to explain to her that it was only a joke. But she didn't. She ran and ran ...'

'So now it's *her* fault, is it?' Daksha snapped.

'There's no need for any more talk, Daksha.' My mother-in-law turned to her eldest daughter and made a solemn pronouncement, 'I don't wish to keep her in this house any longer. She's a bad influence on the younger women of the family. What do you say, Indu?'

Princess Indumayi hadn't uttered a word so far. She had a reputation for being just and fair. I hoped, I expected her to take my part. To tell her mother that she was overreacting to what was, after all, only a girlish prank. But she didn't even glance at me. 'I'll tell Baro khoka to write to her father and ask him to take her away,' was all she said. And with those words she left the room.

I don't know if the letter was written. It probably wasn't because no one came to take me back to Chandipur. I stayed on in the palace. But I was made aware of my disgrace every moment of every single day. Tarinmayi stopped speaking to me. If we came face to face at any time, she turned away. No one bothered to offer consolation or advice. Even the maids shrugged their shoulders and pursed their lips whenever they saw me. I felt totally lost and isolated. I doubt if I could have survived this phase of my life if it weren't for my faithful Chintamoni who remained what she had been. She looked after me with all the old love and care. 'Everyone makes mistakes,' she said, whenever she saw me tearful and morose. 'You've realized yours and that's what is important. Be patient. With time your foolishness will be forgotten and everything will be the same again. And look at the bright side! Think of how it's changed you. You've grown up. You're no longer our naughty, wilful little bourani. You've turned into a dignified lady. A true queen of Bhawal.'

She was right. The incident proved to be a turning point in my life. The fear of being sent away to my father's house in shame and humiliation changed me, in one swift move, from an innocent, playful child to an angry, frustrated, knowing adult. I realized that to survive in this hateful household, where daughters-in-law could be threatened with expulsion for the slightest aberration while sons flouted every rule of decent behaviour, I would have to play a part. The part of a highborn Hindu woman who lived by the rules of her caste and class. I realized another thing. Whatever games I chose to play in the future would have to be games of the mind. Scheming, plotting, sparking off baseless rumours, setting one member of the family against another while maintaining an air of absolute innocence. I made a decision. I would do all these things and gloat over the havoc they caused. I would never be caught. Because now I knew what it took. It took skill and intelligence and I had plenty of both. Added to it was a degree of bitterness I had never dreamed of, even in my unhappy childhood in Chandipur.

Chintamoni was right, too, in her prediction that with time the incident would be forgotten. A couple of months later, Tarinmayi discovered that she was pregnant. It being her first pregnancy there was great rejoicing in the palace and I found myself included in the rituals and festivities that followed. In her happiness, Tarinmayi turned to me again. All was forgiven and forgotten and we were friends once more.

Around this time, I became aware of my husband as never before. Of his presence, or rather, his lack of presence in my life. He was very different from his big, burly, flamboyant brothers. In looks and in everything else. Unlike them, he was small and slight with a thin, piping voice and a hesitant manner. He was neither an alcoholic like the eldest prince nor a womanizer like the second. He had no bad habits. He didn't even smoke an *albola*. His only addiction was paan and scented tobacco of which he ate such vast quantities that his teeth had turned into dark brown stumps.

No sounds of music and dancing or of rowdy, drunken laughter ever came from my husband's rooms on the ground floor. Nor was he, at any time, surrounded by toadies like the older kumars. Curious to see what went on in his apartments, I would often take up his lorgnette and look through the shutters into the yard. Sometimes the door was open and I would see him lying against a pile of silk cushions, his silver paan box and spittoon by his side, deep in conversation with his friend Jyoti Prakash. Jyoti babu would be speaking or reading out something from a sheaf of papers, waving long, white hands glittering with rings. The chhoto kumar would be listening, eyes closed in rapture.

Jyoti babu was allowed entry into other parts of the palace as well. He ate all his meals here and I've often caught sight of him walking down the gallery towards the dining hall. He was tall and portly, very handsome, with a thick mane of hair curling down to the nape, and luxuriant whiskers. He was always well turned out in crimped dhutis with broad borders and muslin kurtas so fine, the rich dark growth on his chest was clearly visible. I had found the friendship a bit puzzling at first and shared my thoughts with Tarinmayi.

'They seem so different from each other,' I said to her. 'Jyoti babu is so much older. And, and, so …'

'It's an old friendship,' she replied, 'starting from their school days. Jyoti dada was Chhoto dada's senior in school. He was a brilliant student and wrote poetry from an early age. Chhoto dada loves his poetry. He is convinced that Jyoti Prakash Mallik is the next Robi Thakur of Bengal.'

'What does he do for a living?' I asked curiously. 'He seems to spend all his time in your brother's rooms. He even has his meals here. Doesn't he have a family?'

'Of course he does. Have a family, I mean. He has parents, a widowed sister, a wife and two sons. As for what he does for a living – he doesn't do anything. He doesn't need to. Chhoto dada supports him. And he is right to do so. If the monarchs of the realm don't extend patronage towards their own writers, who will?'

For some reason I found myself thinking of Jyoti Prakash. Once in a while to begin with, then all the time. Whenever I closed my eyes, I saw him. Striding along the gallery, head held high above massive shoulders, the thick gold chain rippling down his neck and nestling in the dark curls that sprouted from the immense expanse of his chest.

The chhoto kumar, like his eldest brother, spent the day in his rooms but came to the andarmahal faithfully every night. Always at the same hour. Around eleven o'clock. Every night he asked me the same question in the same courteous voice, 'Are you well?' before turning his back on me and going to sleep. Once in a while he bestirred himself and tried to perform his husbandly duty. But his efforts were so tentative, so timid and restrained, that they maddened me. Sometimes I couldn't bear it and pushed him away, my eyes stinging with disappointment. He took my rejection very calmly, as though saying, without words, that this was the best he could do and it was for me to take it or leave it.

But more often than not I yielded, for the desire to become a mother was as deeply ingrained in me as in all other women. Besides, the glorious thought of producing an heir to the kingdom, of being hailed as the next Rajmata and being invested with all the power and dignity enjoyed by Rani Bilasmoni, gave me the strength to endure the unendurable. The baro rani had borne several children but none of them had survived. The mejo rani was sickly and her husband was afflicted with a venereal disease. It was doubtful if she would ever become pregnant. The royal family and the subjects of the kingdom were looking to the chhoto kumar and me to give them the long-awaited heir.

I put up with my husband's clumsy attempts to impregnate me. The only way I could do so was by gritting my teeth, shutting my eyes, and thinking about Jyoti babu. I imagined his hands moving all over my body, the long, white fingers touching my neck and breasts, stroking my face and pressing it against his chest. My limbs quivered with delight at these fantasies. I felt a tautness in my nipples and a melting in my thighs.

But the months rolled into years and I did not become pregnant …

During those years the family suffered a grievous decline. Not only was it denied an heir, the very edifice on which it stood began to crumble. Slowly at first, then so rapidly that the inmates were taken unawares. With no time to prepare for the catastrophe that overtook us, we found ourselves groping in a strange, dark world of which we knew nothing.

Our cycle of ill luck began with the death of the mejo kumar and his wife's breakaway from the family. I don't think she was very keen on leaving what had been her home for seven years. It was her brother who forced her. I went to her apartments on the day of their departure and was shocked by what I saw. Mejo didi lay in bed, white and still as a corpse, her face turned to the wall. The door to her safe was open and her brother was taking out the stacks of cases that contained her jewels and stowing them away in two huge trunks. There was something stealthy in his movements and he was acting in haste as though he feared he would be stopped if he wasn't swift enough. My entry must have startled him for two boxes slipped from his hands and fell to the floor. One was full of bangles and from the other a stream of gold coins came pouring out. They bounced on the carpet and spread in all directions to lie scattered like stars in an indigo blue sky.

With the death of the baro kumar soon afterwards, the estate passed into the care of the Court of Wards. My husband's health fell into a decline and he died two years later. On an earlier occasion, after my father-in-law's passing, the British had taken over the estate on the plea that the princes were minors and had refused to return it even after they had reached adult years. My feisty mother-in-law had started legal proceedings against the rulers and won her case. But Rani Bilasmoni had been dead these many years and there was no one left to fight our battle. Princess Indumayi could have followed her mother's example but she had been diagnosed with asthma and a weak heart. Our doctor, Mahim Dasgupta, had cautioned her against any tension or excitement which, he said, could lead to heart failure. So, there was nothing left for us to do other than accept our fate.

Money became tight, so tight that living in the palace was no longer feasible and the inmates moved out one by one. The three princesses were the first to leave the palace. But they stayed within the complex, settling down in houses received by their husbands in dowry. The baro rani went next. She was a beloved daughter of an illustrious family and was received by them with open arms. When my turn came, I was in a quandary. Where would I go? Returning to Chandipur was not an option. My parents were both dead and my uncle was managing the estate on behalf of my father's minor sons.

I hadn't kept in touch with him or Krishnamohini for years. I had forgotten them and they had forgotten me …

I could have moved in with one of my sisters-in-law. I was invited to do so by all three. But the idea of living on the fringes of someone else's family circle was abhorrent to me. My father-in-law had bought a house for each of his sons in Kolkata. The one belonging to my husband, now legally mine, was a fair-sized bungalow standing on three quarters of an acre of land in Lower Circular Road, a stone's throw away from where Bibhavati lived. Though a total stranger to the metropolitan city, I decided to make it my future place of residence. Bidding a tearful farewell to the rooms which had housed me for nearly a decade and become beloved and familiar, I left Jaidevpur with a small staff of servants. Chintamoni and her family accompanied me. She is with me still.

The house had been kept locked for years and was in a shocking state of disrepair. It took a whole month and a dozen workmen to make it habitable. Walls were stripped of their rotting wooden panels and painted a pleasing shade of green. Floors, thick with dust and grime, were scrubbed and polished and broken windows reglazed. The garden was cleared of weeds and planted with flowering shrubs and vines. The original furniture put up by my father-in-law, slippery horsehair sofas and massive mahogany tables, were despatched to the auction house and light, bright furniture of teak and walnut ordered. Lace curtains and colourful rugs arrived from Whiteway and Laidlaw and Ming vases from Chinese shops selling artefacts and antiques.

When all was done, I looked around in satisfaction. It was my home; my first real home. I was mistress of all I surveyed. The thought sent a thrill through me.

Some months later my uncle, the chhoto taraf of Chandipur, came to see me. Apologizing for not reaching out earlier, he expressed deep distress at my being forced to live alone without a male protector. That, too, in a wicked city like Kolkata.

'You are only twenty-four,' he said shaking his head sadly. 'It isn't safe. And it's highly improper. What will people say?'

'I have never cared for public opinion, Kaka babu,' I answered coolly. 'I care even less now. My guards and servants provide me with all the protection I need.'

'*Na, na*, Aanu. It isn't only a question of physical protection. It is a matter of family prestige.'

'Which family?'

'Well,' he seemed a bit taken aback, 'the Bhawals, of course, and ours too.'

'The Bhawals haven't expressed any concern.'

'But *I'm* doing so. Listen, Aanumoni. You are a young woman with practically no education and very little experience of life. But you have a lot of money. You need someone to manage it for you. Kolkata is full of cheats and scoundrels and rich women get conned all the time. My eldest son, your Harinath dada, is knowledgeable in legal and financial matters. If you wish, he can move in with you. His presence in your household will keep tongues from wagging. It will work well in other ways too. A base in Kolkata will be useful to him and his guidance and counsel will be invaluable for you. Bara bouma is a fine, capable woman and can take some of your domestic responsibilities off your hands. And the children – they have three – will fill this silent, empty house with joy and laughter. What do you say?'

'*Na, na*, Kaka babu,' I smiled snidely to myself and sweetly at him. 'You are doing too much for us already. You are looking after Baba's estate on behalf of my brothers. It's a heavy burden you're carrying and I am truly grateful for it. I couldn't dream of giving you more trouble.'

'It's no trouble ...'

'It *is*, Kaka babu. You know it and I do too. Don't worry about me. The family lawyers and our old Nayeb Moshai are looking after my affairs just as they did during the chhoto kumar's lifetime. And my trusted maid Chintamoni takes care of all the nitty-gritty of the household. I don't have to do anything. As for the children … frankly, I don't like children. They are noisy and troublesome and give me a headache.'

My uncle stared at me as though he couldn't believe his ears. His fat cheeks collapsed like pricked balloons and hung in folds down his chin. His jowls quivered with shock and indignation. 'There's a difference,' he muttered, rising slowly to his feet, 'between paid employees and one's own kin. I came to offer my help. But you don't want it. What else is there for me to say?' He tapped his silver-headed cane forcefully on the floor several times, and walked out of the room.

Kaka babu's plan to gain control over my money was nipped in the bud. But his visit resulted in a breaking of the ice. How or when exactly the process began, I can't say. But communication was restored and members of the family began writing to me and even staying with me when they came to Kolkata. And they came often, the women to bathe in the Ganga and offer puja at shrines and temples, the men for legal and official work. I resented this encroachment on my privacy at first, but since they stayed only for a few days, it seemed churlish to refuse. Then a curious thing happened. I started to look on these visits not as intrusions but as diversions.

The truth was that after the first glow of euphoria at living in my own house on my own terms faded, I began to get bored and lonely. Used to the vibrant atmosphere of the palace, each day packed with rituals and events and teeming with possibilities, my life here seemed to have fallen into a dreary, monotonous routine. I missed the gossip and chatter about saris and jewels, the exchange of confidences with Tarinmayi, the scheming and plotting and settling of scores, the excitement of looking out for Jyoti babu's tall figure striding down the gallery and the leap of my heart when I spotted it. Here, there was no one to talk to and nothing to do. I had no friends in this alien city and my only relatives were my two sisters-in-law, Sarajubala and Bibhavati.

In the first six months of my arrival in Kolkata, I called on them several times, but came back disappointed. Sarajubala lived in a huge, rambling mansion in Boubazar, packed to the gills with so many uncles, aunts, cousins, second cousins, poor relatives, hangers-on, maids and servants that it hummed like a beehive all day. Her apartment was always full of women who welcomed me, plied me with sweets and snacks, but would not leave me alone with her for a moment. It was impossible to have a private conversation, to recall the past with nostalgia and weep and laugh over the present.

Bibhavati's situation was the exact opposite. Her mother had died a year earlier but the house still had the look and feel of a house in mourning. A pall of gloom hung in the air. There was something else, a presence, shadowy and nebulous, lurking within the walls. But the terror it exuded was so real, so pervasive, I could feel it and smell it. The weight of this invisible presence seemed to rest most heavily on Bibhavati and her sister-in-law Sandhyarani. They spoke little and even that little was so restrained, so timidly uttered, it seemed as though they were looking over their shoulders, fearful of being overheard. They looked alike too. One dark, one fair, but both equally careworn and etiolated.

After this it was natural for me to turn to my own kin. They were simple, ordinary folk and stood in awe of me. They, particularly the women, couldn't get over the fact that I, the chhoto rani of Bhawal, was one of their own. I revelled in their pride and admiration and began to look forward to their visits. I even gave in to their persuasion and made a couple of trips to Chandipur. Once to attend Natun thakurma's shraddha and again for my half-brother Bhulon's *upanayan*. And when my turn came to offer a gift to the new brahmin, I hung a *sonar poite*, a bunch of gold wires coiled together to form a chain as thick as a rope, across his torso.

Over the next few years, Harinath dada's wife and I became good friends. She was a very nice woman, wonderfully witty and lively. I also got greatly attached to her youngest child Moni – a beautiful little boy. I sent for him often and kept him with me for months together. I showered gifts on him, pampered and spoiled him, lavishing all the pent-up maternal love that had hitherto lain dormant in my breast. And when he was six years old, I adopted him. It was a formal adoption with all the legal papers in place. His name was changed from Monilal Mukherjee to Ramnarayan Roy, and with that new name he became my true son and heir. I wondered at the irony of life. Kaka babu had wanted my money to flow into his family. He had succeeded, though in a circuitous way. But he hadn't lived to enjoy his triumph. *He must be smiling snidely to himself*, I thought, *from heaven or hell ... or wherever else he might be.*

A year after the formalities were completed Tarinmayi filed a suit against me challenging the adoption. I was convinced that it wasn't her idea. Her husband Brajalal Banerjee was behind it and it was he who had coerced her to sign the papers. Shocked and frightened, I begged Sarajubala to support me. She too had adopted a child and would understand how I felt. She agreed at first and then started to prevaricate. There was no point in asking the princesses to mediate. They were Tarinmayi's sisters and would support her. In utter despair, I turned to Bibhavati.

It was a Sunday and her brother was at home. Bypassing her completely, he put me through a grilling interview. *Who was the child? When did I decide to adopt him? Why someone from Chandipur? As far as he knew, I had never had much to do with my family. Why not someone from the royal line? It was true that the princes of Bhawal had died without leaving any issue. But the princesses had sons who, though from the female line, had the royal blood of Bhawal running in their veins. Why not one of them? And, if at all, I wished to pass them over in favour of my own kin, why didn't I think of adopting one of my half-brothers? Why my uncle's grandson?*

Why? Why? Why? I was so exhausted by Satya babu's cross-examination that I gave up in the middle of it. I got up to leave. Then a curious thing happened. Bibhavati had been silent all this while but as soon as I rose to my feet, she spoke. 'I am with you, Aanu,' she said softly. Her brother shot a warning glance at her but she didn't look at him. 'Your life's choices are yours alone,' she continued. 'No one has the right to question or deny them. You can depend on me for whatever help you need.' She rose quietly and left the room.

The case filed by Tarinmayi dragged on desultorily for several years. Then a new judge appeared on the scene and dismissed it for lack of merit. Through those years and the ones that followed, I often thought of Bibhavati. Of how she had stood by me when everyone else had let me down. Of how she had addressed me by my nickname, Aanu, instead of the formal Chhoto bou that denoted my position in the family hierarchy. It must have taken courage to go against so many people, especially her brother who had made it clear that he didn't want her to be drawn into any controversy pertaining to her in-laws. He was a hard, ruthless man. Who knows what consequences she had had to face?

But she had braved his anger and done what she thought was right. And I? I had been so cruel to her; so spiteful! I had lured the only friend she had in the palace, away from her, with new games and cheap treats from the bazaar. I had spread falsehoods about her and maligned her character.

So, when Satya babu expressed what I thought was Bibhavati's wish that I denounce the sannyasi as an imposter, I agreed. I understood her feelings and sympathized. The mejo kumar had shamed and humiliated her beyond endurance. That chapter of her life was closed and she didn't want it reopened. Not that she was happy under the oppressive rule of her brother. She wasn't. But she lacked the confidence to step into another space. She had brokered an unholy peace with herself, embraced a life-in-death existence. She was content to live it out …

Yesterday when I looked into the greenish-brown eyes of the plaintiff, another pair of eyes floated in my vision. Long, dewy, beautiful eyes looking out of a pale, strained face. I gritted my teeth and, putting my hand on the holy Bhagwad Gita, swore that the man standing before me was not the mejo kumar of Bhawal.

5

Taufique Ali

Kankrajoli Village, Bhawal
1935

A MONTH AGO, A MAN ARRIVED FROM PATUATULI, IN DHAKA, WITH a message from my daughter Rabeya. Her husband Salim had been stricken with typhoid fever. With no other man in the house and no relatives nearby, she was at her wit's end. She desperately needed her parents to come and help her out. Typhoid, I knew, was a highly contagious and debilitating disease and its only treatment was segregation of the patient, a liquid diet and good nursing. It was impossible for our daughter to fend for three small children and an old, half-blind mother-in-law, and nurse her husband at the same time. My wife and I decided that we would leave for Dhaka that very day. She would take charge of the children and the old lady, leaving Rabeya free to tend to Salim. Arriving in Patuatuli, the first thing I did was to speak to the doctor attending my son-in-law and was assured that, though his condition was serious, it was not critical. With proper care he would pull through.

At that time, the city of Dhaka was agog with excitement. Wherever I went – in lanes and alleys, along the waterfront, outside shops and masjids, I found men gathered together in groups discussing the latest situation in the Bhawal sannyasi case. I was excited too. I lived in Bhawal, I had been born there, and knew most of the people involved by sight. Whenever I got a chance, I inched close to the huddling men, trying to glean scraps of information. But it was quite a while before I found the time and opportunity to find out what was happening for myself. The day after Salim was given his first solid meal of rice mush and fish broth, I made my way to the Dhaka district court where the case was being heard.

Entering the courtroom, I was able to find a seat in the third row from where I could get a good view of the witness box. Since there was some time to spare, I got into a conversation with the man sitting next to me. He told me that a number of witnesses, including the two princesses and the baro rani and chhoto rani, had been questioned already and it was rumoured that the woman who would be called that morning was a certain *khemtawali*. I was puzzled. What did a *khemta* dancer have to do with the Bhawal case?

I didn't have to wait long to find out. In a few minutes the judge walked in and took his seat. The lawyer for the petitioner Mr B. C. Chatterjee rose to his feet and the court clerk called out '*Elokeshi Khemtawali Hajir*'. My heart leaped up with excitement. Elokeshi! I had forgotten that the mejo kumar's first mistress had been a khemta dancer, the daughter of the famous Muktokeshi Khemtawali of Chandni Ghat. I had seen her several times in the past, sitting in the phaeton next to the mejo kumar, shimmering in silks and jewels, laughing gaily as the horses galloped down the streets of Jaidevpur. I was a youth of fifteen then and extremely susceptible to feminine charm. Her face came often into my dreams. An oval face with arched eyebrows and crimson mouth, a diamond sparkling from a delicate nostril, a long earring swinging across a powdered cheek bulging with paan ...

I was totally unprepared for the bent old woman who hobbled up to the witness box. The contrast was made even more bizarre by her pathetic attempt to recreate her past image. She wore a rich Benarasi sari but it was frayed in many places and the masses of gold on her arms and around her neck were so obviously imitation that even a child wouldn't be fooled. Patches of lentigo covered her cheeks and her years of paan-eating had blackened her teeth. Many of them had fallen out. Altogether she looked a caricature of her former self.

The trial began with B. C. Chatterjee asking her if she recognized anyone in the courtroom as the mejo kumar and, if so, to point him out. On her waving a hand at the plaintiff, she was asked to identify a photograph taken thirty years ago, at the height of her affair with the second prince of Bhawal. She screwed up her eyes, looked closely at it and admitted that it was hers. She was then asked to give an account of her relationship with the kumar. When it began, how it had proceeded and why it came to an end. She answered with a complete lack of hesitation and spoke with verve and vivacity. Hearing her, I felt I was watching a scene from a play.

'The mejo kumar saw me first in the *naat mandir* of Jaidevpur palace, where I had gone to sing and dance at the festivities celebrating the birth of the baro rani's son. He fell in love with me instantly and made me his mistress. He kept me in his own apartments at first, and then, on his mother's insistence, rented a house for me in Begum Bazar in Dhaka. I lived there for several years. I was well looked after. I had money, jewels, servants, everything my heart desired, and he came to me whenever he could. He was the kindest of men. Not only did he take care of me, he looked after my ageing mother as well. We were deeply in love and remained so even after his marriage.'

'But you did break up eventually, did you not?' B. C. Chatterjee's piercing eyes stared into hers. 'When did this happen? And why?'

Elokeshi shot a glance at the plaintiff and lowered her eyes. Her face turned red with embarrassment. 'We had a fight ...' she muttered.

'Tell us about it. Narrate the circumstances exactly as you remember them.'

'It was after I discovered that he had contracted *para*,' she said slowly. 'My mother, even more than I, dreaded the disease and insisted that I stop sleeping with him. "We are prostitutes," she said. "We can't afford to take risks. What other capital do we have except our bodies? If you don't take care of yours, you'll be starving in the streets. Tell him to go to a doctor and come back only after he is completely cured." When I refused, she took the unpleasant task upon herself. Stopping him at the door the next time he came, she knelt before him and, touching her forehead to the ground at his feet, begged him to stop coming to me. I'll never forget the expression on the kumar's face when he heard her words. His lips quivered and turned white. His eyes widened in surprise. "You, Mukto!" he exclaimed in a bewildered voice. "*You* forbid me to enter my own house! After all I've done for you!"

'"Please have pity on us," Ma begged. "Just think. If Elo gets infected, it will be all over for her."

'"Why? Are you afraid I'll withdraw my protection?" A deep flush rose from his neck and suffused his cheeks as he said this. His eyes glittered with angry tears. "What do you think of me?" he demanded. "Have you forgotten that I'm a prince and your daughter a common whore I picked up from the gutter and treated like a queen?"

'"I haven't forgotten anything, Raja saheb!" Ma said, hastening to make amends. "You have been kinder to her than anyone could have been. We revere you like a god. But this affliction ..." her voice trailed off.

'"This affliction and others like it are part and parcel of the profession you follow. How can I be sure that it wasn't she who gave it to me?" The mejo kumar said.

'I had felt sorry for him so far but his last words made me furious. "I have never suffered from any such thing," I protested vehemently. "I live a clean and decent life. I've allowed no other man in my bed since I've been in your protection. Which is more than can be said of you ..."

'"*Chup kor, mukhpuri*!" Ma rose from her knees and slapped my cheek. It was a hard, stinging blow. "You dare compare yourself with him! Don't you know that women like us must never forget our place. Knock your head on the mejo kumar's feet and beg for forgiveness."

'"Why should I beg for forgiveness?" I demanded, angry tears pouring down my face. "How can he blame me? He knows very well that he has picked up the vile disease from one of the scavenger women he visits on his nightly jaunts."'

At this point, the counsel for the defence rose to contradict the witness. A. N. Chaudhuri's strategy, from what I had heard, was to project the mejo kumar as a decent, educated, cultured aristocrat, totally unlike the plaintiff who, in his opinion, was a rough peasant from the Punjab dressed up to resemble a Bengali gentleman. Elokeshi's comment on the prince's nightly jaunts infuriated the lawyer who lashed out at her for spinning a web of lies.

'The mejo kumar discarded you long ago,' he told her. 'You haven't seen him for nearly three decades. How can you be sure that the man pointed out to you is the second prince? You're lying …'

Elokeshi remained unfazed. 'I'm not lying,' she replied steadily. 'It is true that our relationship ended with the altercation I have just described. He stopped coming to me after that. But I've met him from time to time since then, and kept track of his whereabouts. I had heard of his death in Darjeeling, the rumours surrounding the cremation and then, later, of the sannyasi's claim. I was intrigued and went to meet the man. We recognized each other instantly. "How are you, Elokeshi?" he said to me with a smile and enquired after my welfare. I have seen him several times after that and there is no doubt in my mind that he is the mejo kumar.'

Elokeshi came out with another startling disclosure. She said that an officer from the Kotwali had come to see her and warned her not to testify in the case. He had also offered her fifty rupees for not appearing in court.

Three days of adjournment followed, after which the hearings were resumed. I arrived at the courtroom that morning to find it spilling over with people. It was Satya babu's turn to be cross-examined and the excitement in the crowd was almost palpable. After Bibhavati Debi, he was, without doubt, the principal witness for the defence.

Introducing him as Rai Bahadur Satyendranath Banerjee, A. N. Chaudhuri asked him to open the hearing with an account of himself and of what had transpired on the night of 8 May 1909. *Rai Bahadur*! I was surprised. When and why had he been dignified with that title? As far as I knew, he was an ordinary advocate in the Calcutta High Court with no special claim to fame. Had the title been bestowed on him by the British government for taking their side and denouncing the sannyasi as an imposter?

After a preliminary self-introduction, he went on to describe the events surrounding the prince's death. Denying the charge of wilfully causing it with the active connivance and aid of Ashutosh Dasgupta, he went on to corroborate the defendant's story, now familiar to all. The death, he said, had occurred at midnight, a funeral procession had accompanied the body to the *samsan* in the morning, and the kumar had been cremated with the full honour and dignity owing to him as a prince of the realm.

A. N. Chaudhuri now put Satyendranath Banerjee through a round of questioning with the obvious intention of forestalling the line of attack that he was sure would be taken by his opponent.

'Is it true that Rani Bibhavati Debi had a hysterical fit that night and had to be taken away to another room?'

'No. She sat next to her husband's body all night.'

'Three telegrams were sent from Darjeeling to Jaidevpur. Who sent them?'

'I have no idea. It certainly wasn't me. I saw them for the first time in 1921, after the sannyasi came to Jaidevpur.'

The counsel for the defendants now picked up a worn, leather-bound notebook from the exhibits displayed by B. C. Chatterjee and held it out to his witness.

'Do you recognize this?' he asked.

'Yes. It's my diary.'

'Why did you feel the need to keep a diary?'

'After my return from Darjeeling I stayed on in the Rajbari for some months to comfort my sister in her grief. During that period, I became aware of a conspiracy being hatched against her and, in order to protect her rights, I felt I should keep a daily note of all that was going on.'

'Who was conspiring against her and what was the nature of the conspiracy?'

'The baro kumar and Princess Indumayi were behind it. They were trying to get a Deed of Management executed by which Bibhavati would be made to relinquish her share in the management of the estate in return for a monthly allowance.'

At this point B.C. Chatterjee took over.

'You say you became aware of a conspiracy against your sister. From where did you source the information? Please enlighten the court.'

Satya babu had been totally poised and self-assured all this time. Suddenly his aplomb vanished. His face fell. He was quiet for a few seconds, then pulled himself together. 'These things get talked about,' he answered sullenly. 'Secrets are difficult to keep in a palace teeming with people.'

'Which means you were relying on gossip and speculation. Not hard facts.'

There was no answer.

'The first entry in your diary is dated 20 May 1909. The ones that follow contain recollections of events that had taken place from 7 May onwards. Why did you think it necessary to record events that had happened a fortnight earlier? Did you foresee a case against you?'

'Of course not. It was a harrowing period in my sister's life. I wanted to keep it in my memory. I was afraid that if I didn't put the facts down, I might forget the flow as well as the details.'

'The entries stop on 12 December 1909, the day you took your sister away. It seems that, after the Deed of Relinquishment was signed and the demands made by you were met, you no longer felt the need to remember the harrowing period in your sister's life. Am I correct?'

'Objection, my lord!' A. N. Chaudhuri sprang to his feet and cried, 'Counsel is leading the witness.'

The objection was sustained and the cross-examination was taken up once more.

'Why did you hand over your diary to the Court of Wards?'

'I did nothing of the sort.' Satya babu had recovered his belligerence. 'It was stolen.'

'Stolen?'

'Yes. Along with some old letters and other papers.'

'When?'

'Sometime in November 1912. I don't remember the exact date.'

'Soon after the Court of Wards took over the Bhawal estate?'

'Could be.'

'Why didn't you report the theft?'

'It was only an old diary. Not important enough to make a song and dance about.'

'Very well. Now let us come to the events surrounding the supposed death. Why was Dr Prankrishna Acharya sent for, on the morning of 9th May, if Colonel Calvert had already pronounced that the kumar had died the night before?'

'I don't know who sent for Dr Acharya. I didn't.'

'According to him, it was a woman claiming to be a nurse. A woman who was found nowhere near the body when he went to Step Aside. Who was she?'

'I haven't the faintest idea.'

Requesting the judge to take note of the inconsistencies in the witness's statements, B. C. Chatterjee walked back to his seat. The court was adjourned.

Salim made a speedy recovery, getting back to his feet far quicker than the doctor had thought possible. His youth and general good health were on his side. And, as the doctor explained, the attack was mild and had been attended to fairly early. So far so good. We had done what we had come to do and it was time, in all propriety, to go back home.

'When shall we leave for Kankrajoli?' my wife nagged me every day. 'We came away in such a hurry, leaving the house in a mess. I told Maju bibi to feed the hens regularly but who knows if she is doing so? The floors must be covered with dust and the yard full of weeds. It will take me weeks to get everything back in order again. Besides, it is unseemly to stay in a married daughter's house for too long. It's been nearly a month …'

But I was in no tearing hurry to leave Dhaka. 'You talk as though we came for a holiday,' I muttered.

'No. We came to help Rabeya out in a difficult situation. But it's over now. She is capable of managing her own affairs. Why are we lingering on?'

The truth was that I wanted to attend Rani Bibhavati's trial which, rumour had it, was due in a few days. People were talking about it everywhere. She was, after all, the star witness for the defence. I was immensely excited. I had heard of her great beauty but never seen it and this was such an opportunity! Besides, her strange behaviour after hearing of the return of her husband fuelled my curiousity. What sort of woman was she? I desperately wanted to see her and hear her speak.

'I have some work in Dhaka,' I lied to my wife. 'We'll leave as soon as it's done.'

The anticipated day came. I went early, almost an hour before the scheduled time, but the courtroom was full already. I couldn't find a place to sit and was obliged to attend the entire hearing standing at the back, squashed between two fat men who looked like twins in checked lungis with gamchhas slung across their shoulders. But, from where I stood, I got a clear view of the witness box and could hear every word that was being said. The silence was so penetrating it was almost eerie.

And now a collective murmur, soft as the rustle of a bird's wings, rose from the crowd. I looked up quickly. A slim figure draped in widow's white was making her way towards the witness box. *Subhan Allah!* My first reaction on seeing her was not so much a sense of wonder at her grace and beauty. That too. But what overwhelmed me completely was the stately dignity that exuded from every inch of her person. *Here is a queen*, I thought. *A true queen.*

Through the entire course of her cross-examination by the petitioner's counsel, despite all his efforts to unsettle her, she maintained the same calm and serenity. She took the questions squarely and made no effort to prevaricate. But her manner was guarded. She kept her voice low and answered mostly in monosyllables.

The first round of questioning pertained to the earlier part of her married life. I remember some of the questions put to her. Though not necessarily in the same order, they were as follows:

Q. Did you despise your husband because he was illiterate and a debauch?'

A. No.

Q. Did you feel hurt and humiliated by the fact that he refused to sleep with you?

A. No.

Q. Your reticence is understandable. But in a court of law, you are expected to give fuller answers. Let me put my question in another way. What did you think of your husband's infidelity and loose ways?

A. He was my husband. I do not wish to comment on his character.

Q. What was your opinion of the baro kumar?

A. He was a respected elder. That's all I have to say.

Q. And the chhoto kumar?
A. I don't wish to comment on anyone's character.

Q. Were your husband and the members of his family kind to you?
A. Kind enough. I have no complaints.

B. C. Chatterjee appeared stumped by her unflappable calm. He took a deep breath and tried again.

Q. Are you saying that your relationship with your husband was exactly as it should have been? That there was no discord? No friction?
A. I have said no such thing.

Q. Please answer my question directly. Was your marriage a harmonious one?
A. No marriage is completely harmonious.

Q. Did your husband miss you when you were apart?
A. He may have.

Q. Some married men go to great lengths to please their wives. Was your husband like them?
A. I don't know about other men. I cannot make comparisions.

Q. Did your husband act on your advice?
A. Not always.

Q. Have you ever felt that you were your husband's main concern?
A. No.

Q. Who or what concerned him most?
A. I don't know. I'm not a mind reader.

At this point, the counsel for the petitioner approached the bench and murmured a few words in a low voice. The judge responded by announcing that the court was adjourned for the day and that the hearing would be resumed the following morning.

The next day I reached the courtroom early enough to find a seat within a few feet of the witness box. I wanted to have a better view of the mejo rani to be able to observe her facial expressions.

The hearing began. B. C. Chatterjee abandoned his previous strategy of trying to make the witness confess to a dislike of her husband and in-laws and came straight to the point. Taking her through the events leading to the death of the kumar, he posed his first question.

Q. What was your husband suffering from on the day he died?
A. Severe purging and vomiting accompanied by high fever.

Q. You say you were with him through the entire day of 8 May. When exactly did his condition begin to deteriorate?
A. Around noon.

Q. Did it worry you?
A. Of course.

Q. Did you think he would die the same day?
A. No.

Q. What was the time of death?
A. Around midnight.

Q. Do you know that it is extremely rare for a person to die of gallstones?
A. Yes, I do.

Q. Is it possible that your husband died of something else?
A. How can I say? Am I a doctor?

Q. Stones in the gall bladder do not cause vomiting and bloody stools. Arsenic does. Do you think your husband died of arsenic poisoning?
A. Why should I think that?

Q. Because Dr Dasgupta prescribed arsenic.
A. He must have had his reasons for doing so. What do I know of medicines and their usage?

Q. How long have you known Ashutosh Dasgupta?
A. Since my marriage.

Q. What is your opinion of him?
A. I believe he is an honest man.

Mr. Chatterjee stood undecided for a minute before moving to another tack.

Q. You say that the death occurred at midnight. When was the body brought down from the prince's apartments?
A. In the morning.

Q. Can you be a bit more specific?
A. Between 7 and 7.30.

Q. Are you sure?
A. I didn't look at the clock but I believe it was around that time.

Q. Very well. Now take a good look at the plaintiff. Is he your husband?
A. No.

Q. Rani Satyabhama believes he is.
A. Rani Satyabhama is old and her eyesight is feeble. Besides, she is under the influence of the plaintiff's supporters.

Q. She wrote a letter to you. Why did you send it back unopened?
A. Because I knew what would be in it. An appeal to make me change my mind.

Q. The plaintiff has made several efforts to meet you. You turned him down every time. Isn't it strange that you made up your mind he wasn't your husband even before seeing him?

A. That's not true. I had seen him a couple of times.

Q. Where?
A. In the streets of Kolkata.

Q. Were these sightings arranged?
A. No. They were purely coincidental.

Q. Did you find any resemblance between the two men?
A. None at all.

Q. Is it possible that you've forgotten what your husband looked like?
A. Can a wife forget what her husband looked like?

Q. There has been a gap of nearly twenty-five years since you saw him last.
A. Even so. I remember him quite clearly.

Q. In his conversations with family and friends, the plaintiff has spoken of certain distinguishing marks on your body that only a husband can know of. I'm sure you've received reports. What do you have to say?
A. He is lying. There are no such marks …

Q. Are you willing to undergo a physical examination?

At this point Pannalal Basu interrupted the proceedings with the remark that a physical examination was uncalled for. It would prove nothing and serve no purpose.

B. C. Chatterjee now posed another personal question. Was it a fact, he asked, that the witness had been pregnant at one time? And that the foetus had been aborted and the matter hushed up because the child was not the mejo kumar's?

The mejo rani's face turned as white as paper. Her lips quivered and a blue vein began throbbing in her left temple. She put up a hand to press it down. For the first time in the course of the cross-examination, she betrayed visible signs of shock and fear. She opened her mouth to say something. But before she could do so, Pannalal Basu threw a stern glance at Mr Chatterjee and said, 'I cannot allow this line of questioning. It doesn't have the slightest foundation in evidence. I regret that the topic was introduced and I condemn the charges it led to.'

The cross-examination was over.

Rani Bibhavati's face stayed with me all day and all through the journey back to Kankrajoli. I could think of nothing else. There was a sense of bewilderment as well. She had been so calm and composed through the most difficult parts of the cross-examination. Why did she lose her nerve at the last question? She should have looked her interrogator sternly in the eye and denied the charge as the vilest, most unmitigated rubbish. She should have accused him of bias and shamed him before the whole court. Instead, she had looked petrified. Her eyes had taken on the look of a hunted doe. She had clutched her temple with a shaking hand. Why?

I remembered the stories that were circulated about her after she left the Rajbari. There were hints of an unnatural relationship between brother and sister. Some openly used the word 'incest'. I had neither believed nor dismissed the rumours. I hadn't seen her then; only heard of her. People said she was a beautiful but discontented woman; sickly and nagging. Satya babu, on the other hand, I had met quite a few times. A glib talker, self-assured and good looking in a rough and ready way. But seeing him last week, after almost three decades, I was shocked at the change. Alcoholism and other types of excess were stamped on every line of his vast sagging body and florid face, his many chins and bulging, bloodshot eyes.

I thought of the gossip linking the two and felt an instinctive revulsion. *Impossible!* I thought to myself. *A tissue of lies!* I couldn't, I simply couldn't, imagine the woman I had seen in the witness box with her delicate porcelain skin, her long, dewy eyes and face as fragile as a bruised flower, lying in the arms of her brother. A coarse brute of a man slunk in sloth and dissipation.

6

The Trial Continues

Dhaka District Court
1935

THE DEFENCE COUNSEL, AMIYANATH CHAUDHURI, HAD DECIDED NOT to base his case on testing the plaintiff's remembrance of his past or on the denial of his claim by certain members of his family. Twelve years had gone by, he reasoned, since the man had first arrived in Jaidevpur and there had been adequate time and opportunity for him to have done his networking and been coached in the part that he was to play. Disregarding public memory of the second kumar as an uneducated, wayward youth who had kept mistresses and consorted with singers and dancers from the lowest strata of society, the astute lawyer insisted on presenting him as a cultured Bengali aristocrat and a man of good character and polished manners, thereby creating an image totally inconsistent with that of the plaintiff's, who appeared to be a rough, illiterate yokel from the north. The strategy Amiyanath decided to adopt was a crude, merciless gruelling of the man in the hope that he would lose his cool, forget the lessons he had received, and expose himself for the imposter he undoubtedly was.

But the cross-examination hadn't gone the way he had expected. The plaintiff had not tripped up. It was true that he didn't have answers to many questions. But, as Benoy Chandra Chatterjee pointed out, they were questions on shooting and horsemanship and involved technical terms in English. The plaintiff had been quite open in his admission that he didn't know English. Besides, there were many people present in the court who were ready to testify on oath that neither did the second kumar.

B. C. Chatterjee's strategy was the exact opposite of his opponent's. His plan was to get together a large number of people who would be ready to swear that they recognized the plaintiff as the mejo kumar they had known. These witnesses would be chosen from relatives, friends, employees of the Bhawal estate as well as tenants and other neighbouring talukdars. He wanted his case to draw strength from the sheer volume of people he brought forward. The numbers swelled with every hearing, making the Bhawal lawsuit one of the longest trials in legal history.

The prosecution witnesses were unanimous in their testimony that the kumar could not read or write. All he could do was sign his name in English and Bengali. On being shown samples of the plaintiff's signature, some said that they recognized them as those of the mejo kumar's. Many complained that the Court of Wards had acted against them because they had shown sympathy for the sadhu. Some had lost their jobs. Others had had fake criminal proceedings brought against them. Some had been subjected to the draconian Certificate Procedure and ordered to produce documents proving their ownership of land their ancestors had held for generations.

The witnesses brought by B. C. Chatterjee surprised the court, not only by their massive numbers and the different sections of society from which they came, but also the quality of their recognition. A gentleman called Kumud Mohan Goswami said that the plaintiff had addressed him at their first meeting as Sadhu Kaka, just as the mejo kumar was wont to do. Ramesh Chandra Guha, who had worked on the estate for twenty years, said that the plaintiff's first words to him had been, 'Of course I remember you. You are Ramesh babu, nayeb of Kurmitola.'

Kailash Chandra Chakrabarty testified that he had given the mejo kumar, who was known for his love of birds and animals, a white jackal. The sadhu remembered the gift and had thanked him for it.

Gangacharan Banerjee said that he had been a playmate of the kumars and been nicknamed Master by them because of his glum and studious manner. Of all the kumars, the second one was the most generous and often gave gifts to his friends. Gangacharan testified that even before he had started speaking, the sadhu had smiled at him. 'Where have you been all this time, Master?' he had said. 'Do you still wear the watch I gave you?' Another childhood friend, Jitendranath Banerjee, said that he had seen the plaintiff ride a horse soon after his arrival in Jaidevpur. He had held the reins in his right hand and the whip in his left exactly the way the mejo kumar used to.

A distant relative, Basanta Kumar Banerjee, admitted that to begin with, he had been convinced that the man was a fraud. He had gone to check him out with every intention of exposing him. And it seemed as though he was right … at first. The sadhu had peered at him with puzzled eyes and remained silent for a while. Then, suddenly, his face lit up and he exclaimed, 'You are Basanta dada, are you not?' He had followed this up with enquiries about his daughter Burhi, his wife whom the kumars called Batashi Tharan, and his sister-in-law Kali Tharan. After that there was no doubt left in Basanta Banerjee's mind that the man was indeed the mejo kumar of Bhawal.

Dozens of other witnesses from across the spectrum of Bhawal society were produced by B. C. Chatterjee. Among them were singers and performers from jatra parties who knew the kumar in his heyday, when he was passionate about music and theatre. There were sportsmen who testified to the kumar's love of riding and shooting and complete disinterest in British sports such as cricket and football. Palace employees from guards and chowkidars, footmen and bearers, to stewards and khansamas, mahouts and rifle bearers, even milkmen and tailors, came in droves. All of them said that they were convinced that the plaintiff was the mejo kumar.

And now the day everyone had waited for arrived. Justice Pannalal Basu's court was crammed with people, eager to hear a first-hand version of the strange story that was, by now, on everyone's lips albeit with variations and distortions.

7

The Plaintiff's Testimony

THE MAN WHO CLAIMED HE WAS THE MEJO KUMAR OF BHAWAL STOOD before the people in the court of Justice Pannalal Basu. There were many in the gathering who hadn't seen him before and carried a mental image of a dirty, bearded mendicant with flowing dreadlocks, stark naked except for a tattered loincloth. The reality left them astounded. For the man who stood before them was tall and portly and fair as a *gora*. He was clean-shaven and his hair was combed in sleek, shining waves from both sides of a central parting. In his spotless white dhuti, fine silk shirt and shining pumps, he looked like any sophisticated gentleman from the cultured, wealthy elite of Kolkata. The only two things that set him apart were the spot of sandalwood paste between his brows and the *namabali* falling from the nape of his neck in saffron streams down his chest. There were marks of dissipation on his face but there was also a curious innocence. Especially in the eyes that looked at the assembled people with a direct childlike gaze. When he spoke, it was in the musical drawl, laden with sibilants, of what was known as the Dhakaiya dialect. But his voice had an unmistakable alien inflection, a tinge of rustic Hindi …

Beginning his account with the admission that he had been ailing and was advised by his doctor Colonel Sarbadhikari to spend some months in a mountain resort, the plaintiff went on to describe his journey to Darjeeling, the people who had accompanied him, and the state of his health during his sojourn there.

'I was perfectly fine for the first fortnight,' he told the court. 'Well on the road to recovery. Then one night, in the middle of the third week, I woke up with severe bloating and cramps in my stomach. The doctor who had accompanied us, Ashutosh Dasgupta, put a few drops of some liquid in my mouth after which the pain eased.'

'Do you know what it was?' B. C. Chatterjee asked.

'No, I didn't. I was in too much pain and the relief was so great I fell asleep almost immediately afterwards.'

'What happened then?'

'I woke up feeling much better. Two days went by. Then, on the third night the pain came back again. This time Ashu daktaar gave me some medicine mixed with water. After drinking it I felt a burning sensation in my chest which spread to the stomach and, gradually, to the rest of my body. I started retching and vomiting and the pain became unbearable. I screamed in agony and begged Satya babu to call another doctor. But my pleas went unheeded. I started passing stools mixed with blood from the following morning. The purging and vomiting continued, growing in intensity through the day, till I felt the strength ebbing from my limbs. My thoughts became blurred and confused. At some point, I can't say when, I blacked out.'

'When did you regain consciousness? How many hours later? Can you give us some idea?'

'No. The first thing I remember is rain and hail hitting my body, sharp as stones. I opened my eyes. It was very dark and I could see nothing except some trees swaying in the wind. My head was on fire and my body felt like a block of ice. I tried to call out to somebody to fetch me a quilt. But my tongue was frozen and wouldn't move. All that emerged from my mouth were groans of agony. Then, I don't know when, I fainted again.'

The man fell silent. There was a faraway look in his eyes. As though what he was trying to recall had happened aeons ago. In another life …

'Go on,' B. C. Chatterjee prompted gently.

'Regaining consciousness, I found myself lying on a pile of leaves inside what looked like a cave. My wet clothes had been removed and I was covered with a blanket. The place was warm from a fire that burned in a corner. Three or four men were sitting around me. '*Jai Siya Ram!*' one of them exclaimed the moment I opened my eyes, '*Jai Hanumanji ki! Bach gaya launda.*' (The lad is saved.) He was a large man with a pot belly. I turned my head, painfully, this way and that. All the men surrounding me were naked, ash-coated, with flowing beards and matted hair.

I lay in a semi-conscious state for how long I have no idea. I was unaware of the passing of time. Unaware of day and night. All I remember are faces peering into mine and hands pouring bitter potions and warm milk down my throat. Later, when I was fully conscious and able to sit up, I was fed mashed vegetables and khichdi.

They asked me my name and where I came from but I couldn't remember anything. My mind was totally blank. I felt so weak I could barely move my limbs. Even swallowing the milk and khichdi made my chest ache. Too sick to move, I stayed with the group for about two weeks after which, having nowhere else to go, I accompanied them to Benares. They were travelling mendicants, and took me with them to several other pilgrimage spots. Out of all the sadhus, the one who was kindest to me and whom I loved best was a man called Dharamdas. Since I couldn't remember my name, he gave me one. "You are as fair and handsome as a prince," he said to me one day. "I shall call you Sundardas." The name stuck and everyone in the band started calling me Sundardas …'

'When did you renounce the world and become a sadhu?' A. N. Chaudhuri stemmed the flow. 'Come to the point. The court is not interested in minor details.'

'I never renounced the world in a formal way,' the plaintiff answered meekly. 'That entails the act of throwing one's sacred thread into the sacrificial fire. See …' And now he did a curious thing. Putting his fingers inside his shirt he pulled out his *poite* and, turning to Pannalal Basu, he said, 'See, Judge saheb. I'm still wearing it.'

'Cut out the drama.' A. N. Chaudhuri's voice was sharp and sneering. 'If what you're saying is true, why did you assume the appearance of a mendicant? Can you deny that you pretended to be a naga sadhu when you first came to Dhaka? What sort of hypocrisy was that?'

The plaintiff's face fell. The lawyer's aggressive tone seemed to take him by surprise. Evading a direct answer, he said quietly, 'On a visit to Lord Shiva's shrine in Amarnath, the head sannyasi, Guru Darshandas, asked me if I wished to receive the mantra and become his disciple. I agreed and, following the example of the rest of my peers, got Guruji's name tattooed on my arm. But I only received *deeksha*. I did not renounce the world formally by discarding my sacred thread.' He looked at A. N. Chaudhuri with a plea in his eyes.

'Please tell the court what happened next?' B.C. Chatterjee asked with a touch of impatience. He was clearly miffed by the way his opponent had unsettled his witness.

'What happened next was very strange. After receiving *deeksha*, the fog that had clouded my brain began to disperse little by little. Images from the past came floating into my mind. But they were dim, shadowy and fleeting and melted away before I could make proper sense of them. Such vague recollections assailed me over the next two years, as I travelled with the band to many places in India and Nepal. Then, on a visit to an obscure pilgrim spot called Brahachatra, I had a flash of vivid recollection. I remembered that I came from a place called Dhaka. The name Dhaka stayed with me for several days and I realized that my memory was returning. I wasn't sure if I wanted to share my experience with anyone. I thought about it for many days before making up my mind. I opened my heart to Dharamdas, who informed Guruji.

'Guruji sent for me and, after hearing me out, was silent for a while. "I don't know what advice to give you," he said slowly. "Status quo is a good option since you seem to be happy in your present situation. On the other hand, if you remember who you are, it is your duty to go back to your near and dear ones. They must be pining for you. Think of their joy when they see you again!"

'Finally, it was decided that I would go to Dhaka, locate my family, study the situation and then decide what to do. To go back to my old life or return to the group. "Come back to us if you wish to, my son," Guruji said to me. "You know you are always welcome."

'My brain started to clear dramatically as soon as I reached the railway station in Dhaka. I remembered that I had been there before. Not once ... many times. I saw some faces that looked familiar. Some I even recognized. But I still didn't know who I was. I wandered in the lanes and bazars for some days, then making my way to the river, I parked myself on the Bund. I chose a location from where I could get a good view of Jaidevpur. I kept looking at the Rajbari but didn't know why I was doing so. While sitting there, I attracted a lot of curious glances and comments. I heard people whispering to one another that I looked exactly like the mejo kumar. I didn't understand who they were talking about and refused to respond. When questions were asked in Bengali, I answered in Hindi.

'Over the next three months my memory came back in full. I remembered that the palace had been my home. I remembered my parents and siblings. But I couldn't decide what course to take.

'On the request of my grandmother, Rani Satyabhama Debi, I went to my sister Jyotirmayi's house. I recognized everyone there, including Atulprasad Roy Chowdhury. But I continued to speak in Hindi, insisting that I was a sadhu from the north and no kin to them. I was biding my time. I didn't know if I was mentally ready to make any kind of disclosure. My guru had advised me not to reveal my identity till I was absolutely sure of what I wanted to do. What happened after that is known to everyone present here.'

8

The Naga Sadhus

A GASP OF ASTONISHMENT ROSE FROM THE ASSEMBLY THE MOMENT Darshandas Naga entered the courtroom. He was a giant of a man, six and a half feet tall, with massive shoulders and chest. A huge belly protruded triumphantly from above the flimsy bit of saffron cloth wound about his loins. His face, with its domed forehead, flashing eyes and large beak of a nose was as sharply etched as a Pathan's. His ash-dappled skin glinted coppery gold in the sunlight that streamed into the witness box.

'*Jai Siyaram!*' he bellowed a greeting, and then, raising his hands till they seemed to touch the ceiling, he blessed the assembly. 'May Ramji save and preserve you, my sons.' Turning to Benoy Chandra Chatterjee, who stood beside him, he asked smiling, 'Why did you summon me here, Vakil saheb? What do you want from me?'

The lawyer had been staring at his witness in much the same way as a tiny blackbird would at a mighty eagle. He pulled himself together at these words.

'You are Darshandas Naga?'

'*Ji, huzoor.*'

'Take a good look at that man,' he pointed to the plaintiff. 'Do you recognize him?'

'Why not, huzoor? He is my erstwhile *chela*, Sundardas.'

'Can you tell us when and under what circumstances he joined your sect?'

'It was a long time ago. More than twenty years. Yet I remember everything as clearly as if it was yesterday.' He wagged his large head from side to side.

'Good. Please give us the sequence of events in as much detail as possible.'

'We are *romta sadhus*,' Darshandas commenced his narrative. 'We have no fixed abode. We wander all over the country from one place of pilgrimage to another. Ramji guides us and tells us when and where to go.' His eyes passed over the people in the courtroom as though he wanted to make sure they weren't jeering in disbelief. Then seeing that everyone was listening in rapt attention, he continued with his story.

'We were in Dilli that year on a visit to the Lal Mandir of Shri Digambar Jain. It was a terribly hot summer with burning winds blowing from the deserts of Rajasthan. One night as I lay on my charpoy, in a bylane of Chandni Chowk, tossing and turning and unable to sleep, I heard a voice call out to me from the dark. *Go to the temple of Mahakali in Darjeeling and make an offering on the night of Amavasya. Go, my son. Do not tarry any longer.*

'I set out with my party the very next day. I had no idea where Darjeeling was or how long it would take us to get there. We travelled partly by bus and partly by foot, asking for directions at every step. But, to my amazement, we reached Darjeeling on the evening of *Amavasya*. We made our offerings at the temple and paid our respects to the great goddess ...'

'Do you believe in Kali?' A. N. Chaudhary interrupted. 'She is worshipped only in the east ... or so I thought ...'

'We are Naga sadhus. Free spirits. We make no distinctions between deities. We revere them all.'

'Please proceed.' B. C. Chatterjee shot a cold glance at his opponent and an encouraging one at his witness.

'We tried to find a place to spend the night but the town was very crowded and we couldn't find lodgings anywhere. We wandered around the outskirts and discovered some caves near what looked like a burning ghat. It seemed to be a good omen. For another name for Mahakali is Samsan Kali. It was a bitterly cold night with pouring rain and hail and we were glad to find shelter. Choosing the largest cave, we lit a fire and stretched our fatigued limbs out on the floor.

'But I couldn't sleep a wink. The sounds of wind and thunder, shrieks of nightbirds and howls of jackals kept me awake. At one time during the night, I thought I heard a groan. It was very faint and seemed to come from the burning ghat. I ignored it. Then I heard another groan, a little louder this time, and another. I sat up startled. *There was someone at the burning ghat. And the person was alive.*

'I rose and, wrapping myself in a blanket, went out to investigate. But I didn't have to go far. Just a few yards away there was something lying on the ground. Coming closer, I saw that it was a man bound by ropes to a pallet. The sheet with which he was covered was drenched and spotted with hail. His face was as white as moonlight and his eyes were closed. I touched my hand to his nose and felt a warm mist rising from it.

'Dharamdas! Gopaldas! Devdas!' I yelled. 'Come out and see what's here! Bring a light.'

'Hearing the panic in my voice, the other sadhus dashed out of the cave with lanterns in their hands. 'Quick!' I shouted. 'Fetch a knife and cut the ropes.'

'Devdas ran back and brought a knife. Together we cut the ropes which bound him, loosened the sheet with which he was tightly wrapped and carried him inside the cave. We removed his wet clothes, wiped him dry and wrapped him in a couple of blankets. We fed him warm milk mixed with honey. He had a high fever and, though unconscious, kept threshing his limbs fitfully.

'One of my disciples, Lokdas, had some knowledge of herbs. He made some concoctions and poured them down the man's throat.

They seemed to have helped because after three days he opened his eyes. But he spoke a strange language and didn't seem to remember anything. It was not possible for me to find out who he was and where he lived. We were strangers in the place with hardly any resources and didn't know the local language. Moreover, it seemed to me that a divine hand was at work. God had raised him from the dead and imbued him with life. *Shouldn't that life, so miraculously saved, be dedicated to His service?*

'From Dilli we had intended to go to Kashi but the voice had brought us to Darjeeling instead. As soon as the man was well enough to walk, we decided to redeem our pledge of visiting that holiest of holy pilgrimages. The temple of Kashi Vishwanath. Since he didn't seem to remember anything and had nowhere to go, we took him along with us. He was unable to communicate with anyone at first. Gradually he picked up Hindi and, later, became quite fluent in the language. Since he couldn't remember his name, we had to give him one. Being a very handsome man, we started calling him Sundardas. Out of all my disciples, he was closest to Dharamdas.

'Several years went by. Then, one day, Dharamdas came to me with the news that Sundardas had started recalling his past. He had told him that he came from a place called Dhaka. I sent for Sundardas and advised him to go to Dhaka and try to locate his family. I supposed he had done so for he didn't come back.

'A year or so after he left us, I travelled with my followers to Bengal and visited many temples and shrines. While offering puja in Dhakeswari Mandir, I heard a strange story. A mendicant had come to Dhaka claiming he was a prince of the kingdom of Bhawal and people were flocking to see him. My curiosity was roused and I went too. On seeing him, I was shocked. I recognized him instantly. He was my *chela* Sundardas.'

And now the witness raised his arm and pointed to the plaintiff. 'Vakil saheb,' he announced in a booming voice, 'this man is, without a doubt, the one I met the last time I came to Dhaka. The same man we rescued from the cremation ground. The man who stayed with us for twelve years and whom we gave the name of Sundardas.'

Dharamdas Naga, brought in by the defence, seemed to have been cast in a totally different mould. Two men couldn't have been more different. He was small and slight and his eyes shifted this way and that, like a mouse caught in a trap. His voice quavered uncertainly and he spoke mostly in monosyllables. But he stuck to his story, repeating, parrot-like, the same words over and over again. Claiming to be the chief ascetic of the band, he maintained that the plaintiff was his disciple Mal Singh, a Punjabi Sikh from Lahore. He denied that he and his band had ever been to Darjeeling or rescued anyone from a burning ghat. And he didn't know any sadhu by the name of Darshandas.

9

Excerpts from the Cross-examination of the Plaintiff by A. N. Chaudhuri

Amiyanath Chaudhuri	Are you proficient in English and Bengali? Do you read the newspapers?
Plaintiff	No, I am not proficient in either of these languages and I do not read newspapers.
A. N. C.	Are you aware that Kumar Ramendranarayan Roy subscribed to the *Amrita Bazar Patrika*?
Plaintiff	It is possible that the subscription was made out in my name. But I never read it. My employees did. If they thought some news would be of interest to me, they communicated it in simple Bengali.
A. N. C.	Do you remember studying in Dhaka Collegiate School?
Plaintiff	Of course I do. I was twelve years old.
A. N. C.	Do you remember which class you were in?
Plaintiff	No.
A. N. C.	Was it the eighth class?

Plaintiff	I don't remember.
A. N. C.	Do you remember Shyamacharan Master?
Plaintiff	Yes. His full name was Shyamacharan Guha.
A. N. C.	Do you remember the names of any English or Bengali books you studied in school?
Plaintiff	No. I didn't pay attention in class. I preferred looking out of the window.
A. N. C.	Did you take a slate or paper to school?
Plaintiff	Yes.
A. N. C.	Did you write on them?
Plaintiff	No.
A. N. C.	Not even a scratch?
Plaintiff	Why should I scratch? Am I a tiger?

(Amiyanath Chaudhuri realizes that he is annoying the plaintiff and making him edgy and belligerent. He decides to try another approach. He asks for some papers and hands them to the plaintiff.)

A. N. C.	Take a look at these. Do you recognize the signatures?
Plaintiff	Some of them look like mine but not all.
A. N. C.	These are letters written by Kumar Ramendranarayan to his wife. Did you write them?
Plaintiff	No. I did not write these letters. They are forgeries.
A. N. C.	Were you suffering from syphilis at the time you went to Darjeeling?
Plaintiff	Yes.
A. N. C.	How were you cured?
Plaintiff	I was told by the sannyasis who found me that they had seen signs of syphilis on my

	body. But I don't know if they gave me any medicine for it.
A. N. C.	Your pronunciation of some Bengali words is incorrect. How do you explain it?
Plaintiff	I have a tumour under my tongue. I find it difficult to utter some sounds.
A. N. C.	Did you always have this tumour?
Plaintiff	No. It appeared sometime during my travels.
A. N. C.	The second prince was a keen horseman and racing enthusiast. Do you remember the name of any winner of the Viceroy's Cup?
Plaintiff	I attended a few races and won a cup once. I rode my own horse. But I didn't get any money. I don't remember if it was called the Viceroy's Cup.
A. N. C.	Have you heard of the term 'steeplechase'?
Plaintiff	No.
A. N. C.	The princes of Bhawal played billiards. Can you tell me if billiard balls are made of wood or rubber?
Plaintiff	I don't know. I never played billiards. The baro kumar did.
A. N. C.	You claim you were a good hunter. Can you give me the names of some of the firearms and cartridges you used?
Plaintiff	No. I don't remember the names.
A. N. C.	You don't seem to remember much. Let us proceed to something else. You were shown some letters written by the second prince to his wife Bibhavati Debi. You denied writing them and said they were

forged. What if I were to say that you are not the person you claim you are and were never married to Bibhavati Debi?

Plaintiff — I have proof that I was.

A. N. C. — What proof?

Plaintiff — I knew her body intimately. The big toe on each of her feet was longer than the other toes and there was a tiny ball of flesh, the size of a mustard seed, at the corner of her left eye.

A. N. C. — Such things are easily visible. Anybody could have told you that.

Plaintiff — I know of a certain mark she bears that no man other than a husband can know. She has a scar on one side of her private parts left by a lanced cyst. She had it from before our marriage.

(There is a sudden clamour in the court. Excited voices are heard. Amiyanath Chaudhuri loses his temper and cries out.)

A. N. C. — The plaintiff has been tutored to answer these questions!

(Benoy Chandra Chatterjee is outraged. He leaps up from his chair and shouts.)

B. C. C. — Objection, Your Honour! My opponent is casting aspersions on my integrity. He must withdraw his comment at once or there'll be bloodshed.

Pannalal Basu — Calm down, both of you. The counsel for defence will kindly refrain from making unsubstantiated statements. Restrict

	yourself to facts, Mr Chaudhuri, and proceed with your examination.
A. N. C.	What is the reason for disclosing your identity after so many years? What will you do with the property if you get it?
Plaintiff	I would like to use it for the benefit of my tenants.
A. N. C.	Can you pledge an oath that you will not use the money for your own self?
B. C. C.	Objection! The learned counsel has no right to make such an outrageous request.
P. B.	Sustained. Withdraw your question, Counsel, and proceed.
A. N. C.	I will reframe my question. Are you claiming your inherited assets for your own use?
Plaintiff	Yes.
A. N. C.	How will you spend the money?
Plaintiff	The way rich people do.
A. N. C.	On liquor and women?
Plaintiff	Yes. And elephants and horses.
A. N. C.	Do you still have a taste for these things?
Plaintiff	I'll have to see. I am penniless now. Once I am rich, I will know.

10

Pannalal Basu

Dhaka
1936

THE BHAWAL SANNYASI CASE WOULD COME TO BE THE LONGEST recorded case in the history of British India. The presentation of evidence went on for six years. Over fifteen hundred witnesses were examined. Another three months went by before the closing arguments of the two lawyers were concluded.

Walking out of the court premises on the evening of 30 May 1936, I shot a glance at the three chaprasis following me, their arms weighed down with tin trunks packed with papers. I felt a pang of misgiving. A colossal task lay before me. Would I be able to accomplish it?

I needed to go through every shred of the enormous volume of evidence, separate the relevant from the irrelevant, and arrange all the significant material in proper sequence. A judicious weighing of the pros and cons of each fact would follow, a reasoned opinion formed, after which I would have to write my judgement and type it out without the help of a secretary or typist. The case was highly sensitive and I could take no risk with its confidentiality. I had heard the testimonies of witnesses, day after day and month after month for six long years, and had a good idea of the power of money and influence in inducing respectable, even otherwise honest persons, to bend the truth. There was far too much at stake here for too many rich, powerful and unscrupulous people.

There was also every possibility of my findings being appealed against in the High Court. I could not allow myself to slip, even in the slightest degree, and be made a laughing stock. It was imperative that I present the rationale behind my judgement with clarity and detail, and make my verdict as foolproof as possible.

Sleep eluded me that night. It was stiflingly hot. The air swirled around my body like steam rising from a rice pot on the boil. I lay tossing and turning on the sheets, dozing off from time to time, then waking up with a start and a sudden sinking of the heart. And, over and over again, a feeling of dread swept through me. *Would I be able to accomplish what I had undertaken?*

I rose from bed at dawn and came out to the veranda. I live in a rented house in Tikatuli, built seventy years ago in the Muslim style, with a men's wing in front and a zenana at the back. The house isn't large but it stands on half an acre of land dotted with palms and marble statues weathered by wind and rain and dappled with chalky-white bird droppings. There are some fine old fruit trees as well. Mango, jackfruit, star fruit, rose apple and guava. As I walked out to the tangled garden, that morning a gust of warm air, laden with the scent of mangoes, blew at my face. I looked up. I could see patches of yellow smudging the green of the *kheersapati* tree. My heart lifted. The fruit had started to ripen. The rains would break any day now. I took a deep breath and inhaled the delicious perfume. *I must tell the mali to pick a basketful*, I thought. I love kheersapati mangoes …

I decided to go for a walk. The exercise would clear my head and cool my eyes, burning from lack of sleep. Leaving the city streets behind, I made my way to the river. As I approached the vast expanse of water, I became aware of a palpable change in the atmosphere. The air felt fresher and cooler and smelled of damp earth. The southwesterly monsoon was on its way.

There were a number of boats on the river that morning. Anchored by the bank, close to where I stood, was a fleet of seven, their tattered sails patched over with pieces of cloth in motley shades of green, black and red. A group of women sat in one of them. Young women in voluminous skirts and filthy *kanchulis*. Strings of colourful beads ran down their breasts and wooden combs were stuck in masses of tangled hair. Their arms and shoulders were covered with tattoos and their hands and feet with henna. I knew who they were. They were *bedes*, a nomadic tribe who sailed over the Ganga, from village to village and town to town, displaying their skill in subjugating snakes and making them dance to the tunes of bamboo flutes. *Bedes* followed a wonderfully syncretic faith. Though practising Muslims, they were fervent worshippers of Manasa, the Hindu goddess of snakes. The idea had fascinated me as a child, and still did.

Someone was singing in one of the boats. A rough, slightly off-key male voice came wafting over the waves. I recognized the song. I had heard it in my childhood in my native village of Dakshinpara.

Shaap er bishe jemun temun; prem er bishe du gun dhai
Gourango bhujanga hoye dongshiyachhe aamar gaye
Bish er jwala jemun jwala, prem er jwalai aagun dhai …

Snake poison is nothing; love's poison is twice cursed
The fair one, turned serpent, has lashed my limbs and heart
Snake poison may sting, love's poison is a flame …

'*Kaar bahar*?' I cupped a hand to my mouth and called, 'Whose band?'

'Kamruzzaman Bebajiya's band, Karta moshai,' one of the women stood up and answered. 'We arrived at dawn.'

'How long will you stay here?'

'Three days, Karta moshai.'

'Where do you go next?'

'To Bhawal. To the villages of Rahimpur, Kankrajoli, Nabiganj and Ketuganj.'

Bhawal! I was startled. *What a coincidence!* I thought.

Returning home, I found a strange man at the gate. He looked as though he had been standing there for some time. I thought he was waiting for me and asked him what he wanted. But he shook his head uncertainly and, mumbling something under his breath, walked away. For several weeks afterwards, I saw the same man strolling up and down the pavement opposite, or sitting on his haunches under a tree. He would arrive precisely at eight in the morning and leave at six as soon as the sun began to set. I realized who he was. He was a policeman in plain clothes, appointed by the government to provide security to the judge trying a particularly sensitive case.

I started going for a walk to the river every morning. The physical exercise kept my limbs fit and flexible and the communion with sky, water and earth helped calm my mind. The chaotic jumble in my head started to form a pattern and, gradually, I was able to organize my thoughts and put them in perspective.

The first thing I needed to do was to make up my mind about the two principal characters of the case. The Plaintiff and the Defendant. Amiyanath Chaudhuri had spared no effort in pushing forward his theory that the mejo kumar had been a cultured Bengali gentleman, well-educated and westernized. But the witnesses he produced to support his claim were few. Their testimonies were somewhat vague and they were, quite often, unable to stand up to the test of the piercing questions asked by Benoy Chandra Chatterjee. By contrast, the accounts of the tenants of the estate and the palace servants seemed more plausible. They all seemed to have liked the prince. He had a kind heart, they said, and was generous with his help and money in times of need. Yet they had felt no obligation to hide the cruder aspects of his personality or the true nature of his relationship with his wife. They were also far larger in number.

The Chief Defendant's evidence, I felt, was wanting in veracity. Bibhavati Debi hadn't indulged in deliberate falsehood but her answers to the Counsel's questions had been evasive. Her attempt to portray her life as no different from those of other married women could not be taken at face value. That her husband had continued his liaison with the nautch girl Elokeshi, even after marriage, had been established beyond a doubt. As had been the fact that he came to her, only occasionally, preferring to sleep in his own apartments. On an inspection of the Rajbari, I had been shown the rooms the mejo kumar had occupied. They were well lit, swept and dusted. A large mounted photograph of the prince draped with a garland of jui flowers hung on one wall and a faint scent of incense pervaded the air. The servants, it seemed, were honouring the memory of the prince by keeping his apartment neat, clean and fresh. It was obvious that they associated *these* rooms with his presence rather than the ones which, as a married man, he should have occupied. His wife's.

Bibhavati Debi had maintained, with commendable dignity and composure, that she had no complaints against her husband. But how was that possible? There was no earthly reason for an educated, well-brought-up girl like her to care for a wanton wastrel who neglected her and consorted with other women. The icing on the cake was the filthy disease he had contracted. A disease associated with promiscuous sex. To tolerate him was one thing. To have no complaints at all was quite another.

There were certain rumours about her relationship with her brother. It was this unnatural passion, in the opinion of the petitioner's counsel, that had prompted her to give up all her claims and leave the Rajbari. But I refused to give credence to idle gossip. It was perfectly possible for a recently widowed young woman to wish to leave the house in which she had suffered years of neglect and humiliation, and seek the comfort of her mother's arms. The one thing that puzzled me was her behaviour after her return from Darjeeling. Her tears, her fainting fits, her refusal of food, her self-imposed isolation. What did they imply? True grief? Or the crocodile tears of a consummate actress? Was it possible that her pitiful plight was only a show? Put up with the express purpose of fobbing off uncomfortable questions regarding the circumstances of her husband's death and cremation?

Another thought. Bibhavati Debi had received nineteen lakh rupees from the estate to date. But she had no bank account and no property registered in her name. She didn't pay income tax. Satyendranath Banerjee, on the other hand, owned a large house in Lansdowne Road and had made substantial investments in shares and company bonds. From enquiries about him I gathered that he was a lawyer with a miniscule practice and no other independent source of income. Since neither of the two could produce any documents, not even a scrap of paper to prove otherwise, it was perfectly clear that the entire amount received by Bibhavati Debi had passed into her brother's hands. But why had she allowed him to rob her the way he did? That was the moot question.

Was the sannyasi the second kumar or an imposter? The theory put forward by the defence counsel was that he was a medicine man from Punjab, a charlatan who conned people into believing that he had a cure for sterility. He had attracted crowds of people at the Buckland Bund, not because of his resemblance to the mejo kumar, but because they believed he could cure barren women with fertility pills and potions. Even the zamindar of Kasimpur, Mr Chaudhuri maintained, had sent for him with this in mind. So had the second princess Jyotirmayi Debi. The man had accepted this role for some months. Then suddenly, who knows at whose behest, he had declared himself to be the mejo kumar of Bhawal.

The eminent lawyer's hypothesis had seemed tenable at first. Then, with the emergence of several significant facts, his 'medicine man' theory lost credibility. Not only in the eyes of others. In his own too. I noticed that, in his later arguments, he was not mentioning it. He didn't even seem to like being reminded of it.

What struck me as odd was the almost frenzied denial of a physical resemblance between the sannyasi and the supposedly dead royal. This insistence of the defence baffled me. So many people, from across the spectrum, had sworn to a distinct likeness. It wasn't as if similarity in appearance could be used in court as a proof of identity. I will be the first to admit that it is perfectly possible for two persons to bear a strong likeness to each other while being totally unrelated. Why were the mejo rani and her brother pushing the point of utter dissimilarity with so much force? What were they hoping to achieve by it?

Mr Chaudhuri's contention that Jyotirmayi Debi had originally sent for the sadhu to avail of his skill as a fertility physician, then suddenly decided to use him as a pawn in her conspiracy against the British government, didn't hold water. The princess's servants, and in this there wasn't a single dissenting voice, swore in court that no one in the household or even the extended family needed any such treatment. The man had been sent for because their mistress was a cautious woman not easily swayed by public opinion. She wanted to check him out for herself. Only after examining the marks on his body did she concede that he was her brother. She was a highly religious, orthodox woman and would never have admitted him into the andarmahal unless she was fully convinced of his identity.

I had to agree. It would be totally out of character for a highborn Hindu lady to admit into her household a stranger of whose caste and background she knew nothing and who, if the defendants were to be believed, didn't even look like her brother. Why would she do such a thing? In the fond hope that he would successfully play the role of the mejo kumar in a half-baked conspiracy, fight the British, and restore Bhawal to its former glory? Ten years had gone by. He had been hounded out of Jaidevpur but she had stuck to her resolve of proving to the world that he was her brother. Why?

Rani Satyabhama's conduct, too, had to be taken into account. The widow of the magnificent Raja Rajendranarayan Roy had accompanied the plaintiff to Dhaka after he was forced to leave the estate. Abandoning the comforts of her royal life, she had lived with him in a small rented house. She had never gone back to Jaidevpur but had made her home with him till her end came at the ripe old age of eighty. Why would she do so if she wasn't convinced that he was her grandson? She had also left instructions that, as the last male member of the royal line, he was to perform the *mukhagni* and other rites after her death. And because of his banishment from Jaidevpur, her shraddha ceremony had been held in Dhaka and not in the kingdom of which she had once been the reigning queen. The defence had railed against the decision and called it an enormous aberration. But the event had been a grand affair, attended by many members of the extended Bhawal Raj family and other distinguished persons from both Jaidevpur and Dhaka. From what I gathered, nobody had voiced any objections. What was I to deduce from this?

The response of the ordinary people of Bhawal to the plaintiff's claim was another factor that needed to be examined closely. Their acknowledgement was no actual proof of identity, of course. But it certainly put a lid on the theory of a conspiracy set up by a few interested persons. Unless the mejo kumar's tenants truly believed that he had the right on his side, they would never have risked the ire of their British masters and paid him rent. Besides, they had come forward on their own, to give evidence, unlike the ones brought by the defence. The position taken by the Court of Wards, in the matter of the Bhawal case, was known to one and all. Mr Chatterjee had produced letters to prove that official instructions to organize witnesses for the defence had been sent to the *nayebs* of all the districts. This was also made amply clear from the manner in which they were brought to the courtroom, herded in large numbers, in the custody of government peons. From their looks and deportment, they seemed to have been drawn from poor, ignorant peasant folk who could, I felt, be coerced or threatened into giving evidence in favour of the rulers.

The tenants who deposed for the plaintiff, on the other hand, had come on their own, despite threats and warnings. Many of them carried copies of *K. P. Suits* which could be used against them. They also seemed to belong to a richer, more informed class of society. Of course it was perfectly possible that they were claiming to recognize someone they hadn't known or even seen at close quarters. They were, after all, common people and the man was a prince. A. N. Chaudhuri drove home this point with great force and I had to admit that his hypothesis was not without merit. But, on closer examination of the facts, I couldn't go along with him. The second kumar, according to evidence from both sides, was a man who kept himself visible in the eyes of the common folk. He was often seen driving through the streets in his phaeton, riding his elephant, listening to musical soirees in the naat mandir and attending the *rath jatra* and other village festivals. He was also free and friendly with his subjects, chatted with them and enquired after their welfare.

Of the members of the royal family who had deposed in favour of the plaintiff, the maximum credence, I felt, was to be given to the testimonies of Jyotirmayi Debi and Sarajubala Debi. It was suggested by the defence that, after the investiture ceremony of the third rani's adopted son, Jyotirmayi Debi had lived in fear of the British setting aside heirs from the female line and installing the outsider as a puppet ruler. Thus, she had a material interest in claiming that the sadhu was her long-lost brother.

That could have been the case. In fact, the appearance of the sadhu within a few months of the anointing, gave weight to the claim of the defence. A brother at the helm of affairs would be far more useful to Jyotirmayi Debi than a stranger. But to hatch a conspiracy using a Punjabi double, a man about whom she knew nothing, was too bizarre for words. Only an insane person could conceive of such a thing. And the second princess, by all accounts, was a simple homely woman with plenty of common sense. I was convinced that her evidence was based on genuine recognition. As was the baro rani's. Sarajubala Debi had adopted a son too and could have pressed the rulers to give him the prior claim. But she hadn't done that. After a little initial hesitation, she had admitted that the plaintiff was her brother-in-law.

Another strange thing had happened. No relatives, barring one or two distant ones, had come forward to depose in favour of the defendants. Not even the mejo rani's maternal uncles and cousins from Uttarpara.

The resemblance factor was sorted out quite quickly. Among the prince's insurance papers was a report describing his features, complexion and all the distinguishing marks found on his face and body. A physical examination of the plaintiff had also been conducted just before the trial and a list of details prepared. Comparing the two, I found them tallying on most points. Barring a few. The differences had created quite a bit of excitement in the courtroom. A bony projection on the plaintiff's nose had found no mention in the report of the Oriental Insurance Company and was vociferously denied by the defence. *The mejo kumar had no such thing.* Corroboration by other witnesses was not forthcoming either. The matter was resolved by Colonel Chatterjee, a leading specialist in venereal diseases. It was a syphilitic node, he said, which often appears in parts of the body even after the patient is cured. Dr Thomas and Dr Denham-White, appearing on behalf of the defence, didn't seem satisfied with this theory but did not reject it either.

There were other differences. The sannyasi was two inches taller than the mejo kumar. Medical experts from both sides conceded that it was possible for a man to gain height up to the age of twenty-five. The mejo kumar was twenty-one when his height had been recorded last. The plaintiff had a tiny mole on his penis which had not been mentioned in the insurance papers. It was confirmed by two palace servants and the prince's mistress Elokeshi.

The physical resemblance had been taken care of. It was time, now, to do a comparative study of the two personalities. The defence had never, at any stage of the trial, attempted to test the plaintiff's memory. The line taken was that he was a clever imposter playing the part for which he had been painstakingly tutored for the last ten years. Scrutinizing the man's face, and I did so very often, I found no trace of the astute intelligence required to have absorbed the kind of tutoring that he was supposed to have received. Another thought struck me. If, indeed, the second prince had been as educated, westernized and sophisticated as the defence was making him out to be, it would be insane on the part of the conspirators to choose *this* man to take his place. He was obviously from a rural background. His speech and manner were naive and artless and his eyes appeared dazed as though he was unable to comprehend much of what was going on. Their tutoring, too, was highly flawed. The least they could have done was to teach him to read and write English and Bengali.

Apart from some signatures and letters, the defence could come up with nothing else to prove the prince's literacy. Nine letters supposedly written by Ramendranarayan Roy to Bibhavati Debi were produced in court. They all carried a Dhaka address and were dated over the first six years of their marriage. I studied them carefully and was somewhat surprised by the contents. There wasn't a single expression of a personal or intimate nature. All they contained were details of visits or intended visits to British officials. Why would a fine, vigorous youth write such letters to a new bride still in her teens?

There were some discrepancies in dates as well. In one letter, allegedly written by the mejo kumar, he said that he would be meeting the Laat Saheb on 2 August 1902. The governor, Sir John Wood, was in Kolkata that day, presiding over a meeting of the Legislative Assembly. There could be no question of his meeting the prince in Dhaka. Another letter addressed from Dhaka carried a date on which the prince was actually in Kolkata.

During cross-examination the petitioner had denied having written the letters. The evidence of the handwriting experts, too, went against the defence. S. C. Choudhury, for the plaintiff, was of the opinion that if the acknowledged signatures of the mejo kumar were authentic specimens, then, as per the basic principles of handwriting examination, the letters were written by another hand. Charles Hardinge, for the defence, agreed with the principles applied by S. C. Choudhury but was hesitant in coming to the conclusion that the letters were forged.

The entire evidence produced in court was circumstantial in nature. But the more closely I studied it, an uncanny feeling that the plaintiff was not lying took hold of me. Unless fresh evidence came to light whereby the prince's death and cremation in Darjeeling could be proven without doubt or the identity of the plaintiff as a rough yokel from the north could be conclusively established, there seemed little reason to doubt the veracity of the petitioner's claim.

The Bhawal case, with its many mysteries and contradictions, took hold of my imagination in a way no other case had ever done before. It seemed to have a secret life of its own. The more I tried to distance myself, to treat it like any other case, the closer it impinged on my consciousness. The tighter it wove its tentacles around my brain. Slowly and stealthily, it sucked me into its vortex. Waking or sleeping, I could think of nothing else.

My days were spent hunched over piles of papers, making notes, putting them in order and writing my judgement. Adding a paragraph here, cancelling a word there, deleting whole sentences till each page looked like a poor imitation of one of the poet Rabindranath's doodles. So absorbed was I in my task that even the brief intervals I was constrained to take, for meals and sleep, seemed a waste of time. I had always loved and waited eagerly for the monsoon. But now, the roar of thunder, the crack of lightning and the gurgling joy of pouring rain, sounds that I loved, fell on deaf ears.

And at night, faces floated in and out of my dreams. Satya babu's, fat and florid, bloodshot eyes darting this way and that. Ashutosh Dasgupta's, long and lean with its pointed chin and supercilious smile. The plaintiff's light, liquid, wondering eyes looking out of a face round and rosy like a ripe fruit. Bibhavati Debi's, pale, distant, aloof, almost as though from another world.

I was not presiding over a murder trial but it was important that I come to some sort of understanding about the time and nature of the mejo kumar's supposed death and cremation. Even if I assumed that the petitioner was an imposter, and the kumar did die in Darjeeling, the question remained: *What did he die of?* Colonel Calvert's prescriptions and certificates were presented by the defence as crucial and complete evidence of death by natural causes. However, several contradictions had come to light. In one of the documents the doctor claimed that he had been treating the prince for biliary colic, off and on, for a fortnight. But as per the records of the chemists, Smith, Stanistreet and Company of Darjeeling, his prescriptions had been served only from the 6th of May. The prince had died on the 8th. There was also some confusion about the age of the patient. In one prescription his age was shown as twenty-seven and twenty-five in another.

Ashutosh Dasgupta had stated, on oath, that he believed the prince was suffering from chronic malaria and was treating him for it. However, his prescription dated 7th May had nothing to do with malaria. It was a compound of chemicals containing an element of arsenic. During cross-examination, Ashutosh had declared that he had prepared the prescription as per the instructions of Colonel Calvert. Since there was no way of corroborating this statement, I was obliged to let it pass. But the medical witnesses from both sides were convinced that it wasn't biliary colic or chronic malaria that killed the prince. They were not fatal diseases. Besides, the patient's symptoms were not consistent with either of the two. Nor were the prescriptions prepared by Colonel Calvert and Ashutosh Dasgupta.

The more I pondered over the matter, the conviction, that if at all the prince had died in Darjeeling, it wasn't owing to natural causes, grew stronger. The stomach cramps, acid vomit and bloody flux, described by the palace servants and endorsed by the mejo rani herself, indicated arsenic poisoning. Was it possible that the source lay in the prescription itself? Given in tiny traces to begin with, followed by larger doses? Dr Thomas, for the defence, had admitted that if someone wanted to poison a person with arsenic, the cleverest way would be to get a prescription that was capable of explaining the presence of blood and arsenic in the stools. Was that what had happened? Was arsenic introduced in the patient's regular medicine to serve as a cloak for what was to follow? If true, then Colonel Calvert and Ashutosh Dasgupta were involved. And Satya Banerjee of course.

But a murder has to have a motive. Satya Banerjee's motive was clear enough. He wished to lay his hands on a good sum of money. Money that would never be his until the mejo kumar died and his widow received her share. Which, again, left me with the nagging question: *Why did the mejo rani allow her brother to swindle her the way he did? She was no spring chicken. She was an educated, independent adult. Would he have planned the murder unless he was sure she would do whatever he wanted her to do? What was the basis of this conviction?*

If, indeed, it was a murder or attempted murder, Ashutosh Dasgupta and Colonel Calvert were Satya babu's partners in the crime. He couldn't have carried it out without their help. *But what was their interest in the matter? Money?* Bribery seemed a possible motive where Colonel Calvert was concerned. His reputation was not very savoury. It had been established, quite convincingly, during cross-examinations of several witnesses, that his moral and ethical standards were not very high and that he was in the habit of misusing his position as a member of the ruling class.

But what about Ashutosh Dasgupta? He had been very young then, just out of medical school. Would he have dared to risk his future for just a bit of money? According to the palace servants, Ashutosh and Satya Banerjee were very good friends. They were drinking and betting buddies. It was possible that Ashutosh had incurred some debts which had to be repaid quickly. Another thought struck me. Some of the female members of the royal household had hinted that Ashutosh Dasgupta was attracted to the mejo rani and often accompanied her brother to her apartments. They had caught him throwing lascivious glances at her. Was it possible that he harboured hopes of marrying her once her husband was out of the way? Had he been encouraged in this hope by Satya babu?

No. No. No. My mind was going off at a tangent. Entering the realm of speculation. I realized that I must stop indulging in idle supposition and conjecture. I must pull myself together. I took off my spectacles and polished them with the end of my dhuti. I ran my fingers through my hair and shook it by the roots. I drank a glass of water. *I must focus on the facts of the case and examine them only through the prism of the law*, I told myself severely.

The crux of the matter was that a man, supposedly dead and cremated, had resurfaced twelve years later claiming that he hadn't died. Only been *declared* dead. Was his story acceptable? According to one or two of the many doctors I consulted, it could be. Though highly unlikely, it did not lie totally beyond the bounds of possibility. The heart might stop for a while, then start beating again entirely on its own. I remembered the short story '*Jeebito o Mrito*' by Rabindranath, in which something similar is described.

The young widow Kadambini felt an excruciating pain in her chest one night, after which her heart stopped beating. The master of the house, her brother-in-law, assumed that she was dead and sent her remains for cremation. On reaching the burning ghat, the pall bearers saw that the wood needed for the cremation had not yet arrived. So, lowering the cot with the body on it outside a small leaf hut, they went inside to wait. After a while, to the shock and terror of the men, the cot began to creak and move as though the corpse was changing its position. Shrieking in panic, they ran back to the village and, fearing that he wouldn't believe their story, told the master that the work of cremation had been completed.

On regaining consciousness, Kadambini went back to what had been her home. But it was no longer her home. How can a ghost claim a home? Kadambini's protests that she was alive fell on deaf ears.

The servants scattered in panic at the sight of her. Women screamed and fainted. Then, when her brother-in-law stood before her with folded hands and begged her to go back to the world of the dead where she belonged, all hope of being accepted by the living was lost. Picking up a heavy brass bowl, she hit it forcefully on her head, over and over again, till the blood gushed down her face. 'See! See! I'm alive ...' she screamed and, rushing out of the house, leaped into the swirling waters of the family pond. Her brother-in-law, standing on the balcony, heard the splashing sound her body made on hitting the water, and realized that she had spoken the truth. The story ends with the poignant sentence:

By dying, Kadambini had proved to the world that she was not dead.

The plaintiff's account of his experience was not unlike Kadambini's. Except in one important detail. He claimed that he had lost his memory for over a decade, then regained it, slowly, over the next two years. Was this a likely story? A number of medical men were invited to give their opinion. The defence posed the following questions to Dr Berkeley-Hill, Superintendent of Ranchi Mental Hospital and a pioneer of clinical psychiatry in India.

Is it possible for a human being to retain his cognitive abilities and reflexes while suffering from a total loss of memory?

Dr Berkeley-Hill was of the opinion that it was possible. The condition, he informed the court, was known as *amnesia*. He had studied the subject thoroughly and treated numerous patients over the last thirty years. He had gone through the plaintiff's testimony carefully and was of the considered opinion that, since the kumar had been very young when the events in Darjeeling took place, it is quite likely that his physical processes, capacity for reflex action, and mechanical adjustments had remained unimpaired.

Could loss of memory last eleven years as the plaintiff has claimed?

Dr Berkeley-Hill's answer was that, though he hadn't come across a case like this personally, the longest period of amnesia he had read about had lasted seventeen years.

How did he account for the fact that the plaintiff spoke with a north Indian accent? If he remembered everything else, how could he forget the intonation and modulations of his mother tongue? Was this not selective amnesia?

Berkeley-Hill replied that it was quite natural for people, even with their memories intact, to acquire an accent after a long stint in another country. To speak in the way people around them spoke. He had met many Englishmen who spoke with a Yankee twang after living several years in America.

Why did he think the plaintiff developed loss of memory in the first place? What was the reason?

Amnesia, Dr Berkeley-Hill explained, generally followed severe mental or physical trauma. However, it had not been possible for him to locate the exact cause. He had received no information other than the plaintiff's testimony, which was not very explicit. The latter's loss of memory might have been the result of severe physical suffering or the shock of finding himself, lying on a pallet in the burning ghat, in the middle of a storm.

The doctors appearing for the defence, Major Thomas and Major Dhunjibhoy of the Indian Medical Service, were of the opinion that the condition described by the plaintiff was suggestive of dual personality. The man claimed that he had forgotten who he was, for a period that lasted nearly a decade, but was otherwise normal and adapted to the world around him. That didn't happen, as a rule. But, even if it did, some elements in his testimony were incompatible. The main line of his story suggested a condition of regression, in which he would revert to the behaviour of his childhood, not respond and react like an adapted adult. Again, after returning to his primary personality, he would forget the secondary one. Thus, once the plaintiff remembered that he was a prince of Bhawal, he would forget the part of his life spent with the mendicants.

This reasoning seemed somewhat confused to me. The plaintiff's case did not seem to fit the description of dual personality. For one thing, he had not reverted to the behaviour of his childhood. He had behaved like an ordinary adult who had forgotten who he was but was perfectly content to live the way his peers lived. For another, his memory had not returned suddenly. It had taken the best part of two years. I was no expert on clinical psychology, but Dr Berkeley-Hill's explanation made more sense to me.

All through the monsoon months of 1936. I sat, crouched over my desk, working tirelessly. And as I worked a strange thought drifted into my mind. A flash of intuition. I heard a voice speaking within me, telling me something I had, perhaps, known all along.

This case would be my greatest, most glorious contribution to my chosen profession. Nothing that followed could match it. Therefore, it would have to be my last ...

I was startled and tried to suppress the thought. I was only fifty-three. I had many years of service left. Why should I give up so soon? But the voice echoed and re-echoed in my head. The thought turned into a conviction that grew in intensity till it took total possession of my mind and senses.

Why was this happening to me? Was it a reaction to the relentless hard work of the last three months? The extreme exhaustion I had fought every inch of the way? Did it spring from the fear of an appeal against my verdict? But appeals were quite common, even expected. Was I suffering from a subconscious anxiety that my verdict would annoy the rulers and I might face problems at work? I thought and thought, but couldn't come up with a satisfactory answer.

June passed into July and now it was the third week of August. My work was almost done. I had written my judgment and typed it myself. Only one final revision was left. My chest swelled with elation. I had accomplished a colossal task. The whole of Bengal was waiting with bated breath for the verdict.

The night before the historic reading of the judgement, I told my wife that I was quitting the judiciary.

11

The Verdict

Dhaka District Court
24 August 1936

THE PROCEEDINGS IN JUSTICE PANNALAL BASU'S COURT WERE scheduled to begin at eleven. It was a hot, sultry morning with a heavy cloud cover threatening rain any moment. But the courthouse and the square outside were filled with jostling crowds. People from far and near had been camping through the night, and the whole of Bakshi Bazar had turned into a sea of human heads. Men and women, teachers and students, peasants and aristocrats, writers, photographers, newspaper reporters, idlers, beggars – no one stayed away. By mid-morning the entire stretch from Sankharipara to the church at the corner of Victoria Park was so crammed, shops had to be shut and all traffic suspended. The Bhawal Rajbari and the estate offices were placed under police protection.

As the judge walked in and took his seat, a buzz of welcome from many voices rose from the courtroom. Raising both hands in a gesture requesting silence, he put on his glasses and began reading from the sheaf of papers he carried. A breath-stopping hush fell on the assembled throng the moment his cool, impersonal voice was heard.

I have considered the whole evidence in the case with the utmost care, and the very able argument of the learned counsels on either side has missed, I believe, nothing material that could be argued for and against the identity.

The judgement ran into 525 pages but the judge's conclusions were brief, crisp and clear.

I believe the direct evidence in support of the identity ...

At these words a deafening yell, from thousands of throats, sent a swirl of echoes around the walls of the edifice of justice. Pannalal Basu picked up his gavel to command silence but changed his mind. Putting it down, he raised both his hands again, waited a minute, then continued with his reading in the same aloof, unemotional tones.

It is the evidence of honest men and women, of all ranks and conditions of life, including nearly all the relations ... The witnesses include a great many men of education and position, grave elderly men ... who have nothing to gain or lose and who could not possibly mistake the kumar. It is impossible that these would commit perjury to support an imposter ...

More hollering! And now the shouts had changed to slogans. *Jai! Judge saheb er jai! Jai! Madhyam kumar er jai!* The judge's face remained as impassive as ever. Not a line shifted. Not a muscle twitched. Not the slightest tremor shook his voice as he went on reading ...

Another test, in itself conclusive, is the identity of the body, proved to demonstration and with mathematical certainty by the bodily features, all exceptional, and by the bodily marks, all exceptional, which rest on nobody's credibility. These, in their totality, cannot occur in a second individual, and even if half of the marks go off, the scaly feet and the irregular scar on the top of the left outer ankle ... will be enough to sustain the identity with equal certainty ... Nothing in the mind of the plaintiff shakes this conclusion.

One by one he went over every salient point of the judgement. The personality of the prince versus that of the plaintiff. The relationship between the mejo kumar and his wife as testified by his family and the palace servants. The role played by Satyendranath Banerjee in their lives. The confusion of the doctors over the ailment that had, supposedly, caused the death of the prince. The conflicting prescriptions. The conduct of the mejo rani after her return from Darjeeling and her subsequent change from a grieving young widow to a hard-headed woman, ready to relinquish her title and rights for a substantial payment. Her curious reaction to the sannyasi's claim. The roles played by the officers of the Court of Wards. The conduct of the estate manager F. W. Needham.

Proceeding to the question of whether the plaintiff's declaration was part of a plot to outwit the rulers, Pannalal Basu asserted that nothing had occurred prior to 14th May 1921, the day the sannyasi declared his identity, suggesting a conspiracy. Nor could anything in the man's subsequent behaviour support such a theory. From that date down to this one, he hadn't gone into hiding for a single day. He had kept himself visible, met people and even collected rents. He had brought the estate to a standstill. Yet he had neither been questioned nor prosecuted. On the contrary, his serene self-assurance had sent the other camp into a tizzy. Two days after the declaration, Satyendranath Banerjee had rushed to Mr Lethbridge, Secretary of the Board of Revenue, and arranged to have a letter published in *The Englishman* in which he had introduced himself as the mejo rani's brother and an eyewitness to the death and cremation of the prince in Darjeeling. He had also persuaded J. H. Lindsay to refute the sannyasi's claim and denounce him as an imposter. Which, needless to say, the Englishman had done without a qualm.

Clearing his throat, the learned judge recommenced reading from his papers.

Few imposters would survive this declaration. It created the notion, shared by many witnesses, that the issue was not between the first defendant (Bibhavati Debi) and the plaintiff, but between him and the government ...

Coming to the argument put forward by the defence, he said:

Mr Chaudhuri, with some disregard of these facts, was pointing out the delay in instituting the suit and suggesting that time was needed to fit the plaintiff to play the role. The plaintiff had himself asked Mr Lindsay for an enquiry, twenty-four days after he had declared his identity, and his sisters had sent up a petition even earlier. He was prepared to be faced and questioned then, as always …

Elaborating further, he said:

Conduct speaks and it cannot lie. One sees the dread of the sannyasi even on the 16th of May, 1921, two days after he declared he was the kumar, that sends Satyendra babu post haste to Mr Lethbridge to save the evidence of death; the dread that sends him to Darjeeling … to pin down the witnesses to a cremation; the dread of the insurance doctor's report bearing the kumar's bodily marks … The defendants do not seize upon it to destroy the imposter. They do not call for it … It is the alleged imposter who calls for it and seizes upon it with alacrity just as he seized upon every other document that gave any personal detail …

The judge next considered a point of legal technicality. Did the plaintiff's donning of saffron and keeping company with ascetics disqualify him from the title to his property? His explanation was concise and clear.

Renunciation of the world, when absolute, amounts to civil death under the Hindu Law. The passage does not say that he had been initiated to sannyas, or that he had absolutely retired from all earthly interests, and the passage also adds that the life he led was the result of loss of memory. Retirement into religious life must be a voluntary act to have the effect of death …

I should also add that that there is no evidence that the plaintiff was initiated into sannyas and had undergone the essential ceremony that makes him dead to the world …

The minutes ticked by as the reading went on. The sky had turned darker and rain had started to fall, first in drops, then in sheets, but the gathering, both inside and outside the courtroom, didn't move an inch or utter a sound. Every single person listened in pin-drop silence. Then, towards noon, the voice changed. It became sonorous and charged with emotion as the Honourable Judge read out the decisive sentence of his judgement.

I find that the plaintiff is Ramendranarayan Roy, the second son of the late Rajah Rajendranarayan Roy of Bhawal.

A roar of applause, as of an army announcing victory in battle, rose from the crowd. It dashed against the walls of the courtroom, rattled the doors and windows, and reverberated in eddies, across streets and lanes, parks and alleys, neighbourhoods and marketplaces, till the whole of Dhaka seemed enveloped in a vast volume of sound. The earth shuddered under the feet of thousands leaping and dancing in the rain, ululating, hollering '*Jai! Madhyam kumar er jai! Jai Bhawal Raj er jai! Bande Mataram!*'

So great was the tumult that few heard the last words of the judgement …

There will be a decree declaring that the plaintiff is Kumar Ramendranarayan Roy, the second son of the late Rajah Rajendranarayan Roy of Bhawal, and directing that he be put in possession of an undivided one-third share in the properties in suit … The plaintiff will get his costs from the contesting defendants, with interest at six per cent per annum.

12

Sarajubala Debi

Kolkata
November 1936

WHILE LIVING WITH MEJO THAKURPO, RANI THAKURMA HAD URGED me over and over again to find a bride for him. 'You are a daughter of the famous Matilals of Boubazar,' she said. 'I'm sure there are many beautiful girls in the extended family. Why don't you select one for your brother-in-law? He's lonely and tends to get depressed. More so since the government has restricted him from entering Jaidevpur.'

'Does he wish to marry again?'

'He says he doesn't. But he needs a wife. Since Bibhavati refuses to return …'

'I'll speak to him.'

Ever since they had taken up residence in Dhaka I had been trying to persuade them to come and live with me in Kolkata. I had moved from our ancestral mansion in Boubazar, by then, to a house the baro kumar owned in Ripon Street, and had been living there with my adopted son Pataki and the few servants I had brought with me from the Rajbari. Mejo thakurpo had refused on the ground that he was planning to move court shortly and needed to stay in Dhaka and attend the hearings. But he came to Kolkata often, in connection with the trial, and visited me whenever he could. I also know that he made several attempts to meet Bibhavati. He never mentioned her but I had a feeling that he hoped she might be persuaded to return in the event of his winning the case.

After the pronouncement of the verdict, I made a trip to Dhaka. 'You have won the case,' I told him. 'What are you waiting for? Bestir yourself and get Mejo bou to come back. And if she still holds out let me find a bride for you. It was Rani thakurma's fervent wish that you marry again.'

Mejo thakurpo shook his head. His face flushed with embarrassment. 'I'm an old man,' he said. 'Do you expect me to don a *topor* and marry a girl young enough to be my granddaughter?'

'Of course I do. Many men marry at your age.'

'Don't count me among them.'

'Why not? As the ruler of Bhawal, you'll need a consort. And an heir. Your subjects will expect it of you. You can't disappoint them.'

I knew what was going on in my brother-in-law's mind. I had known him from the time I had entered the Rajbari as a little bride of ten and we had grown up together. There were some strange contradictions in his character. He had taken to his bed women of all ages, religions, castes and classes. He had done so from adolescence onwards without a qualm. But a wife was different; sacrosanct. She had to be respected, loved and handled with infinite delicacy. The thought of deflowering a young virgin wife was abhorrent to him; a violation. He had found it hard even with Bibhavati. Inexplicable, but there it was.

'I see that you are still hankering after Mejo bou,' I smiled. 'I'll …'

'I'm not,' he interrupted. 'Not in the least …'

'Stop pretending and listen to me. I'll make one last effort. I'll go and see her and try to persuade her to come back. But you must give me your word. If she refuses, you will agree to take the vows again. I'll try to find a girl as close to your age as possible.'

A couple of days after my return to Kolkata, I went to 19 Lansdowne Road. 'Sit here and wait,' I told the maid who was preparing to follow me out of the motor car. 'I won't be long.'

Walking up the gravel path that divided a rough, overgrown garden in two, I came to the front door. The sun was setting and the shadows under the trees and bushes were lengthening in the fading light. Clanging the metal rings, I waited. Minutes passed. No one came. I tried again and rapped my hand loudly against the panels. Again, no response. Walking over to a window I tried to peer inside. I could see a large room and a courtyard beyond it. But they were empty. Was no one at home? Had Satya babu taken his family out of Kolkata? I turned and started walking back to the motor car when the door opened. A middle-aged woman, a maid from her appearance, stood within. Her clothes and hair were dishevelled and she was yawning as though rudely awakened from sleep. I was puzzled. What sort of household was this where maids enjoyed afternoon siestas till dusk?

'Who are you? What do you want?' Her voice was rough, her manner discourteous.

'I've come to see Bibhavati.'

'Pishimoni doesn't see anyone.'

'She'll see me. Tell her the baro rani of Bhawal is here.'

The woman's eyes flashed and popped open. She was fully awake at last. 'The baro rani!' she breathed. 'Come. Come in.'

She led me through a dark passage and up a flight of marble stairs that may have been grand once upon a time but was now dull and grimy with neglect. The banister was coated with dust. Guiding me into one of the rooms on the second floor, she called from the door. 'Pishimoni! Look who has come to see you.'

Bibhavati was sitting on a bamboo stool facing a window. Her back was to the door through which we entered. She didn't seem to have heard the maid's announcement for she neither spoke nor turned her head. The end of her thaan trailed across the floor and a soft breeze, blowing from the window, lifted the long strands of her beautiful hair. She sat listless and immobile, a slim silhouette against a square of sky, deepening with the shadows of twilight.

'Mejo bou,' I called softly.

And now she turned and looked at me. Her eyes, in the eerie half-light of the room, were blank.

'Wh-o-o?' she whispered.

'Don't you recognize me? I'm didi … the baro rani … Sarajubala.'

'Didi?' she echoed. There was wonder in her voice.

'Why is the room so dark?' I turned to the maid. 'Switch on the lights.'

'Only one,' Bibhavati murmured. 'Too much light hurts my eyes.'

I pulled up a chair and sat next to her. I stroked her hand and moved the hair gently away from her face. I talked to her for a long time. I begged her to come back to us. But she shook her head. 'It's too late,' she kept saying. 'Too late.'

'It isn't too late. You denied Mejo thakurpo. Why … I can't say. But in your heart of hearts, you know the truth. I can see it in your eyes. He loves you. He's waiting for you.'

'Too late. Too late,' she kept repeating like a parrot. Only once did she utter a full sentence. 'I'm a coward, Didi,' she muttered. 'A weak, miserable coward. But believe me … I've tried. I've fought and failed. I've failed over and over again. I'm tired. I don't have any fight left in me.'

I didn't understand. I thought she was referring to her past struggles with an unfaithful husband.

'You won't have to fight anymore. Mejo thakurpo has changed. He's a different man. You'll be happy with him. All you need to do is come back and take your rightful position as the reigning queen of Bhawal.'

She continued shaking her head as though the prospect was a distant dream. An illusion so far removed from reality that it would melt and dissolve any moment.

A shadow fell across the floor. Satya Banerjee stood at the door. He had changed considerably in the last thirty years. He was monstrously obese now and his chest and arms were hairier than I remembered. Perhaps I was imagining it but he looked more animal than human. He swayed and shuffled into the room, much like a great shaggy bear that had difficulty in carrying its own weight. Still, I recognized him. Perhaps from the odour that emanated from his person. A mixed odour of sweat, alcohol, tobacco and male arrogance. I managed to part my jaws in a weak smile but what I got in return was a growl.

'What's all this?' He glared at me. 'What are you doing with my sister?'

'Doing with her?' I exclaimed, startled. 'Nothing. I've only come to see her.'

'That's a lie. You're trying to brainwash her into going back to that hell. How dare you?' His flaming bloodshot eyes pierced into mine.

I was so shocked at the vehemence of his voice and manner that I sat dumbstruck for a while. Then I gathered myself together. 'Yes, I am,' I snapped back. 'What's wrong with that?'

'Everything. She is nothing to you anymore and you are nothing to her.' Stepping forward, he placed a hand on Bibhavati's shoulder. The sight of that heavy paw on her delicate collarbone sickened me. I was afraid it would break to shards under his fierce, possessive grip.

'Go tell the confidence trickster you and your sisters-in-law have put up that the decision of the trial court means nothing. Nothing at all.' He stamped his foot. 'I'll be moving the High Court shortly. The verdict will be examined by British judges. Then we'll have some fun.'

'Another court? Why are you putting the poor girl through so much stress? Why can't you leave her in peace?'

'Peace! She'll get no peace till the crook is locked up. I'll see the matter to the end. If the High Court lets me down, I'll appeal to the Privy Council in London.'

'Is all this really necessary?'

'It is absolutely necessary. I have taken a vow to expose you. You royals think you own the world. You gloat over your money and entitlements. You treat us like insects. I'll see your pride ground in the dust. Bloody fraudsters and hypocrites. Shame on you. Shame on you all.'

His large body trembled with hate.

Bibhavati hadn't moved or spoken a word all this while. Now she gave a deep, shuddering sigh and stirred slowly. Removing her brother's hand from her shoulder, she said softly, 'Go home, Didi. Don't stay here to be insulted.' She turned and faced the window once again. 'Go,' she said in a trembling voice. 'Leave me to my fate.'

That was the last time I saw her. And that's how I remember her to this day. A thin, wasted, fragile form etched against a skyful of stars.

13

The Appeal

Kolkata
1938

PANNALAL BASU'S VERDICT WAS NOT THE LAST WORD IN THE FATE OF the plaintiff. The defendants lost no time in moving the High Court of Calcutta. The appeal was to be heard by a bench of three reputed legal men. Sir Leonard W. J. Costello, Mr Charu Chandra Biswas and Mr Ronald Francis Lodge. The counsels for the two sides remained the same – A. N. Chaudhuri and B. C. Chatterjee. But, this time, both had a team of eminent lawyers to assist them.

A. N. Chaudhuri, as was to be expected, launched into a tirade against the judgement of the lower court. His contention was that Mr Basu's verdict had been based on what he had called 'direct evidence', though anyone with the slightest understanding of the law would agree that there was no such thing. Ignoring the mass of contradictions in the testimonies, Basu had made up his mind that the plaintiff was the mejo kumar. He had provided no substantial answers to the basic questions regarding the events in Darjeeling. Questions which were inextricably linked to the identity factor.

What was the ailment the second prince had suffered from in Darjeeling? Had he died or only been presumed dead when his body was taken to the crematorium? Did the cremation take place on the night of 8 May or the morning of the 9th? Was the body that of the prince or a substituted one?

The judge, according to A. N. Chaudhuri, had evaded a scientific enquiry. He had disregarded all the evidence presented by the defence and accepted the plaintiff's story down to every improbable detail. The direct evidence the judge had spoken of was the testimony of two witnesses, the dowager queen Satyabhama Debi and the prince's sister Jyotirmayi Debi, one of whom had died and couldn't be submitted to further questioning. Thus, the judgement of the lower court was based on the evidence of one person alone. The plaintiff's story was full of fantastic and utterly unbelievable events. Dying, coming to life, rescue by a group of mendicants, loss of memory, recovery of the same at an opportune moment – all were the stuff of fairy tales. Yet the learned judge had swallowed it, line, hook and sinker! Why? Because he believed that a conspiracy to set up an imposter was impossible. But why was it impossible? Hadn't plots and conspiracies been conceived before? The counsel for the defence urged the learned judges to consider the balance of probabilities on both sides, before giving their verdict. He ended with a plea that, since the trial judge had erred so grievously, it was incumbent on the appellate court to set that judgement aside.

When B. C. Chatterjee's turn came, he dismissed the defence counsel's arguments with thinly veiled disdain. The trial judge, he said, had given far more consideration and taken a far more analytical approach to the question of identity than Mr Chaudhuri, who had merely clutched at straws. Far from coming to a conclusion on the basis of the second princess's testimony, the judge had said, 'Honest belief, even in a sister, is not conclusive though it demolishes the "utter dissimilarity" theory.' He had added that even a single piece of incontrovertible evidence, such as proof of death or that of the plaintiff being a non-Bengali, would be enough to displace Jyotirmayi Debi's evidence. But such proof had not been provided.

No one could question the honesty of the judge's claim that he had based his opinion on authentically recorded physical similarities between the prince and the plaintiff, the opinion of experts as well as the thorough gruelling the plaintiff had been put through by A. N. Chaudhuri. The judge had considered each and every point of difference on their own merits. Had the defence counsel studied the 525 pages of the judgement carefully, instead of picking up stray phrases out of context, he would have done well.

Justice Pannalal Basu, he went on to say, had also considered the matter of the loss of memory and the speech impediment with due care. On both, he had been guided by learned doctors. In conclusion, the counsel for the plaintiff disagreed with the appellants' criticism of the judgement of the lower court and prayed that the appeal be dismissed.

The hearings came to an end on 14 August 1939. The three judges of the appellate court had held consultations over various points of the case while the hearings were on but hadn't reached a consensus. Sir Lionel Costello had proceeded to England on leave soon afterwards, and was unable to travel back to India. War had broken out and the whole of Europe was in turmoil. An entire year went by. And now, Justice Biswas and Justice Lodge decided that it wasn't fair to the parties to delay the verdict any longer. A new rule had been framed which authorized any judge of the High Court to read out the written judgement of another if the latter was prevented, for some valid reason, from doing so in person. It was decided that Lionel Costello's judgement would be sent for and all three would be read out in court. If the findings were not unanimous, the official verdict would be based on the concurring two.

14

The Three Judgements

Kolkata
August 1941

CHARU CHANDRA BISWAS'S JUDGEMENT CONTAINED A CLEAR endorsement of the verdict passed by the lower court. He began by dismissing A. N. Chaudhuri's criticism of Pannalal Basu's analysis and findings. In the opinion of the defence counsel, Basu had ignored the events that had taken place in Darjeeling and based his judgement on the identity factor alone. Terming this a complete misreading of the trial court's judgement, the appellate judge made a solemn pronouncement, 'I do not understand the learned judge as having said anywhere that he must reject the defendants' evidence regarding any of the Darjeeling events as untrue, merely because he had already come to a finding in the plaintiff's favour on the question of identity. On the other hand, it strikes me, the learned judge subjected the Darjeeling evidence to an independent examination … It cannot be denied on a fair reading of the judgement that he held the defendants had wholly failed to prove their case that the second kumar had actually died or that his body had been burned to ashes.'

The next point taken up was the role played by Jyotirmayi Debi. In this matter, Biswas firmly upheld the trial court's stance that she had no motive in hatching the conspiracy as imputed by the defence. The British government had made a token gesture of recognizing the rights of the royal family by anointing Anandakumari's adopted son Ramnarayan. More than two decades had passed since then. The boy of five was now a grown man of twenty-seven. Yet nothing had been done to transfer the administration of the estate to his hands. Everyone in the kingdom realized that the investiture ceremony was only a bluff intended to hoodwink the family and the public. So did Jyotirmayi Debi. There was no reason for her to feel threatened by Ramnarayan. Besides, reviving a dead brother would not advance *her* son's prospects in any way. It was possible, he conceded, that she had made a pact with the imposter to share the spoils if their stratagem was successful. But where was the proof? Nothing of the kind had been hinted even by the defence. Another possibility was that she hated the two younger ranis and wished to harm their interests by foisting a husband on one and dealing a blow on the ambitions of the other. The evidence, however, clearly demonstrated that the second princess was on excellent terms with them both. Neither of the two women had suggested, at any point in their testimonies, that she had borne them any malice or ill will.

Next came the issue of the ascetic's claim and the reaction of the defendants. Referring briefly to Satya Banerjee's frantic visit to Mr Lethbridge, Justice Biswas launched a searing indictment on the conduct of the British officials, J. H. Lindsay in particular. Going a step beyond the line taken by Pannalal Basu, he exposed the prejudice and bias inherent in the man's mental make-up. Deciding that the sannyasi was an imposter even before seeing him was bad enough. Even worse was his hypocrisy in assuring the members of the delegation that met him on 7 June 1921 that he was open to holding a free and fair enquiry without any intention of doing so. Reading from Lindsay's own deposition, Pannalal Basu had informed the gathering that on the question of whether anything had prevented him from holding the promised enquiry, he had replied, 'I don't know. Except my own conviction that he was not the kumar.' Again, when asked if he had conclusive proof of the prince's death before he issued the Imposter Notice, he replied that the only proof he had relied upon was the death certificate.

A fact the appellate judge found suspicious was the defence's inability to produce the official records of that time in court. A. N. Chaudhuri, he felt, had depended more on rhetoric than on documented facts. And the people he had brought as witnesses seemed to remember nothing.

Coming to Satyendranath Banerjee's role in the whole affair, the first questionable fact was his intention in keeping a diary for just a few months. 'One does not,' Justice Biswas commented caustically, 'go out of one's way to keep notes about a true story. But if a person is minded to make a false case, it is often safer to reduce it to writing.' What was even stranger was that the diary had been produced in court, not by the defendants, but by the plaintiff. The former had complained that some pages had been deliberately torn out because it might not suit the opposing party's case. The accusation had remained unproven. But, even if it was justified, it showed up the failure of the defendants. *They* should have been the ones to produce the diary, if it was relevant to their case, and not have to admit it under pressure.

Had the mejo kumar been poisoned? The trial judge, in all fairness, had set aside B. C. Chatterjee's allegation of a conspiracy. Since there was no evidence to prove otherwise, the farthest he had gone was to admit to a possibility that Ashutosh Dasgupta, being young and inexperienced, had miscalculated the amount of arsenic to be administered. It might be accidental poisoning, he had maintained, but not wilful murder. However, the doctor had changed his story so many times that the appellate judge felt that the conspiracy theory had not been put to the proper test and could not be dismissed in its entirety.

Colonel Calvert, too, had had to struggle hard to reconcile his prescriptions with his diagnosis of biliary colic. He was by no means young and inexperienced, yet his conclusions had been full of contradictions. He had attributed the diarrhoea and fresh blood in the stools to 'great strain and spasm due to an impacted stone'. An explanation summarily dismissed in court by medical experts. Major Thomas, appearing on behalf of the defence, was the only doctor who had supported Calvert's theory with a long and involved clarification. He said that pus had passed through the ducts, entered the intestines and caused an inflammatory condition which had re-exacerbated an old, latent dysentery. Terming this a 'fantastic explanation', Justice Biswas repeated a remark made by A. N. Chaudhuri about 'experts who come and support a case provided the remuneration is sufficiently large' and wondered if Major Thomas could be placed in this category.

C. C. Biswas also came down heavily on W. M. Crawford, district magistrate of Darjeeling, for endorsing the death certificate without seeking any proof of its authenticity. Crawford's answer to the question of why he had done so was nebulous in the extreme: 'I do not remember at all the circumstances under which I gave the certificate nor how the details came to be in it.' A shocked and disgusted Justice Biswas was ruthless in his condemnation of such an irresponsible statement. It was not incompetence or even corruption that he alleged. It was faith in a despotic order, a belief in the Divine Right of the white race, which rendered colonial officials unaccountable for any action they took, no matter how immoral. Lindsay, Calvert, Crawford were only a few examples of a habitual wielding of unchecked, autocratic power.

The next matter taken up by the appellate judge were the contradictory statements regarding the date and time of the cremation. It had taken place on the night of 8 May according to witnesses from the plaintiff's side. Even the mejo rani had fixed the time of death at midnight. But according to the defendants, the mejo kumar had been cremated on the morning of 9 May. Dr Prankrishna Acharya had been sent for on 9th morning to Step Aside and shown a longish bundle wrapped in a sheet. He had not been allowed to see the face of the supposed corpse or touch it. Why? The excuse given was that, being a Brahmo, his touch would pollute the body. 'If so,' Justice Biswas wondered, 'why call him at all?' As per the defence's own deposition, Colonel Calvert had examined the body before declaring the prince's death. Was a *firinghee* Christian's touch less polluting than a Bengali Brahmo's?

'Look at the matter from any point of view,' Justice Biswas said without mincing his words, 'there is to my mind no possible escape from the conclusion that the summoning of Dr Prankrishna Acharya to Step Aside had a distinct purpose behind it … The true motive, which was to obtain a death certificate, was foiled by the doctor's walking away in disgust.'

The judge was convinced that the morning cremation, if indeed it had taken place, was a trick played with the purpose of deluding people into believing that the prince had been cremated with full honours. According to Princess Jyotirmayi's testimony, Satya babu had admitted before the baro kumar and the eldest princess Indumayi Debi that the cremation had taken place on the night of the death and no one from Step Aside had accompanied the pall bearers. The servants had refused to go and he and the doctor were occupied in attending to Bibhavati Debi who was in a state of collapse. But in court Satya babu had told a different story. Significantly, even by his own admission, his sister had not performed the last rites of her husband which was her duty and prerogative according to the Shastras. Why?

The defence had been unable to produce reliable witnesses to the morning cremation. Most of them seemed totally confused and contradicted their own statements. Barring one R. N. Banerjee, a known anglophile who always supported the cause of the rulers, now a barrister in the Calcutta High Court. He said that he had carried the body and watched the cremation to the end. But his name was not even mentioned in Satya babu's diary. Besides, evidence produced by the plaintiff's lawyer proved that he was not in Darjeeling on that particular day. He was in Kurseong attending the shraddha of the Raja of Kakina.

Another factor which didn't add up was that, while Satya babu claimed that the prince was cremated with the full panoply of rituals, he wrote in his diary that the funeral party had returned by 2 p.m. The two facts were irreconcilable, since a Bengali cremation is a long and involved process and takes a good ten to twelve hours. There were other discrepancies in his testimony which provoked Justice Biswas to describe him as 'the greatest lying and quibbling' witness he had seen in his whole career in the law.

The appellate judge next reviewed the testimonies of the two naga sadhus. A. N. Chaudhuri had insisted that Darshandas was a fake brought in by the plaintiff's lawyer, as an after-thought, towards the fag end of the trial hearings. C. C. Biswas, however, felt that the very delay indicated Chatterjee's care and caution. He had waited till he had found the right man unlike the defence which had put up a bogus Dharamdas at no notice at all. Depending on Darshandas's evidence, as far more reliable of the two, Justice Biswas made a stunning declaration:

> 'I hold without hesitation that the second kumar did not die at Darjeeling and that his body was not cremated. I hold further, and in doing so I recognize I go far beyond the trial court, that he was the person who was rescued by Darshandas and his companions from the cremation ground, and the sadhu who turned up at the Buckland Bund about twelve years later.

After this his verdict came as no surprise:

> 'I concur with the learned trial judge in his findings. I have read and re-read his judgement several times over and it is no small tribute to the care, thoroughness and vigilant attention he brought to the consideration of the case that I was unable to trace a single error of fact in his statements.'

Though dismayed by the conclusions of C. C. Biswas, the defendants, as well as the British officials who supported them, managed to keep up their spirits. Two white judges were still to deliver judgement. There was no way they would go along with their Indian colleague. Joy surged in their breasts as it became apparent, from the very beginning, that Justice Lodge would fulfil their hopes.

Lodge began with a series of comments on the conditions under which the trial court had held its hearings. The pressure from both sides, the frenzy and hysteria, the enthusiastic support of the plaintiff and the mocking and lampooning of the defendants, he felt, were not conducive to a calm and judicious determination of the issues involved. The large numbers of witnesses, too, had created complications with the enormous mass of redundant material they brought in.

Having said that, he proceeded on a point-by-point rejection of Justice Basu's findings. Two stories, he said, had been presented at court. One by the plaintiff, one by the defendants. Though obvious by any ordinary reasoning that the latter was the more plausible, the trial judge had accepted the former. Why? Because some witnesses from the defence had given false evidence. But does perjury on the part of some from one side guarantee the veracity of all from the other? The judge had clearly played partisan.

But, as every Indian observed, Lodge too was playing partisan. The fact was made amply clear by his motivated defence of the British officials involved in the case. Admitting that Lindsay had been somewhat hasty in concluding that the plaintiff was an imposter, he went on to describe him as a responsible British officer incapable of committing a deliberate act of infamy. Calvert, too, he felt, was more sinned against than sinning. He had said, over and over again, that he did not remember the circumstances of the illness and death, an honest acknowledgement which should have been respected. The man was truthful and upright and didn't deserve the badge of shame pinned on him by the trial judge.

The death, in the opinion of Justice Lodge, was a natural one and the plaintiff's testimony 'wholly unreliable'. It was true that Ashutosh Dasgupta should have prescribed a mild laxative in place of the strong purgative that led to the frequent motions. But it was a mistake not unnatural in an incompetent medical student. It was certainly not made with criminal intent and was not the cause of death. In fact, even the trial judge had conceded that there was no proof of a conspiracy to poison the second kumar.

Regarding the time of cremation, Lodge was convinced that it had been conducted on the morning of 9th May. The trial judge had doubted it on the ground that defence witnesses had given different versions of how the rituals had been conducted and the credentials of the man who had acted as the priest. Lodge rubbished this argument with the words: 'It should be borne in mind that Satyendranath Banerjee and other men of Ramendranarayan's party were young ... and strangers to Darjeeling. They had sought and obtained the assistance of a number of Brahmins ... it seems highly unlikely that they would stand quietly by while some inexperienced young man performed the cremation in direct defiance of the customary rites. In my opinion, contradictions in evidence are natural. I do not think they justify the inference that the witnesses that made them gave false evidence.'

Having established natural death and a traditional cremation, Lodge proceeded to the next point. The rescue. The chief witness on behalf of the plaintiff was Darshandas, whose testimony, Lodge had not an iota of doubt, was false. A man who had lost consciousness due to arsenic poisoning, as alleged by the petitioner's counsel, could not have groaned loudly enough to be heard by someone sleeping in a cave located at least twenty yards away. That, too, on a wild, rainy night. He also found the behaviour of the sadhus extraordinary in that they took the man away with them instead of trying to locate his relatives. The least they could have done was to make enquiries in the local bazaar. Darshandas's account sounded like a fairy tale, a story even a child would have difficulty in believing.

Coming to the plaintiff's amnesia, Lodge accepted the opinion of Dr Berkeley-Hill that the condition often occurred after a severe physical or mental shock. But to admit that loss of memory is possible does not signify acceptance of the plaintiff's story and the doctor had never said that it did. Every fact had to be put to a proper test and this one hadn't. All that the other side had done was to advance the uncorroborated statements of the plaintiff himself. He concluded this point with the words, 'The plea of loss of memory is obviously an extremely convenient one for a person coming forward to claim the identity of a man long supposed to be dead. It helps him to avoid answering questions.' The eminent judge lashed out against what he believed to be Pannalal Basu's irrational and motivated distrust of the chief defendants Bibhavati and her brother.

Admitting the fact that Satya Banerjee had attained wealth through control of his sister's estate, Lodge went on to say that it did not necessarily prove him to be dishonest. Most Indian women depended on their male relatives to manage their affairs. There had never been a suggestion, from any quarter, that he had forced her or done anything against her will. It was true that he had taken her away from her husband's family. But he had done so with her welfare in mind, because he had felt that the atmosphere in the palace was not right for a young widow. Besides, he did not trust her brothers-in-law and believed that they were plotting to cheat her of her property.

Lodge criticized the trial judge for admitting the genuineness of the plaintiff's claim without paying due attention to the testimonies of the defendants. True or not, Lodge was guilty of the same in reverse. In a strident dismissal of the evidence of recognition and physical similarities, he made up his mind that the man was an imposter put up by some conspirators, chief of whom were Satyabhama Debi and Jyotirmayi Debi. The dowager queen's letters, he said, were obviously not the unaided efforts of the old lady. They reveal the cloven hoof of the legal advisor. Nor was he impressed by her desire that her last rites be performed by the plaintiff. Having made a public announcement that he was her grandson, what other option did she have?

As for Jyotirmayi Debi, Lodge felt that the trial judge had been over-considerate with her. He had believed everything she had said on the ground that no highborn Hindu woman, used to a sequestered life, would hatch a conspiracy that involved admitting a strange man into her inner household. It was too big a risk to take, he had said. If caught, she would be charged with perjury and face imprisonment. It was also psychologically untenable. Lodge didn't agree. In his opinion, Indian royals thought they were a law unto themselves. They had huge egos and were eternally seeking greater power. They were seldom fearful of consequences and rarely exercised restraint and caution. And even if, for argument's sake, he conceded that it is 'unusual for a Bengali lady to put forward a Punjabi imposter as her brother, it is equally unusual for a Bengali lady to deny her own husband'.

His verdict was a foregone conclusion:

> 'I am satisfied that the plaintiff is an imposter supported by Jyotirmoyee Debi and others in the full knowledge that he is an imposter. In my opinion, the appeal should be allowed with costs: the judgement and decree of the original court be set aside, and the suit dismissed with cost.'

The score was 1–1. Leonard Costello's verdict would break the tie. Both parties waited with bated breath.

Costello's stance was a bit unclear at first. That, out of the three judges, his position was the least biased was evident from his opening statement. Terming this case as 'most unique in legal annals', he faulted lawyers from both sides for harassing witnesses and making insinuations with regard to their private lives, which was scandalous and should not have been permitted by the trial judge. Commenting on the inability of the defence to make crucial documents available to the court, he expressed surprise at the mysterious, inexplicable way in which they had come into the plaintiff's possession. This point, he felt, should have been examined in greater detail.

Having said this, he made it clear that he did not condone the attacks made by the defence counsel against Pannalal Basu who had expressed himself throughout the judgement in clear, concise and unmistakable terms and in admirable language. A. N. Chaudhuri, it seemed to him, had not read the judgement from beginning to end, as he should have done, but picked up passages at random. It was unfortunate that a learned judge from the appellate court had taken his comments at face value. That he was referring to Lodge was evident from his next statement: 'In my opinion, a court of appeal should be very chary of interfering with the decision of the lower court and even more chary of a wholesale discarding of large bodies of witnesses, however impossible the story they tell may seem to be.'

Going over the details step by step, he expressed praise for the logical working of Justice Basu's mind and the rigour of the presentation of his findings.

The two crucial questions in this extraordinary case came next – the nature of the illness the second prince had suffered and the cause of his supposed death. Costello accepted the trial judge's finding that it was not biliary colic but possible enteritis aggravated by accidental arsenic poisoning. Basu had not found evidence to support the plaintiff's charge that Satya Banerjee and Ashutosh Dasgupta had conspired to poison him. The appellate judge agreed. Satya Banerjee, in his view, was a young hanger-on in the palace, dependent on the goodwill of the princes. Could he have risked losing his advantageous position on the supposition that, after poisoning her husband, he would manage to lure his sister into handing him all her money? Costello thought not.

On the question of the cremation, Costello accepted Pannalal Basu's view that it had been performed sometime during the night of

8 May. 'On a review of all the relevant evidence,' he wrote, 'I see no reason for disagreeing with the finding of the learned judge.'

The story of the rescue was taken up next. The crucial witness here was Darshandas. His bearing and demeanour had impressed the assembly and his account, exotic and romantic as it was, had found credibility in the eyes of the trial judge. Costello saw no reason to question this. The defence counsel had noted many weak links in his story, out of which the chief one was: 'Why did the sannyasis take the man away with them instead of returning him to his relatives?' Costello thought it a good question but was of the opinion that Darshandas had offered an explanation. He had expressed his belief that a man who had been raised from the dead by divine intervention should dedicate the rest of his life in the service of God. This might sound odd in the ears of westerners but which, given the peculiar nature and customs of Indian ascetics, wasn't altogether unacceptable.

The most significant part of the plaintiff's story was his self-confessed amnesia. This had been exhaustively examined by medical experts from both sides and contradictory views expressed. The appellate judge brushed aside both sets of opinions as irrelevant. The important question was: 'Could the story of loss of memory be ruled out simply because it sounded improbable?' Costello thought not. It had been endorsed by Darshandas, an outsider, who would gain nothing by helping to install an imposter in a position of power in a part of the country with which he had no connection. And, even if he wanted to please an erstwhile disciple, would he commit perjury to do so? It didn't seem possible.

As for the conspiracy itself, Costello did not find a scrap of evidence to suggest that there had been one, or that it had been hatched by Jyotirmayi Debi. He wrote, 'On this matter, my mind weighs heavily in favour of Jyotirmayi Debi's evidence. If she were indeed a conspirator, she might have invented a more plausible and credible story.' As for the first rani, Costello found her account 'reasonably convincing'. Sarajubala had changed sides, no doubt, but it was perfectly possible to dismiss a strange story on first hearing and accept it later. She had given detailed accounts of her meetings with her brother-in-law during cross-examination and withstood the onslaughts of A. N. Chaudhuri with equanimity. Apart from these two ladies, sixteen other members of the family had sworn that the plaintiff was none other than the mejo kumar. Costello also gave it as his opinion that it was highly unlikely that an imposter could have been coached and prepared so thoroughly as the plaintiff had supposedly been.

The supporters of both plaintiff and defendants had been on tenterhooks to begin with. Costello's objective, non-partisan stand was puzzling and making everyone anxious. *What route was the adjudication taking? What was the learned judge's final conclusion likely to be?* Both parties were shaking in their shoes.

Gradually the mist started to lift and a clearer picture was glimpsed. As the reading of the judgement progressed, spirits started rising in the plaintiff's camp and falling in the other. Dejection and a feeling of unreality crept over the latter. How was it possible for a British judge to go against his own kind? It was unheard of. They, who had been so confident of victory, now clung desperately to a fading hope.

It is tempting to speculate on the reason behind Costello's stance. Owing to the outbreak of war in Europe, he had been unable to travel back to India. It is possible that, having lived in an English environment for over two years, he had ceased to see himself as the stereotypical white man in India – a superior being destined to rule over a primitive race. The reality of an Indian courtroom, in which he was expected to play a scripted role, had faded from his mind. The image had dimmed and he could see it only as something outside himself. He was no longer a player in the game. He was an objective commentator.

And now the judge came to the matter of Bibhavati Debi's testimony. A buzz of excited voices rose from the courtroom and were quickly silenced. Costello began by making a reference to A.

N. Chaudhuri's contention that an orthodox Brahmin woman would never falsely deny her lawful husband, especially when widowhood in Bengal was such an unenviable state to be in. Admitting that there was some substance in the argument, he couldn't go along with it all the way. Bibhavati Debi's case, he said, was not that of an ordinary Bengali widow's, whose life of enforced abstinence would have improved if a long-lost husband was found again. She had been the wife of a man who had shamed and dishonoured her, spent his time with low companions and loose women and suffered from a foul disease. It was psychologically quite tenable for a highborn, sensitive lady like her to prefer a life of dignity, albeit with some privations, as an esteemed member of her brother's family.

At last the time had arrived for Leonard Costello's concluding remarks. The verdict had been awaited for months and the people of India, nationalists and anglophiles alike, were biting their nails with apprehension. This would see an end to a case fought for eleven years, a case the like of which had never been seen before in any part of the world – fraught with fear, anxiety, and rising and dipping hopes. A sense of moving towards an unknown climax pervaded the entire nation. *Who knew what the end would bring?* Victory for the rulers which spelled indefinite extension of colonial oppression? Or triumph for the cause of nationalism? The fate of Bhawal, as the common man saw it, was a microcosm of the fate of India.

Justice Costello's conclusion caused a sensation through the length and breadth of Bengal.

'No sufficient grounds have been made out by the appellants to justify a reversal by this court of the decision of the First Additional Judge of Dhaka on the issue of fact. I have had the opportunity of reading the greater part of the comprehensive judgement written by my brother Biswas, and I am able to say that I agree with his reasoning generally, and with the conclusions at which he has in consequence arrived. As Mr Justice Biswas and myself are in agreement, the order of the court must be that the appeal is dismissed with costs.

15

Dhara Debi

Kolkata
1946

I AM ONE OF THOSE EXTRAORDINARY PERSONS WHO LIVE IN COMPLETE obscurity and anonymity for the best part of their lives and then, by a curious twist of destiny, are catapulted to a position of prominence undreamed of. Prominence not only in terms of wealth and status but of fame as well as notoriety. Opinion about me is divided. Some people worship the ground I walk on. Others, fewer in number than the first, mock and deride me. But no one can ignore me. I who was nothing, a nobody, find my face in every newspaper today; my name is on everyone's lips.

I said that my story is akin to those of a few unusual people. But no. My story is unique. Because, unlike the others, I was plummeted to the highest point in the vault of fate, then brought crashing down. Like a meteor that shoots into the sky, a flaming arrow, and touches the earth – a pinch of ashes.

I was the third of four daughters and lived with my parents Kalicharan Mukherjee and Tarasundari Debi, in reasonable contentment, till fate played its bittersweet trick on me. My father was exceedingly proud of his illustrious lineage and often boasted of it. His ancestors had been powerful and wealthy zamindars with landed estates in Kushthia more extensive than those of many a local raja. But that was ancient history. Decadent living, failing fortunes and lack of practical sense and foresight had eaten into the family assets over generations, and now there was nothing left for us barring the crumbling old house in Shyambazar in which we lived. Money was tight. There wasn't enough for repairs and maintenance and we spent our days and nights in perpetual fear of collapsing walls and ceilings falling over us.

My sisters were married. But I wasn't. Twenty-nine years old and still unwed! Such a thing was unheard of. Yet it had happened. Exactly why I wasn't sure. I had suffered from *kalajwar* as a child and never regained full health and strength. I remain weak and sickly to this day. My parents may have thought me incapable of coping with my marital duties. That is why they never tried to find a husband for me. Or they may have feared rejection. For all their poverty, they were aristocrats. Incapable of stomaching an insult.

Out of all my father's daughters, I was considered the plainest. I was short, painfully thin, and had very large eyes which, in the opinion of our less compassionate relatives, stared like a ghost's out of a long, pale face. That I had an aquiline nose, wavy black hair, and beautiful hands and feet didn't count.

One afternoon my Phul Pishima came to visit us. Though first cousins, she and Baba looked so alike, they could have been twins. Both had the exceedingly fair complexions, thickset bodies and head-sunk-into-the-neck looks of the Mukherjees of Kushthia. Fortunately for us, all four sisters looked more like our exquisitely beautiful mother than our father.

Hurrying into Ma's room, fairly bursting with excitement, the first thing Phul Pishima said was, 'Have you heard the news?'

'What news?' Ma looked up from her sewing. I sat by her, reading a book. I looked up too.

'The baro rani of Bhawal is looking for a bride for the mejo kumar.'

Ma and I stared at her. The case of the imposter prince or real prince, whatever he might be, was well known to us. The papers had been reporting the story, ad nauseum, for years now. In fact, I had got so bored, I had stopped following it. There had been so many twists and turns, so many conflicting testimonies, I didn't know what to make of it. Of course, the recent High Court verdict had captured my interest once again. I was convinced now that the so-called imposter *was* the mejo kumar of Bhawal. But, even so, what did his sister-in-law's looking for a bride for him have to do with us? Why did Phul Pishima look like a cat that has just swallowed the cream?

'Don't stare at me like that,' she scolded my mother. 'Bestir yourself and start organizing a bride viewing.'

'Bride viewing? For whom?'

'For Dhara. Who else?'

'Dhara! We've given up all hopes of her marriage. Don't forget she'll be thirty in a few months.'

'That's just the point. The mejo kumar doesn't want a young girl. Dhara will be just right for him.'

I stole a sideways glance at Ma's face. It reflected a warring with discordant emotions. Hope sprang into her eyes one moment and despair the next. I felt my ears flame. I dropped my head and pretended I wasn't listening. In all propriety, I should have left the room. But I couldn't move. My body seemed rooted to the bed and my heart was beating fast, so fast that I barely heard her reply.

'You are so innocent, Phul thakurjhi. Even if the mejo kumar of Bhawal wants an older girl, why would he approve of my daughter? As a family we are nowhere near theirs. We have hardly any money. Dhara isn't even beautiful ...'

'She isn't ugly either. Besides, he's nearly sixty. He can't expect to get a beautiful princess with half a kingdom at his age. Anyway, where's the harm in trying?'

'You know your cousin. He is very sensitive about Dhara's looks. He doesn't want her to suffer the humiliation of being rejected.'

'I know. That's why he hasn't made an effort to find the poor girl a husband. And his stupid ego has left her high and dry all these years. Have you given a thought to what will become of her after you both go? She doesn't even have a brother ...'

'How do you know that the baro rani is looking for an older girl?'

'My sister-in-law Bidhubala is a daughter of the Matilal family and the baro rani's second cousin. It is she who brought the proposal. She says that Sarajubala Debi has only two demands. That the girl comes from an aristocratic family and that she is above twenty-five. She has seen many girls and rejected them because they were too young.'

Ma asked a few more questions and fell silent. After a while, slowly, hesitantly, she murmured, 'You must speak to your cousin. If you both think it is worth a try—'

'I certainly do.'

I have no idea of what happened next. I only know that Phul Pishima and her sister-in-law arrived one morning to take me to the baro rani's house in Ripon Street. Being a royal, she wouldn't come to a strange house for a bride viewing. The girl had to be brought to her. It was a family tradition.

The two women dressed me up in my mother's finery. They tried to conceal my flat bosom with a velvet blouse frothing with Irish lace. A dhakai jamdani, crackling with starch, was draped on me in the hope that the stiff folds would hide my narrow hips. My hair was braided and coiled and set with gold-headed pins. Kajal was applied to my eyes and a *teep* stuck on my forehead. Jewels were hung from my arms and neck. I glanced in the mirror and was pleased and surprised by the image that looked back at me. I was almost beautiful.

Conflicting thoughts and emotions swept over me in waves. Was my luck changing at last? Was a new world opening up before me? And if so, did I want to enter it? Another thing. Did I want to put myself on display for the scrutiny of strangers? No. No. I was used to the life I lived. I was content. But … was I happy? Wasn't the prospect of acquiring a husband and children like other women exciting me and sending my pulse racing? Then a sudden sinking of the heart. What if the baro rani turned me down? It would be such a disgrace. How would I bear the ignominy? And … and even if she liked me, who knew what the future would bring?

The thrill of making a brilliant marriage was swamped by anxiety. I was twenty-nine. I was under no illusions about what the married state entailed. Would I be able to cope with its demands? I was confused. What did I want? Acceptance or rejection? I didn't know …

The baro rani was the epitome of gracious kindness. Beautiful and stately, looking every inch a queen in her dazzling white thaan and silk chador, she took my cold trembling hand in hers and led me to a chair. 'Sit at your ease sister,' she said with a smile. 'Don't be afraid.'

She welcomed her visitors as simply as any ordinary housewife would, saw to their comfort and plied them with sweets and snacks. Then, equally simply, she looked at Baba and said, 'Your daughter is beautiful, well educated and the right age for the mejo kumar. She is suitable in every way. Except, of course, that she is very small and slight. I only …' She paused uncertainly.

My father's face darkened. This was exactly the response he had anticipated. It would be followed by an apology and refusal. But, strange to say, my confusions vanished. So did my fears. I knew what I wanted. I wanted her to get over her hesitation and approve of me. I wanted it desperately.

'Please don't take it as a criticism,' she continued quickly. 'I only say this because my brother-in-law is very hefty and powerfully built. I was wondering if …'

'If you give us a little time, say a year or so,' Phul Pishima muttered uneasily. 'We'll try to fatten her up.'

'Oh no … there's no need for that,' the baro rani made up her mind. 'Girls gain weight after marriage. She will too.' Turning her glance on me, she smiled, 'What do *you* say, sister? Are you ready to become one of us? If so, welcome to the family.'

Events moved quickly after that. Sending for an almanac, our hostess handed it to my father.

'Check the *panjika* for auspicious dates, Talui moshai,' she said, 'and let's fix the wedding day. The earlier the better. Preferably next month.'

I noticed, with a leap of the heart, that she had addressed Baba as Talui moshai, a term of respect used for a sister-in-law's father. But Baba stared at her aghast. 'Next month!' he exclaimed. 'That leaves me with no time at all. How can I be expected to organize a daughter's wedding in three to four weeks? I need at least ...'

'You won't have to organize anything,' she interrupted gently. 'You will come to Jaidevpur with your friends and family and stay with us as royal guests. The nuptials will be solemnized in the palace temple and all the arrangements will be made by our staff. The bride's clothes and jewels will be sent to you in advance. So, you see, Talui moshai, you don't have to worry about anything. Anything at all.'

The wedding took place but not in the way the baro rani had planned and my parents had anticipated. The strangest thing happened. The war, hitherto confined to some countries of Europe, came to our door. Suddenly we were caught in momentous times.

Within two months of the bombing of Pearl Harbour, the British had to abandon Singapore and the horrors of the evacuation of Burma began. The rulers turned a blind eye at the massive exodus. There was no concern, no planning. Expatriates, most of them Bengalis who had amassed considerable wealth and property in Rangoon and Mandalay, were taken by surprise. Ships sailing to India were few and evacuees too many. Leaving everything behind, with only the clothes on their backs, many were forced to trek over mountains and through steamy tropical jungles filled with wild beasts, snakes, leeches and mosquitoes. Many died like flies on the way. Of those who managed to survive, some reached Assam and Tripura and some, among them two of my mother's cousins, arrived in Kolkata, more dead than alive. They had lost several members of their families and the ones who remained were sick and famished. The Japanese were at the borders of Bengal and an invasion was expected any moment.

From the top of our house one got a clear view of the steeple and weathercock of the church of Saint Andrews. And further away, in the distance, the majestic Ganga and the long, graceful facade of Howrah Bridge shimmered in silver glory. The most beautiful river and bridge in the world! Though strictly forbidden, I often managed to slip up to the roof in the afternoon, when the inmates of the house were taking a siesta, to stare in rapt wonder on the marvels of my beloved city.

But it was a sad sight that met my eyes these days. The streets teemed with soldiers and army trucks roared through them all day. The houses looked eerie and ghostlike, their windows and ventilators plastered with black paper against air raids. The park in front of the house was ripped apart in places with trenches that gaped like open wounds. Not a single human being was seen because nobody dared to leave the house. Hawkers brought milk, fish, fruit and vegetables to the door. Those who lived on upper floors hung a rope and hauled up baskets of provisions, then lowered them down again with the money.

And now the bombs began to fall. One fell in Hathibagan, named thus because it was the site of the battlefield on which Nawab Siraj-ud-daulah set his elephants loose after wresting Kolkata from the East India Company in 1756. The target was Howrah Bridge, the lifeline of Kolkata.

By a great stroke of luck, the bomb failed to explode. But the attempt spread terror in every heart. An exodus began. People started fleeing the city in thousands. Stations were packed with people and trains ran with passengers sitting on roofs and hanging from doors and windows.

Baba wanted to leave too. But where could we go? The ancestral mansion in Kushthia had been reduced to rubble decades ago, and our kith and kin were scattered in various parts of Bengal. Baba had no idea of where anyone was, having lost all contact with the extended family. The only person living in Kushthia, in a part of the temple which still stood, was a decrepit old aunt. There was no hope of finding refuge with her.

At this juncture, the baro rani came to our rescue. She sent word that she was leaving for Kashi and invited us to join her when we were ready.

We left two days later. The royal motor car took us to Howrah station where we caught a train to Kashi. Dusk was falling as the train snaked into Varanasi station where a carriage stood waiting for us. As the horses cantered down the streets, I lifted the window and looked out eagerly at the beautiful city stretched out in a half moon across the left bank of the Ganga. It could be my fancy, but the innumerable temple spires of this oldest, holiest place of pilgrimage, silhouetted against a pearl-grey expanse, looked like streams of surreal birds making their way back to their nests. The sky was darkening with the shadows of twilight and a thin mist was rising from the river but light shone from the rows of torches that lit up the ghats and the lamps that flickered from windows. This was my first glimpse of a city other than Kolkata and my heart quivered with anticipation of what it would bring.

After an hour or so, the carriage stopped at the iron gates of a vast stone mansion three storeys high. A marble plaque bearing the inscription Bhawal Bhawan, in English, told us we had arrived at our destination. We were met at the door by an elderly woman, a retainer from her looks and manner, and taken to the rooms assigned to us in the guest wing at the back of the house. The baro rani, the woman informed us in Hindi, had arrived the day before and settled herself in the Rani Mahal. She had given instructions that we were to be taken to her after we had a bath and meal.

The mejo kumar arrived a week later. Friends and relatives from Kolkata and Jaidevpur followed and the ceremony took place. My sisters, aunts and cousins came with their families, eager to participate in a marriage they hadn't ever dreamed possible. Although the baro rani's original plan of holding the event in Jaidevpur palace had to be shelved, something she never ceased to regret, the wedding was conducted with a degree of pomp and ceremony unimagined by my side of the family. A priest from Kashi Vishwanath temple performed the rites. All the important people of Kashi were invited to a grand feast. Shawls were distributed to Brahmins and food and money to the poor.

A few days after the ceremony, news reached us that Satyendranath Banerjee had died of a massive heart attack. But prior to his death, he had sent a petition to the Privy Council, the final court of appeal in India, to reverse the verdict of the Calcutta High Court.

But the news that followed was stranger. The Board of Revenue, unwilling to pursue the matter further, had requested Bibhavati Debi to withdraw the petition. The defence lawyer A. N. Chaudhuri, it was rumoured, was so disappointed by the verdict of the High Court that he had driven down to the riverfront and flung his brief into the water. But to everyone's amazement, and particularly that of the baro rani's, Bibhavati did not withdraw the petition.

The threat of a Japanese invasion had receded by this time but, the case being sub judice, the mejo kumar was still barred from entering Jaidevpur. In consequence, we returned to Kolkata and settled down in a house belonging to the baro rani, on Vivekananda Road. Not only did she give me a home, Sarajubala Debi played a valuable role in my life. Over the years, she became my sister, friend, guide and mentor. I don't know what I would have done without her.

I had been warned by so-called friends and well-wishers that marrying the mejo kumar of Bhawal wouldn't be a fairy tale come true. There would be many glitches, many hurdles, many tears and regrets. We were so mismatched! He was thirty years older than me and thrice my size. He was an illiterate debauch with a history of promiscuous living and venereal disease. How could I, a simple girl from an educated, enlightened Kolkata family, put my trust in such a man? How long could I be happy with a fine house and servants, saris and jewels?

I am a very private person and find it difficult to express my deepest thoughts and emotions. But I have to say this. The prince was a most gentle and loving husband. He had a large heart and his warmth and generosity were felt not only by me but by everyone around him. Though uneducated, he was not uncouth. He had all the refinement of a thoroughbred aristocrat. He was a simple man, honest and straightforward, and I felt totally at ease with him.

We lived like any ordinary upper middle-class couple. We kept a small retinue of servants. A cook, a gardener, a man of all work, a driver and a maid. Having lived among ascetics for twelve years, the kumar was used to simple food. He ate fish sometimes but preferred daal roti or rice and vegetables. I liked cooking and often tried my hand at the north Indian dishes he had eaten during his twelve years with the band of sannyasis. He was very religious. His mornings and evenings were spent in the puja room. And once a week, without fail, he visited the Kali temples at Thanthaniya and Kalighat to offer prayers.

The Privy Council verdict took very long in coming. But news kept filtering in. The mejo kumar held meetings with his lawyers every three or four days, and they kept him updated. I didn't enter the room. I stood outside the door and listened. I could hear only snatches of their talk but I persuaded my husband to fill in the rest. He was hesitant at first. He was afraid, perhaps, of raising my hopes and having them dashed. Then gradually, as it seemed to me, he started enjoying our conversations and hearing my views.

'Pankaj Coomar Ghose has left for London,' he said one day. He seemed a bit worried.

'Who is he?'

'He's Sasanka Coomar Ghose's son. Sasanka Ghose was one of the defence lawyers during the Dhaka trial and knows all the intricate details of the case. Pankaj babu won't play a prominent role, of course. He'll only assist the King's Counsel, Mr Page.'

'Who will argue on your behalf?'

'D. N. Pritt.' The muscles of his face relaxed a little. 'He is a brilliant lawyer and has a reputation for justice and fair play. He has sided with natives before. He defended a revolutionary named Kishori Lal in a Privy Council appeal some years back and got it dismissed.'

The first question before the Judicial Committee of the Privy Council, the lawyers informed the prince, was whether or not to grant leave of appeal. Mr Pritt argued that the issues raised in the petition had already been examined by two courts and did not merit re-evaluation. But Mr Page managed to convince the Council to reopen the case on the ground that some evidence had been improperly admitted and some improperly judged in the two courts of India. The appeal was allowed and the process began.

The hearings were held over twenty-eight sessions, the longest in the history of the Privy Council, and were regularly reported in both English and Bengali newspapers. I liked to keep abreast of events and read the *Amrita Bazar Patrika* regularly. Now I started sending out for English papers as well. Looking out with an eagle eye for the tiniest thread of information pertaining to the case, I would share it with the kumar. And it was this mutual interest and the discussions that followed which brought us closer together in trust and reliance.

'I have fought for more than twenty years to establish my identity,' he said to me one day, 'but sometimes I wonder if it was worth the effort. I was quite happy as a member of Guruji's band. I travelled to so many places and learned so much about people and different ways of living. I could have spent the rest of my years ...'

'No,' I interrupted. 'Once you realized *who* you were, it was your duty to reclaim your identity. No one should live a lie.'

'But the strain of waiting, fearing and anticipating has been too great. I doubt if I can endure it much longer. I have a feeling this long struggle will come to nothing. The English stick with their own kind.'

'Not always. Leonard Costello didn't.'

'What do you think will happen now?'

'How can I say? What do I, a mere woman, know of the technicalities of the law?'

'Don't call yourself a mere woman,' he sounded quite annoyed. 'I, too, was brought up to look upon the opposite sex as weak in body and lacking in intelligence. Foolish, feeble and in need of male protection. I had no qualms about keeping them locked away in the andarmahal. But now I realize how wrong I was. After all, wasn't it the women of the family who insisted that I fight for my rights? Who challenged the British officials and played a proactive role in the case? My grandmother, sisters and sister-in-law ...'

'But it was also the women of the family who let you down,' I said. 'Don't forget that the chhoto rani and your wife refused to acknowledge you.'

'The chhoto rani recognized me alright but pretended not to. She is an ambitious woman who wants Bhawal for her adopted son. She believes that the *abhishek* ceremony Ronaldshay and Lindsay conducted is proof that Bhawal will be handed to him on a silver platter once the courts denounce me as an imposter. Poor woman! She has no idea that the whole thing was a supreme bluff. As for Bibhavati ...' He paused a few moments, a sad little smile flickering on his lips.

'What about her?'

'She's a good woman. One of the finest I've known. She's ...'

I felt a sudden stab of jealousy. 'Why then,' I burst out, 'did she behave the way she did? Why did she deny you?'

'It's complicated,' he sighed. 'In a way, it was my fault. Our marital relationship was strained. I was used to older women and she, poor girl, was too young and innocent. She had no idea of how to lure a man and hold him. She kept waiting and waiting ...'

His voice trailed away. Then, making a clicking sound with his tongue, he continued, 'Her whole life has been a nightmare, a living hell. She lost her father before she was three and, to fill the void, put her brother in his place. And he, under the pretence of loving and protecting her, played on her emotions in many devious ways. He exerted a mysterious power over her. He practically held her in the hollow of his hand.'

He paused for a minute and continued, 'I was careless and thoughtless at the time. It was later, while living with the sannyasis, that I learned to look inwards. To pause and reflect. I realize now that life would have been different for her if she had married an ordinary man, faithful and loving, and a good father to her children. Instead, she found herself locked in the andarmahal of a feudal household with a husband who had no use for her. Deprived of all dignity, freedom and self-respect, it is no wonder that she felt stifled and alienated. Can we blame her for turning to her brother for comfort?'

He paused again, then continued slowly, 'I could have removed her from his insidious influence if I'd shown her some consideration and compassion. But I didn't. I neglected and humiliated her. A time did come – it was during our stay in Darjeeling – when we started to understand each other's needs. When I thought, and I'm sure she did too, that she could shake off her brother's malignant power and make a new beginning with me. Unfortunately, we weren't given the chance.'

'It proves she has no will of her own,' I muttered sullenly. 'She's weak, spineless.'

'I don't know what she is now but the woman I knew wasn't exactly spineless. She was gentle and sensitive, with a horror of confrontation. She allowed Satya babu to have his way with her simply because she hated scenes and arguments. And, for the same reason, she never fought for her rights as a wife. If taking the line of least resistance is cowardice … yes, you're right. She was a coward. But I prefer to retain my earlier opinion. She was too civilized, too refined, to stoop to her brother's level and take him on. You didn't see her in the dock, Dhara. She was the target of so many vicious attacks. She was accused of incest and an aborted pregnancy. But the grace and dignity with which she withstood them was the most amazing thing in the world. I've never seen anything like it.'

'Do you believe the allegations?'

'No.'

The hearings dragged on. Days passed into weeks, weeks into months and months into years. The cause of the delay was obvious. The war was over. England had won. But the country was left reeling under the blows struck by the enemy. German aerial action had devastated the port of London, her docks, and many industrial, residential and commercial areas, including the buildings in the historic heart of the city. It was reduced to a pile of rubble and thirty thousand citizens had lost their lives.

The arduous process of reconstruction had begun, but there were many hurdles. Most of England's able-bodied men had either died in the war or returned maimed and wounded. A shrinking labour force, combined with a shortage of building materials, had rendered the process painfully slow.

The public was suffering in many ways. Old industries, dating from Victorian times, had collapsed and new ones, started during the war years, weren't faring much better. Investments were yielding very poor returns. Long queues and rationing, even for essentials, were frustrating and embittering people. With the bombing of communication links, movement was impeded. England's economy was in the doldrums. As was her morale. The disintegration of the Empire, upon which the sun never set, was at hand. Even the most stubborn, the most obtuse Englishman couldn't deny this reality.

In circumstances such as these, it wasn't possible for the members of the Privy Council to proceed at their customary pace. Unforeseen glitches appeared. Gaps between the hearings grew longer. We understood the constraints but the delay was fraying our nerves. My husband, even more than me, was losing patience. He had turned sixty-two last year. How much longer could he be expected to wait for justice?

Gradually a change came over him. He, who had been the calmest, most patient of men, grew restless and irritable. He lost his temper frequently. He shouted at the servants for the slightest dereliction of duty and quelled me with a look if I tried to intervene. The muscles of his large, round face started to slacken and wrinkles appeared around his mouth and the corners of his eyes. His once-healthy appetite diminished and he was eating less and less every day. Sleep was erratic and came fitfully. Sometimes he slept all day and stayed awake all night. I've often come upon him, at dead of night, pacing up and down in the garden or sitting in his armchair on the balcony staring at the sky. And more and more, he began withdrawing from people. He stopped meeting his lawyers. They dished out the same stale news, he said. But what was more worrying was that he even turned away his friends.

'Why did you refuse to meet Pataki?' I asked him the day he sent the baro rani's adopted son away. 'He must have brought news from Didi.'

'I'm tired, Dhara. I don't have the energy to talk to anybody.'

'But to turn away Pataki!' I exclaimed. 'What will Didi think?'

'I know. I should have made the effort …' There was a tinge of guilt in his voice. Then, shaking his head, he added, 'Everyone who comes to me asks about the case. They don't know that I've lost all hope. That I can't bear talking or even thinking about it. My father was a great man, a great ruler. We were his worthless sons. But of the three I was the worst. I've done nothing good in life. Achieved nothing. All I've done is hurt my near and dear ones. I ruined Bibha's life.'

'You haven't ruined mine …'

'Who knows?' He smiled at me. 'I may do so yet.'

And now physical symptoms started to appear. Dizzy spells – fortunately they lasted only a few minutes – and heaviness and discomfort in the abdomen. The doctors we sent for thought they might be caused by indigestion. They gave him pills and advocated a light diet. He felt better for some days, then the trouble started again, accompanied by breathlessness and irregular heartbeat. The kumar had suffered from asthma as a child and we were told that it was a recurrence of the same.

He had good days and bad days and it was on one of the former that the news arrived …

It had been raining incessantly for three days and nights. But that morning the skies had called a truce. The clouds parted at dawn, bringing the promise of a gorgeous day. I stood on the balcony, watching a crimson sun rise slowly, spreading beams that turned to gold across the sky. A damp breeze blew from the garden, laden with the scent of rain-washed jui. I inhaled deeply. Suddenly I felt a presence beside me. It was my husband. I was surprised. He never rose so early.

'Is anything wrong?' I asked. 'Are you feeling uneasy?'

'No. No. In fact, I feel a little better this morning. Thank God it has stopped raining.'

He sat in his armchair, stretched his legs, and breathed in great draughts of the clean, pure air.

'I'd like to have breakfast here,' he turned to the servant who stood in attendance. 'Tell the cook to make luchi and halua.'

'The doctor has forbidden fried food …' I murmured.

'It's only for today. One day's indulgence won't kill me. What do you say, Dulal?' He smiled at the young man who hastened to obey.

He had just started on his third luchi when the purr of a powerful engine was heard and a deep blue Minerva came skimming along the drive. 'Who is this?' he muttered. 'People have no sense of time …' Suddenly his voice changed. '*Arre!*' he exclaimed. 'It's Sudhamoy babu. At this hour! I wonder …' He rose and walked towards the railing. I joined him just as the car door opened and Benoy Chandra Chatterjee's son stepped out. His father had died three years ago and he had taken over the case. He looked up at us and waved a piece of paper.

'Raja moshai!' he shouted, his usually sombre face creased in an ecstatic smile. 'A telegram from London! The ordeal is over. We've won.'

I was standing close to my husband, my head touching his arm. The address 'Raja moshai' fell on my heart like the beat of a mighty drum. I felt the huge body next to me jerk violently in a series of spasms. It swayed from side to side and would have fallen if Dulal hadn't darted quickly to his master's side and caught him in his arms. Between the two of us, we led him to his chair. My heart was racing madly and my hand shook as I poured a cup of tea and held it to his lips. 'Drink this,' I said. 'It will steady your nerves.' He sipped gratefully at the hot brew. The shivering stopped and, in a minute or two, even before the lawyer had joined us, he was himself again.

Over breakfast, Sudhamoy babu shared the details. The telegram had come at one o'clock and he had spent the rest of the night in telephone calls with his contacts in London. He didn't wish to disturb his client at that unearthly hour since the latter was having health issues and needed his night's rest. Besides, he wanted to bring the news in person.

The final hearing had been held the day before, on 30 July 1946, at the end of which Baron William Watson Thankerton, who was heading the Committee, had read out the judgement which was unanimous. Thankerton's observations were brief and succinct.

He had begun with the comment that, unlike the judges of the Trial Court and High Court of India, he and his colleagues, Lord du Parcq and Sir C. Madhavan Nair, had been disadvantaged by being unable to inspect the plaintiff. The Board, he continued, though committed to reviewing the findings of two concurrent courts, was not obliged to do the same with those of two judges and that a dissent by a member of the appellate court did not obviate the practice. The Board made an exception, now and then, but was always reluctant to depart from it in cases which involved the manners, customs and sentiments peculiar to another country. But, due to the unusual magnitude and complication of this particular case, a review had been undertaken.

The evidence, after the most cautious and careful re-examination by all three members, had yielded nothing new. The appellant had failed to establish valid ground for her claim. The appeal was thus dismissed.

My heart gave a tremendous leap. My husband had finally established, in all three courts of law, that he was who he claimed to be. The legitimate heir and successor to his father. He was Raja Ramendranarayan Roy, ruler of the kingdom of Bhawal.

As soon as Sudhamoy babu left, I said to my husband. 'Have a bath quickly and get ready. We must leave for Cornwallis Street at once.'

'Why?' His eyebrows came together. 'Why at once?'

'I've pledged one hundred silver rupees to Goddess Kali of Thanthaniya temple. I vowed to make the offering the day the news of your victory came.'

'It has turned very hot and humid. Why don't we go in the evening when it's cooler?'

'Didn't you hear Sudhamoy babu say that the newspapers are working overtime to bring out an afternoon issue? The news will become public in a few hours and we'll be mobbed. Better leave now before the streets get crowded.'

I bathed and dressed carefully in a red-bordered *garad* sari. I put sindoor in my parting and alta on my feet. I set out the offering of flowers, tulsi, fruits and sweets on a silver tray. Placing the coins in four neat stacks in the centre, I covered the whole with a piece of lace I had crocheted myself. My husband too, I noticed, had taken special care with his appearance. He wore a fine muslin dhuti with a broad gold border and a kurta of muga silk embellished with diamond buttons. Rings set with precious stones flashed from several fingers.

Sitting in the car, as it wound slowly in and out of the streets of North Kolkata, he began outlining his plans for the future. He would leave for Jaidevpur in a day or two, he said, and hold meetings with officials and important tenants who would help him in the work of administering the estate. Bhawal had suffered immensely. It had fallen to rack and ruin ever since his father died. He and his brothers had done nothing to improve the condition of their subjects. Yet they had shown the royal family the greatest loyalty. Looking back on the past, he felt humbled and ashamed. He had been selfish and obtuse. But he would make up for his past neglect. He would open schools and clinics in every village. Good roads were a must too. The village paths turned to rivers of mud during the monsoon and people had a tough time going about their daily activities. Bhawal needed a bank and a good modern hospital. How would it be if some palace wings were converted for the purpose? There were so many! We didn't need such a colossal dwelling house, did we?

I listened to him, nodding from time to time, but my eyes were fixed on the moving scene outside the window. People were stopping in their tracks and glancing curiously at us. And, gradually, they began standing in knots and whispering to one another. Some pointed to the car and even moved towards it. I realized that the news had leaked from the press and started percolating through the city. 'Go faster, Satish,' I urged the driver. 'We must reach the temple before more people get to know.'

The car picked up speed and we arrived at our destination. But, to our dismay, hundreds of people were there already. They made a rush towards the car and tried to surround us. Several voices cried out together:

'*Oi to!* There's the Raja of Bhawal!'

'The mejo kumar?'

'He's the Raja now. He has won the case. A telegram has come from London …'

'Which case? The prince turned sannyasi who died in Darjeeling?'

'Was *supposed* to have died, you blockhead!'

'*Arre!* Look … look. His wife is with him.'

'Which wife?'

'The second one, of course!'

'She's quite plain. Not like the first.'

'But she's a good woman. So I've heard.'

'She comes from a very poor family.'

'And she's thirty years younger …'

'I wonder why he married her!'

'I think we should go back,' Satish said, 'and come again in the evening.'

'I think so too.' His master shot a glance at the pushing, jostling crowd and muttered uneasily, 'We'll never be able to make our way through all these people. Even looking at them is making me uncomfortable. I feel a bit queasy.'

My face was flaming with humiliation at what I had just heard. Still, I didn't want to leave. I had come with an offering to the temple and was determined to make it. Taking it back would be disrespectful. It would annoy the goddess. I glanced at my husband. His face was very pale and there were beads of perspiration on his brow.

'You sit in the car,' I said to him. 'I'll go with Niru and make the offering. Don't worry. We won't take long. Come,' I beckoned to the maid who accompanied me wherever I went. 'Let's go.'

'Wait a moment,' he stopped us. 'Gurupada babu is coming.'

I looked out of the window to see the head priest come huffing and puffing down the path, a copper plate heaped with flowers in his hands. He was preceded by two of his helpers who rushed forward and opened the car doors. Gurupada babu greeted his royal guest with folded hands, marked his brow with consecrated sindoor and hung a hibiscus garland, taken from the breast of the goddess, on his neck.

'Come, Raja moshai,' he beamed at us. 'Come, Rani ma.'

'The crush …' My husband hesitated. 'So many people! I'm not sure …'

'Don't be afraid. They'll disperse in a minute. Come with me. It's only a few yards to the porch.'

We stepped out gingerly. It was very, very hot. A huge sun, blazing out of a metallic blue sky, rained white-hot beams on our heads. The air was so heavy with moisture it was almost tangible. I felt as though I was walking through clouds of steam.

We proceeded towards the temple, the head priest leading the way. The other two flailed their arms and pushed and shoved to make a passage for us. 'Step back,' they shouted. 'Make way for the Raja and Rani of Bhawal.' The mass of densely packed humanity receded and surged forward involuntarily like waves on a sea shore. Their sweat-soaked bodies threatened to swamp ours. Their breath was foul in our faces. My husband walked ahead of me as we inched our way towards the temple. I saw that he was breathing with difficulty and his feet were slipping and faltering. His kurta was clinging to his back in a great dripping patch. Suddenly I felt a cold hand at my heart.

You should have gone back, a voice hissed in my ear, *what you're doing is dangerous … dangerous … go back … go back … dangerous … go back …*

Sometimes the echoes seemed to come from far off, sometimes from within my own self. And now my heart was thumping madly and my hot body turning to ice. We had almost reached the temple entrance when a wave of panic swept over me. Clutching my husband's arm, I tried to turn him around. And, at that precise moment, the vast figure crumpled like a collapsed balloon and fell with a tremendous crash. I fell with him, scraping my knees on the rough stony ground.

The tray flew from my hands and apples, pomegranates and silver coins rolled about, scattering in different directions.

He died two days later.

From 31 July, the day the telegram arrived from London, streams of men, women and children had started converging towards Kolkata. Friends, relatives, local zamindars, important tenants and ordinary subjects came to felicitate their monarch on his victory and remained to mourn his death. Pannalal Basu, now estate manager to the zamindar of Panchet, travelled a hundred miles to offer his respects and so did several officials from the district court of Dhaka. The raj purohit, chief priest of the royal temple in Jaidevpur, arrived in time to chant the *Tarak Brahma* in the dying king's ears and pour gangajal down his throat. Guru Darshandas, too old and infirm to come himself, sent three sadhus of his band to prepare his erstwhile disciple for the final journey.

The baro rani had taken up residence in the house on Vivekananda Road from the day of the fall and it was she who made the funeral arrangements. She had wanted to cremate the new king in the royal cremation ground of Jaidevpur where all his ancestors had preceded him. But that was not feasible, as everyone pointed out. The distance was too great and the weather too hot. She did the next best thing. Sending for the raj purohit, she expressed her wish that her brother-in-law's last rites be conducted with all the requisite sacraments and ceremonies owing to him as the ruler of Bhawal. Her instructions were followed to the letter. The three sadhus washed and prepared the body to the accompaniment of Vedic chants. They dressed the now-acknowledged Raja of Bhawal in the ceremonial robes of velvet and brocade worn by his predecessors on state occasions. Pearls were hung around his neck and a jewelled turban set on his brow. Masses of his favourite flowers, jui and rajanigandha, were strewn on the sandalwood bedstead on which he lay, ready to begin his journey to the land of no return.

His love of music being well known, bands of kirtaniyas had arrived from different parts of the city and taken up their positions at the head of the procession which would accompany him to Nimtala. As soon as the royal bier emerged from the house, to the solemn chanting of '*Bolo Hari! Hari Bol!*', one of them burst into a soulful rendition of 'Mathur', the heart-rending tale of Radha's loss and bereavement when Krishna leaves Brindavan for Mathura.

I stood at an upstairs window and watched them take my husband away. My marriage had lasted just a little more than three years …

Suddenly someone from the crowd shouted, '*Jai! Sannyasi Raja'r jai!*' Others joined him, then more and more and more, till the voices reached a crescendo. '*Jai! Sannyasi Raja'r Jai! Jai! Sannyasi Rajar jai!*' Springing from the throats of thousands of common people, the vast volume of sound drowned both chant and *kirtan*.

Fading slowly, as the procession moved on, the words kept echoing and re-echoing in my ears.

I smiled. The people of Bengal had given Raja Ramendranarayan Roy, ruler of the kingdom of Bhawal, a new name. A name that would go down in history. A name he would be known by for all time to come.

Sannyasi Raja!

Acknowledgements

First, my deepest and sincerest thanks go to Professor Partha Chatterjee, author of *A Princely Imposter?* His book was a treasure trove of information on the Bhawal case. Almost all the facts I used were sourced from his book. I also thank him for providing an exhaustive bibliography of English and Bengali books written on the subject. Some of them offered valuable insights into the ethos and ambience of the times.

My gratitude to Waqar Khan for sending me photographs and a link to all his articles on the case. We also had some lively conversations in which he shared reminiscences about some of his relatives who were close to the royal family.

I thank the writers who wrote about the Bhawal case in the *Daily Star*, *Dhaka Tribune* and other Bangladeshi journals.

My heartfelt thanks to Phalguni Matilal, a relative of the baro rani of Bhawal, for the family anecdotes and insights into the personalities of some of the members of the royal family that he so generously shared with me.

I thank my niece Swati Bhattacharya and my friends Monmoyee Basu, Antara Datta and Neeman Sobhan for reading the first draft of the novel and giving me many useful suggestions.

Last but not least, my grateful thanks to Teesta Guha Sarkar of Pan Macmillan India for her meticulous yet sensitive and unobtrusive editing of the manuscript.

